Garden of Lilies

Lilies of the Underground Trilogy
Book 3

Steven Hamilton

Cover Design and Interior Formatting by BespokeBookCovers.com

Please visit our website:www.insidepassagebookroom.com

Other Novels by Steven Hamilton

Dragon Slayers

McSally and Company

From Where I Stood

Journey Home

Steeno Six

Twisted Truth

Lilies in the Dark (Book 1, *Lilies of the Underground*)

Seeds of Light (Book 2, *Lilies of the Underground*)

Acknowledgments

My deepest gratitude goes out to those who helped bring the second of three novels in this trilogy to completion. My Thursday Writer's Group—Gretchen Day, Richie Goldstein, and J. J. Waller:

Thank you for the long hours, hard work, and, most important, the critical feedback on my work. To my editor, Diane Luehrs: Once again I am in your debt. I am forever grateful that you see things that I manage to overlook. As always, I am grateful to Peter and Caroline O'Connor of BespokeBookCovers.com for the remarkable work they do. Not only do they produce beautiful covers, but also all the internal formatting for this book. They make my life so much easier. Finally, once again, to my beautiful wife, Mary. She not only nudges (gently) but also edits and keeps me on track.

Special Thanks

Following from the second book in this series, we continue to encounter Boris Bunin. He is a Russian mob boss in New York. Boris appears courtesy of author Richie Goldstein. Bunin is a central character is Goldstein's Sasha Kulaeva trilogy, *Crime on the Alaska/Russian Border*. Richie was kind of enough to grant permission, for which I am grateful. His fictional work is engaging and paints vivid images of the complicated web of organized crime and law enforcement in Alaska. All of Richie's work is available on Amazon. Visit his author's page on Amazon https://www.amazon.com/author/richiegoldstein.

Author's Note

This is a work of fiction. The characters are fictional and not inspired by true events. While some organizations in the story exist in the real world, characterizations are presented to move the story forward. They are in no way meant to be true representations of the actual organizations.

One element of this novel that does reflect our society is the blight of domestic violence. The horrifying events that I've portrayed in this novel are all too common. One has only to keep up with current events to understand this.

As of this writing, my home state of Alaska has the third highest rate of domestic violence in the United States. If you look at the data, it is striking. In the top tier states more than 40% of women report experiencing domestic violence at some time in their lives. These numbers hold across multiple data sources. That our culture tolerates this evil is an indictment of who we are. It is not a pretty picture.

The Story So Far...

A violent husband guns his wife down in a law office parking lot. Reverend Janet Polasky, who is there to accompany the woman to an appointment with a divorce attorney, witnesses the murder in horror. That nightmare infuses the minister with a sense of purpose. Certain that it is her calling, she sets out to help abused women who fear for their lives—help them disappear. Her plan is to give them new lives in new cities and states.

In addition to inspiring Janet to action, this tragedy robs twelve-year old Abby Miller of her mother. The grandmother, Roberta Klein, assumes custody, but it quickly becomes evident that the woman is herself so grief-stricken that she struggles to care for the young girl. Janet feels a duty to help the young girl survive the traumatic event.

Meanwhile, working on her idea of rescuing women, she scores a quick initial success securing funds from a wealthy businessman to accomplish this mission. Then Janet suffers her first brutal defeat. As she moves to save

Luellen Pickering and her children, the woman's husband manages to locate and murder the kids. Despite the resources and passion, Janet's efforts aren't enough. Once again, violence destroys a family.

Janet begins to understand that she will not be able to carry out the day-to-day work of rescuing women and their children. After all, she has responsibilities to her church. On the recommendation of a friend, Detective Dee Martin, Janet hires a woman who has gone through domestic violence trauma herself. Valentina Gomez had just spent ten years in prison for killing her abusive husband.

Things begin to take shape. Janet establishes organizations to comply with requirements—payroll, taxes, expenses, banking, and other elements that go with any enterprise. Spiriting women to safety requires a sophisticated infrastructure.

Along the way, she encounters Leah Bowman, the wife of a local gang leader. Leah comes to Janet for help through Detective Martin, who is attempting to get the woman to testify against her husband. Leah claims to be trying to escape him, although she is by no means the victim of his abuse. Despite her reluctance, Janet allows her to stay in a rented condo that they have access to. The world turns upside down when the husband comes looking for his wife at the condo. Conveniently, Leah isn't there. Janet is. As she stares down the barrel of the man's gun, her world once again flips. Anton Bowman, gang leader, and his two associates are themselves killed by an unseen shooter from just outside the condo.

Janet suspects, although she has no hard evidence, that this had been Leah's plan all along—to lure her husband into a trap and kill him without exposing herself. Janet sweeps the traumatic incident from her mind. She already has too many other irons in the fire.

Meanwhile, Janet's funding source—billionaire Greg Stottman—struggles with his own problems. His niece, Dani, for whom he is legal guardian, becomes involved with a controlling and abusive boyfriend, Billy Robinson. Compounding the problem is Dani's rejection of her uncle's help. In his desperation to keep her safe, Greg turns to an old college acquaintance who operates mostly on the wrong side of the law. Rico Enretti is known as the *go-to guy* for anything desired but not legally allowed. Rico recommends a security expert with unique talents.

Enter Dimitry Kazarian. Kaz accepts the task of keeping Dani safe while he and Greg together strategize a longer-term solution. Their plans are dashed when Greg discovers that Dani's boyfriend is regularly beating her. Greg and Kaz find where they are staying and physically remove her. This, however, didn't end the saga. Within weeks, Dani runs away, leaving a note telling Greg to leave her alone.

During this time, another woman comes to Janet for help. The circumstances, however, make this a seemingly impossible case. The woman, Lucy Young, is married to Janet's board president at the church, Rob Young. The minister begins the delicate balancing act of remaining professional while interacting with him and, at the same time, working to help his wife escape. Despite her efforts, though, Janet suspects that Rob knows of her involvement.

He enlists the help of his cop brother, Phillip Young, who attempts to strongarm Janet to find the runaway wife. When his first attempt fails, he accosts her on the street while she is on an early morning run. He comes for Janet and there seems to be no possible escape route. Suddenly, Leah Bowman shows up. She has taken over her husband's gang operation and, as luck would have it, Phillip Young is on her payroll.

The cop and his friends retreat, but Leah warns Janet that the road she is on will lead to increasingly dangerous situations. Because Janet helped her, Leah promises friendship; a resource that Janet is reluctant to accept.

During this time, Valentina Gomez—Val—escorts Lucy Young to safety in another state. Despite their efforts at secrecy, Val finds that she is being followed... two states away. The breach is traced back to a tapped telephone in the office of the attorney who helped set up Janet's organization.

Greg once again calls on his friend, Rico Enretti, to find a technical wizard who can unravel the mess. Eisen, a very expensive tech contractor, quickly finds the bug on the phone system and traces it back to its source—Seattle attorney Reba Stillings, who has made a name for herself advocating for men's rights, especially men accused of domestic violence. There are hints and signs that this powerful lawyer is providing the technical means for men to track down and sometimes kill their runaway wives. There is no hard evidence of her involvement, though, so she is free to continue her crusade.

A phone call brings Greg Stottman's life crashing down around him. His niece, Dani, has been brought to the emergency room. She's been beaten, shot, and left for dead. There is no doubt who was responsible, but Billy Robinson has long since disappeared. What he left behind, was a young woman whose world has been turned inside out. Dani struggles, alternately blaming Greg for the entire event, and defending Billy. With Janet by his side, Greg tries to talk to her but begins to understand that there is a very long road ahead for his niece.

During the investigation into Dani's shooting, we are

introduced to Detective Charlotte Wharton of the King County Sheriff's Department. She butts heads with Greg as she investigates the case. He has a strong inclination to try and find Billy Robinson and dispose of the man himself. Greg's clumsiness in this endeavor, though, brings Wharton down on him as she warns him off.

Tired of tiptoeing around the issue, Janet finally confronts Rob Young. With his wife safely relocated, she has to deal with the reality that she has a violent, abusive husband as the president of her church's governing board. She takes a bold approach. Accompanied by Kaz, she meets with Young and gives him an ultimatum—resign from the board and leave the church or she will bring the entire issue into the public eye. The coup is successful, although Janet is under no assumption that it was the end of the issue.

Meanwhile, her involvement deepened with Abby Miller, the young girl whose mother's murder started all of this. The grandmother's mental health has deteriorated, leaving Janet to try and fill the empty spot in the girl's life.

With all of these issues and problems converging, Janet feels increasingly stretched. The magnitude and pace of events suggested that the entire mission was an impossible dream.

Then it gets worse. Janet's next client is the wife of a popular U. S. Senator who is running for re-election. His public persona is one of caring and concern for victims of family violence. In private, he abuses and batters his own wife, Bonnie. Unfortunately for Janet, Senator Corel soon has Janet in his crosshairs. His hired contractors kidnap and murder Sue Hartman, the director of DV services for King County Washington, among others, in an attempt to gain information.

As the days and weeks pass, the senator drifts steadily

toward paranoia until he is on the verge of a psychotic break. He begins to order the deaths of his opponents and even allies that he feels have betrayed him. Janet is first on his list. She barely avoids capture and death when Kaz intervenes and kills her assailant. Meanwhile, Corel's main contractor, Dylan Strauss, becomes increasingly concerned about the senator's unraveling and warns him off on several occasions.

A new character enters the story. The mysterious man, known only as The Sniper, is stalking and murdering domestic violence workers and advocates. We learn that he is part of a larger hate group that has embarked on an ambitious campaign to cripple services and take revenge on women who assist battered wives.

Upon return from a mission, The Sniper finds a visitor at his remote cabin—a long lost cousin from his childhood, Billy Robinson—the same man who assaulted Dani Stottman and left her for dead. The Sniper quickly learns that Robinson has committed several murders and is on the run. He makes a calculated decision, though, to take his cousin in, give him protection, and train him as an assistant.

Things go well at first as Billy successfully completes his initial tasks, including one assassination. Then everything goes awry. The inept cousin botches an attempt on the life of one of Janet's friends, Aylin Freyberg. He then goes after Greg Stottman and his niece, Dani, in an effort to tie up old loose ends from his prior life. In true Billy Robinson fashion, though, he messes that up as well and is captured by Greg and Kaz.

With a sense of resignation, The Sniper, who watches the capture from a distance, kills his cousin with a long-range shot.

Meanwhile, Senator Corel, who has managed to keep

up his façade, cruises to victory in his bid for re-election. In celebration, he finalizes arrangements to have his enemies and former allies killed, including Reba Stillings and Dylan Strauss. In his blind rush to revenge, he overlooks a crucial rule of contract killing—never turn on your own contractors. Word of his effort apparently spreads and his life is unceremoniously ended as a result.

During this time, Abby Miller, the young girl whose mother's death started Janet's journey, is deteriorating. She has trouble at school and her grandmother, who is her guardian, is also suffering from grief. Janet works with Greg, the man who has funded her project, to get Abby moved into a private school.

A spark of hope emerges as Dani, Greg's niece who was assaulted and nearly killed by Billy Robinson, meets and befriends Abby. An arrangement is quickly struck for Dani to drive Abby back and forth to her new school. This friendship is a ray of light in an otherwise dark world for both Abby and Dani.

While all of this develops, Janet begins to suspect that Greg Stottman has more than a professional interest in her. Being widowed for ten years, she finds herself unwilling to go down that road, feeling that she's not quite ready to set the memory of her late husband aside. She begins to wonder, though, if there might come a time when she is ready. If it does come, is Greg Stottman—CEO and billionaire—the man that she would like to spend the rest of her life with.

The final thread that haunts Janet is her relationship with the church council. Several of the members begin to dominate discussions about the philosophy of domestic violence services. It comes to a head as they maneuver a vote to roll back their support for battered women and give more consideration to the men who assault them. Janet responds and manages to orchestrate a defeat for them. In the process, though, she is introduced to a new face—Nicholas Trowbridge. Although he says little at that tense meeting, Janet is left with the nagging sense that he is not simply a bystander. There seems to be a darkness within him that she is certain will show up again in the future.

1

Everything looked wrong. Valentina Gomez sat in her Toyota Highlander, in the rundown one-building apartment complex parking lot. The woman she was supposed to meet lived in the second unit from the right on the ground floor. The windows adjacent to the door were dark. Although it was only five in the afternoon, the overcast sky and light rain hurried the encroaching dusk.

The parking lot was half-full. Another car pulled in. A young man got out and trudged across the lot toward a unit on the far left. As he entered, an inside light popped on, revealing movement in the apartment. The unit that held Val's interest, though, remained cloaked in darkness.

Maybe she's afraid and is trying to make it look like there's no one home. Val was there to escort the woman away from a violent husband—take her to safety in another town. Val's boss, Janet Polasky, had said that the husband was supposed to be at work until after seven in the evening. *Two hours yet.*

Her gut, though, told her that something was very wrong. She couldn't shake a dark sense of foreboding. She saw nothing to confirm or eliminate the suspicion. Still, the entire situation screamed *trouble*. She reached over into the glovebox and removed her Glock nine-millimeter handgun. As a felon, she shuddered at the thought of getting caught in possession of the weapon. It would be a surefire ticket back to prison.

She muttered, "Better prison than dead." Retrieving a shoulder holster from the rear seat, she strapped it on. Holding the handgun in her right hand, she slammed a magazine into place and released the slide. The loud click reassured her—a round chambered. She set the safety, holstered the weapon, and exited the car.

Taking one last look around, she searched for the unnamed, unseen threat that gnawed at her. The last light of day faded. The single glaring light in the parking lot cast just enough illumination to paint a dreary, copper-tinted picture of a neighborhood bathed in poverty and despair. The constant rain added to the sense of misery.

"Might as well get this done." She skirted the perimeter of the lot to the right, preferring to approach the apartment via the walkway alongside the building. She saw no point in advertising her arrival, on the off chance that things had already gone wrong inside.

She reached the far side of the lot, made her way toward the building, and started along the walkway. Her destination was the second unit in. As she cleared the first unit, she peered into the window of the second one—darkness. She could see nothing.

Drawing a deep breath, Val took one last long look around and then tapped lightly on the door. No answer. She banged the door, louder. She heard the clinking of a chain and a click. The door cracked open and a woman's face appeared, her eyes full of fear. She shook as she stood with the door slightly open.

Chapter 1

Val tried to look past her but could see nothing. "Ruth? I'm Val. Are you ready to go?"

The woman glanced furtively to her right, licking her lips. "Uh, I've changed my mind. You need to go."

Before Val could react, the woman silently mouthed what appeared to be, "Help me!"

Val's mind raced. Removing her gun, she clicked off the safety and spoke loudly, trying to insert some annoyance for effect. "Well, okay, I guess. If you don't need anything else, I'm going to——"

With no warning, she stepped back, raised a bended leg, and kicked the door with every ounce of strength she could muster. It gave way, hurling the woman back. Val lunged through, her eyes searching for the target she knew would be there.

Everything shifted into slow motion. Ruth, the surprised woman tumbled back across a small table and rolled toward the wall.

Val caught movement at the back of the room... too late. She saw a flash as pain shot through her left chest and shoulder. The sound, though, seemed muted. The room spun. The ceiling whirled. Colors danced across her field of vision. Another flash—more pain, this time in her thigh. Darkness hovered at the edge of her vision.

Val felt her own gun coming to bear on the movement, as though it had a mind of its own. She stared in quiet curiosity at the small sight at the end of the barrel. Then it was there. Looking down the gun barrel, she saw him. Her finger reacted, squeezing, again and again.

Pop! It sounded as though it came from miles away, barely discernable to her ear. Pop! She had the vague sense of weapon recoil. No matter. Pop! Vivid colors continued to swirl in front of her. The darkness on the edges closed in. Pop! Her finger would simply not be still. Pop!

She felt herself flailing backwards, her legs collapsing. A scream managed to pierce the shell into which she had retreated. The blackness overpowered the colors and silence swallowed her.

It didn't feel so bad. She floated there, seeing herself lying on the floor. *No! I won't die this way. Dee, please help me. If you can hear, please come.* She almost laughed, although she wasn't sure whether or not spirits could do that. How could Dee hear her? Why would she expect her lover to come to the rescue, especially after their last argument. *I'm sorry, Dee. I should have told you.* She understood, though, that it was too late for apologies.

No! I won't die like this. She struggled to concentrate… on anything. She would survive this. She had to. Then there was nothing.

2

The meeting had been set for nine in the evening. Reverend Janet Polasky waited in the leased condo —the one that had seen three men die in front of her and had provided safety and shelter for Bonnie Corel after she left her abusive senator husband. Gregg Stottman's nice, Dani had stayed there, recovering from the trauma that had assaulted her life over the past nine months.

Dimitry Kazarian, her security chief, sat beside Janet. The woman on whom they waited had wanted a one-on-one meeting with the minister. Everyone involved in the project had agreed—no way. The stakes were desperately high. Strangers simply did not get to meet with Janet Polasky alone.

Kaz ran his index finger around the rim of his cup of steaming coffee as he stared out the window. "She didn't give you any clues as to what she wanted?" He asked the question without looking at Janet.

"I assume it's about helping a woman. Maybe she needs help. Other than that, I have no idea."

"She didn't give you a name or anything?"

"Tahira. That's all she said. She spoke with a heavy accent—sounded Indian, Pakistani, or maybe Afghani." Janet paced the living room. She went over the conversation she'd had with the woman. It had revealed nothing other than she wanted to talk to Janet and that it was urgent. She stopped and faced Kaz. "Do you think it could be a ruse—someone trying to get to me?" She couldn't bring herself to say "kill me" although that's exactly what worried her.

Kaz tilted his head for a moment as though carefully considering the question. "Seems like a lot of trouble to go through. It's no secret where you work. If she wanted to ambush you, why not do it at the church without alerting you?"

Janet returned to the pacing. Although she was expecting it, the doorbell startled her. She moved toward the door, but Kaz motioned her back.

"Let me have a look." He pulled back the curtain and stood for a moment considering whatever it was that he saw. "She's alone. At least I don't see anybody else. Go ahead, answer it."

He moved across the room and stood at the threshold of the kitchen, his hand behind his back. Janet knew he held a handgun and could respond in the blink of any eye if there was trouble.

She opened the door.

The woman standing before her wore a light gray wool coat, charcoal slacks, and a black hijab. Her dark almond-shaped eyes were set into her brown face. She glanced furtively around, as though worried about who might be watching. "We spoke on the phone."

Janet opened the door wider and stepped aside. "Come in, please. Can I take your coat?" She gestured toward the couch.

As the woman shed her outer garment, she eyed Kaz suspiciously.

"This is Dimitry Kazarian, our security officer." Janet hung the coat up. "I'm Janet Polasky, although I guess you figured that out yourself."

The woman smiled weakly. "Yes. Thank you. I am Tahira Kushk."

"Can I offer you something to drink—coffee, tea, water?"

"Tea would be lovely." Tahira sat, smoothing out the invisible wrinkles in her slacks.

"Sugar or cream?"

"Just tea, please."

With steaming cups on the coffee table, Janet drummed her fingers on the arms of the overstuffed chair. After a moment of silence, she said, "You said you needed my help."

"Yes, that is true."

Janet prodded, "And?"

Tahira stared into Janet's eyes as though trying to read something within. She touched her index finger gently to her high cheekbone. "I… there is a woman that I am trying to help. She wants to escape her husband."

"I assume violence is involved."

"I fear that is the case."

"Have you tried the King County Domestic Violence Network? They can provide emergency shelter, protective services, legal assistance, and a host of other services. It's what they do." Janet forced a smile.

"This is a special case. This network of which I speak cannot do what needs to be done." Tahira's voice was soft but firm. She never took her eyes from Janet's.

"Why me?

The nod was barely perceptible. After a moment,

Tahira responded, her voice less urgent and almost conversational. "I know who you are. I know what you do."

Somehow that bothered Janet, although she couldn't say why. After all, the people who came to her for help were supposed to know what she did. "May I ask how you came by this information?"

Tahira offered the faintest of smiles. "I would prefer, at least for the moment, to maintain confidences. I will say only that I trust my source."

"Fair enough… for now." Janet sighed. "If we decide to move forward together, we will revisit the question." She sipped her tea and cleared her throat.

"What is it exactly that you think I can do that the DV network cannot?"

Tahira shook her head and glanced away for a moment. "Before we deal with specifics, I need some assurances."

"About what?"

"First, that you are willing to help. Second, that you will honor her confidentiality."

Janet shot back immediately. "On your first point, I can't promise anything until I know more about what she needs. Secondly, yes, confidentiality and privacy of our clients is a core element of what we're about. Let me say this, Miz… Kushk, did you say it was? You strike me as a smart woman. You know that I can say anything I want. In the end, you will either trust me or you won't."

"You are spoken of in the highest regard, Reverend Polasky. I rather expect that such a person does not gain this respect by lying or by going back on her word. For that reason, I ask the questions and will take your answers on good faith."

"You have my answers. Now, some specifics, please.

Where is she now? Is she in a safe place? How soon will she need this help? I'd also like a rundown on her husband."

"Hmmm, well…." Tahira again considered Kaz, seemingly reluctant to speak in front of him.

Janet asked, "Is there a problem with Mister Kazarian being here?"

"It is just that I am not used to conducting business with men present. You will excuse me if I seem overly cautious. Where I come from, such situations can turn deadly."

Before Janet could speak, she felt her phone vibrate in her trousers pocket. She pulled it out and looked at the screen. "Excuse me, please. I need to take this call." She stood and eased into the kitchen as she connected.

"Hi Dee. I'm in the middle of something right now. Can I call you back?"

The voice on the other end screamed. "THEY SHOT HER! God, Janet, they shot her."

3

Kaz drove. The trip from the condo to the hospital seemed a blur to Janet. She phoned Greg Stottman, her funding source who had since become a close friend, to let him know what had happened. Otherwise, silence prevailed. Dee had not been able to provide much information on the phone other than the fact that Val had been shot. From what Janet was able to infer, the woman that Val had been sent to help wasn't seriously injured.

The possibility of this event had haunted Janet on and off since the beginning. In recent months, the danger had grown more real with attempts on her own life and the disappearance of Sue Hartman, the director the King Country Domestic Violence Network. Now this. Her employee had been shot and according to Dee, was in grave condition. Greg and Kaz had both warned her.

Val had been armed as both men had suggested. That hadn't saved her... or had it? She wasn't dead. What happened to the man? Dee hadn't said. If the other woman had survived, though, then either he was dead or ran away. At this point, there were simply no answers.

Chapter 3

They found Dee in the waiting area outside the surgery center, her eyes swollen and red. Janet rushed and embraced her. Dee sobbed while Janet held her.

After a moment, they separated. Dee wiped the tears from her cheeks.

Janet asked, "Is there any update? How's she doing?"

Dee appeared as though she wanted to speak but simply shook her head.

They sat in padded chairs facing out the window into the darkness. Midnight had come and gone. Daylight would not arrive for hours.

Greg arrived about fifteen minutes after Janet and Kaz. His questions were the same as Janet's. There were still no answers.

Just after three that morning, a doctor came out and briefed them. Val's condition had been upgraded from grave to critical. They were doing everything possible. Time would tell. He uttered the expected cliches and then disappeared back into one of the rooms leaving behind silence and uncertainty.

Janet grasped Dee's hand. "She's improving. Val's a fighter. She'll make it."

Dee nodded without enthusiasm. "She's a felon and she had a gun. That's all they care about." Her voice was flat, the words bathed in resignation.

"Who?"

Dee looked up. "The detectives. That's what they said once they found out who she was and checked their records." Her voice grew angry. "Val might die. If she does survive, though, they want to send her back to prison. Jesus Christ, Janet. How the fuck does that kind of thing happen?"

"Don't worry, Dee. We'll make sure that doesn't

happen." The words came easily to Janet, although she had no idea how she might fulfill that promise.

Dee's shallow laugh was full of bitterness. "You haven't seen it. The machine doesn't care. Val's just a woman and a felon. It will chew her up and spit her out as though she was nothing."

Janet mindlessly repeated the promise. "No. They won't. Not this time."

Greg touched Janet's arm. When she looked up at him, he stood and nodded away from the group. "Let's talk."

They huddled in a corner of the waiting area. Greg said, "I might be able to help with this."

"How so?"

"We know a U. S. Senator. Maybe it's time to establish a relationship."

"Bonnie Corel? You think she can help?"

He responded, "It's worth a shot. This is not a federal issue, but she was appointed by the governor when her husband died. That means that she has access to him, and he does have the power to make things happen."

Janet arched her eyebrows. "I don't know, Greg. The two of you didn't hit it off that well as I remember. Why would she get involved in something that's not really within her area of influence?"

"Every relationship begins with some small step, often transactional. We didn't hit it off because there was no real reason we should have. I needed nothing from her, and she didn't need anything specific from me. We were introduced and came to know each other, that's it. Now I need something from her. It will require some political capital on her part, but it will create a relationship that she can leverage later."

Janet's laugh was mirthless. "So, you want a favor from

her, and, in return, you'll be her friend and return some unspecified favor in the future. Is that it?"

He laughed. "I wouldn't have used those terms but, yeah, I suppose that describes it pretty well. Look, Janet, that's the way the world works. Even the greatest friendships often start with some transaction. Look at us. It started out because you needed some money for a worthwhile project. Who knows where these things go?"

She studied his face. In a passing moment, she wanted to ask him where their relationship was going. This, however, was not the time. "If you think it'll help, then, certainly. I appreciate it."

He grasped her hands and squeezed. "Of course."

A wave of warmth swept over her. Janet felt reassured… and safer.

4

The Sniper got out of his truck and stretched. It had been a long drive from southern Idaho to Spokane, Washington. He'd left before dawn, forging through an early season snowstorm. By the time daylight made its appearance, he reckoned there was at least a foot of snow, with more in the forecast.

The McDonald's parking lot, though, was well-plowed and salted. He stood for a moment, as he considered the building beneath the golden arches. Just how was this supposed to work? What he was here to discuss could hardly be considered idle chit-chat appropriate to a fast-food joint. The thought crossed his mind that this could be an ambush—a set-up. He knew beyond any doubt that his life hung in the balance. On the other hand, if they wanted to kill him, they would have done already. Besides, a crowded spot like this wouldn't be the best place for an ambush.

It had been a long, twisted journey that took him from being a U. S Army sniper in Afghanistan to his current plight as an out-of-favor assassin for a shadowy organization in the Pacific Northwest. As he sat in his truck, his mind traced the path. Everything, it seemed, had changed —gone to shit—when he'd reluctantly agreed to help his idiot of a cousin, Billy Robinson. What ensued was a failed hit followed by the kid's failure to clean up some loose ends. It ended up with his cousin's capture and the Sniper being forced to execute him.

So, here he was. He'd fallen from grace with the organization that had paid him so well. Now, he was the target. Except that they'd contacted him suggesting that things could be *made right*. He had his doubts but *no guts… no glory*.

"Hmmm. Might as well get to it." He felt the Smith and Wesson .38 handgun in his coat pocket. It wouldn't be that easy to get to but carrying it in plain view would be decidedly worse.

Opening the restaurant door, he stepped in, stopped, and scanned the dining area. His contact sat in a window booth on the far side. The white shirt, red down jacket, and gray ball cap were exactly as described to him. He made his way to the counter and ordered—quarter pounder with cheese, large fries, and a coke. Grabbing his receipt, he eased over to the booth and slid in opposite the man.

His contact looked to be in his mid-fifties. He had gray hair cut short on the sides, but the ballcap obscured the top of his head. He carried what looked to be about fifty to seventy pounds of excess weight, evidenced by an ample stomach that rolled onto the tabletop.

"My order will be up in a minute." The Sniper wasn't sure what else to say. The meeting had been called by his contact. He didn't know this guy's name. He had no intention of introducing himself, although he suspected that the man already knew his identity. The organization knew everything about him.

His contact nodded and took a sip of his cold drink through a straw. "No hurry."

The silence was unnerving, but the Sniper was determined not to fill the empty space with idle conversation. Until the man said what was on his mind, there was little to talk about. In those few minutes, the Sniper replayed the past few months' events. He'd had some successes and a few major screw-ups. Mostly, he figured his major fuck-up was placing trust in Cousin Billy, whom he had been forced to kill. In retrospect, he should have killed the idiot the day he showed up at the cabin. *Regret won't solve anything. Everything is always clear in the rearview mirror.*

A voice rang out from the counter. "Number two one three."

"That's mine. I'll be right back." The Sniper did his best to keep his voice even, trying for a touch of ambivalence. He returned to the table a moment later with his lunch in hand.

As he unwrapped his sandwich, the other man cleared his throat. "Thanks for making the trip over. Much appreciated."

The Sniper nodded and took a bite of his burger.

His contact continued, "Sometimes things go sideways. Regardless of the planning and care, there's always the possibility of that random hiccup." He grimaced and shook his head.

"True enough." The Sniper popped a French fry in his mouth.

The man glanced around, presumably to make sure no one was within earshot. "You have a chance to make this right."

Something seemed off but the Sniper couldn't put his finger on what it was. Maybe it was the eyes—not unpleasant but… they seemed empty. The man's calmness and sense of serenity unnerved the Sniper. Still, the words sounded good. Everything could go back to the way it was before.

No. The Sniper had a long and productive relationship with his gut. It rarely let him down. The man was lying. This wasn't about amends for a screw-up. The Sniper had become a loose end. His mind raced. He snuck a glance around the room—no danger that he could spot. Still, he was certain that he was being set up. At this point, though, there was no reason not to play along. In fact, it was better to convince the man that there were no suspicions. "I'm listening."

A folder slid across the table, ending up in front of the Sniper.

"He's not an enemy. In fact, he's our ally and a personal friend of mine."

The Sniper placed his hand on the file but kept it closed. He arched a single eyebrow and cocked his head in question.

The man continued, "Unfortunately, his vices—sins of the flesh—have turned him into a liability. Everything you need is in the folder." He picked up an oatmeal cookie from his tray, considered it for a moment, and took a large bite, devouring half of it at once.

"And after this?" The Sniper queried.

"All is forgiven." The man paused and narrowed his eyes before continuing. "Additionally, I can make it worth your while—twenty thousand."

If there had been any doubt at all about what really going to happen, it ended with that offer. The Sniper was on the outside and wanted back in. The obese man sitting across from him had to know that. There was no need to offer such a generous package. In fact, the Sniper had fully expected that whatever task he was to be assigned, there would be no compensation. It was, he thought, easy to offer a large payment if there was no intention of follow-through. And so, the game continued.

The Sniper put on his most enthusiastic face. "That's very generous of you, and I hope you know how much I appreciate this second chance." He poured the bullshit on thick. "I won't let you down."

His contact smiled broadly. "We have great things ahead of us. It will be good to have you by our side."

The Sniper probed. "This offer, you've cleared this all the way to the top?"

The man frowned and stared back. "I'm the only one you need to worry about."

The Sniper back-pedaled. "No offense intended." He picked up his last French fry, dipped it in ketchup, and popped it in his mouth. Swallowing, he wiped his lips and stood. "I should be headed back. It'll be slow going through this storm. I'll contact you when it's done."

He was amazed at the serenely pleasant look on the man's face, but there was no hiding the intent. Redemption was not on the table. The fat mass of betrayal was only interested in whoever was described in the file folder and the Sniper's death. And yet he looked as though he sat at the right hand of Jesus.

Why the charade? The Sniper wondered why the man would go to this much trouble. With the resources controlled by the *Strength is Truth* organization, making someone disappear wouldn't pose a problem. Perhaps he would find the answer in the folder he carried with him as he pushed through the restaurant door and out into the winter storm.

5

The Sniper stared at the photo in the open folder—a pasty-faced weasel, from the look of him. He muttered, "Millard Conyers." The brief narrative indicated that he was pastor of a church in the Seattle area— New Life Ministry of the Nazarene. *Such a pompous name.* When he thought about it, though, it was a good match. According to the instructions, the pastor made a monthly journey to Portland, staying at the Hilton downtown. This area was known to be his sexual playground. This is where the target was supposed to die.

"Why do they want this guy dead?" The Sniper muttered to himself as he stood and began to pace the room. He couldn't have cared less about Conyers. The situation was complex and had to be dealt with as such. His contact had said that the man had to die because his sexual adventures had made him a liability. "Maybe."

The truth was, though, that the man's vices were of no interest to the Sniper. The only connection he felt to the man was that they were both condemned. If his enemies wanted this man dead, then perhaps there was value to be found in him. The Sniper paced. *The enemy of my enemy is my friend.* "Hmph… not exactly the kinda guy I want for a friend."

"I suppose the fact that we both have a bullseye on our back gives me more in common with him than with the people who want him dead." He rubbed his hands together as he shuffled around the room muttering to himself.

"What are the facts?"

First, the organization, or at least a part of it, wanted Conyers dead. Why? "I don't know why? Does it matter?"

Yes. It mattered, but the Sniper decided to defer that thought until later and deal with his own issues. *They*—the organization for which he had labored and risked so much —wanted him dead. How did he know that? *I saw it in his eyes.* No, that was not good enough. How did he know? *Why offer me a lot of money to do something I'd do for free just to get back in? We all know I want in.*

The Sniper had asked his contact whether this operation was sanctioned by those above him. The response had been curt but revealing. No one above the contact mattered. "So, does my contact want me dead or does the entire organization want me dead? For that matter, what about Conyers? Is it just between him and the contact or is the good pastor truly on the outs with everyone?"

Another possibility found its way into the Sniper's thoughts. "What if Conyers is really the important target and I'm just a loose end?" That would be a sweet arrangement for the organization—get rid of a crucial target and, at the same time, eliminate a loose end, all without spending a penny. The answers to these questions all seemed to be tied up in his contact. Without knowing more about him, everything else was a dead end. *I could just go ahead and do the hit and take things as they come. After all, fore-warned is forearmed.*

This would be satisfactory but not optimal. The target, Conyers could be leveraged. He likely knew more about the organization than the Sniper did. If he could get to the man, preferably down in Portland, then perhaps the two of them could explore options of mutual benefit.

The first task, though, was to learn the identity of his contact—the one who wanted him dead Undoubtedly Conyers would know it. After all, the contact said that the pastor was a friend. He whispered under this breath, "No. Better to do this on my own. I may have a use for this chump later. For now, though, I'll get the information myself."

Since Conyers was a pastor in the Seattle area, then it would follow that his contact likely resided in that area as well. After all, they were friends, according to his contact. Maybe he attended Conyers' church. The Sniper thought again about the nature of the organization *Strength is Truth*. They bantered a lot of Bible stuff around. Everything was bound up in religious mumbo jumbo.

"No, the contact isn't a part of Conyers' church. He is at the very least, a peer—another preacher maybe?" How many churches were there in the Seattle area? A quick Internet search turned up just under fourteen hundred—too many to check one at a time.

"I'm going to assume that he's not one of those liberal leftist preachers." Another Internet search narrowed down the number of churches, excluding the more liberal denominations like Episcopalians and Methodists.

So it went. He worked the problem logically until he was down to under a hundred churches. "Okay, then. Let's have a look." He plowed into the list, pulling up the website for each church in turn, checking out their board of directors and their minister. It took just under an hour until he hit paydirt.

He stared at the face that he'd seen in the McDonald's over in Spokane. He whispered to himself with an air of superiority. "Well, well, Reverend Carl Broward. It is indeed a pleasure to make your acquaintance."

It felt right. The Sniper was back in business. No more running and hiding. He would take the fight to his enemy, just like he'd done in Afghanistan.

6

It wasn't that Janet had forgotten Tahira Kushk. With Val in the hospital facing the double-barreled tragedy —hovering near death and in danger of going back to prison if she survived—every bit of attention Janet could muster was focused on that. Three days after the initial meeting, the minister carved out the time to meet again, this time in a non-descript office in University Heights.

"I'm truly sorry for letting it go this long," Janet apologized, "but one of my employees was shot and nearly killed. It's occupied all of my time over the past few days."

Tahira folded her hands in her lap. "I understand. Where I come from, these things are everyday events. It can almost seem as though they are part of day-to-day life, and yet in each case, a human life hangs in the balance. I pray that your employee recovers."

"That reminds me. You've twice used the phrase 'where I come from.' May I ask, where are you from?"

"I have lived in many places, but I started a rescue mission such as you have in Kabul, Afghanistan. I fear that in that part of the world, such services are far less valued than they are here."

Janet's laugh betrayed her bitterness. "I wouldn't say that our services are that welcome here either. The women we serve may appreciate us, but few others do." Her memory floated back to the confrontations with Carl Broward and Millard Conyers at the Church Association.

She continued, "But, we do what we must. You said that you have a client who needs our help. Could you please tell me about her situation?"

Tahira seemed far less tentative than she had at the last meeting. Maybe the woman had had time to think things over or maybe it was just that she hadn't trusted Kaz. In any event, she spoke freely. "The woman is married to a man who comes from old money, as you Americans say. He is a federal judge, although he is not accomplished or ambitious. His father, however, is a very different tale. He is politically powerful and spares no expense in protecting the family name. My client is terrified that if she tries to leave, he will simply make her disappear. I would like to help her disappear in a very different way."

"Are there children involved?"

"No, but there is a family complication. The woman's father also lives in the area. She would be reluctant to leave him behind. Also, as you might guess, if she were to disappear without him, her husband's family would likely use him as leverage."

Janet pondered the problem. "Tell me more about the woman's father."

"He is a widowed schoolteacher. The two of them are close, so it is likely that she will want him to accompany her."

"I confess that we've not had to deal with a situation like this before. From what I've heard informally, though, such arrangements usually involve never contacting friends or family again. I'll do some addition checking and let you know."

Tahira stood. "It seems that our meeting is finished, then. I have my tasks ahead as do you. At our next meeting, I will be prepared to give you details, including names and locations. I will speak to you within two days, if that is acceptable to you."

Janet considered what she needed to do and responded, "That may be optimistic. To get the information we need could take as long as a week. Let me know if anything comes up that requires us to move immediately. Otherwise, let's plan on meeting again this time next week. Is this a good location?"

"No. I rented this space for the day only. I will let you know where to meet next."

"Meanwhile, I'll get my other employee lined up for this."

Tahira eyed Janet for a moment before speaking. "Thank you. About your employees—it is not my place to comment on who you utilize. I will say honestly that I am not at ease with men being a part of the service. My experience is that, when things go badly, men tend to stick together."

"I appreciate your candor. Mister Kazarian, whom you met last time, is an employee. He plays a crucial role in our operation. Without him, we are unable to do the things we do. If you cannot bring yourself to work with that, I understand. I cannot, though, simply cut him out of the arrangements."

The dark-skinned woman drew her mouth into a tight line. After a moment, she nodded. "It seems you have me at a disadvantage. If I want to save my client's life, I will have to bow to your wishes. Just know that I do so reluctantly."

"Understood. And you should know that I risk the lives of my employees reluctantly as well. If what you say is true, then everyone involved in this will be in danger. We'll be, as they say, all in this together."

7

Kaz spotted Detective Charlotte Wharton across the small park. She sat on a bench clutching a disposable cup with both hands. Stopping to watch her for a moment, he was struck by what seemed a sense of calmness. He could see her breath as she exhaled. The detective remained still for the most part, lifting the cup to her lips every minute or so. Otherwise, she seemed a fixed part of the environment.

The idea of meeting with her had been a long shot. While Greg and Janet were caught up with Val's shooting and the aftermath, the problem of the hit list that included Janet seemed a larger issue. Greg had provided Kaz with contact information for Wharton but had otherwise seemed preoccupied. When Kaz contacted Wharton, she also seemed ambivalent about meeting. After some cajoling, though, she had agreed.

As he considered her, he went over in his mind one more time what he wanted from her. It would be a hard sell.

Suddenly he was aware that she was returning the

stare. After a moment, she offered an almost imperceptible nod. He stopped by a small kiosk and purchased a cup of coffee before wandering over to sit beside her. "Nice day," he quipped, "considering it's the middle of winter."

"I'm not accustomed to doing business on a park bench, Mister Kazarian. What can I do for you?"

"Thanks for meeting with me. I thought this might work better than your office." He held his cup up. "At least the coffee's better and I'll bet the scones they sell over there are better than the donuts."

"I didn't realize you were an aspiring comedian."

He laughed lightly. "More of a hobby than a vocation."

"Again, what do you want?"

"All business, huh? You need to lighten up, Detective. Life's too short to stay that tightly wound."

"When I need that kind of advice, I'll consult a therapist."

Kaz smiled and took a sip. "Have you learned anything else about Robinson's death?"

Her reply carried a hard edge. "I don't discuss ongoing investigations with civilians."

"It's not an ongoing investigation, Detective. Robinson was wanted for assault and murder. He's dead, end of case. His death unfortunately didn't happen in your jurisdiction. Unless I'm missing the mark, your superiors are chomping at the bit for you to leave it behind and get on with your active caseload."

"My workload is none of your business."

Kaz ignored the remark and continued, "It's like an itch that you can't scratch. Your suspect is dead, and, for all your passion, you accomplished nothing in your *investigation*, as you call it. You want answers but the King County Sheriff's Department isn't going to pay you to find them."

After a moment's silence, she spoke again, the anger and distaste still coating her words. "Just what line of work are you in, Mister Kazarian?"

He gazed out across the park with its brown grass, staring at the bare branches on trees on the other side. "Security."

"In certain circles, that's a euphemism for a hit man. Is that what you are, Mister Kazarian, a hired killer?"

"Have you ever killed anyone, Detective?"

"That would also be none of your business."

He nodded, smiling softly. "Oh, but it is. You're a public servant. I'm the public. I think it's reasonable for me to ask that question. Have tax dollars ever paid for you to take a human life?"

"For the last time—what do you want?"

Kaz turned toward her. "I have a problem, Detective. I need information. I can work on my little issue alone, if necessary, but I thought that working together might allow both of us to get what we want. The beauty is that we can do all of this *off the books*... and without breaking any laws."

She peered deep into his eyes, as though contemplating some enormous puzzle. "Before we go on, I need to know more. For starters, what is it you intend to do with any information we gather?"

Kaz sighed. "I suppose that's a fair question. You were at the meeting about that hit list and the website. Janet Polasky is the next name of that list. I intend to fix that."

"Why? Is she something special to you? Lover?"

He burst out laughing. "Seriously? That's the best you can come up with?" He grew serious. "No. That's not it at all. I work for her—security—as I said before. The people that are after her have a history of hitting their mark most of the time. The last attempt, the one on the Freyberg woman, was a screw-up—totally out of character. This gives us an opening. I want to capitalize on it."

"What does that mean—*capitalize on it*?" She raised her cups to her lips with both hands, taking a sip. "Are you going to go out and start killing people?"

Kaz grew exasperated. "What's this fascination you have with killing? I told you at the meeting when we first met, I don't know what we're going to do with the information—maybe turn it over to the cops. It might also help us design better security. What I can tell you is that I'm not a vigilante."

His next words came out with what he thought was the perfect amount of harshness. "If that's not good enough for you, then we're done here, and you can go out and find your own information."

She softened. "What makes you think I have anything to offer?"

He sighed. "Can we just stop the posturing for a minute. I'm asking for help. In return, I'm willing to share any information that I find… and I promise you I will find information. I'm asking you because I believe that this hit list and the people behind it are connected in some way to Billy Robinson. Look, whoever killed the kid was a pro. I was there. It wasn't a casual, haphazard hit. It was a precision shot, quickly taken, after which the shooter melted into the night without a sign."

"Yes, but Robinson's dead and, with him, any answers that we might have gotten. If you'd been able to protect him that night, it might be different."

Kaz's eyes narrowed. "I'll let that one pass. In my experience, though, there are usually multiple sources of answers. We just need to go at it a little differently."

"What makes you think Robinson and the hit list are connected?"

"His cousin, the one you said was killed in Afghanistan —what if he wasn't killed? What if he made his way back and is existing off the grid. He was from Idaho. We know that at least one of the key players behind their operation is in Idaho. We know that they're radical right-wing fanatics. From what little I've learned about Robinson's cousin, he could fit the bill."

"That's a lot of speculation, Mister Kazarian. You have no solid evidence of the connection."

Kaz laughed. "I'm not preparing a court case, Detective. I'm trying to protect my employer. You, I might add, are not working on a case that's likely to end up in court, at least not in the near term. We both want answers. I think that, working together, we can put the pieces of this puzzle together."

Wharton shook her head. "As you so aptly put it, my superiors are not anxious for me to devote time to this."

"I'm not asking for your official time. This is after hours work."

She remained silent and lowered her gaze, running her finger around the rim of her cup. After a moment she took a deep breath and turned her attention to him. "I need to think about it. Sharing information like this could get me into a lot of trouble."

"I understand." Kaz felt a sudden kinship with her. She was trying to sort it out. He could see it in her eyes. "I can only promise you that I know how to protect my colleagues. I will respect whatever decision you reach." He took out a card, scribbled his private cell number on it, and handed it to her. "If you need to reach me.

8

It felt wrong. Janet knew that she needed to move forward, connecting Aylin Freyberg, the new employee, with the new client. It was the right thing to do. With Val lying in a hospital bed close to death, though, it seemed insensitive. In the end, Janet understood that leading any organization, especially one that rescued women in danger, involved keeping things on track despite all adversity. There would be time to sort things out, even grieve, if necessary, later.

Aylin Freyberg pulled up a chair in front of Janet's desk. The winter sun had just risen, and the two women sipped on coffee.

"Are you sure you feel well enough to work?" Janet queried the woman.

"Do you have a client for me?"

Janet responded, "I've been waiting to make sure that you're fully recovered. The last thing I need is for you to collapse on me."

Aylin snickered. "Not likely. So, what's the deal? Is she ready to go?"

Janet put a hand on Aylin's arm. "Let's slow down. It's not that simple. I've got some preliminary legwork to do before we start moving anyone anywhere. There's some political power at play. It won't be a simple *grab and run* job."

"Okay, what's our first move, then?"

"*My* first move is to investigate a way to get this woman a new identity. That's one of the complicating factors. Her husband's family is not going to sit idly by and let this happen. She needs to disappear completely and come back as someone else entirely."

Aylin probed, "How are you going to manage that?"

"Like I said, figuring that out is my first step."

The woman shot back, "It doesn't seem like you've thought this through very well."

The remark rubbed Janet too hard in all the wrong places. "Let's get something straight, Aylin. I've run up against some near impossible situations thus far and, with some very competent help, manage to figure them out. If you want to be a part of this, you're going to have to acquire some patience. We take things as they come—plan where possible and recognize solutions when they present themselves. I'd love it if we just had this playbook that gave us all the answers. Sadly, it doesn't work that way. If this isn't to your liking, I understand, but if you want to stay with me, you'll need a lot more flexibility than you're showing now."

Aylin brushed away the comments with a wave of her hand. "Don't get your knickers in a bunch. Just point me in the right direction and stay out of my way."

The comment only made things worse. "First, and you need to remember this, I will never *stay out of your way*. I'm responsible for these women as well as the safety of all my employees. You'll have a lot of responsibility, but you will never call all the shots. Second, I won't always know right away what the *right direction* is. As I said, we take it as it comes."

Aylin's face turned deep scarlet. She drew her mouth into a tight line and glared at Janet. After a long, tense moment, she averted her gaze and muttered, "Whatever."

Janet thought for a moment to try and rebuild a bridge to the young woman. They shared a passion for helping abused women. Most of their values aligned. Instead, she pushed ahead with the discussion. "We have all your paperwork done and your direct deposit is set. Did you get your health insurance card?"

The woman nodded. "Yeah."

"Okay, next step—we'll get you set up with a cellphone and some burners. Once that's done, we can go over when to use each." Janet paused for a moment, watching for reaction. She saw none. "Sometime over the next few days, our security director will contact you. He'll equip you with a weapon—a handgun—and train you."

Aylin shot back, "I have that covered. I own a gun already and I know how to use it."

Janet ignored the comment. "His name is Dimitry Kazarian."

An icy silence filled the room. Janet reinforced her expectations. "I'm sure you've heard, but my other employee is in ICU right now with multiple bullet wounds. She'd be dead right now if not for her ability with her weapon. I'm not leaving anything to chance, Aylin. Dimitry will be in touch. If you want to use your own weapon, we can consider that, but he *will be* providing the training. That's not negotiable."

"I heard about her. That's why I'm prepared. It's my life we're talking about here and I get to decide how I protect myself."

Janet's voice rose and she hurled the response back. "This isn't just about your life. It's also about the lives of our clients. You may well be able to look after yourself, but these women will be depending on you. Just so we're clear, they are not *your* clients—they are *our clients*. I have a responsibility to them as well."

"I need to go. I have a bunch of things to take care of." Aylin stood and put on her jacket.

Janet tried to salvage the conversation. "Hey, look, I'm not trying to be some kind of dictator. You know as well as I do, we're in uncharted territory here. We take things as they come and it's important that we stay on the same page."

Aylin turned her back on Janet. "Let me know when we're ready to go with this client." She left closing the door a little too firmly behind her.

9

First order of business—gather information on Carl Broward. He was the primary contact within the organization, *Truth is Strength*. The Sniper had everything he needed on his target, Millard Conyers. More would be gathered later. For the moment, though, Broward was the enemy— priority number one.

Daylight was still an hour away when he eased his pick-up onto the main road headed north toward Coeur d'Alene, where he would intersection I-90, which would take him to Seattle. It would be a grueling trip with icy roads most of the way. Sleeping in the back of his truck, washing up in restrooms, and living off fast food would not make the trip any easier. He figured it would take him at least three days of surveillance to get what he needed. The one bright spot was that fast food restaurants and coffee shops all had wi-fi access these days.

It was just after ten that evening when he parked his truck across the street from the Bellevue Baptist Temple, north and east of downtown Seattle. This was Broward's church. The parking lot was well lit but deserted, just as the Sniper had expected.

He muttered to himself, "Hmmm, big fucking church." The campus included what seemed a main gathering place —*the church*—along with four smaller buildings around it. From the signage, they appeared to be a school, a youth activity center, a media center, and another unnamed structure. Bellevue seemed a wealthy town and Baptist Temple certainly fit in well. The place screamed *money*.

After about fifteen minutes of idle observation, he made the journey to a nearby McDonald's. According to the sign on their door, they were open until midnight. He ordered a quarter pounder with fries and a coke and parked in a back corner of the restaurant. Accessing the web, he went to the temple's website and quickly found what he wanted. Yes, they had church-provided housing for the minister. It didn't take long to find the location. *Tomorrow.*

Finishing his meal, he drove to a nearby Wal Mart, which was open 24 hours a day. Parking about mid-way back in the lot, he settled in for the night. He'd learned long ago that the 24-hour box stores were very lenient about overnight parking.

The next morning, he parked on the street a half-block from Broward's residence and watched. Thus far, he'd seen nothing that surprised him. At 7:45, the garage door opened, and a beige Mercedes sedan backed out. As it passed him, he noticed that a woman drove it. "The Missus," he muttered.

Five minutes later, a Chevy Tahoe departed the residence with Carl Broward at the wheel. This was his target. He followed at a discrete distance, confident that the church was his destination. The first minor surprise came when the Sniper watched the minister pull into the lot and park beside the beige Mercedes that he'd seen leaving their house earlier.

"Must be a family affair." A quick check of the church's website produced a roster of the staff. There she was—Rhonda Broward, Administrative Manager. The Sniper wondered in passing if maybe they had children who were also feeding at that trough.

An hour later, he made a. Micky Dee's run, loading up with a couple of egg McMuffins, hash browns, and coffee, along with several bottles of water. Returning to the church, he parked on the other end of the street and watched as he ate.

And so passed the day—ordinary, uneventful. The two Browards—husband and wife, he assumed—left within ten minutes of each other. He followed the minister, who went straight home. When he arrived the garage door was open, and the Mercedes was parked. "What's that all about? Driving separate cars going the same place."

Carl Broward left home again around eight that evening, making his way to a non-descript building that turned out to be the King Country Church Association. The Sniper recalled that Broward's bio on the church website indicated that he was currently the board president of the association. "This could be helpful," he muttered. It could be the case that some of Broward's confederates were also involved in the association.

The Sniper took out his camera. In the low light, it would work better than his cellphone, which was not high-end. He photographed every person coming and going to the structure over the next few hours. He'd try and sort out the pictures later and cross-check them. Something might come of it.

10

Janet sat with Val every day, although the woman wasn't able to speak much and didn't really appear to be aware of everything that happened. By the end of the fourth day, however, she became more lucid. Sipping water through a straw with Janet's help, she mostly engaged in small talk. It was as though she wanted to avoid any conversation of substance.

The minister, however, felt a growing sense of urgency. Events were occurring and the situation was evolving by the day. Sooner or later, they had to face the elephant in the room.

"I know you're probably not feeling up to it, Val, but we need to discuss some things."

Val turned her head to stare out the window into the bleak Seattle winter day. "What's there to discuss. It happened. Not much I can do to change that."

Janet forced the conversation. "No. We can't change what happened, and I'm not particularly interested in trying to second-guess anything you did. We do, however, need to plan our next moves. This isn't going to go away simply because we don't want to talk about it."

Val jerked her head around too stare at Janet. "What?" The single word came out as a challenge. Her voice softened. "What do you want from me?"

"I just want to talk about where we go from here."

Before Val could respond, Janet continued, "We have two different immediate issues and a host of others that are percolating. First, the issue of the gun and your status. No matter what else happens, I'm not prepared to let them send you back to prison."

Val's laugh was laced with bitterness. "And just what is it that you think you can do about it? Somehow I doubt that the police, the DA, and courts care much about your opinion."

Janet shot back immediately, "Maybe not, but sitting back and just waiting for things to happen doesn't strike me as a particularly smart approach." She scooted her chair up closer to the bed.

She continued, "I suspect that this is one of those instances where the DA may well decide it isn't worth the trouble. I mean, if we choose to make a spectacle over this, the public is likely going to come down on your side. After all, you protected yourself *and* saved a woman's life with that gun. The women's rights people are certainly going to be with you, and most likely the second amendment ones will be in your corner, even if reluctantly. I'm guessing that, with a little strategic pressure up front, we can keep this from even becoming an issue."

Val waved away the thought, turning her attention back to the bleak early afternoon sky outside.

Janet took a deep breath and continued, "If we play our cards right, we might be able to accomplish two things at once. It's possible that we could get the governor to issue a pardon for you at the same time as we convince the DA not to act on this. It would let you off the hook as well as allow you to carry a weapon in the future."

"Yeah, right. That's gonna happen." The sarcasm was thick.

"Do you have any better ideas?"

Val sighed. "Cut me loose. What you're doing is too important to let it get all wrapped up in his mess. If I'm out of the picture, there's little reason for your program to be at risk."

Janet retorted, "It's *our* program. It's not just me and it's bigger than both of us. I need you, Val. Think of it as me being selfish. I can't do this by myself, and there's no one else I can depend on right now. It's in both of our best interests to meet this head on."

Val smirked, "And both get our heads bashed in."

Janet patted Val's arm and then leaned back in her chair. "All I'm asking is that, just for now, trust me."

11

It didn't take long. Janet heard back from Greg a week after he offered to speak with Bonnie Corel. What surprised her most, though, was the response.

"Bonnie called back this morning. The governor is willing to entertain the discussion. There's a catch, though." His tone softened as he ended.

"And?"

"He wants to meet with you in person."

The stipulation stunned Janet. "Why? There's likely nothing I can tell him that he doesn't already know about the case. I mean, it's been investigated by the police. As for Val being a felon, that's a matter of public record. What could he want with me?"

"I couldn't say. You could always meet with him and ask that question."

Janet could hear that he was attempting to inject some humor into an otherwise dark conversation. "I don't know, Greg. I'll have to talk to Val about it. After all, this entire thing is about her. She should have some say in it."

"I understand that. Still, I'm not sure what harm could

come of it. Like you said, he already has the ability to know most everything about the case. Besides, he might be able to offer some help or, if nothing else, a different perspective. You have to admit, it might be a nice thing to have Governor Ethridge in your corner."

"I'll give it some thought and get back to you."

The laugh that came over seemed genuine. "As much as I enjoy talking with you, I have a number that Bonnie gave me. You might do better contacting the governor's office and speaking with them directly… I mean, once you reach a decision."

* * *

"No, Janet." Val's face seemed bathed in exhaustion. Her eyelids fluttered as she tried to keep them open. "It's too risky. Keeping these women safe means that we need secrecy. If what we do gets out, then we won't be any more effective than the existing shelter system." She turned her head toward the window and closed her eyes.

Janet glanced over at Dee who, at least for the moment, kept silent. "Of course I'll always consider your wishes, Val. Keep in mind, though, that meeting with the governor could prevent you from going back to prison. Besides, I can control the flow of information. He knows a certain amount. I have the option of holding back anything I don't want him to know."

"Forget it. They're not going to send me back to jail. You said it yourself. It would be a PR nightmare for them. Remember, we're talking about self-defense and protecting an abused woman. The issue they have with me is a technicality—a felon having a weapon. In today's environment, what with all the second amendment stuff going on, it would likely blow up in their faces. Nope, just let it go."

Janet mulled over what Val had said and found herself mostly in agreement. "What about the future, though. You might slide by on this one, but the next one might not go so well."

Val grimaced and offered a shallow laugh. "I had a job before this one. I can go back to bookkeeping. It's boring but a hell of a lot safer."

Dee jumped in. "No, Val. You can't go back to that. It's not who you are."

Janet sat dumbfounded. Dee had been the very one who wanted Val out of the business. When Val was shot, Dee blamed Janet and the job. Why the sudden turn-around? Janet asked, "I thought you wanted her out of this job?"

Dee closed her eyes, appearing to sort out some kind of explanation. "I want her to be safe. I don't want to have to worry every night whether she'll be coming home or not. Mostly, though, I love you, Val, and I want you to be who you are. As frightened as I am about you being hurt on the job, I'm terrified at the thought of you having to give up what you were meant to be."

Val reached over and took Dee's hand. Her words came out soft and measured. "I appreciate that, Dee. We have to think about a bigger picture, though. It's not fair to anyone to hold my needs above theirs. Besides, I'm not totally sure what I'm meant to be, other than with you." She turned her head toward Janet.

"No, don't meet with the governor. It doesn't buy us anything we don't already have, and poses a huge risk."

"I'll consider it, Val. We'll just take things as they come. If the DA decides to move against you, we'll get with DV advocates around the state to step up the PR. As for the job, let's see where this goes first."

Chapter 11

* * *

The next morning, Janet overslept and arrived at the church office a half-hour later than usual. Her desk was exactly as she had dreaded. Full to overflowing with work that should have been attended to already.

She shook her head and quickly turned her attention to the stack of mail on her desk. As she stared at it, she realized that the pile contained at least three days' worth. She had neglected to go through it on Monday and Tuesday. To the side of her inbox sat a stack of telephone messages that she'd not responded to. She leafed through them—the church association, a note to call her board president, Gayle Rountree, from two days prior, and several from congregation members.

She picked up the phone and dialed the intercom. "Margaret, were there any other calls or visitors that I might have missed in the past few days?"

"Let's see, Fred Adamson dropped by and wanted to talk to you… didn't say what it was about. He said he'd get back to you later. The guy that tunes the piano called asking if he could put it off until next month. I told him that it would be fine. I think that was it. Why?"

"Nothing. I'm just trying to catch up on everything." She suddenly felt sick to her stomach. In that moment, she knew exactly what her board president wanted to talk to her about.

12

J anet forced herself to take a bite of the Russian tea biscuit and chew slowly. She savored the flavor for a moment before taking a sip of tea and then setting her cup down. "How have you been, Maddie?" Creeping up on the real discussion seemed a good idea.

Maddie Kavanaugh, Janet's old friend and mentor, though, was having none of it. "I suspect a lot better than with you. What's got you in a bunch, Dearie?" The old woman's eyes sparkled and her faced offered a peaceful smile.

Janet knew it was no use. Maddie had long sense learned to read the subtle signs of distress. Maybe that was why the minister treasured her friendship so. "It's complicated, as always." She laughed briefly.

"Why do I always have to remind you? The best stories always are. Now, you pour it all out while I enjoy these biscuits."

Janet started off slowly, picking up speed. She related the account of Val's shooting, the unexpected complications, and Greg's offer to help. By the time she finished, she wondered if maybe her version was so convoluted that no one could understand. Miraculously, though, Maddie seemed to get the gist of it.

"Well, I have to admit, you do bring me the most entertaining problems. I shudder to think how boring things would be without your exploits. Seriously, though, while it seems challenging, it's not as bad as you make it out to be. Your boyfriend's explanation seems right to me. The governor already knows or could know everything he needs to. Without getting into details, which I doubt he could even remember if you told him, there's little else to be said."

Janet fired back, "Exactly. Then why meet with him at all?"

"I don't know, Dearie, lots of people would give anything to have a private audience with the governor. You never know, he might have something to offer you?"

"He has nothing to offer that I need. Beyond that, even if he did have something, it would come with strings attached."

Maddie burst out laughing. "Oh my, you still don't get it. Everything comes with strings attached. Even God puts conditions on his offer of salvation and the governor's hardly going to do better than God."

"Like I said, though, the governor's got nothing I need."

"How do you know? You haven't spoken with him yet."

The argument frustrated Janet. "I'm just trying to avoid an awkward confrontation. He's going to want information that I don't want to provide. Right now, things are, I don't know... tense. I would hate for a confrontation like that to make things worse. I don't really want to be on the governor's bad side."

Maddie shrugged. "Let's leave that for a minute. Say

that you do decide to solve this on your own. You certainly might be able to keep this employee… Val is her name? You might be able to help her avoid going back to prison. That doesn't solve the gun problem in the future. If you want your employees to carry weapons and she can't do that, what's going to happen with her? Are you going to fire her?"

"It's not like that. I mean, no, I don't intend to fire her."

Maddie shot back quickly, "Then you're going to let her continue without carrying a gun?"

"Of course not. We'll need to work something out, that's all."

"What does that mean—*work something out*?"

"I don't know. I'm taking this one step at a time. The first thing is to keep her out of prison."

"I understand that, Dearie, but keep in mind that how you do that might affect what she does in the future… for work, I mean."

A thought struck Janet out of the blue. "Maybe I'm looking at this wrong. Everyone agrees that keeping her out of prison probably won't be that hard. The employment, though, is another matter. I've been assuming that the only thing Val could do is escort women. I haven't considered other possibilities."

Maddie cocked her head, her eyes wide. "Like what?"

Janet grinned. "I don't know right now, but I think I might have some ideas."

The old woman beamed. "Well, good then. I'll send you a bill for my consulting services."

Janet's grin turned into a laugh. "You do that, Maddie. I'll gladly pay." She popped the rest of a tea biscuit in her mouth. As she finished her tea, she added, "And, by the way, he's not my boyfriend."

13

The Sniper turned the question over in his mind. The most important issue for the moment seemed to be —did the his death sentence come from Carl Broward or was there someone else—someone higher on the food chain that who dictated it? In the end, it seemed that, short of asking Broward directly, the most likely source for an answer would be with Millard Conyers. *Time to go to work.*

Once he'd arrived in Portland, where he was supposed to make the hit, he set up to watch Conyers. Surveillance presented problems that the Sniper hadn't had to deal with in the past. The pastor had checked in to the Hilton Hotel in downtown Portland, parking his vehicle in the parking garage. Since camping outside the man's hotel room was out of the question, a choice had to be made—watch the car in the garage on the off chance that he would be traveling around the area by vehicle. The other option would be to surveille the front door of the hotel assuming that the pastor would be engaging in his play nearby and walk.

The Sniper decided to watch the garage. There was nothing within blocks of the hotel that appeared to give opportunity for *sins of the flesh*, as Broward had termed it. Conyers' portly build suggested that the man didn't walk much of anywhere. There was one other possibility—that the pleasures would be delivered to the pastor's hotel room. This would present a problem, since scores of people came and went through the hotel lobby every hour.

The revised plan that emerged represented a compromise. The Sniper would watch the car for the first day of the three-visit. Fortunately, the temporary parking permit in Conyers' window displayed the effective dates.

The Sniper checked into the hotel, although it created some additional challenges. He didn't have a credit card, which the Hilton required for check-in. He ended up having to purchase a Visa gift card and convince the staff that it was the best he could do. Fortunately, the evening shift desk attendant wasn't terribly conscientious. Purchasing a parking permit for the three days, he situated his truck about twenty feet from Conyers car. So began the waiting and watching.

It didn't take long. Within an hour, Conyers came into view, waddling mindlessly across the parking area to his car. He gave a perfunctory look around before getting in and starting the car.

Christ, man. Did it ever occur to you that someone might be watching? On the other hand, the pastor's obliviousness worked to the Sniper's advantage. With a little caution, the man could have made this a lot more difficult.

The Sniper followed Conyers out of the parking garage after about a thirty-second delay. He exited on to 6th Avenue SW, which, being a one-way, meant a right turn only. Easing into traffic, The Sniper could easily see Conyers white Ford Expedition six cars ahead. This was turning out to be a piece of cake.

The trip took less than ten minutes. Conyers parked on

a side street and entered a two-story gray house just outside the downtown area of Portland. The Sniper parked about a half block away and settled in to watch. His trusty binoculars gave him all the detail he needed. A couple of men came and went. Presumably, this was a queer hook-up spot.

When enlightenment came, it hit like a truck. The Sniper watched a man arrive with two boys, neither of whom appeared to be more than ten or twelve years old. They appeared, at least from a distance, to be Asian. The escort walked behind them, a hand on each one's shoulder. Opening the front door, he nudged them both through.

Kiddies? The Sniper felt revulsion wash through him. It would be a pleasure to kill this piece of shit. He forced those feelings aside, though. This development worked to his advantage. Conyers, when confronted, would do probably do anything, give any information at all, to extract himself from the shithole that he wallowed in.

The minister left the house about an hour after he entered, a relaxed smile on his face. He got into his car and drove straight back toward the hotel.

The Sniper had no need to follow him. At the first straightaway, he passed Conyers' vehicle with a burst of speed. Making straight for the hotel, he parked in an out-of-the way corner, got out of the truck and leaned against a concrete stanchion out of the light.

Five minutes later, the minister's Expedition came around the corner. After getting out of the truck, Conyers started for the elevator. At just the right moment, the Sniper stepped out in front of him. The pastor's eyes grew wide. For an instant, he appeared to search for the best escape route.

With a broad smile, The Sniper said, "Good Evening, Reverend Conyers. You've been a very bad boy."

14

The morning turned out to be productive. By early afternoon, she'd gone through the mail and returned the pending phone messages. She began to almost feel caught-up. The impending meeting with Gayle preyed on her mind, though.

Her board president showed up ten minutes early. After a few pleasantries, they settled into the meeting behind closed doors. Gayle fidgeted with a note pad as she appeared to compose her thoughts. Finally, she spoke, beginning slowly and haltingly. "I've been meaning to connect with you for the past week." She forced a shallow laugh. "It seems the older I get, the more scattered I become."

Janet smiled and nodded without comment.

"Anyway, we've got some things coming up that need attention. The first thing is that I want to get a jump on the budget a little early. It's only January, I know, but I'd like to have things finalized by the end of May."

Janet scribbled a note on her lined pad. "No problem. I can get started on that right away. Do you see the budget as a continuation of this year's or do you think things need to change?"

"I think we can start off looking at the one we have now. Speaking of that, though, it looks like we're slipping into the red for this year. Contributions are down. I'm sure the sluggish economy's not helping, but we do need to try harder."

Janet understood clearly that the "we need to try harder" referred to her. This was the part of the position she liked least—pushing the congregation for more money. It felt a little sleazy, despite understanding that it was absolutely necessary. "I can add a pitch to the Sunday services. We can also put a blurb into the programs."

Gayle hesitated, and then added, "You may have to do some home visits, too."

The words hit Janet hard. She had no problem visiting congregation members but making a sales pitch in the guise of a home visit felt more like trying to sell used cars. "We can look at that too." Janet finished up the note and looked at Gayle.

"What's next?"

The board president's face reddened. She averted her gaze, her mouth drawn into a tight line. "I also wanted to talk about things in general. I know that you've had a tough year, what with Hanna Miller dying and the man who tried to kill you. I was wondering... the board was thinking, that maybe you're feeling a little overwhelmed. I mean, your time here at the church has been kind of hit and miss."

She hurriedly added, "You do wonderful work, Janet, you really do. We were just wondering if maybe you should take some time off to get things straightened out. We can bring in a temporary minister."

Janet was stunned at the suggestion. "No, I don't think

I need that. Things are settling out now and I should be able to catch up. As for the funding, I'll get right on it."

Gayle continued apologetically, "We're just worried about you. We know that you're capable. It just seems like you've been overwhelmed with everything that's happened." She paused and then added, "And I...we know that you've got a lot going on helping abused women."

Janet's first inclination was to push back. On quick reflection, though, she realized that Gayle was right. She'd been consumed with her project and all the attendant crises. The reality hit hard. Continuing into the future, it would not grow any less demanding. In effect, she was trying to work two full-time jobs. A part of her knew... had always known that it wasn't sustainable.

"I understand, Gayle, and I appreciate your honesty. You're right, I've been trying to do it all. Things have to change." Janet paused for a moment before continuing. "Tell you what, I'm going to take a close look at this over the next several days. How about we connect on Friday and I can fill you in?"

Gayle looked relieved. Her color returned and a smile found its way onto her face. "That would be fine. Just shoot me a text and we can set up a time."

After her board president left, Janet settled back into her chair, confronting the reality of the commitment she'd just made. She knew what she had to do... sort of. How she was going to do it, though, eluded her.

* * *

Every minister with any experience knew about this element of the job. They knew about it coming into the position, and it was never far from the highest thing on the list. Janet seen her father, a retired Methodist minister, grapple with the problem year in and year out. Distilled into its simplest form, it was the classic business problem. A church had to bring at least as much revenue as it expended. Absent that, the house of worship would go under.

She sat across from the elderly couple clutching her cup of steaming coffee with both hands. As the three of them made small talk, Janet struggled to summon up the words that she'd so carefully authored that morning. This was little more than a sales pitch, although she frankly had no product to offer.

"It's great to catch up on things. Even with coffee hour after the services, I don't seem to spend them time with congregation members that I'd like to." Janet took a sip and then set her cup down on the coaster.

The throwaway line made her feel even worse—like she didn't pay attention to people until she needed money from them.

The man, Victor Thomas, offered a warm smile. The glint in his eyes suggested that he knew exactly what the visit was about. "How's the budget coming along?"

Janet sighed as sadness washed over her along with the realization that he was trying to make it easy on her. "Truthfully, it's…" she paused for a moment before mentally discarding her prepared speech. "Not good. We'll get through this year by dipping into the contingency fund. Next year—it just doesn't pencil right now."

He shrugged. "Inflation bites at all of us, I guess. No reason the Lord's house would get preferential treatment. Would it help if we upped our monthly contribution?"

"That's kind of you, Victor. I appreciate it." She felt like a used car salesperson. She had planned for the visit, creating a script designed to separate this couple from some of their money. Instead, they willingly offered it.

Betty interjected, "We can afford it, and there are others that can as well. This is our church. God gives us his blessings but it's up to us to keep the doors open and the bills paid." She patted her husband's knee. "Would you like more coffee?"

These meetings occupied the rest of the day and most of the next. By evening on the second day, Janet had secured commitments sufficient to close the fiscal gap... barely. She felt conflicted about it. Some members had made it easy on her—like Vic and Betty Thomas. Others struggled to convey the message that they themselves were stretched to the limit. A few had even been indignant, musing aloud that St. Luke's wasn't supposed to be like one of those megachurches. All in all, it had drained her spirit.

With all of that, she also felt the pull of her project and the dilemma in which she found herself. On top of the issue with the governor and his desire to meet, the need to solve the security problem haunted her. Something simply had to give.

15

K az took a deep breath and began the conversation that he knew would lock him in place. It had been a hard decision over which he had agonized for nights. "Thanks for taking the time to get together. Hopefully we can get this done and all get back to work." He sat with Janet and Greg in Greg's office.

Kaz continued, "Janet, I know that we've worked together more or less with the understanding that I'd probably take the job. I feel like it's time to formalize it, though. My contract with Greg," he nodded toward Stottman, "is finishing up and the timing is right."

Janet responded, "That sounds good. I assume we need to go over the specifics. I understand that Greg's spoken to you about the health care insurance. Given your mother's situation, we probably need to adjust what we currently have to cover it."

Greg interjected, "Yes, we talked about. If what you currently have in place is not sufficient, then you should amend it. I'm certain that we have plenty of funding in place to cover that plus the salary."

The remainder of the conversation went quickly—pay, insurance, vacation, retirement, etc. Kaz leaned back in the chair as they finished up. "Okay, that should do it. I'll swing by the accountant office and complete the tax forms and insurance stuff. After that, I guess we get to work."

Janet responded. "There are a couple of things that are at the top of the list. The first is a new employee—Aylin Freyberg. She says that she has a weapon. I need you to check it out and make sure it's the best one for the job, as well as providing orientation and training for her."

Kaz took out his phone and pulled up his Notes app. "Do you have contact information for her?"

The minister provided the information and then added, "When I spoke with her, she seemed reluctant on the training thing… She seemed to think she had a handle on it. I'd feel more comfortable, though, if you'd go over things with her. She can be a little headstrong, so be prepared."

"Got it. I'll give her a call and set a date and time. If nothing else, we'll go out to the shooting range, and she can show off her skills." He smiled and added, "You said there were two things."

Janet took a deep breath. "Yes. Do you remember the woman that we spoke with, Tahira Kushk?"

Kaz nodded.

"We need to get moving on that. The hitch is that it looks like we're going to have to find a way to get the woman a completely new identity."

He responded, "I can tell you that any identity you get on the black market will only hold up in the easiest of situations. It would never get past an investigation. If you want to get something that truly works, you'll need to get a legitimate ID. To my knowledge, the only way to get that is through the Feds."

Chapter 15

The minister sighed. "Yeah, I know. I conveyed that problem to Tahira when we spoke earlier in the week. I was hoping that you might have some ideas."

Greg chimed in, "It's not like we didn't know this would come up sooner or later. I could talk to Rico Enretti about it. He might know something."

Kaz said, "If I'm understanding correctly, this likely isn't a one-time issue. It's probably going to crop up again in the future. I'm not sure that Enretti has the resources to pull something like this off, but he might be a good place to start. I think it's time that I met Rico in person."

16

The Sniper watched with mild amusement as Pastor Millard Conyers stood in the middle of the hotel room. The pudgy man's eyes darted back and forth from the Sniper to the door to a cellphone on the dresser. He clearly had no idea what he was in for.

I'm guessing the weapon doesn't do much to reassure him. The .38 handgun, in this case, served no useful purpose other than to get the man's attention and make sure he didn't do something incredibly stupid.

After moments of long, awkward silence, the Sniper spoke. "Don't worry about the gun. It's here to make sure things go smoothly. You and I are going to become very well acquainted over the remainder of the weekend. If you play your cards right, you might just live to see Sunday night."

Conyers' head twitched as he shuffled in place. "What do you want?"

"It's a little complicated, so let's take it slow. First things first. Sit. You're gonna have a heart attack if you don't calm down."

"Who are you and what do you want?"

"You're repeating yourself. You already asked that question, and I told you we're going to take it slow, so that you can understand everything. This brings me to my second point. I don't like repeating myself, so stop asking the same questions over and over. In fact, just stop asking questions altogether. Let me do the talking."

Conyers backed up to the bed and sat, shoulders slumped. His eyes registered total defeat.

"Better." The Sniper set his handgun on the small round table by the window and pulled a chair around so that he was sitting directly in front of the minister.

"You and me, we're entirely different people. We live in different worlds, and we have different, how do you say… *preferences*. Honestly, though, I don't care who you're fucking. I don't care what you believe in. I don't give a royal shit whether you live or die. We do, however, have one thing in common. We're both marked for elimination by a certain organization with which we once had good standing. You do know what organization I'm talking about, right?"

Conyers stared, eyes wide.

"You can talk now. Just answer the question."

The ministered stuttered, then recovered, apparently trying to appear confident. "I belong to several organizations, but I've never seen you around any of them." His words, though, came out reeking of uncertainty.

"Don't play *catch me—fuck me*. You know exactly what organization I'm talking about."

The minister stared down at the floor, as though trying to come up with a coherent answer. "I don't know. Maybe."

The Sniper laughed. "This is going to take forever if you keep this up. You know that you've never seen me around any church or even anything closely related. Take a wild fucking guess."

Conyers nodded. "Okay. I get it."

"Good. As I said, we're both slated for elimination. I was directed to take care of you. Unfortunately for them, I'm not as stupid as they think. I know that, after you, I'm next. I'll spare you the back story. Now, I could have gone ahead and plugged you right there as you came out of the fun house and then taken my chances. On the other hand, I think we might come to a mutual understanding that will be far more beneficial to both of us."

The minister rubbed his right hand across the polyester comforter on the bed as he appeared to process what the Sniper had just told him. A look of disbelief dominated his face. "If I could ask one question, who gave you the assignment to...." His voice faded as though he couldn't bring himself to even consider the possibility that he was marked for death.

"You tell me. Who in the organization would be in a position to give such an assignment?" The Sniper arched his eyebrows and cocked his head.

Conyers squirmed. "Well, uh, it could have been one of a couple of people that I know of. Maybe there are others that I don't know."

The Sniper probed. "Who might these couple of people be?"

The minister rolled his eyes, appearing exasperated. "Look, I get it. You have the gun. You call the shots, but this is stupid, this back-and-forth crap. You know who gave you the assignment. I don't. Why keep badgering me about it?"

"Fair point. See, you can think things through when you try. To cut through the bullshit, your old pal Broward gave the instructions."

Conyers eyes widened as though in disbelief. "Carl? Why? I don't understand."

The Sniper's laugh was genuine. "In his own words, the sins of the flesh have turned you into a liability for the organization... or words to that effect. I think he knows about your playdays down here... or at least he thinks he knows. I'd be willing to be he doesn't have a clue what you're really into. That's not the issue, though. Over the next day and half, you and I are going to work on this problem. Let me start by saying that there's more to this than appears on the surface. You're going to help me get to the bottom of it."

Conyers, apparently emboldened, challenged, "What makes you think I know any more than you do?"

The Sniper stood and stretched. He picked up his handgun and stuffed it into a coat pocket. "It's been a long day. We should both get some rest and take this up tomorrow. So, here's the deal. I was supposed to eliminate you down here this weekend. If you bolt from the hotel and return to Seattle, they'll figure I failed and send another hitter after you. You'll be dead within a day. You can run, you can hide, you can do anything your little heart desires. In the end, though, you'll never be safe until we solve this little problem. Understand?"

The minister nodded his assent.

"Good. Excellent. I don't need to watch you. Trying to run... get away... would be one of the more stupid things you've done. With that said, what say we reconvene in the morning at about nine o'clock. We'll order up some room service for breakfast and get cracking."

* * *

The Sniper half-heartedly chewed the bit of scrambled egg and then dropped the fork on to his plate. "You'd think for these prices, they could figure out how make fluffy \eggs."

Conyers sat at the table displaying no interest at all in the food. "You know, I've had the night to think about it and I figured something out."

"Do tell."

"You said that Carl ordered this because of what I was doing down here. I don't believe that's the case. The exact nature of my… preferences, as you put it, aren't something he would know. Yes, he knows I come down here for what he calls *dalliances*. He's known about them for years and it's never been an issue. As far as he knows, nothing's changed."

The Sniper tore off a piece of toast and popped it in his mouth. "I only know what the guy told me. He may well have other reasons, but, honestly, none that concerns me. The only thing that matters is that he wants you dead. After that, I'm next on the list. I aim to fix it, and you're going to help."

The minister scooted his chair up closer to the table and set his plate aside. Putting his hands on the tabletop, he said, "Let's suppose for a moment that I do agree to help."

The Sniper interrupted him before he could continue. "That's rich… *supposing that you agree to help.* Let's get one thing straight. You'll help or you'll die. I prefer the help, but I won't lose a minute's sleep if you take the other option."

Conyers continued as though he hadn't heard the threat. "Like I said, if I help, it won't be as easy as just fixing things or killing Broward or whatever you have in mind."

"That's why we're having this little conversation. There are a lot moving parts. In my line of work, I survive by paying attention to even the smallest and most insignificant ones. Now, in the spirit of cooperation, why don't you tell me what you know about the organization. Specifically, I'm interested in the structure, leadership, and funding."

Conyers leaned back in his chair and ran his hand over his balding head. "Okay, structure. First thing to know is that the one big organization, the one I think you're referring to, is simply a part of a much larger network of groups. They each have different purposes and operate most of the time independently. In fact, people working in one group might be totally unaware that there are other groups."

The Sniper was familiar with such structures. They weren't unlike terrorist cells. Each cell was kept completely insulated from others. "What kind of other organizations?"

"Well, let's see. If what you say is accurate, you've been active in what we call our outreach cell. This is a key thrust because it's where we are able to effect rapid change in society. We also have a political wing. They do nothing but leverage assets among politicians. This is our most expensive effort, since buying off congressmen and senators takes a lot of money. It operates out of a political action committee, the Council on Safe and Healthy Families, and has no visible links to any other parts of the organization."

The Sniper sat back facing the window. With the curtain open, he could see the early December rain pelting the glass. It was a comforting sound. He closed his eyes and focused on what Conyers was saying. "If Broward is in charge of your little corner of the organization, who runs the big picture?"

"I'm not certain. Carl talks in very general terms about

how there is a boss, but he's never told me who it is. Also, if it matters, he plays down the boss's role, as though Broward himself is actually calling the shots."

"Does he?"

Conyers paused, stood, and walked over to the window, parting the drape. The dreariness of the gray, rainy Sunday morning appropriate to the conversation. "Sometimes, maybe. The small stuff—routine—he can make snap decisions. If something else comes along—something more complicated or important, he delays saying he'll think about it. What I think he's doing is talking to his boss about it. He just hates to admit that he's not calling all the shots."

The Sniper laughed. "This is where it gets interesting."

"Why? Is this important?"

The Sniper responded, "Yeah, just a little." He rolled his eyes and shook his head, hoping that Conyers could detect the sarcasm. "It could spell the difference between life and death. Broward is the one that gave me my instructions regarding you. Unless I'm mistaken, he's also the one that's convinced that I have to go as well. If we're going to fix this, then he has to die. On the other hand, if this was a decision handed down to him by someone higher up the food chain, then they both have to go... and that will greatly complicate things."

Conyers considered him for a moment. "So, that's it. You want to kill these guys?"

The Sniper laughed. "You seem shocked. You know, when Broward told me to kill you, he was as calm as a cucumber--munching on an oatmeal cookie, it was as though he was doing nothing more than ordering a pizza. Trust me, if you want to live, Broward and maybe the boss are going to have to die. End of story."

Chapter 16

The minister swallowed hard and glanced around the room, as though some grand truth would present itself. "What next?"

The Sniper shot back, "Money."

17

Minimalist. That's the only way Kaz could think to describe Rico's office. A rickety desk sat close to the back wall with barely enough room for the chair, which itself appeared to be on the verge of falling apart. Two wooden, straight-backed chairs sat in front of it. Two four-drawer file cabinets appeared to have come from a surplus outlet. Beyond that, nothing.

Rico Enretti sat, hands folded on the desk. "It's a pleasure to finally meet the esteemed Dimitry Kazarian in person."

"Thanks for making the time." Kaz had a feeling the meeting wouldn't produce what he really needed. His only hope was that it would give him a *next step*.

"How's Mister Stottman doing? I assume from what he's told me, that the two of you are getting on nicely." Rico's faint smile and calm demeanor gave the impression of confidence; of being in control.

"He's good," Kaz paused a moment before adding, "and I appreciate your recommendation."

"Everybody's got a make a living."

Chapter 17

Kaz thought it an odd statement, but let it go. "Anyway, we've run up against a problem that I'm afraid we're going to need some help with."

"Sounds promising. Hopefully, you've come to the right place." The smile never left his face.

It occurred to Kaz that Enretti may or may not know what Greg… and Janet were up to. Sadly, the best way to approach this seemed to include the sharing of that information. "Are you familiar with what Mister Stottman and his associates are trying to do?"

"In very general terms, yes."

"We've come to a point where we need to secure a completely new identity for someone—one that will hold up to any amount of scrutiny."

Rico allowed a laugh to escape. "Sadly, magic tricks are outside my area of expertise." He grew more serious. "Getting a new ID in and of itself doesn't present problems that can't be solved with money. Some IDs are better than others and, as you might expect, the quality is highly correlated with price. Unfortunately, nothing I can facilitate would be completely impervious."

"The clients we serve are not people that want the freedom to wander back and forth across legal boundaries. They're women who want to start their lives over, you know, get a job, rent an apartment, buy a car, or get a credit card. An arrangement that has them always wondering whether discovery is around the next corner or not won't work."

Enretti tapped a pen on his desk as he appeared to idly consider the problem. "What you're looking for is a legitimate ID. That means a birth certificate that resides in some state record system, a social security card issued by the U. S. government, and an educational record that checks out if anyone decides to go looking. In short, you're trying to invent a new person from birth. As much as I'd love to take your money, it's simply not something I can do."

Kaz suspected as much. "I appreciate your honesty. Could you, by chance, offer me some ideas on where I might go next?"

"If you truly want to go forward with this, I can get something started. Let me say straight away that, once I get it started, that will be the end of my involvement."

Kaz understood. Rico was, in some ways, a facilitator and sometimes only a mere catalyst. If his reputation was to be believed, he had the ability to *get the ball rolling* before stepping away and completely disengaging. "I think it's fair to say that we need to move forward. I imagine this would be a rather expensive proposition."

Rico again laughed. "That I can't say. I assure you that I will be compensated for the referral, albeit through back channels with which you will have no contact. Beyond that, you'll simply have to take it a step at a time."

"You got a name?"

"Do you by chance have access to the encryption app *Gobbledeguk*. It's rather expensive, but I find it impervious to curious ears."

"Yes, and?"

Rico continued, "Keep the app running over the next few days. Someone will contact you."

18

Yes, Janet had told Val that she would abide by her employee's wishes and not speak to the governor. It wasn't exactly a promise, though… more of a statement of intent. On top of that, Janet had the right to change her mind. After all, talking to the governor would not bring additional risk to Val. If anything, it would help her. The downside would be the risk of being forced to reveal more information than she wanted to about her operation.

Greg sat across from her in the church office as Janet laid out the dilemma. He kept quiet as Janet talked her way around the various issues, offering only nods and *hmmms*. "Part of the problem is that you called in favors to get this audience."

He shook his head. "Sunk costs. Yes, I called in favors, but that's true whether you talk to the governor or not. The only hitch, and it's a relatively small one, is that Bonnie used up some of her political capital in setting this up. Not following through might decrease the likelihood that she'd help you again in the future. All things equal, that doesn't strike me as particularly crucial right now. If something comes up in the future that's so important that you need her to go to the mats for you, she'd probably do it on principle."

He shifted in his chair. "No, the consideration needs to be what's the best course of action—the one most likely to produce the results you want. As I understand it, you don't want Val to go back to prison. That's your primary goal. You would also like to facilitate her being able to carry a weapon in the future, which would mean a pardon from the governor. Ask yourself, is he likely to give her a pardon? I doubt it. Too much political baggage attached to that."

She leaned back in her chair, tilting her head back to stare briefly at the ceiling. "I guess I knew that. What about sending her back to prison?"

"First, don't worry about what the cops are saying. They're looking at the issue from the standpoint of closing a case. Sending her back to prison gives them a checkmark in the win column, which is all they care about. The DA would normally make the decision about how to proceed. In this case, I'd lean toward them ignoring it… maybe giving her a lecture about the law and letting it go at that. The governor could certainly move that process along quickly and even give some political cover to the DA."

Janet asked, "And if I don't talk to the governor?"

"He probably does nothing and the DA will make whatever decision they're going to make based on how things look at the moment. My guess is, though, that if they decide to proceed against Val, intervening would be more difficult since it would make the DA look wishy-washy. In my opinion, influencing the process before it gets to that point produces the best chance of success."

Janet got a sick feeling in the pit of her stomach. "What happens when he begins to ask the probing questions?"

Chapter 18

Greg laughed. "First of all, the governor is not likely to be interested in the details of your operation. He has more important issues on his plate. Second, you might respond to questions by providing information that, quite frankly, is already known. For example, you help women escape from violent partners. Tell him the story about Hanna Miller. Those things aren't secret. A fair number of people know about them. Anything that's widely known is certainly knowable by the governor. Finally, you can decide at any time to turn off the flow of information. You can say, truthfully, that you're uncomfortable providing more information or you can check you watch and say that you have another appointment coming up and have to leave. It's unlikely he'll want to schedule another meeting with you to get more details on something he doesn't care about to begin with."

Janet considered his words and could find no flaw in his reasoning. "Val was really opposed to my talking to him. What do I say to her?"

"She's your employee. You're the boss. It's not like you're doing something that could hurt her. The issue is the security of your operation, and that's your responsibility. She may not like it, but it's your call."

19

The small, plush conference room intimidated Janet. The furniture, the art, and even the carpet screamed *opulence*. It was the governors meeting room and was clearly not designed for large groups. The small, oval table anchored six overstuffed chairs. A faint lemon aroma hung in the air along with a smell that Janet could only describe as *power*.

She had been sitting for about five minutes—a receptionist had ushered her to the room and offered coffee, tea, or water, which Janet had refused. She just wanted to get this over with. As far as she could imagine, state government had nothing that she needed. Why the governor wanted to meet with her remained a mystery.

The door opened and two men swept in. The first, short and thin, held out his hand. "Thank you for coming in, Reverend Polasky. I'm Charles Ethridge."

Janet found it curious that he didn't refer to himself as *governor*. She stood and took his hand for a moment. "It's my pleasure, Governor."

"I hope you don't mind. I asked my advisor for faith-based initiatives to sit in with us. This is Nicholas Trowbridge."

Janet didn't need the introduction. This was the same man that had sat in the church association conference room the night she had taken on the board… and won. He hadn't changed at all. He stood at least six feet with a trim build. His full head of dark, perfectly coifed hair was stylishly trimmed with touches of silver at the temples.

"It's a pleasure to see you, Reverend Polasky. It's been a while. I'm anxious to know more about what you're doing."

Alarm bells went off for Janet. This was exactly what she'd feared—having to provide details to a public figure who could make their own decision about what to disclose. She nodded, smiled, and sat.

Trowbridge quickly seized control of the meeting. With his hands clasped on the table in front of him, he caught and held her gaze as he spoke. "I understand that you witnessed an unfortunate murder about a year ago. I can't imagine the trauma that it caused." His voice was soft but firm, his eyes intense.

Janet took a deep breath. "Yes. It shattered a lot of lives, not the least of which was the woman's young daughter, who's still trying make sense of it all."

"Would it be fair to say that this event was the catalyst that motivated you to begin providing the services that you do?"

It was fair question, although for some reason, it made her uncomfortable. Janet tried to think two or three steps ahead. *Where's he going with this?*

Trowbridge had a pad in a rather expensive-looking folio out and had scribbled a few notes.

The governor sat quietly, his hands lying still on the table.

Janet glanced at both faces before crafting an answer. "As you noted, the incident took a toll on a lot of people. It's hard to live through something like that without it affecting you." It was a non-answer and she knew it.

Trowbridge narrowed his eyes and turned his head slightly to the side. After a moment, he smiled again and nodded. "The women you help—can you tell me a little about them, for example, what criteria do you use when deciding whether to help them or not?"

Janet steeled herself. The showdown was coming faster than she expected. "I hope that understand, Mister Trowbridge, but I'm reluctant to talk about it. I've already had the children of one potential client murdered and an employee nearly killed. The stakes for these women are incredibly high, and their safety depends to a very large extent on secrecy."

His eyes again turned intense, his mouth drawn into a tight line. After a moment, he responded, his voice slightly louder but still even and controlled. "Reverend Polasky, I'm not the enemy here. What you're doing has enormous value for society, but it also brings many unintended problems. I'd like to think that we here in the governor's office can help."

Janet felt her worst nightmares closing in. "I appreciate that, and I don't mean to be confrontational. I don't see what the state's interest in this is. You're not funding it and unless I'm missing something, there are no professional licensing requirements. What kind of help do you envision providing?"

Trowbridge's smile broadened and he gestured toward her with open hands. "Well, for starters, there's no reason why we can't find some funding for you. You've done an incredible job so far but think about how much more you might accomplish with additional money as well as the combined intellectual resources that we might bring to bear."

Janet forced a smile despite the growing nausea. "That's very kind of you." She nodded perfunctorily toward the governor. "I believe that we have sufficient funding." She noticed the look on his face hardening. She continued, "On top of that, there are existing agencies and networks that could use the extra funds. I don't in any way want to compete with them. As for the advice and information, I assure you that I remain in close contact with professionals in the area. They do an excellent job of providing guidance."

He tapped on the tabletop with his fingers for a moment as he considered her. After a brief moment of silence he spoke, his voice quiet but pointed. "Let me ask you a question, Reverend Polasky. What's going to happen when you spirit one of these women and her children away from what you consider to be a dangerous situation, and her husband reports it to the police as kidnapping? You're essentially taking children from their father without his consent or any legal basis. That's a crime, you know."

Janet shot back quickly, "What makes you think I'm *spiriting women away*, as you call it?"

"Secrecy around things like this doesn't hold. Surely you know that. I know quite a bit about what you do." His face softened and corners of his mouth turned upward with the hint of a smile. "I'm not criticizing you. I'm merely saying that you can better address these potential problems with the state as a partner. We can give you advice on what's legal and what's not. Through our relationships with the AG, we can grease the wheels, so to speak. The state has considerable law enforcement capacity. All that can be mustered in your support."

The governor continued sit without speaking, his face betraying no sense of his thoughts.

Janet searched for a way out of the discussion. What she wanted was an avenue that didn't involve an unpleasant confrontation. It seemed clear to her that this man was not backing down. She sighed, averting his gaze and focused for a moment on one of the art works hanging on the wall. Finally, she gave up. This was not going to end pleasantly.

"Mister Trowbridge, if you don't mind my asking, why is this an issue for the faith-based initiative program? What I do is in no way affiliated with my ministry. I'm sure there are lots of good faith programs out there that need financial help more than I do."

He glanced over at the governor who continued to show a neutral face. Finally, he dropped his hands on the table and donned his faux smile again. "We seem to have gotten off on a bad note, and for that I apologize. I assure you, Reverend Polasky, we just want to help. Tell you what, why don't you give it some thought and maybe talk it over with your funding source? Here's my card. We can perhaps get together in a few weeks and continue this. After that, we can explore the issue of your employee and any potential legal potholes." His smile faded, his face donning a look of determination. He nodded toward the governor.

There was little doubt in Janet's mind that this was a threat.

Governor Ethridge suddenly smiled and stood. "It was so nice to meet you, Reverend Polasky. He turned and left followed by Nicholas Trowbridge, leaving Janet alone in the room.

20

Janet slouched into the overstuffed chair in Greg's living room. It had been a grueling day, and she wanted nothing more than to put it behind her. Despite her fatigue, Greg needed to know about the turn of events in her meeting with the governor.

"Actually, Governor Ethridge said next to nothing. It was almost as though he was a spectator at a sporting event. No, the real meeting was with Nicholas Trowbridge. I think you've run across him before." Janet remembered the account of Greg's meeting with the man some months before.

Greg sat on the end of the sofa, his elbow resting on the arm. "What a pompous jerk. What was he doing at the meeting?"

"Get this. He is the governor's new advisor for faith-based initiatives." Janet found herself wondering if her faith was in any way related to Trowbridge's dogma.

She continued, "I'm surprised that the governor would throw in with this guy. Ethridge, as far as I know, has always been more progressive. Trowbridge seems to be somewhere to the right of Genghis Khan."

Greg laughed. "I can't argue with that." He grew more serious. "These are some really strange times, at least in terms of politics. I suspect the governor has a couple of reasons. First, I think he's probably angling to be viewed as someone who can bring various sides together to find solutions. He could also be trying to pander to some slice of the far right... kind of hedging his bets. Whatever it is, Trowbridge is nothing but trouble."

Janet nodded. "He's slimy. I'm sorry if that sounds judgmental, but I could feel the hypocrisy oozing out of him. He tried to suck up to me by telling me how important my work was and how much the state could help. What he wanted, though, was more information on what we do and how we do it."

Greg arched an eyebrow. "How did it end up?"

"The best way I can describe it is that he apologized for the tension, and suggested that we meet again in the future to continue the discussion." She went on to describe the threat.

"How do you intend to handle it?"

The question surprised Janet. She thought that, with Greg's experience and position, he would immediately offer a solution. It felt good, though. The decision was hers and he recognized that. "I believe that I've gotten everything I can get from the governor. I'd bet that they're not going to prosecute Val, although they're equally unlikely to pardon her. That means that, while she won't be looking at prison, she won't be able to carry a gun, at least not without breaking the law."

"And?"

Janet shot back, "And what? I don't need anything else from them. I'm going to lay low and ignore them."

Greg shook his head and leaned forward. "Just to play devil's advocate, that may work in terms of your current issue with Val. What if they decide to come after you in the future? Remember, there are lots of potential legal potholes in the work you do. Pissing the governor off may not be your best strategy."

"I thought about that. Regardless of whether I talk to Trowbridge or not, those potholes are there and there's no way that he's going to be able to bail me out if I fall into a legal black hole. Besides, any conflicts with the state would likely originate in the Department of Law, where Trowbridge has little power, as far as I can tell."

"Greg stared at her for a moment and then leaned back. "I see your point. You have nothing to gain and everything to lose." He offered a smile and a nod. "You're turning into a master strategist."

Janet laughed and then stood. "I need to be getting home. It's been a long one and I've got a full day ahead of me tomorrow."

Greg stood and moved closer to her, taking her hands in his. Though not unpleasant, it caught her off-guard. The jerk in her arms was certainly an unconscious reaction.

He drew back, letting go of her hands. "I'm sorry. I didn't mean to startle you." His eyes widened.

"No, you didn't. I mean, I guess that I'm just a little jumpy after the day I've had." She reached and took his hands. "Thanks for listening. It really helps to have someone I can bounce things off of."

He eased closer. "Any time… you know that."

She could see the emotion in his eyes. Janet struggled for the words to defuse the sexual tension that had suddenly built. She forced a brief laugh. "Yes, I know, and I appreciate it."

He gently squeezed her hands. Shivers went up her arm. She felt the tingling into her shoulders and downward through her chest to her stomach. Her throat constricted and she struggled for breath. No words came. Neither did she pull her hands away, though.

What came next was not really expected although it really was. He released her hands and caressed her face, before moving his arms to embrace her.

Janet felt it happening in slow motion. The desire built. She could feel the fire kindling as she struggled to pull back emotionally.

Their lips met and parted. Janet closed her eyes, swimming in delicious darkness as she felt herself being pulled closer. Her arms found their way around his neck and her thighs ground against his.

Then it was over. The kiss ended. Her tight embrace loosened. She pulled herself back away from him. Taking a deep breath, she whispered. "I can't, Greg."

He started to speak but she, but she put her finger on his lips. "It's not that I don't feel it. Right now there are too many things in my way."

He appeared to struggle for breath just as she had. "Such as?"

Janet took another step back and smoothed the non-existent wrinkles in her pants. "I'm not even sure where to start, but for starters, you have to know that I'm still struggling with my feelings for my husband. It's been ten years, I know, but somehow it doesn't seem long enough."

She held up her hand to forestall the response she knew would come. "Second, you're the funding source for my project. A romantic relationship between us could change things." Janet wasn't actually convinced that it was a good argument, but it was what came to mind.

"Finally," she sat in the chair and gestured toward the

couch for him to sit. "We come from different worlds, Greg. I'm the minister of a small church that barely makes ends meet. I live payday to payday and buy my clothes at the box stores. You're…," she paused searched for the right words. "You have money and power. Your world looks nothing like mine. Yes, I'm attracted to you, but once the shiny wears off, what is it we have in common?"

He took a deep breath as he appeared to think about what she'd said. In a way, that surprised her. Janet was accustomed to people having immediate answers to arguments. Greg seemed to actually be listening to her.

"I have money, yes. Being the CEO of a large company, yes, I have a certain amount of power. I promise you, though, that these things don't define me. You've seen how I live. Do I strike you as living an opulent life? I buy my clothes off the shelf too. I don't have a private plane or vacation homes in Europe. I drive a two-year old Camry and live in a condo. In my professional life, I do what is expected of me in order to succeed."

He paused as though to reconsider. "You have to know, though, that even in those roles, I have boundaries. I'd like to think that my values drive my behavior." He swallowed and took a deep breath. "I love you. You—Janet Polasky. It's not about you being a minister, or how you live, or how often you're paid. It's you. I could go on all day about what all I love about you, but, if nothing else, I would hope that we can get past this *money* thing."

The danger passed. Her breath became measured. She re-asserted control over her emotions. "I understand all that, Greg, I really do. It's not that I don't have feelings for you." She was careful not to use the word *love*.

"I can't give you any explanation other than I have to work through this in my own way."

Janet left feeling conflicted. On her way out, she turned

and looked down the hallway at the door to his bedroom. She could have been walking through that door rather than the front door to the outside. This was, however, not the night.

21

Kaz examined the weapon—a Glock 9-millimeter. The weapon was equipped with an aftermarket magazine. "Nice. Fifteen in the mag and one in the chamber. That should do it." He handed the gun back to Aylin Freyberg. They sat alone Kaz's studio apartment.

The scowl on her face never changed as she took the weapon from him. "Let's just get this over with. I gotta lot going on and I'm sure you have better things to do."

Kaz put his hand gently on her arm. "Hang on a second. To start with, I can assure that I have absolutely nothing more important on my plate right now that get you oriented. Also, there's nothing else that you're going to do, at least not with regard to your job, until we finish. You need to lose the chip on your shoulder."

He sat still, his gaze locked with hers as though each were waiting on the other to blink. Over the years, Kaz had learned the value of patience. He easily outlasted her.

"I don't need you to tell me what's important and what's not. Janet says that I have to get this orientation. So be it. That doesn't give you the right to bully me. I don't take shit off anyone."

He laughed. "Well, that's good, because I have no intention of giving you shit. We should hit it off nicely."

She glared at him.

Kaz continued, "Now that we have that out of the way, let's talk a little about that gun of yours. How long have you had it?"

Aylin drew her lips into a tight line, her body tensed for a moment, before she responded. "I got it about a month ago, when I got out of the hospital. I'm not about to get caught like that again."

"From what I was told, you were attacked by a sniper. You never saw him nor did anyone else around you. Tell me, then, how is that weapon going to keep that from happening again?"

"You let me worry about that. I have to do this, so let's get it over with."

Kaz shook his head and smiled. "We are *getting it over with*. This little chat is a part of it." He paused for a moment, letting the silence settle in. When he continued, he injected more seriousness into his words.

"This isn't just about your life. Reverend Polasky is trusting you with the lives of people who have come to her for help. Once you're connected with them, their safety is your responsibility. Having the weapon will help, as will body armor. Nothing, though, will ever come close to protecting you and your clients like good observational skills and sound judgment. We'll work on the weapon skills later, but for now, we're going to talk about the softer skills, so to speak."

Kaz could see that the woman was fuming but, at least for the moment, held it in check. He leaned back on the sofa and reached for his coffee cup. "We'll go to the range this afternoon. I'll walk you through a proficiency exercise and then we'll do some judgmental training, you know, the old *shoot—don't shoot* exercises. This morning, though, I'd just like to talk to you."

"About what?" She spat the question as though it were a projectile meant to destroy Kaz.

"Oh… a number of things. First, let's talk about that chip on your shoulder. I suggested when we first started that you lose it. You apparently haven't. Tell me, then, how did someone like you become so enraged such that it blinds your judgment."

She hurled the response with no delay. "My judgment is fine. I just don't have patience for assholes like you. I had a husband that beat me down. Not gonna happen again."

"I'm not your husband and it's not my style to beat people into submission. I find discussion—rational discussion with engagement by both parties—produces the best results. Can I assume, then, that your anger stems from your experience with your husband?"

He saw the slightest flicker of softening in her eyes. "That's part of it. What I went through at the Church Association didn't help. They fired me because I wouldn't kowtow to their warped way of looking at domestic violence. Getting shot was the icing on the cake."

"The anger can help. You just have to combine it with good observational and judgmental skills, while channeling to get the best results."

Aylin stood and paced the room, looking alternately out the window and down at the floor. "What are you, some kinda shrink?"

Kaz responded softly, "I have a master's in psychology, but I'm not a practicing clinician, if that's what you're asking. I'm employed in a security role. That's why I'm talking to you about this. I promise you, Miz Freyberg, while the gun might help in a pinch, you and your clients will be safer by a country mile if you are able to spot trouble in advance and avoid it."

She shot back, "On the other hand, if I kill some abusive motherfucker, that'll be one less asshole in the world. That feels like success to me."

He leaned forward, his hands on his knees. "You weren't hired to reduce the number of abusive partners in the world. You were hired to keep clients safe and escort them to new lives. What I'm going to tell you is, I believe, exactly what Reverend Polasky would say. Avoid shootouts if at all possible. Killing another person, be they good or bad, is the absolute last resort."

One corner of her mouth turned up slightly as she narrowed her eyes. "I can keep my clients safe. You don't need to worry about that."

"Oh but I do. It's my job. There's something that perhaps you haven't thought of. If you get into a gun fight, regardless of how it turns out, there's going to be a lot of public exposure. There will be questions that demand answers. You'll force more of what we do into the spotlight. That's not good. We do our best work by remaining in the dark."

Before she could retort, Kaz continued, "Let's get some closure on this topic, shall we. It's really this simple. If you want to work on this project, you're going to do it our way. And by *our*, I mean Reverend Polasky's and my way. Period. If you can't bring yourself to join this team, I understand and wish you well. Otherwise, let's get some lunch and then go to the shooting range."

22

J anet pulled her chair up close to Val's bedside. "I hear they're letting you out of here tomorrow." The time had come for Janet to make the changes.

"I guess." Val's response, indeed her entire demeanor, lacked enthusiasm.

"I met with the governor and one of his staff. They don't like me very much, I'm afraid." Janet forced a shallow laugh. "Mostly, I think it's that faith initiative guy —Trowbridge. Unfortunately, he and I have some history. Just lousy luck that he ended up with Governor Ethridge's ear."

"And?" Val's interest had picked up only slightly.

"Bottom line, my gut tells me that the gun charges won't be happening. They don't have the appetite for the bad publicity they'd get. They're not saying much, but I suspect they'd like it to just go away on its own. I guess we're getting the next best thing. The state AG will prob- ably instruct the local prosecuting attorney not to even entertain the case."

Val stared for a moment, her eyes searching Janet's. "I sense that there's a *but* coming up."

"Yeah, there is. The governor's not willing to issue a pardon, which means that you carrying a gun is off the table."

"It doesn't matter much. Bookkeeping wasn't such a bad gig. At least nobody was shooting at me." She turned her head toward the window. "At least we saved a few of them, right?"

Janet put her hand on Val's arm. "We're going to save a lot more. We're just going to have to make some changes."

"I'm not going back into this unarmed. That night...," she swallowed hard, "it was.... Even armed, I was barely able to save myself. There's no way to do it without a weapon. It's not fair to me or to the clients."

"I agree." Janet took a deep breath. "I'm going to ask you to look at a bigger picture for the moment. We can come back to the gun thing later. We've never spoken about this, but running this organization has stretched me to the breaking point. I have a full-time job at my church and, as it turns out, keeping this project running has turned into a full-time endeavor. I can't keep doing it." She paused, looking for some reaction.

Val shrugged, "I can imagine."

"You, on the other hand, have plenty of time and knowledge but you can't carry a gun. Voila! The solution presents itself."

"I'm sorry, Janet. I don't follow you."

"It's like this, Val. You can lead the organization—do the hiring, manage the budget, meet with potential clients and referral sources, all the back scene stuff. You hire people like yourself and Aylin to do the actual escorts. We just have to put protocols in place for arming them and making sure they're trained. Kaz can handle that part for you."

"Wait, am I hearing this right? You want me to take your place?"

"In a nutshell, yes. I will remain around as an interested party, maybe chair of your board of directors or something symbolic like that. I just won't have the time to devote to hands-on work."

Val stared down as she appeared to process the information. "Have you spoken to your funding source about this?"

"Greg Stottman is totally onboard with it. If you must know, I've also talked with an old friend whose advice and judgment I value above just about anyone else's. This move is perfect, Val. It solves both of our problems and ensures that the leadership of this project will be in the hands of someone who understands exactly what has to be done."

"I don't know. I'm not really a boss type of person. I'm not sure I can do that."

"What do you say we give it a shot. Once you're out of here, we can look for a small office you can work out of. Besides, Dee will be thrilled to get you off the streets."

23

Despite her misgivings, Janet had promised. Gayle, her board president, had confronted her in a gentle way about the church ending up on short end of Janet's allocation of time. Now that she had a tentative solution, she needed to make good on the promise to fill her president in. The problem, of course, was that Janet hadn't discussed her plans with anyone else other than Val.

"I'm sorry it's taken me so long to get back to you." Janet started to explain but let it go. It didn't matter anyway. She was here and needed to make good on her word. The thing is, it wasn't just a promise to inform her president. No, she needed to recommit herself to the congregation. The only way to do that was to shed the mantle of responsibility for her project with abused women.

Gayle nodded and refrained from speaking.

Janet waded in. "As you know, the past year I've been working on a project to help victims of family violence. After Hanna Miller died, I felt that I couldn't turn away as though it never happened. Lots of other stuff got in the way and, well, at the end of the day, I've been overextended. You pointed out to me in our last meeting, quite rightly, that I needed to be spending more time on church matters."

She paused, but then quickly continued. "I told you that I'd find a way to solve the problem. I've come up with a solution, at least in principle. I still have to make sure all the players are onboard, but I think it's going to work. Effective sometime in the next week, I'm going to be passing the leadership role in my organization on to one of my employees."

Gayle spoke for the first time. "I'm happy that you managed to find a way to make more time for the church without ending your efforts. By the way, how is Hanna's daughter doing? I think her name is Abby?"

"Probably as well as we could hope for, given the circumstances. Frankly, I'm more worried about her grandmother. Roberta Klein used to be an active congregation member, but she's withdrawn over the past few years. Her situation has worsened considerably since Hanna's death. I'm trying to arrange for mental health care for her, but I'm not sure how willing she'll be to accept it."

The smile that had been a constant on Gayle's face throughout the meeting faded. She furrowed her brow as she appeared to find the right words. "That has to be hard. I'm wondering if maybe passing this off to a social worker or even a public guardian might be a better way to go. This could easily turn into a huge time sink."

Janet bristled with anger. Roberta Klein was a human being. She hurt and she needed help. Gayle was treating it like a distraction. Rather than argue, though, she nodded. "I'll certainly give that some thought."

It was none of Gayle's business how Janet went about addressing the issue. The only thing her board president had a legitimate concern over was the amount of time the minister dedicated to the church. Janet was determined to fulfill her responsibility to the congregation, but she was not about to sidestep her responsibility to the older woman. Congregation member or not, Roberta Klein needed help, and Janet was called to provide it.

She pivoted to the other sensitive topic. "Oh, and I wanted to let you know that I did a bunch of congregation visits like you asked. We've got the budget covered for the remainder of this year and all of next." She started to add that the years following that would find them right back in the same situation they had just gotten out of.

"That's wonderful, Janet. I had all the confidence in the world. I think if we can just stay focused on the important things, we can keep our collective heads above water." The smile had returned.

Janet wondered, however, if her idea of *important things* was the same as Gayle's.

24

The first, most fundamental rule in solving a puzzle such as the one confronting the Sniper—follow the money. He poured another cup of coffee from the carafe that room service had brought up. Settling back in his chair, he started the process. "Tell me about the funding."

Conyers stared at him for a moment, as though not sure how to answer. Finally, he shrugged. "What about it?"

"Come on now, don't start fucking with me. You've been tolerable up until now. Don't screw it up. Where does the money come from?"

The rotund minister paced back and forth across the room, occasionally glancing over at the Sniper. "I guess what you're asking me is where the big bucks from. I mean, we get lots of contributions from different sources. A lot of the conservative activist groups chip in from time to time. It's mostly symbolic with them." He stopped pacing and considered the Sniper before continuing. "I figure it makes them feel good about themselves without having to sacrifice too much."

The Sniper stifled the urge to kick the shit of this yahoo. "Yeah, the big bucks. That's what we're after."

Conyers remained silent for a moment, staring at the Sniper as though running the calculations in his head—*tell him or don't tell him.* After what seemed like minutes, he sighed and plopped down on the bed. "Trent—Randolph Trent."

The name resonated with The Sniper. "*The* Randolph Trent?"

"Old money and sympathetic to our cause."

The Sniper inserted the information into his planning. "Okay, he's the money. How much does he get involved in the planning and decision-making? Is it possible that he's Broward's boss?"

"I don't know for certain. Carl makes a show of controlling a lot of things, but any time a sensitive or important issue comes up, he defers... says he needs to *think it through.* My guess is that he runs those things through Trent or someone else."

"Assuming you're right, it's probably safe to assume that Trent was at least in agreement with the decisions regarding you and me. That means that we have to deal with him too."

The Sniper drained the last of his coffee from the ceramic cup and poured another from the carafe that room service had provided. "Let's go back to the money itself. As you know, I got paid in cash, and I'm sure that I'm not the only one with such arrangements. That means that at least part of your funds are kept in cash. How much is that and how do you get it?"

Conyers scratched his chin and stared at the floor for a few seconds. "As for the amount, I don't know for sure, but I'd bet it comes to about a quarter mil a month."

Chapter 24

"So, what? Trent just delivers you guys a bag of cash every month?"

"No, nothing like that. You have to understand, too, that the northwest is just one region. The organization spans the entire country… and maybe even has some stuff overseas. Once a month we send two couriers to pick it up and bring it back."

"Now we're cooking. Where do they pick it up?"

Conyers stared thoughtfully for a moment, as if trying to decide whether to give it all up. Finally, he sighed. "Saint Louis area."

The Sniper's mind raced. "Where in Saint Louis?"

"No idea. That kind of information is kept close. As far as I know, only Broward and the couriers are in on that."

"Who are these couriers?"

"They're guys that work in some other part of the organization. I've only seen them a couple of times and then it was a quick look. They must be part of the central administration."

The Sniper laughed. "*Central Administration.* That sounds pretty high falutin. Where might we find this *Central Administration?*"

"Broward goes to a coordination meeting once a month. Sometimes it's in Seattle. Other times it's in other locations. If you want to know about how things are organized, that's the place to be."

The Sniper probed. "So, if I crash a meeting, I stand a good chance of seeing the couriers?"

"I couldn't say for sure, but it's probably your best bet. I can't see how you'll get into the meeting, though. They're very tightly controlled."

"You let me worry about that." The Sniper downed the remainder of the coffee in his cup and stood. "Okay, I think we've done just about everything we can. Here's the deal, Conyers. Broward paid me to execute you. He's under the impression that this is the weekend it happens. If you go back home, he'll know you didn't get wacked, and he'll probably send someone else after you. In short, you can't go home, at least until we neutralize things. Do you have a wife? Kids?"

"I don't actually live with them. We stay married for appearances, but we live very different lives."

The Sniper smirked, "I'll just bet you do. Anyway, it's going to take me a few weeks to figure all this out. That means that you're on your own until then. You have any place you can go?"

"My family has cabin on a lake over in Idaho. As far as I know, nobody goes over there anymore. I suppose I could hold up there for a while."

The Sniper tossed a burner cellphone on the bed. "Take this. Destroy your current one and dump the remains in the river. If anyone calls the burner number, it'll be me. Just in case, though, just answer the phone with a simple 'yes.' I'll identify myself and we can go from there. If it's anyone else, hang up and destroy the phone."

Conyers stared at him for a moment before quietly asking, "You said you'd identify yourself. What is your name?"

The Sniper shot back, "Don't worry about it. You'll know who I am."

"What are you going to do next?"

"I'm going to a meeting."

25

Dani Stottman pulled into the driveway. The house was cloaked in darkness. With only three weeks until Christmas, she would have some time off from taking Abby back and forth to school. In her heart, though Dani wasn't that excited about it. Seeing the young girl had become an integral part of life.

She sat in the car for a moment and stared at the wood frame house. With the dismal December weather and late sunrise, the darkness gave the appearance that the home had been long abandoned. It didn't overly concern her, since this was more or less the norm. Dani couldn't help but wonder, though, about the effect that it had on Abby. The young girl's life seemed bathed in darkness, both literally and figuratively.

Abby answered the door after only a short delay. Rather than come outside, though, she stood in the threshold. "Grandma won't get out of bed." Her voice was tentative, as though she wasn't sure about the words.

It didn't seem that unusual. Roberta Klein was occasionally up and about in the morning when Dani arrived, but not all the time. Abby had never seemed particularly worried about before. Today seemed different, though.

"She didn't get up with you this morning?"

Abby looked perplexed for a moment. Her gaze dropped to her shoes, and she stood perfectly still. "Well…," the young girl paused as though putting her thoughts in the right place. "She didn't get up yesterday. Last night I asked her if she was okay. She just turned over in bed."

Alarm set in. Dani knelt and put her hands on Abby's shoulders. "Do you mean that she didn't get up at all yesterday, even after you got home from school?"

The young girl nodded, her gaze still fixed on the floor.

Dani's thoughts raced. Was Roberta sick? Had Abby eaten in the past day? "What did you have for dinner last night?" She eased past the young girl, into the living room.

Abby muttered, "Peanut butter sandwich."

"You stay here, Abby. I'll check on your grandmother, okay?" She tiptoed down the hallway, afraid to make a sound. When she got to the first bedroom door on the left, she knocked gently and then cracked the door open.

"Miz Klein, are you okay? Can I come in?" She felt horribly out of her element.

No response.

In the dim light, Dani could see a lump of covers on the bed. Presumably Roberta Klein was beneath. "Are you awake."

"Yes." It came out more as a sigh than a response.

"Are you alright?"

"Yes."

Dani probed, "I'm going to take Abby to school. Can I get you anything before I go?"

"No."

Chapter 25

She backed out of the room and returned to Abby. "Let's get going. We don't want to be late."

Abby didn't move. "Are you going to help Grandma?"

Dani struggled to process everything. What could she do? "I'm going to call Reverend Polasky. She'll know exactly what to do. I promise you."

Finally, the young girl turned and crept toward the door, her movements seemed bathed in uncertainty. "Okay."

On the way to school, Abby remained silent until they were nearly there. Just as Dani made the last turn before pulling into the parking lot, the young girl turned and asked. "Is Grandma going to die?"

The question hit Dani had. She struggled to catch her breath. Pulling into the parking lot, she switched off the ignition and turned toward Abby. "No, Abby. Reverend Polasky will know what to do, but your grandmother is not going to die." She reached over and held the young girl's hands. "Thank you for telling me about this. It's the very best way to help her. I'm going to call Janet as soon right away. Things will be fine, you'll see."

Abby looked away, seeming transfixed by a stand of trees next to the school. She sat as though anchored in place, unwilling or unable to get out of the car.

Dani got out, went around, and opened the passenger door. "What do you say I walk you to the school? Would that be okay?" She reached over and clicked Abby's seat-belt. Touching the young girl's cheek, her words came out as little more than a whisper. "Come on, Abby. Let's go."

Back in the car after walking Abby to the front door of the school, Dani pulled out her phone and made the call.

"Janet, there's a problem."

26

J anet sat quietly and watched as Dee took a seat and
adjusted her chair. Judging by the taciturn look on the
detective's face, this was not a social visit.

"Thanks for making time to see me, Janet. I know that
you're busy now and I'll try to make this brief." The tone
was all business.

Janet leaned back in her chair, her hands resting on the
arms. Peering into Dee's eyes, she tried to fathom what had
come over the woman. "We've been best friends for years,
Dee. Of course I've got time to see you. What's this all
about?"

The detective nodded slightly. "Do you remember me
telling you about the men who were killed? There have
been several of them over the past few months. All of them
had been charged with domestic violence but, for one
reason or another, either charges were dropped or the cases
dismissed."

"And?" Janet struggled to make the connection
between these distant events of which she had almost no

knowledge and the foreboding demeanor that Dee was exhibiting.

"There was another one last night. Same MO. The pressure's building on this one. The current thinking is that it's a lone vigilante exacting vengeance on perpetrators who have seemingly dodged legal consequences. As you could probably guess, they're going to be focusing on domestic violence advocates, survivors, and professionals to begin with."

Janet wanted to lash out. After all the crap that survivors and advocates had to put up with, after the hit list of DV workers and associated assassinations, after the deaths suffered by these women—after all this, it seemed that the legal system wanted to pile even more tragedy into their lives. On the other hand, murder is murder. With someone killing these men, it only made sense that the police would focus on people with motive. "So, what you're saying is that I'm a suspect now?"

Dee shook her head. "Not really. They're probably going to come talk to you, but as of this morning, there really aren't any real suspects yet."

"Do the police have any evidence at all?"

"I'm not supposed to discuss the case," she shrugged her shoulders and stared out the window for a moment, "but there is something that I believe has already been released. The killer is using a nine-millimeter handgun."

Janet had heard the term before, although it meant little to her other than a type of gun. "I don't own any kind of weapon."

Dee's eyes searched Janet's for a moment. "Val carried a nine-millimeter."

The minister forced a shallow laugh. "Except that Val was in the hospital last night."

"I know. Also, the police have the rounds that she fired

the night she was almost killed. They've already compared them. Val's gun isn't the murder weapon."

Janet spread her hands, palms up, and smiled. "That's that, then. We know it's not Val. I don't own a weapon. I'll assume for the moment it's not you. What's the problem, then?"

"Nothing really. I just wanted you to be aware of it and to expect a visit. I'm sure they'll ask you about Kaz. I'm not sure what kind of weapon he carries but given the work he's been doing for you and his former profession, they might want to take a closer look at him."

"That's a load of BS, Dee. It's not Kaz."

Dee put her hands as though warding off the anger in Janet's words. "I'm just delivering the message, Janet. I'm not the one that has to be convinced."

* * *

"Have a seat, Kaz. There's something I need to talk to you about."

He pulled the chair up close to Janet's desk and sat. "Sure, what's up?"

Janet went through the information that Dee had conveyed. Kaz, for his part, listened, his face devoid of expression. "I'm sure it's not going to be a big deal, but I didn't want you to get caught unaware."

"Not a problem. I carry a nine-millimeter and I'd be happy to have them compare ballistics, although they have my rounds from that shootout in the church parking lot. If they're that interested in me, likely they've already compared them."

Janet nodded, "Oh yeah, I'd forgotten about that."

Kaz dropped his gaze for a moment as he seemed to consider some other problem. "There is one thing, though.

Aylin Fryberg also carries a nine-millimeter and more than enough rage for something like this."

Janet sat stunned. She hadn't even considered that angle, and yet it made perfect sense. Ever since the showdown at the church association, the woman had been practically blinded by anger. It was so bad that the minister was feeling some trepidation about even using her. Kaz's report on the orientation and the chip on Aylin's shoulder hadn't reassured her. "Do you think it could be her?"

"Offhand, I'd say there's no evidence that points directly towards her. She's not the first person to feel that kind of rage. As you're coming to find out, lots of people carry nine-millimeters. It's a popular gun. In any event, if the police do interview her as you indicate they might talk to me, they'll ask her for the weapon so they can compare ballistics. If she's smart, she'll hand it over without a fuss." He smiled and shook his head. "I'm betting it won't go that way. In any event, I'll chat with her first, but I'm not sure she'll listen to me. Hell, I'm not sure she'll listen to anyone."

27

Her cellphone rang just as she pulled into the church parking lot. Janet parked and connected just in time. "Hello."

Dani's words poured out sending waves of nausea though Janet. "When I went to pick Abby up to take her to school, her grandmother was still in bed. The house was dark. Abby wasn't dressed and hadn't eaten breakfast. I managed to get her to school on time, but I have to tell you, Janet, I don't think her grandmother's doing well. What am I supposed to do about it?" When the young woman finished a moment silence set in.

Finally, the minister took a deep breath and gave the only response she could. "Thanks, Dani. There's nothing you can do beyond what you're doing. Take Abby to school and be her friend. Roberta's going to need something far beyond what either you or I can give her. I'll get on it right away." She started to end the conversation, but added quickly, "Oh, if you don't hear back from me by the time you go to pick Abby up from school, give me a call."

Janet raced into the office. "Margaret, I've got an

emergency. Abby's grandmother is ill. I need to get over there right away." It was the only explanation she could think of on the fly.

"Is it serious?" The church secretary asked, concern in her eyes.

"I don't know. I just found out and I need to get over there. Can you hold the fort down for us?"

Janet found the house dark, just as Dani had described. She knocked, waited for few seconds and then opened the door. Taking a moment to get her bearings, she eased through the stillness of the living room down the hallway. In the bedroom, she found Roberta Klein just as Dani had left her.

"Roberta, it's me, Janet Polasky."

Silence.

Janet could see the slight rise and fall of form on the bed. Abby's grandmother needed help immediately. This could not wait. "Miz Klein, can you get up so we can talk?"

"Nothing to talk about." The words sounded hollow... empty. The huddled form on the bed didn't move.

Janet had clearly stumbled into treacherous waters. She had to make a choice—try to help Roberta Klein or call for professional help. The minister was keenly aware that a call for help—911—would set events in motion that she wouldn't be able to control.

What's the worst that could happen? Janet knew exactly how it could go wrong. EMTs and police would show up. They would likely take her to the emergency room where some doctor would call for a mental health professional who would likely recommend a psychiatric hold pending evaluation. Abby might well be shuffled off into some Children's Services emergency residence.

"Roberta, please. Would you at least agree to listen to

me?" She started to add "for Abby" but decided against putting anything more on the woman's shoulders.

The lump of covers shifted. The form rolled over and Janet could see Roberta Klein in the dim light of the December morning. Gradually, the woman pushed the covers off and slowly sat up in bed. Her head hung and her shoulders slouched.

A brief touch of optimism swept over Janet. Such a small step, but it was a start. "I'll make some coffee. We can sit and talk for a while." She put her hand on Roberta's shoulder.

Ten minutes later, the two women sat in the gloomy kitchen, each with a cup of steaming coffee in front of them. Janet searched her soul for a conversation starting place. She knew what they needed to talk about. How to get the discussion started in a way that didn't send Roberta scurrying for the safety of her bed was another matter entirely.

"Abby seems to be doing well with her studies. I think the new school suits her well."

Roberta furrowed her brow and stared into the cup of coffee without speaking.

"Truthfully, though, it's getting harder and harder to get her to go to school." Janet reached over and took Roberta's hand in her. The old woman didn't react.

"She's afraid to leave you alone. She's worried for you."

Miz Klein mumbled, "Nothing to worry about. My life's over. She needs to take care of herself."

Janet clinched her jaw. *As if Abby is capable of taking care of herself. For God's sake, the girl's thirteen years old.* "I know it seems that way to you but try to consider it from her point of view. You're the only family she has left. Without you, she's alone. She needs you and, quite frankly, I think you need her."

Roberta jerked around so that she stared directly into Janet's eyes. "What do you want me to do? I couldn't save Hanna. I can't save Abby. I can't even save myself."

Janet softened her gaze and squeezed Roberta's hands. "No, maybe not by yourself. There are people that can help. You simply have to be willing to accept that help. I'm begging you, Miz Klein, open your heart to help, both for you and for Abby."

Silence.

Janet continued, "I have a friend who's a therapist. She'll meet with you if you agree. Please."

"I can't afford no *therapist*." The words were bathed in resignation.

"You don't have to. It won't cost you a dime."

More silence.

Janet waited.

"I don't know. Maybe. What do I need to do?"

28

Kaz knew the conversation wouldn't be easy. He and Aylin had yet to find any common ground for a productive discussion. He'd known people like her before —outsized chips on their shoulders and determined to fight about the most miniscule of issues. They either got over it or flamed out. He hoped that she'd ultimately come around. So far, though—no such luck.

"What is it?" She made no effort to hide the impatience and annoyance. "I've got a lot to do."

He considered confronting the attitude again, but knew it was fruitless, especially given what he had to discuss with her. "Are you familiar with the assassinations that have been going on, the murder of men involved in domestic violence cases?" He tried to keep the tone in his voice neutral and non-accusatory.

"Why?"

Kaz stared at her for a second before responding quietly. "Why? Because I understand that the investigation has turned toward domestic violence workers, advocates, and victims. That's shorthand for—the police will be interviewing you, me, Janet, and Val. I thought you might appreciate the courtesy of a heads up."

"Are you accusing me of killing them?" She stood, hands on her hips glaring at him.

"No. I don't recall making that accusation." He suppressed a smile.

"What are you saying then?"

"Sorry, I didn't think what I said was that complicated. The police are interviewing DV workers, advocates, and survivors in connection with the case. That includes you, so I was simply offering the courtesy of an advance warning. Clear enough?"

She dropped her gaze and turned away. "What am I supposed to do?"

He broke out in laughter. "Right offhand, I'd say that you should answer their questions. I certainly intend to, and I believe Janet will do the same." Before she could hurl a response, he continued. "Since they have the bullets from the assassinations, they'll no doubt ask for your weapon so they can compare ballistics."

She exploded. "That's bullshit! They've got no evidence that I was involved. I have a second amendment right to carry that gun. It's none of their business."

He narrowed his right eye as he shook his head. "Bad approach. It won't be hard for them to get a warrant. If they're forced to go that route, I'd bet that they'd make assumptions about you. You may clear yourself in the end, but not before they drag you through the mud."

"So, you'd just have me roll over like an old, tired dog. Do whatever they say. Is that it?"

He smiled. "I think that just about covers it." He grew serious. "Aylin, I'm trying to help you here. Unless you destroy the gun, they're going to get it and test it. Assuming that you're innocent, you'll get past it a lot easier and faster if you cooperate. There's no upside to picking a fight with them."

"They don't go to these lengths to get the men who beat up and kill women. God forbid, though, that one of us fights back. They'll put us underneath the jail."

"Look, I get that you don't like me or even trust me. That's too bad but I'm not going to lose any sleep over it. I'm trying to help you to help yourself. Honestly, Aylin, you really need to learn how to pick your battles. If you continue to fight everything and everybody that comes along, you'll find yourself with no allies. More importantly, nobody'll trust you. Given what's ahead for you and our clients, you're going to need all the trust you can get. Do yourself a favor, when they come to talk to you, let them have the gun. They'll test it, it will be over, and you can go back to work."

29

Kaz found the building with little trouble. It was exactly as described by the woman who'd requested the meeting—two story, older but well-kept, brick façade, and bars on the windows. The rickety elevator took him haltingly to the second floor where he quickly located the third door on the right. He knocked once, opened the door, and entered.

She sat at a desk with two men parked against the wall beside the window facing him. "Come in, please, Mister Kazarian. Have a seat." She gestured toward a wood frame armless chair in front of the desk.

He glanced around and half-smiled. "I love what you've done with the place."

"Cute but an over-used cliche." The black woman in the executive chair wore what looked to be an expensive wool silk blend forest green blazer over a cream silk blouse. Her black hair framed her face and fell just below her ears. She appeared to wear little make-up, opting for a more natural look. She stood and offered her hand. "Leah Bowman."

He took the hand, held it for a moment and then released it, sliding into his chair. "I've heard the name. If you don't mind my asking, how did I come to your attention?"

She laughed. "Information is the new currency, or haven't you heard. I make it my business to know what's going on around me."

"And just what is it that's going on that involves me?"

Leah's demeanor remained pleasant but neutral. "You're asking a lot of questions around the area, and you're not that subtle about it."

Kaz considered the two men, neither of whom seemed in a high state of readiness. On the other hand, both looked as though they could handle themselves in a tight situation. They stood with their hands behind their backs with what appeared to be disinterested looks on their faces. Something told Kaz that underestimating them could be fatal. "Yes, well, I'm looking for something specific. I assure you that I had no intention to stepping on your toes."

"Be at ease, Mister Kazarian. I don't mean this as a confrontation. I believe that I might help you."

"How is that?"

"Before we start, let's agree on some ground rules, shall we? I'm happy to talk to you and discuss how we might help each other. In return, at least for today, I would expect that you would participate in the conversation. My help is, of course, predicated on some benefit to me. I hope that doesn't come across as unreasonable." She smiled warmly.

"You have me at a disadvantage, Miz Bowman. I know of you, generally speaking, but I have no idea what you're getting at right now. That said, I'm happy to talk to you to the extent that it doesn't cross any of my own professional lines, if you know what I mean."

"Understood."

Chapter 29

She turned and nodded to each of her guards in turn. "If you'd like to get a cup of coffee, I'll let you know when we're finished here."

The two men answered in unison, "Yes, Ma'am," and departed, closing the door behind them.

"You can speak freely, Mister Kazarian. I assure you that I have no recording devices and trust that you don't either. You've been asking around about an enterprise in the central Idaho area." She arched an eyebrow.

Kaz shrugged. He knew, of course, that Leah Bowman controlled much of the drug and prostitution business in western Washington. Just in the past year, she'd killed her husband, who previously ran the enterprise, and taken over his operation. No doubt she was into other ventures as well. He saw no reason that she should be concerned about his inquiries, unless of course, her empire extended beyond what he knew.

"Mister Kazarian, when I said that I expected some participation on your part, that included you actually speaking. I'm not here to give a lecture."

"What is it you want me to say? What you've stated is essentially true, although I'm unsure how you came by this information or, for that matter, why you're interested."

She smiled and nodded. "That's better. I may have some information that'll help you. For example, I know of this venture that you seek. They distribute different products in the Idaho and eastern Washington region. Those products include illegal substances, non-taxed tobacco, alcohol, and marijuana, as well as people."

"And you're willing to provide me with that information?"

"Quid pro quo."

"I assume the 'quid' is the information you have. What is the 'quo?'"

"Later. I will assure you, though, I have no intention of asking you to cross a legal boundary. First, though, a full disclosure is in order. I know about you and your effort because you're working on behalf of Reverend Janet Polasky. Let's just say that I have a soft spot in my heart for the preacher lady. That's the reason we're having this conversation… that and the fact that you may well be able to do me a favor."

"I guess that would depend on the favor."

She drummed her fingers on the desk. "Yes, of course it would. So, back to this mystery organization. I presume that your interest has little or nothing to do with the activities I spoke of. My sources tell me that you're after a specific person who may be involved."

"That's correct."

"So here we find ourselves, Mister Kazarian. I believe that I can indeed help you in that regard. In return, I would like a small, insignificant favor. There is man back in New York with whom I understand you are acquainted—one Boris Bunin."

Kaz froze as he registered the name. "I'm sure that many people know Mister Bunin. I have no professional relationship with him."

"My favor is simple." She took out a business card, scribbled a number on the back, and handed it to Kaz. "If you happen to cross paths with him at some point, would you mind giving this to him along with my warmest regards?"

"You want me to connect you with the Russian mob in New York?"

"What I'm asking is straightforward. Simply give him the card and tell him that I send my warmest regards. If he asks any questions, you may simply defer."

Kaz turned the card over in his hand as he considered

the request. "I can't say for certain when I'll be back there. It could be months."

"Given that your mother is in a nursing institution back there, I doubt that it will be too many months." She smiled and arched her eyebrows.

Leah Bowman clearly had reliable sources. He thought about what he was being asked. There was little doubt in his mind what this was about. Leah Bowman wanted to partner with Boris to manage the entire Northwest enterprise, possibly even the entire West Coast.

On the other hand, he was not being asked to facilitate it. Any arrangements that might lead to such a partnership would be made between the two of them. He was simply giving Boris a card and a greeting. If Leah wanted, she could easily send that through the mail.

"Let's say that I might be willing to do that. What makes you think it will mean anything to him? After all, as I said, he and I have no professional relationship." He knew it was a losing argument.

"I'll take my chances."

Kaz stuffed the card in his shirt pocket. "Okay, your turn."

Leah leaned into the desk, her eyes intense. "The man you're after goes by several nicknames—The Hitter, The Shooter, The Sniper, and The Crusader. He divides up his time and effort into three areas, as far as I can tell. First, he distributes heroin, fentanyl, and some other products from a pick-up point in Boise up through Coeur d'Alene and over to Spokane. Second, he does contract killings, mostly low-level stuff. Finally, in his Crusader role, he does hits on women who work in domestic violence services. I believe it is in this particular area that you are concerned."

Kaz made the decision on the spot. "Yes. As you said, I work for Reverend Polasky. You know, of course, what she's into. As it turns out, she's the next name on the hit list for this guy."

That got a rise out of Leah. Her face went stony, her eyes betrayed alarm. "I hadn't heard that."

"I intend to get this guy before he gets her."

Leah regained her composure quickly. "Then you'll need some additional information. The enterprise that you're looking into doesn't operate in ways that you might expect. Don't look for the contacts and networks in seedy strip malls or old abandoned warehouses. You need to be looking at churches."

"Which ones?"

"I'm guessing that you can figure that out for yourself. Based on what I've heard, things are in flux right now. Your man is coming off a failed hit. Additionally, I think you might have met a relative of his, you know, the one who was shot that night when he broke in on you. That little screw-up further damaged your man's standing with his organization. He has no friends right now. The time, Mister Kazarian, is right."

30

Kaz eyed the detective. Wharton looked different than before. Dressed in blue denim jeans, an azure pullover hooded sweatshirt, and running shoes, she came across as more approachable and relaxed. The Saturday afternoon crowd at the small coffee bistro was sparse. One young woman sat in a corner, notebook computer open, undoubtedly connected to the free wi-fi as she sipped on what appeared to be the smallest drink available in the place. Two young men occupied a window table. They were engaged in what sounded like a heated political discourse. All in all, no one seemed interested in the two new faces.

"Thanks. I'm glad you signed on for this." Kaz held his black ceramic cup of steaming coffee with both hands.

Wharton glanced around the room and nodded almost imperceptibly. "I wouldn't say that I've *signed on*, as you put it, Mister Kazarian. I'm here mostly because I don't have anything else going on today. Let's see where it goes before we celebrate." She offered a slight smile with the words.

"Fair enough. I guess, before we get into the thick of it, my friends call me Kaz. It's easier than Mister Kazarian."

"Okay." She took a sip from her cup.

The one-word response grated on Kaz. "Would it be acceptable for me to call you Charlotte, or do we need to stick with the *Detective Wharton* moniker."

She laughed. "Whatever makes you comfortable."

"Charlotte it is."

Wharton pulled her chair closer to the small table and leaned in, her eyes fixed on Kaz. "Now that we have the important stuff out of the way, perhaps we can move on to some of the more mundane issues, such as, where do we start?"

Kaz idly rotated his coffee cup back and forth as he tried to visualize the path they should take. "I guess, to start with, we need to compile what we know. As luck would have it, you're the current keeper of the information. You know the background on Robinson's cousin."

"I can take a look at the file we got from DOD. I'm not sure how much I can legally share with you. I don't think there's anything classified about it, per se. Still, it is an official document and I'm not sure whether it's appropriate for public disclosure."

Kaz shot back, "We're not talking about public disclosure. This is you and me. I certainly wouldn't ask you to disclose information that's confidential or anything. I would ask, though, that you trust me enough to share official unclassified information." He held his hand up as though to ward off the expected pushback. "Before you start on me, I promised that I'd be sharing information with you. Here's what I've learned. The guy we're looking for operates out of central Idaho." Kaz summarized what Leah Bowman had told him.

She stared at him for a moment. The bored, agitated

look he'd grown accustomed to from Wharton was gone. Her eyes screamed *interest*. "How did you come by that information?"

"An informant of mine. As we go on, I might be able to share their identity, but for now I promised anonymity." He, of course, had promised no such thing, but it gave him an easy out for the moment.

"Okay, getting back to me sharing information. Let's say that I do share with you. Are we going to have some kind of repository for everything we gather? If so, what protections are we going to set up? If I disclose official correspondence, I'd hate to see it show up in the newspaper or, even worse, in the hands of the very people we're going after."

"Fair point. The answer to the first question is yes. This is likely to get complicated and we're going to need to have some way of storing, organizing, and accessing the information. As to the second question, I'll check with Eisen, the technology geek working for Stottman. I'm sure he can set something up for us."

Wharton tapped her index finger on the table. "See, this is what I'm talking about. We haven't even gotten started and you're already proposing to share the information with someone else. Maybe we should back up and be clear about the extent to which what I'm giving you will be disclosed."

"First, I want to be clear with you, this isn't just about information that you're providing. It goes both ways. As I've demonstrated today, I'll be bringing stuff to the table as well. Your concern is well taken, though. To answer the obvious question, I suggest that the circle of knowledge include Greg Stottman, Eisen, and Reverend Polasky. I see no reason it should go beyond those three."

"Why does the minister need to know?"

Kaz laughed. "Her name is at the top of the hit list. I think that maybe she deserves to know what progress we're making."

The detective turned her head toward the window, seemingly lost in thought. After a moment, she responded, "I'll concede the basic point, but I would ask that we share only what's absolutely necessary for her to know in order to remain safe."

With sigh, he responded, "Agreed."

"Then it seems that we each have an assignment, so to speak. I'll review the material that I have and bring what I can to our next little get together. You're going to talk to this Eisen guy and come up with an information security plan."

"Done." Kaz gulped the rest of his coffee. "Oh, and one other thing... and please don't take this the wrong way. I think it would be best to not bring our little project to the attention of your colleagues at the sheriff's department."

She eyed him with what looked like an air of amusement. "Okay for now."

31

The app notification sounded no different than any of the other standard smart phone notification alarms. The icon flashed and displayed an option to connect. Kaz touched the word *yes*, and put the phone to his ear. "Hello."

The voice carried what sounded like a heavy Eastern European accent. "Can you talk now?"

Kaz was amazed at the clarity of the signal that was being filtered through the encryption app. "Yes."

He eased over and sat on the couch. "May I put you on speaker? I am alone in my apartment."

"If you wish."

Kaz made the change to the external speaker and set his phone on the coffee table. "There. Can you hear me?"

"I understand that you are looking for some very specialized services."

Kaz explained to the disembodied voice much as he had to Rico. When he finished, he fell silent.

After a moment, the voice responded. "We can help,

but first we must discuss the conditions. We understand what it is you want as well as why you want it. We know about your organization and what you do."

"Uh… may I ask how you came by this information?" It occurred to Kaz, though, that he's basically laid it all out for Rico. There was no reason to believe that Enretti hadn't passed that on. The response, though, caught Kaz off-guard.

"We make it our business to know many things. Before we commit to a course of action, we must ensure that our goals are aligned. I trust that makes sense to you."

The voice hadn't really answered the question. On the other hand, Kaz was the one that needed the impossible service, so being hardnosed about information acquisition hardly seemed appropriate. "Yes, it does. Before we go on, though, how much, roughly speaking, will this cost?"

"It will cost you nothing, if you are speaking in terms of cash. We would, however, like to establish a relationship with you. We may, at some time in the future, need your services."

"Really? You would possibly like us to help women escape violent partners?"

The voice responded, "We can discuss that when the need arises. For now, we should begin working on this specific problem. I will contact you again in seventy-two hours. I will need the existing names of the two individuals, their dates of birth, and social security numbers. I assume that they currently reside in the U. S. state of Washington. With that, we can take care of the rest."

* * *

Seventy-two hours later, to the minute, the encryption app

on Kaz's phone flashed and the notification alarm sounded. "Yes?'

"You have information for me?" The same heavily accented voice asked.

Kaz checked the sheet in front of him. "The woman is Gwendolyn Trent. Her father's name is Joshua Lambert." He provided the dates of birth and social security numbers, as the voice had requested. "Do you need addresses?"

"No. One final thing. Are there any preferences to location of their new life?"

"None that I know of." Kaz realized that none of them had thought that far ahead.

"One week. Same time. I will have detailed instructions."

Kaz jotted down the note. "I do have one other question. My associates would like to know more about this relationship that we're entering. We have no idea who you are, where you are, or what kind of business you are in. You know much about us, so we think it only fair that we understand who we're dealing with." He tried to come off as confident but non-confrontational.

"You ask for the impossible in terms of the service you want. I would think that you would happy enough to accept that service at face value."

Kaz put on his most conciliatory demeanor. "I mean no disrespect. Believe me, we are grateful for what you offer to do. Caution suggests, though, that we at least know who we are working with, especially if there are expectations of future collaboration."

The line fell silent for a moment. "I will pass your request on. Perhaps I can give you an answer when I call back in one week."

* * *

"I don't like it." Janet sat at the kitchen table in the parsonage with Greg and Kaz. "I appreciate what they're offering to do, but it sounds to me like they want a blank check in terms of some future favor."

"True enough." Kaz drummed his fingers on the table. "On the other hand, they do know what business you're in. It would seem that, if they want something, it would be in that vein. I may be wrong, but it could be that they will just be another referral source."

Greg chimed in, "Whoever the *they* is. There has to be a reason he didn't want to tell you anything."

Kaz considered the proposition. "I don't know. You have to realize that what they're prepared to do breaks any number of major laws. Given the fact that these new identities will be impervious, there likely is good reason for their caution."

Janet added, "The very fact that they're likely going to have to break laws is what worries me."

Kaz shook his head. "You knew going in that what we wanted was legally impossible. Unless you could convince the feds to do it, there's just no legal way to go about it."

She tilted her head back, eyes closed and sighed. "I know."

Greg said, "The dilemma isn't that complicated. If we want to move them to a new life where they don't have to look back over their shoulders every day, this is the only avenue that I know of, short of them trying to live off the grid."

Kaz added, "Living off the grid's not an option for them. They would have to pay for everything in cash. That would be a nightmare, and sooner or later, one of them would need medical care. No, they either need to keep their identities and hope for the best or we go down this dark road. It's that simple."

Janet pushed back from the table and stood. "Like it or not, I guess we go."

32

Kaz took the issue of the assassin seriously. He may have screwed up the hit on Aylin, but by all accounts, he had been flawless before that. His take-down of Billy Robinson had been textbook. No, he could not be ignored, even if he had dropped out of sight.

The two of them, Kaz and Eisen, sat in the privacy of Kaz's kitchen. "I know it's a tall order, but I need to try and find some footage of this sniper. We've reached the point where we need some idea of what he looks like."

"Okay, any ideas about a starting point?" The look on Eisen's face screamed *skepticism*.

"We have to assume he's communicating… or was, at any rate, through the old website. That means that he's accessing the web. If he's doing it from some private residence, likely he's using VPNs and the dark web. He does, though, travel for work. That means that he probably needs to access it from public wi-fi spots. From what I know, he works both in the Seattle area and makes runs from southern Idaho up to Spokane. My money's on Boise as a spot where we're likely to find him. I'd start with coffee shops and fast-food joints on the north-south interstate that offer free wi-fi."

Eisen rubbed his chin as he stared at the tabletop. "I've got the connection records for the website archived. I could crosscheck for the IP addresses used by any of those spots. Who knows, we might get lucky."

* * *

Kaz tossed the file folder on the coffee table. "I spent some time with our tech god, Eisen. It didn't take him long, but he came up with some interesting info."

Detective Wharton, seated in an overstuffed chair on the other side of the table, picked up the folder and perused its contents. "Give me short version first."

Kaz laughed. "I sense that you don't enjoy my company... that you'd prefer to get this over with."

"This isn't a social outing for me, Mister Kazarian. I agreed to work with you, but that doesn't include warm and fuzzy, okay?"

"I doubt that anyone's going to accuse you of *warm and fuzzy.* Anyway, there's some pretty good stuff in there, at least in terms of a starting point. Eisen was able to determine that the IP used for communication between who we think is the sniper and his organization is at a fast-food joint down in Boise."

She closed the folder and considered him for a moment. "I kind of thought that we knew that already."

"We knew that it was in southern Idaho. Eisen pinpointed to a McDonald's, which was used regularly. It gets better, though. There's a bank and a credit union across the parking lot. Both have ATMs out front... ATMs with video surveillance cameras."

Wharton shook her head. "That's gonna require a warrant."

"Not to worry. The credit union scrubs its videos after ninety days, so it's not going to help us much. The bank, on the other hand, keeps theirs in archives for one year."

"Still doesn't solve the warrant problem."

"I might agree, except for the fact that we don't need to get the video from them. We know the exact times of communication. With that, I was able to come into possession of the specific files we need."

Wharton narrowed her eyes. "That would imply that you broke the law."

"I didn't do anything except look at some files that were given to me. Now, you can assume that those files were stolen... or not. Your choice. If you want to go through them with me, though, they are right over there on my computer." The corners of his mouth turned up in a smile and he arched his eyebrows.

"Are you asking me to be complicit in appears on its face to be a felony?"

"I'm asking you if you'd like to see some video footage. I don't know exactly how it was obtained. Truth be told, I probably wouldn't understand if I were told. You can view them with me if you'd like. Otherwise, there's not much for us to do here tonight."

She fell silent. Staring at the file folder in front of her, the detective appeared to be weighing her options. "You see, this is what I was afraid of. We start out skirting around the edge of legality. Before you know it, we end up stepping over the line."

Kaz laughed. "You're overthinking it. I have some video files. Do you or do you not want to see them?"

Wharton sighed. "Let's have a look."

As they scrubbed through the video files, Kaz was glad

that they'd been able to pinpoint the times. Going over hours and hours of these files would be mind-numbing. Still, having to focus beyond the immediate area of the ATM was painstaking. When he tried to zoom in, the poor quality video pixelated, obscuring any useful information.

After going through four different time windows, Kaz pointed to the screen. "I think that's our guy. He's in all of the footage and I don't see any other good candidates."

"Yeah, assuming that the time frames are accurate. If they're not, it could just be another fast-food junkie."

Kaz leaned back in the straight back chair. "Nope. It fits. The time is right. Look at the guy... watch how he acts. See that," he pointed to a distant figure on the screen, "he looks around when he gets out of the truck. He pauses and surveys the entire parking lot. Also, he's carrying a small daypack that perfect for a computer. That's our man."

Wharton studies the frozen frame for a moment. "Assuming you're right. How does this help us. We can't see any detail on his face and the license plate on his vehicle is unreadable. It appears, from the color scheme, to be an Idaho plate, but that's about it."

Kaz had to admit that she was right. They could make out the shape of the guy as well as the relative size and color of his truck. There were no details, though.

"I agree. Tell you what. Let me get back with Eisen and see if he can work some magic on these specific scenes. Maybe we can grab enough for either some kind of facial recognition or, with luck, a plate number."

She folded her arms. "Uh, I see a problem ahead. Any kind of ID through facial recognition would come through law enforcement. That would mean, at least for me, stepping solidly over that line. Maybe we could grab some public information from a plate number, if we can get that."

"I promise you, Charlotte, I'm not going to ask you to do that. I have a hunch that Eisen has far greater technical resources at his disposal than anything you could come up with. Let me see what I can do."

33

I t didn't take long. Two men strode through the front door of the Hilton Hotel in Portland. The Sniper mused on the irony that this was the same hotel where he and Conyers had spent the weekend planning the strikes on the organization.

Both men wore dark slacks and leather jackets. The more he looked at them, the more confident he became. They had close-cropped hair, muscular builds, and steely, focused looks on their faces. Also, from the way their coats fit, it seemed clear the two were wearing body armor. They were the ones.

He had already reported back to Broward that he'd made the hit on Conyers and hidden the body so that it was unlikely to ever be found. If the pervert managed to keep a low profile, that should buy him a few weeks. Hacking Broward's e-mail had given him the location of the time and location of this meeting.

He knew how get at Broward when the time came. He had the identity of the money man—Randolph Trent. All he had to do at this point was to identify the couriers so that he could track them to the cash pickup location. Killing his two targets was only part of the plan. The Sniper intended to get his hands on some serious cash.

He discreetly snapped photos of them, although it was unlikely to give him any meaningful information since he didn't have access to facial recognition software.

The made for the elevator, scanning the lobby as they went. They were professionals. The Sniper fiddled with his smart phone, as though scanning texts or e-mails. When the elevator door closed with the two inside, he casually made his way over to watch the display to see where they got off.

It took only a few seconds—third floor. *Probably the location of the meeting.* He returned to his seat and waited. The two emerged from the elevator twenty minutes later and headed straight for the front door. One of them carried a briefcase that they had apparently acquired upstairs. As they exited the hotel onto the street, the Sniper eased over to the door and watched them. They turned right, walked about ten yards, and then crossed the street.

Following at a discreet distance, he saw them approach a black SUV. The Sniper turned toward the side and put his phone to his ear and gestured with his hand, as though having a heated discussion with someone. One of the men opened the passenger side back door and tossed the briefcase on the seat before closing and locking the door. After a perfunctory survey of the environment, presumably to spot anyone tailing them, the two headed farther down the street, entering a small restaurant.

The hunch had paid off. He had one more task to accomplish. He reached into his coat pocket and pulled out a small black box no bigger than the palm of his hand.

Chapter 33

Extending an antenna, he powered it on. A red LED began flashing slowly on and off. He held his phone in his other hand and began to wander down the street trying to appear totally engrossed in whatever was on the phone.

As he passed the SUV, he dropped the phone onto the ground. "Shit," he muttered just loud enough for anyone close by to hear. The phone bounced and slid underneath the vehicle. As he reached to retrieve it, he attached the small black box, which had a magnet affixed, to the underside of the wheel well. Standing up, he wiped off the phone, swiped and punched the screen a few times, and then shrugged to signal any random observers that the phone appeared undamaged.

"Are you okay, buddy?" The voice came out of nowhere.

A middle-aged, overweight man stood staring at him. "Looked like you had a heart attack."

The Sniper stole a quick glance down the street in the direction the two couriers had gone. He saw no sign of them. Turning back toward the man, shook his head and laughed. "Not hardly. Yeah, just dropped my phone." He held up the device for the man to see. "I'm surprised it didn't shatter the screen."

The guy shrugged and turned away, calling over his shoulder, "Have a good one."

As he turned to leave, he saw one of the two men walking briskly toward the car. Had they seen him? Maybe they saw the entire incident.

Naw. If that were the case, they would both be coming. He sauntered away from the car, his attention focused on the phone.

Ten minutes later and three blocks away, he powered up an app on his phone, punched in a few settings, and then studied the display. A smile stole across his face as he thought to himself, *gotcha*. He could only hope that they didn't perform an electronic sweep of the vehicle before they left for St. Louis.

34

I n that moment, everything changed. Kaz felt as though the ground itself had been pulled from beneath him, allowing his body to be battered about by dark, tumultuous storms. The few words that the person on the other end spoke had sliced into his heart and devastated him.

"When?" Did *when* really matter? Despite having no details, he knew everything that mattered.

Still, the answer came. "Earlier today, about an hour ago. She developed a respiratory infection yesterday and it worsened overnight. She passed quietly in her sleep." The woman's voice was soft, the words coming slowly, as though in no hurry to be spoken.

Kaz took a deep breath. "Okay, I'll be on a plane as soon as I can, maybe a few hours. It'll probably be tomorrow morning before I can be at the center."

He had known it would come eventually. He'd even thought about it—how she would pass, how he would find out, and how he would react. All of the questions and uncertainties paled before the one unavoidable reality—his mother was dead.

* * *

Kaz leaned his head back against the airline seat as he spoke. "You didn't have to come with me, you know." He wanted to say more, but, as had been the case over the past six hours, words simply refused to come.

Greg Stottman replied in a soft, almost reverent tone, "I wanted to come. You've been by my side through everything—the mess with Dani, the attempt on Janet's life, and the kid that came for me. It only seems natural that I should be with you now."

Kaz shook his head. "Those things—that's what you paid me to do. This is different."

Greg laughed and it came across as genuine. "You gotta know, Kaz, there is no amount that I could have paid you that equates to what you've done for me. You can say whatever you want, but I'm just gonna chalk it up to friendship."

"Thanks." Kaz had lots of acquaintances and colleagues but no real friends. The closest he came was his relationship with the Russian mob boss—Boris Bunin. "I guess I owe Janet a debt of gratitude as well. The memorial service will mean a lot more in her church than it would in some random church in Brooklyn. I appreciate her offer."

The next twelve hours were a blur. They landed just before midnight and got to the hotel just after 1:00 a.m. They were in and out of the nursing facility the next morning before 10:00 a.m. and on to the mortuary.

"We'd like to offer our condolences on your loss." The man with thinning gray hair dressed in an expensive wool blend suit, folded his hand on the desk in front of him. "I know these discussions can be difficult. To help you navigate through this, we've prepared a few options from which to choose." He held a slim three-ring binder in his hand for a moment before handing to Kaz. "Whichever option you choose, you can be assured the services will be provided with the utmost respect and quality."

Kaz nodded as he stared at the unopened binder in front of him. "What I'd like is a simple cremation and container suitable for travel. The memorial will be held in Seattle. How soon can you get this done?" He felt nauseous for even having the discussion. His mother had died while he was away. Now here he was discussing her as though she was nothing more than a financial transaction. He wanted to sit by himself, stare out the window at the East River, and cry.

The man pursed his lips for a moment as he considered the question. "Mid-morning tomorrow." His tone had shifted from quiet and respectful to all business. "We accept checks, direct account withdrawal, credit card, or, if you prefer, cash."

Before Kaz could speak, Greg slid a credit card across the desk. The man took it without speaking.

While he was out of the room, presumably ringing up the charge, Kaz said, "You didn't have to do that. I had it covered."

Greg smiled. "As you've no doubt discovered, there's not a lot I do well in this world. It seems a small gesture in the big scheme of things." He shrugged.

"Thanks."

An hour later, they picked at lunch—deli sandwich and side salad for each of them. Early spring in Brooklyn had a way of bringing gray, raw days and this one proved no exception. Kaz could find no appetite. "I need to go see a guy after lunch. Shouldn't take more than a couple of hours." He forced a smile. "Maybe by dinner time I can manage an appetite."

Greg took a bite of his sandwich and followed it up with deep draught of beer. "Who're we going to see."

"*We* aren't going to see anyone. This is one I need to do by myself."

Greg set his glass down on the table and stared for a moment.

Kaz continued, "It's no big deal—just an old family friend that you'd probably be better off not knowing."

35

The bear hug came as expected, although it seemed not as robust as Kaz had remembered them. Boris Bunin's face looked old and haggard. His body sagged and his dark hair was thinning and tinged with gray. The bags under his eyes betrayed sleepless nights, which Kaz would have never imagined. The *old Boris* would never worry that much about things.

The old man laughed. "Please sit. You look so frail that I fear you may fall over on my floor." The laugh, though, seemed more a ritual than evidence of true emotion.

Kaz took the offered chair and bowed his head briefly. "It is good to see you again, Boris."

The Russian clapped his hands together and grinned. A bottle of vodka and two shot glasses magically appeared, along with dark brown bread, blocks of cheese, and dried fish. "You look famished, at death's door even. Eat, drink. You need more meat on those bones."

Boris's demeanor softened. "You are always welcome here, my friend. I fear that you spend far too much time away doing who knows what kind of work, that is obviously beneath you. You need to be here among your people." He paused for a moment before adding in a quiet, reverent tone, "I grieve with you the loss of your dear mother."

Kaz nodded feeling the tendrils of encroaching sorrow. His eyes averted, he responded with as much brevity as he could. "Thank you. It's hard." In that moment, he recalled that Dylan Strauss, the mercenary with whom he had shared a conversation only months prior, had told him that Boris' wife had been killed. This must be the source of the Russian's relative timidity.

"I understand that you only recently lost your wife. I regret that I never had the honor of meeting her. Still I offer my condolences."

Boris hardened for a moment, before softly replying. "Thank you for those kind words. Sadly, there are no words that can wash the pain from my heart."

"I cannot imagine."

A forced smile broke out on Boris' face. "Enough of this. I'm sure you did not come to hear an old man wail and cry."

Kaz reached into his shirt pocket and retrieved a business card. He stared at it for a brief few seconds before handing it Boris. "This woman provided me with information I needed. In return, she asked that I give you this with, as she put it, her *warmest regards.*"

Boris stared at the card for a moment. "Hmmm. Leah Bowman. Yes, I've heard of her. If my sources are to be believed, she's the brown woman that murdered her husband in order to gain control of his enterprise. Cold, Dimitry, cold indeed."

Kaz forced a smile. He recognized a hint of approval, even respect, in Boris' words.

Boris continued, "I admit that I am surprised that you

have taken up with such a person. You will not even consider working with me, an old and trusted friend, but you have no reservation about this woman."

"I'm not working with her. I have nothing to do with her enterprise." Kaz lowered his tone and volume. "I work with a group of people who try to protect women whose husbands beat and kill them. The woman who runs the organization, she ended up on a hit list managed by people who would like to perpetuate the assault and killing of strong women. Miz Bowman was able to give me information on the Sniper who's making the hits."

Boris considered him for a moment. "My Larissa was a strong woman. She was killed because of that."

Alarms went off in Kaz's head. *Here it comes.*

"The police officer who killed my Larissa, she was allowed to retire in peace with a pension. She lives her life as though nothing happened. I ask for nothing more than justice."

Kaz sat forward, wringing his hands in his lap. "You ask for revenge, Boris, and you know quite well that it is not something I do."

Boris stared daggers at Kaz. "I know that your mother died in Brookdale, barely able to remember who she was. She was put there by some punk looking for a nothing more than a handful of change. Yet you refused to avenge her. This piece of street shit walked free while your dear mother was fed every meal and had her diaper changed regularly. I find your willingness to accept this and move on with your life troubling. Why would a real man behave this way?"

Kaz had known it was coming. This wasn't the first time Boris had tried to guilt him into a revenge favor. "Come now, Boris, we have had this discussion before. It was not successful back then. It will not be successful today.

My mother has passed. No matter what happens to the person who put her there, it does not change anything. I made her life as good as it could be. Killing her assailant would not have made it any better."

Boris suddenly relaxed and smiled. "I had to try. You cannot blame me." The smile morphed into a laugh.

"I would never blame you, Boris. You have always been a friend to me. I value that. So, I will give you this gift. Forget that police person. She is likely a miserable soul who trusts no one and no one trusts her. Killing her buys you nothing but more trouble."

Boris shot back, "Trouble I can handle. It is just like my current troubles with the law. My case is plodding along, but it will soon disappear. There are too many people in high places who have skeletons lurking in their closets. I will be thoroughly chastised by the system and sent on my way with admonitions to be a good boy. One dead cop, more or less, will not change that reality."

"Boris, I tell you as a friend. What you are talking about is a solution in search of a problem. She is no danger to you, but if you screw it up, it could complicate your life. Keep Larissa in your heart and move forward. Live your life and celebrate the love that the two of you had."

"You sound like a fucking greeting card, my dear friend."

Kaz laughed. "Perhaps I'll go to work for Hallmark."

The two men rose and embraced. As the parted, Boris said, "Do not be such a stranger. Come, visit. We should have meals together, you and I."

"That would please me."

As Kaz started for the door, Boris said, "Wait, I have something for you." He eased over to his desk and took pen in hand, scribbling on a piece of paper. As he handed it to Kaz, he continued, "This is the name of the name of the shit who assaulted your mother. Not to worry, he has long since passed from this life. I just thought you should know."

Kaz stared at the paper for a moment. "Did you—"

Boris cut him off, "No. I had no part in his untimely demise. He apparently picked on the wrong person. Still, it is nice to know, is it not?" He offered a broad smile.

"Oh, one other thing. If the opportunity arises, I should like very much to be introduced to this Leah Bowman woman. Perhaps you might drop a good word for me."

Kaz couldn't help but roll his eyes. "You have no shame, Boris."

"Be well, my friend."

36

At first glance, there seemed nothing about the house that was extraordinary. As the Sniper studied it closer, though, the signs were clear. For a residential home in an economically depressed section of East St. Louis, Illinois, the lights around the structure kept every square inch illuminated. Video surveillance cameras were affixed at each corner of the house and constantly swept the entire yard, including the street out front. Like other homes in the area, the windows were fitted with bars. Unlike the other homes, though, a high-end electronic lock secured the front door.

"Best bet is to get inside before raising any suspicions." The Sniper spoke as he peered through the binoculars. "That means a night assault is out. If anything so much as moves after sunset, my guess is that they'd be on it in a few seconds." He lowered the binoculars and turned to face Conyers.

"Daytime. We approach like we belong there." He gestured toward the large canvas bag visible in the cap that sat over the truck bed. "I have a toy that'll get us through the digital lock in about ten seconds. I don't see a camera targeted specifically at the lock, so I'll go through the motions of punching numbers in while my box does its magic. Once we're inside, my guess is that we'll be confronted by at least two security guards who'll check our IDs against a list of expected couriers. That's when the gloves come off."

* * *

The Sniper lay awake in the semi-dark, staring at the ceiling. The sleazy motel room reeked of stale tobacco. The intermittent illumination from a nearby lounge was wasted. There was nothing in the room worth seeing.

Conyers snored in the main full-size bed while the Sniper camped out on what passed as a sofa. Along with all of the concerns about the security at the cash disbursement site, there was also the issue of the minister. Whatever qualifications the man had with regard to his religion, the Sniper was certain that they did not include combat, marksmanship, or even composure under pressure. Unfortunately, though, it was a two-man job. In order to access the house, they would need to appear legitimate That meant two couriers.

So far, everything had gone well—no… things had gone extraordinarily well. He had easily identified the two couriers at the meeting that Conyers had described. They had not found the tracking device, which worked perfectly. The two had led the Sniper and Conyers directly to the cash distribution site with no hiccups.

The Sniper had stolen a couple of Illinois license plates and affixed them to the truck, which he figured would help avoid unwanted attention. They had parked on the street at a discreet distance and watched the house for two days, coming and going at various times and shifting positions to avoid notice. On the first day, four sets of couriers came and went. There were five sets on the second day. The arrival of couriers was in no way unusual, but they didn't come in droves. Because of the difference in intervals, the Sniper assumed that there was some kind of master schedule.

He had done as much as possible to assure that Conyers knew what to do. The minister's job was simple. Once the action started, shoot as many people as he could. He would be carrying a Smith and Wesson 9 mm automatic handgun. That meant eight rounds in the clip plus one in the chamber. He would have an extra clip, giving him a total of seventeen rounds. If he needed more than that, they would probably both be dead anyway.

The body armor was tight…extremely tight on Conyers. It was, however, necessary. The guards, if they had any training at all, would fire at the midsection—chest and stomach. The Sniper cautioned him that, if he was hit where the body armor covered, it would be painful and knock him off balance but would not be fatal. "You need to recover quickly and keep firing. Our only hope is to take them all out before they know what hit them."

He had done as much as he could, and yet here he was —wide awake at 2:00 a.m. staring at the ceiling. *It's been too easy. I'm missing something.*

The sun found its way through the curtains and lit up the room. The bedside clock displayed the time—7:25. *Showtime.*

37

Kaz sat against the wall in a straight-backed chair. Val rolled her office chair back from her desk and leaned back, her hands laced behind her head. Aylin sat in a chair in the corner, appearing to want nothing more than to disappear.

The two male police detectives had pulled chairs up to Val's desk. The older one did most of the talking. "We'll take these in for ballistics testing and get them back to you as soon as we can." He slid the two handguns into individual plastic evidence bags.

"In the meantime, we do have a few questions for you."

Val's words exuded calmness and non-commitment. "Okay."

"Was your organization involved with any of these men's wives?" The detective stared at Val.

She glanced at the list for a moment, rubbed her chin, and slid the paper back across the desk to the man. "No."

"Take another look. Are you certain?"

Her gaze dropped briefly to the paper before returning to the detective. "Yes, I'm certain."

"Do you know of anyone who might have been involved in these cases?"

Val placed her hands flat on the desk and leaned in. "I told you, we were not involved in any way. What some other hypothetical organization or person may or may not have done is not something I can comment on. I'm sorry, but I can't help you."

The younger detective shot back. "You may want to reconsider. In case you're not up-to-date on this case, we're looking at the deliberate assassination of seven men... *men.* These are not crimes of passion. We have no reason to believe that it was self-defense. The victims appear to have been chosen simply because they were men. We can make the case here for domestic terrorism. You know what that means?"

Without waiting for an answer, he pulled his chair even closer to the desk a stabbed his index finger on the desktop. "The rules change. We're talking about enhanced interrogation, maybe even an all-expenses-paid excursion to Gitmo. Unless you want to be in on that party, you should reconsider your answer."

Kaz couldn't help smiling. He'd seen this dance before. The kid was taking a calculated risk by trying to intimidate Val. If she folded, he won, although it wasn't clear what he would win since Kaz was certain that Val didn't know anything.

On the other hand, if she stayed the course, the kid would end up looking like an idiot. Kaz tried to diffuse the situation. "Look, Detective, we're cooperating as much as we can. You have our weapons. We've told you—truthfully and completely—that our organization was not involved with these men or their cases in any way. There's simply nothing else we can say. We don't know any more than that."

Chapter 37

He glanced at Val to see her staring daggers at him. He shrugged it off, figuring he could speak with her later. The most important thing for the moment was to bring this interview to an end.

The older detective resumed the questioning. "Take it easy. We're just trying to make sure we have all the information. Myself, I find it hard to believe that we have seven identical murders, all apparently linked to domestic violence suspects in one way or another, and no one in the field knows anything. I mean, usually there's something. One of your clients, a disgruntled worker, even rumors… anything." He turned toward Aylin.

"I understand that you were shot a few months back and they never caught the person that did it." The older man arched an eyebrow, his lips curling in a subtle smile.

Aylin's face turned red. She clenched her jaw and leaned forward as though about to unload on the detective. A quick look toward Kaz offered him the opportunity to offer a slight head shake. He tried to convey the message *don't rise to the bait.*

She nodded curtly. "That's right."

The detective offered a humorless laugh. "That's gotta suck. I also hear that your ex-husband allegedly assaulted you. We could check with him, I guess, but I understand that he's dead. Stroke of luck, I'd say."

The color on her face deepened and she glared at him.

He stared back at her, as though waiting for the dam to break.

Suddenly, Aylin relaxed. "You have my weapon. Test if you need to, but please return it when you're done. She smiled and nodded.

The detective retorted, "I have to say, something about this whole group here," he waved his hands around the room, "doesn't ring true. There's more than you're telling me. The thing is, I chew up people like you and spit them out regularly. I promise, this is not over. If I find that you're concealing anything, you'll regret it."

Val held a hand up toward Kaz, as though to silence him. "I've been honest with you, Detective. We've not worked with any of those cases, and I personally have heard nothing… nothing at all… about the killings or individuals who may have been involved." She stared for a moment at the younger of the two.

"As for you, I can assure you that your petty threats don't impress me. I spent ten years in prison. I know your tactics and I know what you're capable of. Save yourself the time and energy. I know better than to lie to the cops, but I also know that I have no responsibility to help you. Now, are there any other questions?"

The older one subtly shook his head at the younger, warning him off. "We'll be in touch, and we'll have your weapons back to you as soon as possible."

After the cops left, silence enveloped the room for a few minutes. Finally, Aylin spoke. "For fuck's sake, Kaz, could you have been any more solicitous of those assholes? Hell, why didn't you just give 'em a blowjob while you were at it?"

"Knock it off, Aylin," Val stared at her. "While you may want to fall on your sword here over this, the truth is that it's just a distraction. We had nothing to do with those deaths and, as far as I know, we don't know of anyone who is involved. We've got work to do and I don't need for this to drag on."

She continued, "And Kaz, while I appreciate your effort to help, I can speak for myself."

He nodded, "Apparently."

38

Janet closed her eyes and reiterated her response to Detective Dee Martin. "I'm telling you, we don't know anything… period. I wasn't there at the interview, but from what Val, Aylin, and Kaz told me, the two detectives tried to strong-arm them. That's crap. They told the truth and were rewarded with accusations."

"I'm not saying they did anything wrong, Janet. I'm just trying to convey to you that this thing has traction. Yes, they are talking domestic terrorism. The governor has even weighed in on it. They're talking about bringing in the feds. Trust me, this isn't the one that you want to go to war over."

"How many different ways can I say this, Dee? We are not going to war over anything. We cooperated completely. I don't know what else you'd have me do."

After a moment of silence, Dee spoke quietly. "Okay, I understand. Look, if you do hear something, no matter how seemingly minor, let me know. You don't want to be caught on the wrong side of this one."

Janet felt her phone vibrate and saw the notification

that she had another incoming call. "I gotta run, Dee. I promise I'll let you know if I hear anything."

The number didn't trigger specific caller ID. It was just a 509 area code—eastern Washington. "Hello."

"Is the Reverend Polasky?"

"Who's calling?"

"Reverend Polasky, my name is Charles Owen. I live over in Spokane. My sister is Luellen Pickering. I think you know her."

Luellen Pickering was the woman who approached Janet the previous year looking for help getting her and her children away from an abusive husband. Unfortunately, the husband had found the kids and murdered them before being killed by the police himself.

"Uh… what can I do for you, Mister Owen?"

"It's about Luellen. You know, of course, what happened to her kids. She had a mental breakdown after that, but I haven't been able to convince her to stay in treatment. She got out of the hospital about five months ago and is behaving really strange. I'm trying to get her to go back in, but so far, she refuses."

"I'm sorry to hear that, but what is it you would like me to do?"

"I don't know. She talked about you from time to time, about how you tried to help her. Then, a couple of weeks ago, she disappeared, and I haven't heard from her since. I think she might try to contact you, given that you seem to be the only person she trusts. I was hoping that, if she does, you might convince her to go back into the hospital. I'm afraid that, in her state of mind, she might try to harm herself."

* * *

Days passed. The issue of Luellen Pickering was quickly obscured by the scores of other problems biting at her ankles. Despite what her brother had said, the woman thus far had not contacted Janet.

Kaz sat in the parsonage living room across from Janet. "No problem at all. What did you want to talk to me about?"

Janet sipped her tea. "The meeting you had with the police, you know, you, Aylin, and Val—I was curious to hear your version."

He eyed her suspiciously. "Have you spoken to Val about it?"

"Yes. I wanted to hear your account, though."

He glanced briefly out the window. "I'm not sure it would be any different than what she told you. Just a couple of cops on a fishing expedition. Truthfully, there was nothing more we could have told them."

Janet started to probe a little deeper when the doorbell rang. She froze in place, staring at Kaz.

He shrugged back, as though to say he had no idea who it could be.

She eased over to the front window and looked over toward the door. "Hmmm, it's Luellen Pickering."

"I give up. Who's Luellen Pickering?"

Janet shook her head. "She's a woman we tried to help. In fact, she was our first case. Unfortunately, her husband located her kids that she had stashed with a neighbor and killed them. The police shot him right after that. Her brother called the other day saying that she was having some mental problems."

She opened the front door. "Hi, Luellen. It's good to see you. Would you like to come in?" The woman's face was gaunt, her eyes sunken, and her body frail almost to the point of collapse. Her long slacks and blouse were wrinkled, and she looked as though he just climbed out of bed.

Luellen seemed stuck in the threshold of the front door. She gently swayed back and forth as if in some dream state. She had yet to say anything.

"Come in, please. It's cold out there. I can make you some tea."

The woman shuffled haltingly through the door. A combination of fear and anger haunted her face.

Janet gestured toward Kaz. "This is—"

Luellen Pickering reacted instantly. She drew back in a revulsion, her eyes wide. Almost immediately, she stepped forward. At the same time, she went into her purse with her right hand and drew out and handgun, pointing it toward Kaz.

She screamed, "You took my children. Where are they? Where are you hiding them?" She trembled as she advanced on Kaz.

Janet tried to intervene. "No, No, Luellen, he is a friend of ours. He does not have your children."

She appeared not to hear. "Tell me now or…." She raised the gun, her finger on the trigger.

Kaz, after a brief moment of surprise, seemed to enter a calm, almost spiritual state. He eased toward Luellen, his eyes glued on hers.

She stopped and tensed up. Her finger drew tighter on the trigger.

In instant, Kaz's hand shot out. He pushed her arm up deflecting the aim of the gun. At the same time, his other hand went out and twisted the weapon from her grasp before stepping back.

Janet rushed in and put her arms around the woman. "It's okay, Luellen. Kaz is a friend. He won't hurt you. No one's going to hurt you."

Chapter 38

Over the course of the next hour, Janet talked her down. In the end, Janet agreed to drive the woman to the hospital.

Three hours later, the minister trudged through her front door, ready to fall into bed. She had gotten Luellen Pickering admitted to the psychiatric ward where hopefully she could get some help. It occurred to Janet, though, that the woman had pulled a gun. Could this woman be the assassin that had killed those men?

She plopped onto the couch and pulled out her burner cellphone. After punching in Kaz's number, she sat and waited.

"How'd it go, Janet?"

"She's admitted. Hopefully they can help her. I assume that you're thinking the same thing I am, though. What did you do with the gun you took from her?"

"What gun?"

39

J anet closed her eyes briefly and promised herself that she would tread carefully. Dee Martin wanted to talk and there was little doubt in Janet's mind what it was about. "Come in." She gestured toward the chair in her office.

The detective had a grim look on her face. Her lips were drawn into a tight line and her eyes intense as she considered the minister. "Look, Janet, we go back a long way, but what I need to talk to you about is serious. You've gotta be honest on this one."

Janet feigned surprise. "Of course I'll be honest. What is it?"

"Luellen Pickering."

It had been four days since Janet and Kaz had disarmed the woman and gotten her admitted to the hospital. Four days since Kaz had taken the gun from her and then refused to discuss it. "What about her?"

Dee leaned toward the desk with her hands flat on the top. Her voice was hard, cutting as though she were interrogating a suspect. "You know damn well *what about her.*

You got her admitted to the psych ward. What was that all about?"

Janet slowly explained. "First of all, you know perfectly well what it was about. She lost her children to an abusive husband. You were there, remember?"

The detective appeared impatient. "I get that. Yes, I remember. What I mean is, how did this latest development come about?"

Janet shrugged. "It was pretty straightforward, I guess. I got a call from her brother. He told me that she'd left the hospital over in eastern Washington. He was afraid she might be suicidal. He asked to try and convince her to be readmitted if she contacted me. She came to see me several days after that and I convinced her to go to the ER."

"Why'd you take her to the ER?"

Janet shook her head. "What's this about, Dee? You know her story. You even predicted way back then that she might be suicidal. What's so earthshaking now? She's back in the hospital and hopefully she'll get the care she needs."

"You didn't answer the question. Why the ER? Was she suicidal or maybe you thought she might be threat to other people?"

Janet shot back, "Neither. She seemed disconnected, like she'd had some kind of break with reality. She just kind of stood around in a daze as though she had no idea where she was. Knowing her background, it just felt right to access emergency services."

Dee's voice softened. "I told you before, Janet, this case with the vigilante murders—those men—this is serious stuff. They're talking domestic terrorism, FBI, and who knows what else. As much as I may sympathize with what Luellen went through, you have to admit, she's also the perfect candidate for these killings. What did she say to you? Did she confess to them or even indicate that she might be responsible?"

Janet held up her hands as though to ward the detective off. "You know as well as I do that I'm bound by clerical confidentiality standards. I can't reveal what someone told me within the sanctity of our spiritual conversations." He held up a finger as though asking Dee to hear her out.

"I will tell you that she never mentioned killing anyone."

"Do you know whether or not she has a gun?"

Janet winced at the question. "I honestly do not know whether she has a gun or not." It wasn't a lie. Kaz had taken a gun from her. She had—past tense—a gun, but whether she currently had one or not was an unknown.

Dee continued to probe. "So, what you're telling me is that she didn't say anything that might give you cause to think she could be involved."

Thus far, Janet had not lied, at least not technically. This question, though, would not be so easy to finesse around. "Dee, I'm not a detective. I'm a minister. She didn't mention killing anyone or talk about any of the men. If you need a deeper dive into her thoughts, you need to ask her yourself."

"I can't. She's not accepting visitors and, of course, the mental health staff at the hospital are being less than cooperative."

Janet took to the offensive. "And so now you're here browbeating me. I don't know anything." That was, perhaps a lie.

She continued, "It seems simple to me. If Luellen Pickering is the killer, then she's in a locked psychiatric ward and won't be committing any crimes so long as she's there. If she gets out, you can pick her up and question her. I don't see the problem."

Dee's voice got louder. She punched her index finger on the desktop. "*The problem*, is that when she's released, she could easily continue the killing before I pick her up."

"That's absurd, Dee. You're speculating based on speculation. Your entire argument is based on an assumption that she's the killer. You don't know that any more than I do."

"What I know, Janet, is that you're choosing your words carefully. I know that you don't want to lie to me, but I suspect that you would also like to protect Luellen. I'm telling you, though, keeping information from me is no better than lying."

Janet felt the heat rising in her face. The anger built. "Tell me, Dee, how often does this kind of pressure get applied to get at a man who beats or kills his wife? How many times does an entire department get deployed to apprehend a man who might or *might not* be abusing his children? You do this when men are the victims but, if a woman is hurt, the system doesn't seem to care very much. The cops don't enforce TROs. They don't protect battered women. Hell, they don't even do a good job of prosecuting the men who perpetrate violence against their families."

Dee pounded her fist on the desktop. "I don't need a lecture from you, dammit. I have a responsibility to the rule of law."

Janet knew that she should back off, but the anger would simply not let her. "Did that responsibility include watching them send Val up the river for ten years?" She knew the instant she uttered the words that it was a mistake. Janet wanted desperately to take the insult back.

Dee's eyes grew wide. She opened her mouth as though to speak, but the words never came. Tears filled her eyes. She stood, turned, and left the office, slamming the door behind her.

Janet shot up from her chair and through the reception area in time to see Dee disappearing down the hall. "Dee, please. Come back. I'm sorry."

The detective stormed through the exit door without answering.

40

Janet held the plate of Russian tea biscuits out for Maddie. "I got the last ones they had, so enjoy."

Maddie took two, placing one on her saucer and taking a bite out of the other. "Sinful. Anything that tastes this good…. Mmmm."

Janet took a small bite of her biscuit followed by a sip of tea. "Well, all I can say is that we'll have to pray for forgiveness." She offered a half-hearted laugh. She'd come in search of wisdom that had nothing to do with cookies.

After a moment, Maddie moved the conversation along. "So, what is it that brings Reverend Polasky to my home bearing sinful treats in the middle of the week?" She wiped her mouth with the linen napkin while eyeing the second biscuit.

"Why do I need a reason to come see you?"

Maddie shot back, "You don't. I sense, though, that today is one of those days when there is a purpose." She arched an eyebrow and smiled.

Janet nodded as she considered the women—her

mentor and one of her best friends. "I suppose I need to practice my poker face."

Maddie's eyes sparkled as she laughed. "No, Dearie. Your complete honesty and lack of guile are parts of what makes you you. Now, what is it?"

Janet recounted the events related to Luellen Pickering, ending with her confrontation with Dee. As she told the story, it sounded worse than when she'd rehearsed it in her head.

"Well, now, that is quite the pickle. We can judge the rightness or wrongness in a few minutes, but let's clear up a couple of things. First, you lied to the good detective. Of course, you know that, or we wouldn't be having this conversation. Second, it sounds like you feel like this Kaz fellow has put you between a rock and a hard place. Maybe it's his fault."

Janet felt her spirits drop. She'd hoped that Maddie would come down squarely in her corner. It seemed as though the old woman was going to just pile on to an already bad situation. The conversation, though, took a different turn.

Maddie continued, "Now, let's see if we can tease out the bigger picture, shall we? You refer to this detective as your friend. It should be clear, though, that she didn't come to you as a friend. By all appearances, she came to take advantage of a friendship in search of answers about her case. Were you right in not helping?" The old woman laughed. "Only you can answer that. It seems to me, though, that when you look at the entire picture, this woman, Luellen, is in a place where she can't hurt anyone. Lord knows she needs help after what she's gone through. Where is she most likely to get this help—in the hospital or in prison?"

Chapter 40

She cleared her throat and continued, "The police have the responsibility for investigating crimes. They know where she is, and they know the realities of having to work around the mental health system. That's their problem; not yours."

Janet responded slowly, "I understand all of this. The other thing I'm struggling with, though, is the way that Kaz took the gun and is refusing to even acknowledge its existence. It's as though he's trying to shield Luellen from the responsibility for what she's done."

"I'm sure he is. The police, though, can make their case without the gun. Granted it will be harder, but they can do it. Here's what I think, and keep in mind that it's just my opinion. The police and prosecutor have nearly unlimited resources in their quest to solve the crime. The woman, on the other hand, has only the goodwill of a few people and possibly an overworked public defender."

Maddie paused and took a sip of tea. "I'm not condoning what she might have done, and I do think that she will someday have a reckoning with God. In the purely secular sense, though, she does at least deserve to be on even footing with the authorities. The police have a long way to go before they can charge her with anything. Once they have enough, though, this woman will be trampled and ground up by an uncaring system without so much as an afterthought. For my money, you have a duty to protect life. If this woman is a threat to others, then shielding her is a problem. If, on the other hand, this is only about punishment for past actions, then you have no moral obligation to help the police do their job. Keep in mind," she said with a twinkle in her eye, "there might be a moral obligation not to cooperate. Only you can decide where that line is."

"One last thing. This detective is a friend. By your own account, thing went sideways the last time the two of you spoke. Your challenge will be to repair the damage without jumping on her wagon to solve the case."

41

The Sniper had learned as much as he could. They had watched the house for two days and two nights. They had observed the comings and goings of the couriers. He'd kept meticulous count of the staffing, both day and night. During the day, there would be what looked like five guards and a couple of others, presumably the guys who handled the money.

The guys that passed as guards were clothed in all black. Their stocky appearance indicated that they probably wore body armor. When they came and went, there were no weapons visible. The Sniper assumed that the weaponry remained in the house. It made sense.

After parking the truck, the two of them—the Sniper and Conyers—sat in silence for a moment. What went through Conyers' mind was anybody's guess. The Sniper mulled over the likely organization and distribution of guards. At least two or them would be stationed at or near the front door. Anyone gaining entry to the house would have to clear these two before getting anywhere near the money. As for the other three guards, the Sniper wouldn't know until he was there.

What about the money? How would it be stored. No doubt there was a safe most likely with a sophisticated lock system. During the day when couriers would be coming and going, hopefully the safe would remain open. Getting to it without getting killed was the trick.

He and Conyers gained access to the cash distribution house without a hitch. The black box did its job in under ten seconds, while he fumbled around the keypad like he knew what he was doing.

They entered into a dimly lit corridor with a desk blocking their way. One of the two guards stood, an annoyingly bored look on his face, and said, "You guys are early."

Few things truly provided the Sniper with pleasure. One of them was watching the expression on someone's face as reality hit. It was that bored look that made it all worthwhile. The Sniper slipped his hand into the leather satchel he carried and withdrew a 9 mm automatic handgun fitted with a silencer. He could feel himself smiling. As he brought it to bear, the Sniper watched the realization sweep across the guard's face. That was all there was time for. He nailed both guards before they could unholster their weapons. The silencer dulled the sound although others in the house would certainly have heard it.

That was the last of the low-hanging fruit. The element of surprise had been spent. From here on out, it would be a pitched battle. A door opened to the right and two men poured into the hallway, one after the other, hurling themselves to the floor and rolling. The first defender came up, his assault rifle spraying automatic fire for a few seconds.

Out of the corner of his eye, the Sniper saw Conyers

go down. He was surprised that the obese minister had lasted as long as he had. Turning his attention to the defender, he knew that the burst of automatic fire had probably emptied the clip. He came up, his pistol grasped in both hands. He could see the look of terror in the man's eyes that came with the realization that he'd fucked up royally.

The squeeze of the trigger was followed by a muted pop as a hole appeared in the man's forehead. One down, two more guards to go.

He turned his attention to the other guard who had emerged from the side door. He didn't come out with a hail of automatic fire. Instead, he rolled into the hallway, coming up while bringing his rifle to bear on the Sniper. Whatever the young man's plan, he never had a chance to execute it. The Sniper put a round into his throat. Another one down.

One more to go. The Sniper wondered in passing at the wisdom of equipping guards with automatic rifles for indoor combat. Hand guns, or at the very least, shotguns would seem more appropriate.

The house fell silent. Was the final guard holed up in the same room as the other two or somewhere else? The Sniper slowly turned, his eyes searching every nook and cranny. The door into what was likely a kitchen was closed. In the other direction, a room at the end of the hallway was fitted with what appeared to be a steel-reinforced door —closed at the moment and probably locked from the inside. The noise from the firefight, though, could not have been missed by whoever was behind that door.

The Sniper looked again at Conyers. He was still moving, struggling to get into a sitting position. They both wore black clothing, so it was impossible to gauge the severity of the man's wounds, but it appeared as though his entire left upper side was saturated in blood. An unwanted thought intruded into his mind. *Maybe I should finish him off. Loose ends can spell disaster.* The Sniper's eyes, however, continued to scan the room.

From down the hall, a loud click cut through the silence. The Sniper whirled in that direction, his gun coming up in search of a target. Nothing.

Then he heard it. Everything shifted into slow motion. He had taken the bait. Exposed in the hallway with no cover, his mind acknowledged how this would play out. A louder sound came from behind him. He knew it was the kitchen door being thrown open.

He began his turn, all the while cursing himself. His mistake was amateurish... a noob move. The initial click at the end of the hall had been a diversion, obviously coordinated with whoever was inside the room. The unlocking of the door had drawn his attention.

He brought his gun around as he whirled, but in his mind he knew it was too late. The owner of the gun behind him had already acquired his target. The end had arrived.

Microseconds ticked by as though they were hours. The man's face came into view—the self-satisfied half-smile which said in clear, unmistakable terms—*gotcha.*

Two shots rang out, one after the other. The snide grin evaporated. His expression changed from satisfaction to surprise just as blood sprayed out from his face.

Stunned, the Sniper continued to turn, only to see Conyers sitting, his back to the wall, and allowing his weapon to drop into his lap. This loose end... this disgusting excuse for a man... this revolting asshole had just saved his life.

Quickly recovering, he ran to the end of the hall and threw the now unlocked door open. Two men cowered against the wall. Clearly these guys were not intended to be guards. There were a couple of handguns on the table, but neither man appeared anxious grab one.

With his own weapon trained on them, he made a quick decision. "Here's the deal. You have one chance to walk out of here alive." He eased back into the hallway and picked up the leather satchel. Reaching in, he withdrew the canvas duffel back and tossed it to the two guys.

"Keep your mouths shut and fill this up. If you can manage that, we can end this little party without any more unpleasantness, okay? Can you do that?" He smiled coldly at them.

As they finished and shoved the bag back in his direction, he could see their eyes widen as they tried to do the calculus. He could hear the questions they were asking themselves. Had they done the right thing? What they apparently wanted was to live. Had their actions helped them or hurt them in that regard?

He nodded to them. "A deal's a deal. Give me your phones."

They complied.

The Sniper smashed them with this heel. "Stay put. We're going to take our leave now. If I see either of your faces looking out a door or window at me, I'll reconsider. Otherwise, have a nice day."

42

What Janet had to do seemed perfectly obvious when she had spoken with Maddie. Later, as she steeled herself for the conversation with Dee Martin, things seemed considerably less clear. Dee was her friend. She had been the one standing beside Janet during some of the darkest times of her life. There should be nothing that can't be worked out between friends.

And yet, as Maddie pointed out, Dee had not come to her as a friend. Instead, she came leveraging the friendship in order to solve a case. That Janet was not at liberty to reveal what Luellen Pickering had said seemed lost on the detective. She considered it as a simple, moral situation. If Janet knew anything about who killed all of those men, was she morally bound to convey that information?

"Thanks for making the time, Dee. I don't like the way that we left things." Janet centered her cup of coffee directly in front of her, adjusting it so that the handle was on the right. It kept her hands busy.

"We've been friends since forever, Janet. I would have thought that you'd have more faith in me." Dee held

Chapter 42

Janet's gaze, although the look seemed carefully contrived as neutral.

"It's not a matter of faith. You asked me to betray the confidence of someone who spoke to me as a minister. I'm bound by a covenant of confidentiality. I went out on a limb and told you that Luellen had not said anything at all about killing anyone or even getting even. It's not like I'm hiding some monumental confession from you."

Dee shook her head. "If that's the case, what's the big deal about just telling what she did say or do."

Janet shot back, "You didn't come to me as a friend, Dee. You viewed me as an information source and leveraged our friendship to get it. Also, I would never expect you to reveal confidential information from your job."

Dee countered, "And yet I've done exactly that several times. You never had a problem accepting inside information from me."

"I never demanded anything like that. Everything you've given me in the way of information was freely offered. Dee, I understand that you're under a lot of pressure on this. Look, if you think Luellen was somehow involved, you know exactly where she is. Work through the staff there and try to get in to see her. After all, she knows you. You're the one that tried to help her last year."

"I get the sense that there's something you're keeping from me. Maybe that something would hurt Luellen, or it could help her. Either way I'm not going to hang her out to dry. Whatever you may think, I was profoundly hurt when Val went to prison. I saw what the system did to her, and I would never do that to another woman."

Janet shook her head. "From what you've told me, I'm not sure it would be your decision to make. I don't know who's driving the train on this case, but I bet it's not you. I've always known you to have a good heart. I can't say the same for other cops that I've encountered. They want to close the case. I believe in my heart that if they could close it by railroading Luellen, they would do it in a heartbeat, whether she was truly guilty or not."

Dee appeared as though she wanted to take issue but held her words for a moment. With eyes downcast, she spoke softly. "I understand your feelings. As much as it may seem an overused cliché, these things are more complicated that they appear. Yes, there are cops that would willingly send an innocent person up the river in order to close a case. Yes, there are misogynist cops who would gleefully screw a woman to help a batterer get off. These are realities that I can't deny."

Dee tapped her fingers on the table. "I'm not that way. One thing you should know about me by now is that I have no problem defying authority. I know Luellen Pickering. As you said, I tried to help her. I saw what happened to her kids and I watched her melt down. Frankly, I'm surprised she isn't already dead. I can only tell you that I will do anything I can to help her. If she did commit these murders, she'll be better off by a country mile building a credible defense based on mental illness rather than simply stonewalling the issue."

Janet was exasperated. This was not going the way she intended. "What is it you want from me?"

"I want to know what you're hiding about this case. Believe me, the guys that are working this case know about Luellen. Her name came up in a search of DV victims. They know she's in the hospital suffering some kind of mental breakdown. They will eventually find a way to get at her. She simply won't be able to hide behind the hospital doors forever."

"So, you think I can give you this smoking gun that will seal, at least in your mind, her guilt. I'm supposed to believe that you're going to take this and use it to help her. Do I have this right?"

Dee shrugged. "Pretty much, yeah."

"First, I don't have any such information. I'm not sure what gave you the idea that I do. To be perfectly accurate, you know as much as this case as I do... more, in fact. You know as much about her possible involvement as I do. I'm not sure how much clearer I can make that."

Dee sighed and shook her head. "Okay, I can see this is going nowhere. Here's the thing, Janet. If it comes to light that you've obstructed this investigation, I'm not going to be able to help you. They'll come after you with a vengeance."

She stood to go. "I'll keep trying to get in to see her. I hope for your sake that you're being up front with me."

43

J anet stared at Kaz with incredulity. "Do you really think you can get away with this?" The silence of parsonage enveloped them for a moment.

"Get away with what?" He looked at her as though genuinely confused about the conversation.

"Come on, Kaz. Don't do this. You know exactly what I'm talking about. She drew a gun on you, and you took it away from her. You have to know that she's most likely the one who's been killing those guys."

He narrowed his eyes for a moment before reverting to that injured innocent look. "Could I perhaps get a cup of tea?" A slight smile stole onto his face.

Ten minutes later they sat facing each other. Steam rose up from their cups, softening their view of each other. Janet broke the silence. "Let's start over. You know—"

Kaz interrupted her. "We actually know very little, Janet. You might suspect some things, and you might be correct. Here's some things that I know. First, if you hang her out to dry, she won't get a fair shake. The system, in this case, is wound like a tight spring, ready to snap on whoever happens to trigger it. No one… no one at all will speak up for her."

He continued, "Second, there is no purpose other than retribution in prosecuting her. It will not make the world a better place. In fact, one could argue that she did the world a favor." He held up his hand as though forestalling an objection.

"Before you say it, no, I am not advocating vigilantism. I'm saying that what's done is done. If the police find her, so be it. I can think of no good reason to help them, though."

She shook her head. "And you think you can prevent this by pretending that nothing happened? What are you going to do with the gun?"

"What gun?"

Janet waved him off. "Cut the crap, Kaz. You can't make all this go away by simply stonewalling it."

He laughed. "You'd be surprised what you can make go away by stonewalling things." He leaned forward, cupping his tea in both hands. "Yes, the police may eventually find their way to her. If they do, it will likely be through the hospital. Then what they're faced with is a mental patient who has had a complete psychotic break. Likely there is nothing she can say that would be taken seriously by a court. It's possible that the police will get a court order for disclosure of hospital records, but even those will be presented within the context of a patient who has completely lost grip on reality."

"What if they find out you have the gun?"

"Any kind of information about a gun, which may or may not exist, would come from the woman herself. As I said, she's a mental patient with no grasp of reality. If it comes to conflict of testimony between her and me, who's version do you think will prevail?"

His tone softened along with his eyes. "Yes, Janet. They may eventually discover that she's the killer. When that happens, though, she will be a woman who is not competent to stand trial. If the police find their way to her through other means, such as you or me, I suspect they will try to disregard the mental illness diagnosis. No, if they are to find her, it's better that they do it through the mental health system. As for me having a gun that may or may not have belonged to her... it will be her word against mine and I have no reason to lie."

Janet stared at him for a few seconds. "Except that I was there."

"Yes, you were." He held her gaze without flinching.

After a moment, he continued, "You knew when you hired me that I was not averse to wandering across legal boundaries from time to time. I've done it before, and I can say with near certainty that I'll do it again. You've seen first-hand the brutal realities of the world we live it. All we can do is what we believe to be the right thing."

44

Janet felt the weight of the day. Her body and mind were bathed in fatigue. The relentless pressure of fundraising for the church never gave her a minute's respite. This had all been complicated by the Luellen Pickering case. Four visits to congregation members during the day had left her frustrated. She'd had to beat back anger on several occasions when members acted as though they were doing her a favor by attending church. In the end, she reminded herself that these were all good people doing the best they could.

She passed on dinner, having no energy to eat much less prepare anything. Instead, she opted for a hot shower and a book. Just as she turned on the shower, she noticed the display on her phone indicating an incoming call... from Greg. "Hi, Greg. Thanks for returning my call." She turned off the shower.

Janet felt inexplicably odd. Standing there in the nude talking to him felt strange though not unpleasant, even though she knew he couldn't see her.

"My pleasure."

Is that excitement in his voice? She became even more self-conscious in her nudity. "Actually, I was hoping that you might have some time, maybe tomorrow evening. I'm struggling with some financial stuff related to the church and I could use your advice." She turned away from the mirror and looked down at the floor.

"Absolutely. Is seven okay?"

Janet responded, "Perfect. I'll drop by your place, if that's okay."

It wasn't as though she never expected to have these feelings again. It had been ten years since she'd lost Mark. Before this, though, she successfully kept sex out of her mind, for the most part. Since *the kiss*, though, those feelings had crept back in, seeming to take advantage of every opportunity. Talking to Greg while standing nude in the bathroom definitely opened the door.

She forced the emotions back. Janet had a lot going on and needed to focus. She turned the shower on and stepped in. The sensation hit her like a speeding train. She thought about his words, especially the tone of excitement, while the hot shower pelted her breasts. She'd not felt this for years. The ache inside and the building passion blocked everything else out. Her hands found their way on to her stomach and then slid farther down.

After the shower and she shut the water off and stepped out. She dried herself and slipped into a terrycloth robe as she replayed in her mind what had just happened.

Lying in bed watching the shadows of the tree branches dance on the walls in her bedroom, Janet considered her feelings. It wasn't as though she hadn't felt sexual arousal in the past ten years. It was just that she'd been able to successfully ignore it. After all, there hadn't been an actual person attached to it. Although it hadn't been easy, she held to the notion that sex in the absence of someone special was meaningless.

Things had changed. Almost without her noticing, Greg had become the center of these feelings. He'd made no secret that he felt she was special. And… he felt special to her. It made a difference.

Janet glanced at her bedside clock. She was stunned to see that she'd lain there for two and a half hours. She forced her eyes closed and willed sleep to come. No such luck. She found it difficult to banish the thought that the next evening would bring change. Did she really want that change?

45

The escape had been relatively clean. The only real point of contention had been Conyers' need... or rather desire to go to a hospital. It had, of course, been out of the question. Emergency rooms and trauma centers would report a gunshot wound to the police. The minister agreed, under much duress, to the first aid that the Sniper could provide along with a few days' worth of oxycontin. After all, he'd taken a shot to the shoulder—hardly a life-threatening wound.

They'd made their way to the south and east for a few days—enough to reassure the Sniper that no one was hot on their trail. After that, they turned and headed for home.

The Sniper mulled the irony over in his mind as they covered the final hundred miles to his cabin in central Idaho. It was hard to imagine anyone deserving to die as much as Conyers did. Not only was the man a queer, but he was also queer for little boys. He was a despicable excuse for a human being.

Yet this same piece of shit had saved his life. After

being shot, Conyers had had the presence of mind to shoot the final guard, who had gotten the drop on the Sniper.

For his part, the Sniper had dragged the man to safety. He had nursed the pervert's wounds and provided food and drink. In another life/another time, he would have put a bullet in the man's head on principle. After all, he'd killed his cousin Billy—his own flesh and blood—for the relatively forgivable sin of getting caught. Now, here he was going above and beyond expectations to care for this guy.

He shook his head as he glanced over at the man. Conyers had fallen asleep again, his head resting against the passenger side window. *Why bother with him?*

The truth was, Conyers, whatever he might be, was the only human being on earth that the Sniper could trust at the moment. Everyone else who knew about the Sniper wanted him dead.

What was most confounding, though, is that he'd never needed companionship before. It wasn't that Conyers was a strategic asset of any importance, and he damn sure didn't have a magnetic personality. Sure, he'd been on the raid and had done his part. That he'd taken a bullet said nothing about the man's value. It was random luck.

He did save my life, though.

On the other hand, that was obviously a self-serving action. Without the Sniper, Conyers would never have escaped. It was a simple transaction. Conyers had saved his life, and he returned the favor. No more debts were owed.

The minister moaned and shifted in his seat After a moment, he muttered, "Are we just about there?"

"Another hour and half or so."

"What then?"

"Things are gonna move fast. We walked away with just over eight million dollars. Those guys are most certainly going to want it back. We have to get Broward and Trent before they can mount that effort."

Conyers seemed to ponder the idea. "How would they even find us?"

The Sniper laughed as it occurred to him that Conyers didn't have a clue about the real world. "For starters, they know who we are. That place had surveillance video of every square inch and it's not like we're strangers to them. They also know that I live somewhere in central Idaho. It won't take 'em long to find us."

The Sniper could sense Conyers staring at him. After a moment of silence, the man asked quietly, "What're we gonna do?"

"Pretty simple. We have to get them before they get us. By that I mean Broward and Trent. They're the ones calling the shots, unless you left out some crucial information. By taking them out, especially Trent, we throw the entire organization into confusion. That'll give us time to figure out our next steps."

They rode the rest of the way in silence. As they approached the turnoff to his cabin, the Sniper slowed. Through the bare branches, he could just make out some features of the structure. More importantly, he could see that there were no vehicles in the driveway. He eased past the turnoff and continued on for about a half mile.

He pulled over into a small dirt road and followed it around a bend before coming to a stop. "You wait here. I'm going to go in through a back way and make sure everything's okay."

The Sniper backtracked to the main road and followed it back toward the cabin from about a quarter mile before sliding into the woods on a game trail. He followed that for a hundred yards or so until he came to a steep drop-off.

Some 200 feet below the bluff, a small creek cut its way through the rugged, snow-covered countryside.

Following the bluff, he crouched and eased forward five to ten yards at a time, stopping to carefully scan the area ahead as well as listen for any telltale noise. He didn't really expect anyone to be there, but he was worried about any surveillance that might have been set up just to alert the organization to his return. It had been nearly a week since they'd hit the cash house—plenty of time for them to pull that off.

He stopped at the edge of the clearing where his cabin stood. He followed every line of the structure with his eyes. He studied every tree. Seeing nothing, he slipped over the edge of the bluff and found enough footing to move past the clearing while remaining out of view.

Coming up on the other side, he went through the same exercise with the same results—nothing. Things didn't add up. The two of them had not used disguises or even masks at the cash house, so certainly the organization knew who they were. His contacts within the group knew roughly where he lived. Why had they not set up surveillance video cameras?

The Sniper worked his way back to the truck. When he opened the door and got in, Conyers was staring wide-eyed at him.

"What? What's wrong?"

Conyers shook his head. "I was just looking at the news." He held up his smart phone. "It's Broward. He's dead."

46

J anet sat on the sofa while Greg lounged in his overstuffed chair. "I appreciate you taking the time to talk to me." She had figured that if anyone could give her decent business advice, it was Greg Stottman.

He burst out laughing. "Seriously? Come on, Janet. You know how I feel about you. I'm never going to pass on a chance to talk to you."

She ignored the subtext. "I need some business advice."

He arched an eyebrow but said nothing.

Janet poured out the description of her financial dilemma with the church. He listened without comment or even visual reaction.

When she finished, he turned his gaze toward the window, his face serious, as though he was considering some deep philosophical challenge. Finally, he spoke. "You're dealing with what every business owner or non-profit director goes through. It's driven by the need for growth. They secure funding and then promptly realize that, with even more money, they could do so much more.

It's a never-ending cycle. I don't know much about churches, but it strikes me that they have a slightly different problem. You have a congregation that sees the church as a spiritual sanctuary of sorts. Intellectually, they realize that it takes money to run it, but it seems almost a contradiction—spiritual matters and money don't go together, at least in some minds."

Janet related her experiences with the congregation members—the differences in reaction among them. "In some ways, it seems unfair. Those who make it easy on me end up bearing the brunt of the burden while others contribute little."

One corner of his mouth turned upward in what seemed a cynical smile. "You knew this already. You've been a minister for well over a decade. This can't be the first time that you've noticed this."

"No, but it seems worse this time... maybe because I've got so many other things nagging at me. I can't seem to catch my breath."

Greg exhaled and shook his head. "Well, the financial problem is pretty simple. You can do one of two things. You can keep doing what you're doing—managing expenditures and pressing for more contributions. That's what I'd call the line of least resistance and probably what most small churches do."

She queried, "And the other thing?"

"You know the funding mechanism for your project, right? We put an obscenely large amount of money in an investment account, and you operate on the income from that account. It's not a complicated model."

It was Janet's turn to laugh. "So, your solution would be to come up with millions of dollars for an investment account so that the church could live off the income. Am I getting that right?"

"Pretty much."

"No offense, Greg, but you've lived too long in a world of wealth. I'm sure coming up with those kinds of dollars isn't hard for you, but I'm barely able to get enough to operate on, much less to fund an investment account."

He leaned forward, his hands clasped on his knees. "That's because raising operating money isn't the same as trying to fund an annuity account. You have to go about it much differently."

He raised his index finger. "First, for a fund such as this, you're soliciting one-time contributions. People who donate in these circumstances have an expectation that you won't be coming back for more. It makes a difference. For another thing, hitting up every congregation member won't help you much. You might look for wealthy members who might be willing to include the church in their wills. You can also look for business connections where an owner might be willing to contribute to such a fund. Churches, after all, can make a community for vibrant and desirable to live in. Bake sales and car washes won't do it for you."

In that instant, it struck Janet. Greg was inviting her to ask him for money. *No. I'm not going there.* She leaned her head back and closed her eyes. The problems all swirled around in the darkness, giving her no peace. Finally, she opened her eyes. "Okay, thanks. I have some ideas. I'll just have to give it some thought."

As if reading her mind, Greg asked, "Why haven't you asked me for money?" His tone was casual, as though a comment made in passing.

"You've been very generous with my project, and I want you to know how much I appreciate that. You're not a member of my congregation, though. I just don't want to...." She couldn't find the words, or at least she didn't want to say them. *I don't want you to be my personal bank.*

He offered what sounded like a sincere laugh. "I have to tell you, this is a first for me. I have someone sitting here in front of me who's not willing to take more money. What are you afraid of—that you're going to owe me and I'm going to demand something... something in return?" He seemed to stumble on those last words, but the meaning seemed clear.

Was that it? Was she afraid to be more in his debt than she already was? No. It was something else entirely. Suddenly she understood. She wanted more from him—not his money, but.... Her eyes teared up and she felt as though her throat were constricting. *I'm not ready for this.*

Then it happened. She began to argue with herself. *Why not? If not now, when?*

"No, Greg. I'm not afraid of being in your debt. After all, I already am. You've single-handedly funded our project. More than that, you've been there for me every step of the way. There's no way that I could ever owe you more than I already do."

"Then what is it?"

This was it. Her stomach did somersaults. She searched in vain for some quick response. It was time.

She stood and moved over to sit beside him. She took his hand in hers and leaned against him. "I need you to know that... it's not about your money." As the words came out, she realized how stupid they sounded.

He put his arm around her and drew her closer. "I know that, Janet. I've known it all along." He stroked her hair gently with his other hand. "You're not driven by money."

She snuggled into him. "How do you know?"

He laughed softly. "If you were, you'd be on a very different career track. There's no money in being a

Methodist minister. You could start one of those big glitzy megachurches, but that's not you."

She wanted to respond, but words seemed unnecessary. Janet closed her eyes and let the warmth pass into her.

His hand moved from her hair to her cheek—his brushed it softly.

Janet lifted her face.

The kiss came naturally. At first, a gentle touch of the lips. Then another. His arms embraced her as he turned, pulled her closer to him. They kissed deeply and a feeling long pent up inside Janet found its way out. She put her arms around his neck. His hands found their way to her back and beneath her blouse. She pressed closer, harder. The dam broke.

* * *

Janet lay with her head on his bare chest, the covers only half over them. She felt his heart beating as she soaked in the warmth of his body. Finally, she glanced over at the digital clock display on the bedside table. Groaning, she eased away from him and sat up. "I should be going. Tomorrow's a workday."

Greg reached up and pulled he back down. "For me too, but that's tomorrow. This is now." He kissed her again. "Stay the night. We can get up early and you can make it work in plenty of time."

"Believe me, I'd love to, but I can't start spending the night with you." She half-laughed. Not everyone in my congregation is as *open-minded* as me. People would talk."

"That's okay. My business partner has been talking about this for months."

She sighed and smiled, although she knew he couldn't

see it. "Well, I suppose we've given her something to talk about, then."

47

The incoming call interrupted the small talk. Val, Kaz, Janet, and Eisen had gathered in anticipation of the call from the mysterious party who had agreed to help with the new identification. Val hit the *connect* icon on her phone, set it for speaker, and set it on the center of the table. "Hello."

"You have this set for speaker, may I ask who all is in the room?"

Val responded, "I'm Val Gomez, and I'm here with Dimitry Kazarian, whom I believe you're familiar with. Janet Polasky, who began this project, is also here along with our technical consultant, who goes by the name Eisen."

The voice sounded almost cheerful. "Ah yes, Mister Eisen. We are familiar with his talents. It is good to contact with you directly."

Eisen arched an eyebrow. "Thank you."

The voice reverted back to an all-business tone. "I assume that you have some questions for me."

Val spoke hesitatingly, "Well, I guess my first question would with regard to your identity. Who are you?"

"If you are referring to me personally, I am of no significance. My employer, at this point, prefers to remain anonymous. I hope that you understand. I will assure you that, if I told you their name, you would not recognize it."

Val responded, "The difficulty I have is that you are offering this generous service with strings attached. I worry that at some point in the future when the debt comes due, we might find ourselves allied with a less than savory lot. I mean no offense, but not knowing anything about you, I have to plan for the worst."

"I will convey that concern to my employer, although I am not sure what will come of it. I am able to assure you that they are most certainly not an unsavory lot, as you call it. They prefer to do their work in the shadows. I will add that my employer has been aware of your efforts from the beginning and find themselves aligned with your objectives."

Val shrugged as she glanced around at the others. "Okay, I think we can leave that for now. Hopefully we can come back to it later. We do have some other questions, most of them technical. I'm going to let Eisen take it from here."

Eisen sat up straighter and leaned in toward the phone. "We've been talking about a new ID that will hold up to close scrutiny, meaning a deep-dive investigation. Is the ID you're offering going to do that?"

"Yes, because it's not a fake ID. The documents will be real. There will indeed be social security accounts. Their final destination will be Orlando, Florida. The driver's licenses will be issued by the State of Florida. Birth certificates will have the original copies on file with the Florida

Bureau of Vital Statistics. In other words, your clients will be new, quite legitimate people."

Eisen shook his head, appearing enthralled with the concept. "If you don't mind my asking, how will you pull that off?"

"My employer has… relationships everywhere. There are people in the various organizations that are all too happy to help. I will leave it at that."

Silence fell over the table for a moment. Val was overwhelmed at the magnitude of what seemed to be transpiring. "I guess I'm struggling to understand how all this happens for free."

A hearty laugh came over the speaker. "Nothing is free. Forms of currency vary across the world. We are not asking you for money. Neither are our associates at these organizations reimbursed in that way. Again, though, perhaps we can leave this discussion alone. You know what you need to know."

Eisen spoke again, "Okay, yeah. I get it. I do have a more technical question. Even with new driver's licenses, there's still a danger. Licenses these days have digital photographs affixed. The images are a part of the DMV database in all states. This is all public information. A person could, if so inclined, download the databases from all states and filter them through facial recognition software. Using AI as an adjunct tool, they could conceivably find our clients."

"An excellent question, Mister Eisen. We have thought of that. The photographs that will be used for the licenses are based on their existing Washington licenses. We have, though, tweaked those photos, both in terms of age and facial ratios, which are the basis for comparison. To a casual observer, the photos will appear to resemble the clients. Because of the changes we've made, though, facial recognition software, even with AI assistance, will have a less than five percent change to make the connection."

Eisen laughed. "You guys must have some great toys."

"Is there anything else?"

"This is Janet Polasky speaking. From your accent, I assume that you're located somewhere outside of the United States. How is it that you knew about my project? We don't advertise and we've tried to keep this as close as possible."

"In very general terms, Reverend Polasky, my employer makes it their business to stay informed regarding efforts to combat domestic violence. Let us say that it is a special significance to them. Beyond that, I am not at liberty to discuss it."

Janet continued, "I'm more than a little uncomfortable with that. We've had one client whose children were killed, and Val Gomez was nearly killed herself. Remaining obscure and in the shadows is our best protection. It's disturbing that your employer, who resides not only outside our state but in a different country, could be so familiar with what we do."

"Understandable. The reality is, though, that my employer does know. You should also be aware that your efforts, while they may seem independent and isolated, are anything but. There are dedicated people all over the world attempting similar feats of heroism. There is a virtual garden of lilies out there offering new lives for battered women."

Janet's eyes widened. "Garden of lilies? How did you come by that term?"

Val studied Janet. The question seemed odd. *Why did that term—garden of lilies—strike a nerve?*

"A simple colloquialism. It seems a good way to conceptualize the efforts, would you not say?"

After the conversation ended, Val put the question to Janet. "Why did that strike you, I mean, the term?"

Janet responded, "It's just that, when I first started out, I envisioned the lily exactly as they used the term. I saw what we were doing as a way of offering a rebirth or resurrection to these women and their children. It seemed odd that they would hit on the same metaphor"

Val sighed. "Maybe you didn't keep things quite as close as you thought you did." Before Janet could object, Val continued, "Or maybe it's just a coincidence."

48

The players filled the parsonage living room. Janet had carefully selected each person to attend this meeting that had multiple purposes. In her heart she knew it would be one of the most monumental gatherings of her life.

She started with the easy part. "Most of you know each other, but in the interests of making sure we're all on the same page, I'll do introductions."

The minister started on her left. "This is Aylin Frey-berg. She'll be the operative working directly with Gwen and her father, Jason Lambert. Next is Greg Stottman. As most of you know, he's the funding source for our project and has been with us every step of the way."

She turned slightly. "This is Dimitry Kazarian—goes by Kaz. He handles our security and has been the contact person for all the arrangements we're going to discuss tonight. Sitting on the couch over there is Eisen. He's done all our tech work so far and can give us advice on what to do going forward. In the chair beside the coffee table, this Tahira Kushk. Gwen Trent initially contacted her for help.

Miz Kushk came to me and, well, here we all are. Finally, and I saved her for last, is Val Gomez."

Janet took a deep breath and dropped the bomb. "As some of you know, running this project has stretched me to the limit. I've tried to balance my duties to my congregation at Saint Luke's with the burden of keeping our clients safe. I can no longer do this. As of tonight, I'm passing off the leadership of this project to Val. She's been with me since the beginning. She's escorted clients to safety, and, as some of you, she was almost killed helping a woman. Starting now, she's in charge of day-to-day operations. I'll remain involved in a supportive and advisory capacity, but I can no longer do the direct coordination."

The room fell silent. Of all the those present, Aylin looked the most disconcerted. Her eyes darted about, and she pursed her lips. She stared for a moment at Val then back at Janet. Finally, she spoke in a soft voice. "I wasn't expecting this. I agreed to work with the project because it was something you were doing. Nothing against you, Val, but I don't know you. You'll be asking us to risk our lives and the lives of our clients. I'm just not sure about this."

Janet hadn't seen this coming. She gathered her thoughts before speaking. "I understand your concerns, Aylin. If you need to bow out, I'll respect that. I will say, though, that Val had to make the very decision you're talking about when she came onboard. She had a job before this. She didn't know me or anything about what I wanted to do. What made it even harder is that I needed her to commit and get to work immediately. Things were difficult, but we trusted each other and it worked out. That's where you're at, Aylin. I need you to get to work. You know what we want to accomplish. Val has a proven track record. In terms of understanding the nuts-and-bolts problems you'll face, she's much better informed than I am."

Janet paused and her voice softened. "If this doesn't work for you, I understand and wish you only the best."

Aylin to a small step backward and lowered her head. "I can stay, I guess. I just wish that you'd discussed this with me ahead of time. I mean, you've obviously known about this for days, maybe even weeks."

Everyone else remained dead silent. Janet considered the woman for a moment before deciding not to engage in that particular conversation. "Okay, then, if there's nothing else with regard to Val taking over, my final act as leader will be to turn the floor over to Kaz. He's going to walk us through what will be happening with Gwen Trent and her father.

Kaz stepped forward and nodded, offering a tight smile. "There's a lot that's going to happen and I'll go over each part again with those that are involved. The people helping us have set things in motion. We have a few days to refine our local operations plan. Once we start, it'll happen fast. Last things first. Miz Trent and her father will be relocating to Orlando, Florida. As far as I know, there's nothing special about that. To be honest, I don't know how that location was selected, but it was."

Tahira raised her hand. "Mister Kazarian, may I ask, is that decision final?"

Kaz nodded. "For now, yes. It's possible that at some point in the future, they might be able to relocate. At this time, though, we are setting them up there. What that means will become clearer as we go on."

The Afghani woman nodded.

"So now to the operation here. The first order of business will be for Miz Trent to prepare." He turned to face Tahira. "You're in direct contact with her, so you'll need to pass this along. She should not bring anything she doesn't absolutely need. She'll get new clothing and personal items along the way and when she gets to her new destination. I believe that she can get her bare necessities in a small backpack. I say this because she will need to move quickly from place to place."

Tahira jotted notes on her pad. "Very well."

"Next. This next part is important. She is not to convey any information to her father. I understand this could create some problems between them, but the stakes are simply too high. He must be kept in the dark. When she's ready to go, please inform me."

"Yes, I can do that."

"Aylin, this next part will involve me and you. When we get the word that Miz Trent is ready to go, we will go to the school where her father teaches and abduct him."

There was an audible gasp in the room, but Janet couldn't tell where it came from.

Kaz continued, "Yeah, I know. That sounds bad, but we need for everyone to be surprised. We have to assume that Miz Trent's in-laws are not so detached from reality that they don't suspect something. She and her husband have had problems in the past. In all likelihood, her husband's father, Randolph Trent, has some surveillance in place. The man didn't get to where he is by leaving things to chance and he has made clear to Miz Trent that she will not be leaving her husband."

Aylin asked, "How is this abduction supposed to work?"

"Good question. We're going to grab him at the school where he teaches. We can talk more about the details, before this happens, but my initial thoughts are that I'll engage the receptionist. I'll distract them while Aylin makes her way down to the classroom. We'll time it so that this all happens right at the change of class period, so the confusion will be on our side. I figure we can add to the confusion by pulling one of the fire alarms. That'll throw the entire school into chaos."

He paused and then continued, "While I'm doing that, Aylin, you give him a quick explanation, and move him toward a rear door at the school, maybe a loading dock for supplies. I'll meet you along the way. We'll drive away using a pre-set route."

"If they've got any surveillance set up, as you suggest, won't they see this go down and follow us?" Aylin seemed genuinely engaged at this point.

"Yes, they might. That's why Val is going to be stationed on the route about three blocks away. She'll watch for any signs of pursuit. If they're on our tail, she'll create a distraction. If things are clear, we'll move to an underground parking lot about three miles away and transfer to another vehicle. Leaving there, we'll travel south through downtown Seattle on I-5 and rendezvous with Tahira and Miz Trent at a short-term rental unit that we will have swept for any video or audio surveillance. After that, it's simply a matter of Aylin moving them to Orlando by car. You'll use hotels that don't have video cameras reserved along the way. Avoid areas where you might be picked up on camera. Obey all traffic laws and generally try to stay on the interstates, going with the flow of traffic."

Aylin asked, "What about when we get to Orlando? What do we do?"

Kaz took an index card from his notepad. "Go directly to this address." He handed the card to Aylin. "The entry code for the electronic lock on the condo is there beneath the address. Inside the condo, you'll find everything you need—new social security cards, driver's licenses, credit cards, etc., along with instructions on how to access financial resources. They'll be provided with sufficient funds to live for two years, three if they economize. After that, we can reassess, but I think the expectation is that, with the new lives, they can find employment. The condo, a new car, which will be in the garage, and new furnishings will all be paid for up front."

Aylin turned her gaze toward the front window and stared, as though she were running things over in her mind. "This all sounds too simple. I'm more than a little uncomfortable not having any idea who's behind all this."

Kaz sighed. "We've conveyed that very concern to our benefactor. Unfortunately, for now we've gotten all the information we're likely to get."

Janet, for her part, was amazed. This complex, dangerous operation had been put together in less than a week. The best part was that everyone involved seemed ready to go.

49

Kaz endured the uncomfortable silence on the ride. He'd somewhat understood Aylin's unpleasant demeanor during her weapon orientation. The impertinence when he'd given her initial instructions on how to handle dangerous situations was tolerable, only because he knew her background.

Nothing had changed, though. The woman remained hostile. Although it appeared that he was the target of her anger, Kaz knew better. Aylin's issues went much deeper than mere annoyance. He toyed with the idea that he should recommend to Val that they not use her. As much as he hated *soft language*, there was no way around the fact that *not using her* was a euphemism for firing the woman, which seemed a rather drastic step.

On the other hand, her state of mind could easily put her as well as clients at risk. *Let's see how the meeting goes.* "Do you have any concerns that we should talk about before we get there?"

"Nope." She stared out the side passenger window.

"Aylin, you can take this any way you want, but I'm

going to lay it out for you. Once we get into this, you're going to be that woman's only link to the rest of the world. How you treat her will matter. You can be as pissy as you want with me, but once this process starts, you need to soften up. She's going to need someone to talk to and to understand."

"I'm not being pissy. I just don't like you."

"It's completely irrelevant whether you like me or not. I don't care how you feel. I care how you behave and what you say. Your job carries no small amount of relationship building. So far, I haven't seen any attempt on your part to connect with me… or with Val for that matter."

"Janet hired me. She must have had a reason. I don't know Val. Maybe she's okay; maybe not. The monkey's on her back to prove herself to me."

Kaz burst out laughing despite the seriousness of the topic. "You have that one exactly backwards. You're the one that has to prove themselves. Val's already done that. She's escorted a woman to safety and saved another's life while nearly sacrificing her own. She's paid her dues. You, on the other hand, have done nothing but complain. I'll give you that you're good with a weapon, although I worry that you're far too anxious to use it."

"Why don't you get off my back. I've done everything you've ordered me to. I have a job to do, so back off and let me do it. I'll take care of my client."

Kaz shot back with what he hoped was an unmistakable tone of authority, "She is not *your* client. She is our client. Never forget that. She didn't come to you for help. She came to Miz Kushk, who approached Janet. You're the last person to arrive at the party."

They passed the remainder of the trip in silence.

Kaz pulled into a parking spot on the street in busy section of University Heights. "The office is in that complex." He pointed to what appeared to be a set of row houses. "Second floor… the blue one."

Val and Tahira had already arrived and were engaged in what seemed light conversation. Kaz shed his coat and hung it on a coat rack by the door. "Sorry we're a little late. We got held up in construction."

Val responded, "Construction… what else is new? There only seems to be two seasons around here—dead of winter and road construction season."

Once everyone was seated, Val started things off. "I think we all know each other from the other night. What I hope to do here today is come up with an executable plan. Once we wade into this, there won't be any time for pauses or uncertainty until we have Miz Trent and her father in a safe house."

She turned toward Tahira. "Have you spoken with Miz Trent about our tentative plans?"

"She seemed fearful about the abduction plan and wanted to forewarn her father. I told her no, for fear that his behavior might be affected enough to tip off anyone watching. I want to reiterate, I do believe that the Trent family probably has him under some type of surveillance. Gwendolyn told me that things have been tense."

Val responded, "Good call. If this goes the way we want, Mister Lambert will be surprised." She looked at Kaz and Aylin. "That means that you're going to have to connect with him, get him moving quickly, and reassure him at the same time. Any thoughts?"

Aylin jumped in. "I'm not sure why this is a two-person job. All I have to do is get to Mister Lambert and lead him to car. I can talk to him along the way. Having two people strikes me as making us more noticeable, which is one thing we don't want."

Val responded, "You raise a good point. I want two of

you, though, because you're going to have multiple things all happening at once. We have no way of accurately predicting how things will unfold. I could go over ten different scenarios with no confidence that any of them were valid. Kaz is our security officer. He'll call the shots during this operation. If it were me, I'd have one person holding Mister Lambert's arm and talking to him while the other person ranged out in front by a few feet guiding the progress and watching for trouble. In the end, though, you will have to flexible, taking things as they come."

Aylin started to object, "But—"

Val cut her off. "I want both of you on this. That's my decision. Now, let's get down to specifics."

Kaz could have sworn that he'd seen a brief smile wash over Tahira's face.

50

Dani Stottman turned left rather than right, as she normally would when taking Abby home from school. On this day, though, the two of them needed to talk. For the first time since she'd entered into this arrangement, transporting Abby Miller to and from private school, Dani was tasked with negotiating a sensitive conversation.

"What do say we grab a cup of hot chocolate?" The December day was overcast and raw. The weather hadn't quite decided whether it wanted to rain, snow, or just remain gloomy.

Abby, who had been extraordinarily quiet, nodded. "Okay." The response lacked enthusiasm. It was as though the young girl were being asked to do chores.

They pulled into a strip mall and Dani parked in front of one of the many boutique coffee shops that dotted the area. "This place makes the best muffins, too."

They split a blueberry muffin, and each cradled a ceramic mug of hot cocoa with whipped cream topping. "Abby, you know that your grandmother's been kind of sick lately?"

"I guess." The young girl stared at her cup.

"The good news is that she's going to get some treatment at the hospital."

Abby shrugged.

Dani felt a knot form in her stomach. The discussion wouldn't have been so bad with another adult, or even a teenager. She felt the weight of responsibility on her shoulders. This was playing out to be a sensitive conversation.

"That means that we need to talk about where you're going to stay while she's there, you know, until she gets home."

Abby's voice was soft, and hard to hear as she kept her gaze lowered toward the table. "Can I stay with you?"

"That's certainly one possibility. Here's another idea. You could continue to stay there at your grandmother's house, and I could come live with you while she's away. Would you like that?"

Abby mumbled, "What if she doesn't come back?"

Dani reached across the table and took Abby's hands in hers. "Of course she's coming back. That's the whole point. She's going to the hospital so that she'll get better."

"She got sick when I had to live with her. Maybe she'll get better if I'm not around."

This sort of turn had been Dani's worst fear. She was simply not equipped to deal with these kinds of conversations. The truth was, that Abby herself probably needed mental health counseling. "You know, Abby, we've talked about this. Your grandmother was hurt when your mother died." Dani avoided drawing attention that it had been Abby's father who had killed her mother. "You didn't cause that. In fact, you're the bright spot in her world."

Dani forced a broad smile. "Actually, you're the bright spot in my world, too."

Abby didn't respond and her face gave no clue as to

what she was thinking. She stared at the steaming cup from which she had not taken a sip.

"You haven't touched your cocoa. You don't know what you're missing, Miss Abby." Dani blew across the top of the liquid and then took a long sip, followed by a bite of the muffin. "And if you don't eat your half, I'm just liable to steal it." She laughed.

Abby looked up into Dani's face, her eyes dry but full of pain. "I guess we can stay at Grandma's house, if she says it's okay." Her voice was barely loud enough that Dani could make it out above the din of noise in the small shop.

"That sounds good, Abby. It'll be like a really long sleepover, huh? We can watch movies and have popcorn... well, after you do your homework." Dani struggled to keep an air of lightness in the conversation.

"Things are going to get better for you and your grandmother. Just wait and see."

51

Janet should have known. After all, she herself was bound by a covenant of confidentiality. Still, the answer frustrated the minister.

"I'm sorry, Janet, but you know the drill. I simply cannot talk to you about her case without her permission." The therapist put up her hands as though to ward off argument. "If it's that important, I can ask Miz Klein to sign a release, which will enable me to have a conversation with you."

Janet sighed, "It'll have to do. There's no way that I can help plan for Abby if I have no idea what's going on with her grandmother."

"You know, without discussing the case, I can offer you this. The responsibility for the young girl will fall to State Children's Services. It's good that you're engaged and I'm sure that will do wonders for Abby, but planning and implementation are in the domain of the state government."

* * *

"Greg, there's something that we need to talk about... something that I don't think either one of us has considered." Janet held his hand as they sat together on his sofa.

He took her hand with both of his, caressing them gently. "Sure. What is it?"

She paused a moment and gathered her thoughts, needing to get this right. "It's about Abby."

"What about her?"

"I think I might have told you that her grandmother agreed to inpatient mental health therapy. I suppose it's possible that it will help enough that she can go back to raising Abby. I'm afraid, based on what I've seen of her, that she may end up hospitalized for an extended period. As of right now, she's not able to take care of her granddaughter."

He continued to hold her hand in his, keeping his silence.

"The bottom line is that Abby may end up as a ward of the state." She stopped there to let the information sink in.

After a moment's silence, he responded softly, "So, I assume that means that they would place her in a foster home, assuming that the grandmother will ultimately recover. If that recovery doesn't pan out, then... what? Would they put her up for adoption?"

"I don't know how it works. I'm guessing that the adoption part would hinge on whether they terminated Roberta's custody rights. That would be a hard pill for her to swallow, regardless of her condition. My immediate concern is the foster care thing."

He turned to face her. "What do you intend to do?"

She closed her eyes and turned away from him. "I don't know for sure, but the thought crossed my mind that she could come live with me, at least until things get figured out."

He stopped caressing her hand, but didn't respond verbally.

Janet continued, "Since we—you and I—are, I don't know, *closer* now...." Her words trailed off into silent expectation.

A brief laugh escaped his lips. "And you think that I might have some reservations about it?"

She smiled. "The thought crossed my mind."

"Janet, I've been connected with Abby since the beginning of all this. Dani, my niece, has become Abby's best friend, taking her to and from school. Your project helped to get her into that school and we talked about it then." He paused and squeezed her hand. "Regardless of how I feel about you, there's nothing I wouldn't do to help her if I can."

Before Janet could answer, he continued, "As fortune would have it, though, you and I are... how do you put it? *Closer?* I love you and although we haven't discussed it, what I hope for is that we start a life together. The word *marriage* comes to mind, although I suspect that you feel it's a little early to have that discussion. As far as Abby goes, though, I'm all in and I trust you."

* * *

Dani Stottman sat in the overstuffed chair across from Greg and Janet. The young woman brushed back a lock of hair from her forehead. "I hate to break it to you," she grinned as she shifted her gaze back and forth between the couple, "but this thing between you...." She pointed first and Greg and then Janet. "I knew about this months ago. It's not news to me."

Greg protested, "Regardless of what you think, Dani, this *thing*, as you call it, wasn't happening months ago. It's… recent." He squirmed in his seat as he seemed to struggle for the right words.

Dani laughed. "Oh, it was going on alright. Maybe you didn't realize it, but it was plain as day to everyone else." She shrugged and looked shyly at Janet. "Sorry about that."

He waved his hand as though to dismiss her words. "Be that as it may, that's not what we wanted to talk to you about. The thing is, it looks like Abby may be living with Janet, at least temporarily while her grandmother gets treatment. That means that you'll need to pick her up there at the parsonage instead of at her house."

Dani furrowed her brow as she stared back at the two of them. "I have a better idea. It'll serve the same purpose but be a lot easier on Abby. How about I temporarily move into her grandmother's house. I can watch over her, take her back and forth to school, and also be there for her if she needs to talk. We can do things and have fun together."

Janet interjected, "Thanks for the offer, Dani, but things may get complicated really fast. If the state takes over custody, I'm not sure how they'd feel about placing her with you. Also, if Roberta doesn't respond to treatment over the long term, it may lead to something more permanent."

"I assume that you're talking about my age. Why don't we talk to Roberta about it now? I mean, she's still living in the house. Maybe I could move in to help out with things. That way, if she does have to go into the hospital or something, it wouldn't end up being disruptive. The state might not even get involved."

52

Kaz parked the maroon Nissan Pathfinder on SW Hinds Street, about two blocks from Madison Middle School. Checking his watch, he turned to face Aylin. "One-thirty. Fifth period ends at two-fifteen. Any last-minute thoughts?"

Her response caught him by surprise. "Supposedly, he doesn't know anything about this. Sidestepping, for now, that we're catching him off-guard, what happens if, in the long run, he doesn't want to go along with this. I mean, he has a good life here—good job and all. Maybe he'd rather stay here and lose contact with his daughter."

It was an excellent question. Kaz hadn't expected a positive engagement on the subject. "Yeah, I see your point. That does present a dilemma. Here's my best guess. We grab him and get him to the safe house where he's able to talk to his daughter. We sort it out then. If he wants to go with her, we move as planned. If not, then we come up with a strategy for returning him home… with the understanding that he may well find himself in a very uncomfortable situation, should Trent's thugs come after him."

Chapter 52

"What time is Tahira going to connect with Gwen?"

"I think she said right around two. The pick-up point is roughly a half-hour from the safe house. We might well beat them there, depending on how clean our getaway is."

Aylin stared out the passenger window into the early January weather—mixed rain and snow. After a moment, she turned back toward Kaz and remarked, "I think we should toss the idea of setting off a fire alarm. If we grab him between classes, we can hustle along in the general flow until we get to the hallway leading to the loading dock. That'll be less noticeable."

Kaz thought about it for a moment. She raised a good point. "What about the ruckus that's going to go down when we breeze past the receptionist desk without signing in? If they're like most institutions, they'll assume something's up and sound a general alarm."

She countered, "What about this? You stop at the receptionist desk and engage whoever's there. Take your time. Do some kind of convoluted question or request. While they're distracted, I'll make my way down to his classroom. The period will end, and kids are gonna come pouring out of the classrooms. We can connect at the intersection of hallways just up from his classroom and go from there."

He had to admit, her's was a better plan. "Okay, let's do it. We'll approach the desk two minutes before the end of period. The timing should be perfect. The only hitch will be how to disengage from the receptionist and head down the hall. That's going to alert her, but she probably won't have time to activate an alarm before we're out the back. Besides, intruder alarm lockdowns are usually meant to keep people out rather than locking them in."

Aylin nodded and went back to staring out the passenger window.

Kaz started the car. "Let's move in closer and survey the parking lot. With any luck, we can spot any kind of surveillance Trent's people might have in place." He navigated the last two blocks slowly, finding parking spot on the side street within view of the parking lot.

He reached into the back seat and grabbed a pair of binoculars, handing them to Aylin. "Take a look."

She scanned the lot several times before she handed them back to him. "Far side, near the edge of the lot. That dark blue Chevy Tahoe looks like it has occupants."

He raised the glasses to his eyes. "Bingo. That's them." Setting the binoculars on the floor at her feet, he continued, "This'll work perfect. We can approach the loading dock from this side and not be exposed to them. Our exit path takes us near them, but not that close. I'm hoping that our diversion's in place and ready."

Val planned to park three blocks away on the exit route facing the school. She would see anyone coming after them. Her job was to get her vehicle crossways in the street if they were pursued. The plan was that she would appear to be turning around and doing a poor job of it. That would give Kaz and Aylin time to take some side streets and disappear.

Aylin noted, "Ten minutes to end of period. I think it's time."

53

Kaz approached the receptionist desk with confidence, Aylin trailing slightly behind and to his right side. They had parked their vehicle back near the loading dock and walked around to the front entrance. The woman at the desk stared at her computer monitor as though trying to solve some profound problem.

From behind, he heard Aylin whisper, "The classroom is down the corridor to the right."

He nodded without turning his head. As he reached the counter, he cleared his throat, alerting the receptionist to his presence. Summoning his best smile, he announced himself. "Good afternoon. I'm Gerard Tompkins. I was supposed to pick up some materials here. I'm gonna be substitute teaching tomorrow and the teacher said he'd leave the materials at the front desk."

As the receptionist searched around on her desk, Kaz could sense Aylin drifting to the right and down the hallway. *So far, so good.*

The young woman glanced up, a confused look on her

face. "I don't have anything here. Normally they don't leave class materials with us. Who's the teacher?"

Kaz drummed his fingers on the counter as he narrowed his eyes. "You know, I don't recall his name, but I think I'm supposed to be down in room one eighteen." He looked to both sides as though searching for the placards on the wall that showed which classrooms were down each hall. He knew, of course, that room 118 was to the right. That was Joshua Lambert's classroom.

"If it's okay, I can go down there and see if he's in." He turned and started down the hallway without waiting for an answer.

From behind, he heard the receptionist call out. "You can't go down there without a pass. I need you to sign in."

Then the bell rang. Within seconds, students poured out of the classrooms, moving in all directions. Kaz knew the receptionist was unlikely to chase him through this mess. He did hope, though, that she wouldn't feel the need to sound the general alarm. They'd planned for it, but it would certainly complicate things.

Luck was still with him. As he made his way down the hall, he saw Aylin and Josh scurrying along, weaving in and out of the traffic flow. It was at that moment that Kaz knew something was wrong. She wasn't talking to him, and he seemed to be accompanying her willingly. *Fuck! He knew about it in advance.* Security had broken down. Assuming that his daughter told him over the phone, there was every reason to believe that their adversaries now had that information.

His mind raced. He figured that, by the time they reached the loading dock, the place would be crawling with enemies. The only saving grace is that they had not shared the specific plan with Gwendolyn Trent. Another thought occurred to Kaz—it was unlikely that Trent's thugs would know Kaz or Aylin by sight. *Maybe… maybe.*

"Hold up." Kaz pointed to a janitor's closet. "In there, let's go." He could see the confusion on both of their faces. As they hurried inside and shut the door, he pulled the cord that turned on a single light bulb.

"Mister Lambert, did your daughter by chance let you know that this was going down?"

"Uh, yeah. She called last night. Just told me to be ready and not to resist… that everything would be okay."

Kaz sighed. "We have to assume that Trent's guys know, then. They know who you are, and they're aware that your daughter would like to leave the marriage. In all likelihood, they've found a way to monitor your phone calls."

"That's not possible. We were using cell phones. There aren't any lines to tap."

Kaz had to restrain the laughter. "We can talk about it later, but for now, they know. Here's what we're going to do."

Just a few short minutes later, Kaz opened the door and took a quick look around. "All clear. The kids are back in class. Go."

Josh Lambert, dressed in a pair of coveralls and wearing a baseball cap pulled down low, left the closet, pushing a mop and bucket lazily down the hall toward the loading dock.

Aylin had remained quiet but cooperative thus far. "This is going to be tight."

Kaz grimaced. "Tell me about it. You remember everything?"

"Let's do it."

They left the closet just after Lambert and started toward the main entrance. Aylin carried a three-ring binder in her hand. As they approached the front of the building, she opened it and began speaking in normal, almost bored tone. "The new class schedules are going to disrupt the flow for students that have been around for a while."

Kaz responded as they exited the building. "That's easy," he spoke loud enough for people around him to hear as he pointed to the open page in the binder. "Administration has to allow for orientation days. Otherwise, it's not gonna work."

Aylin shook her head, responding to his comment. "If they don't get their head out of the collective asses, the shop steward's gonna be all over them."

There were several men wandering the parking lot, eyes on the exits. Kaz steered within ten feet of a couple of them, glancing up long enough to nod and return to the conversation. "I'm telling you, Susie, I'm not anxious walk that picket line. I got bills to pay. Let's try to schedule a meeting with Johnson next week."

Aylin went along with it. "We can try, but it may be too far along. I'm not sure they'll be willing to change things."

The wandering men glanced at the two, but their attention didn't linger. Kaz and Aylin reached the car and got in just as the loading dock door opened. Lambert pushed his mop bucket out and sat down on a box of something or another, looking as though the bored look on his face was forced.

Kaz started the ignition. "We need to get him before he cracks. He's not looking too good." He eased the car out of its parking space and generally in the direction of the back exit from the lot. At the last moment, he turned gently and came to a stop at the loading dock.

Lambert stared for a moment, as though unsure of what to do next. Then, suddenly, he sprung into action.

Chapter 53

Jumping off the platform, he opened the back door of the car, leapt in, and closed the door behind him. "Go."

Kaz was careful not to burn rubber in his attempt to get away. He eased down on the accelerator and the car picked up speed. He check ahead and to the side, before checking the rear-view mirror. "Gig's up. Here they come." He gunned it.

They flew down the side street and turned right on a main throughfare. "Val should be just ahead. If we can make it to her, we should be home free."

The dark blue SUV they'd seen earlier was nearly on them and gaining. In his peripheral vision, he saw Aylin reach into the glove box and pull out the two handguns they'd brought along. *Please don't let us have to use them.* Kaz could imagine the trouble that would erupt if they got into a shootout here in the south Seattle suburbs.

One block to go. Kaz caught side of Val's highlander, exactly where he expected it. He clenched his jaw and floored the accelerator to open up the distance between him and the pursuing SUV. As he pulled away, he saw Val's car ease out into the road. He shot by her with barely a glance. In the rearview mirror, he saw her end up blocking the entire road. The blue SUV didn't make it past.

As Kaz turned onto another side street, he glanced into the rearview mirror and his gut tightened. A small sedan had jumped the curb and bypassed the blockade. "Shit. Okay, Aylin, get ready. I'm gonna try to lose this guy. If we don't, I'm gonna turn down a side street and slam on the brakes. Come out of the car with your weapon drawn, but don't fire. I think we can talk 'em down."

He turned his head slightly to speak to their passenger. "Lambert, when I slam on the brakes, open your door on the passenger side. It'll give Aylin some cover. Don't get out of the car.

221

Eluding their pursuers didn't work. The small sedan was too maneuverable. "Okay, I'm gonna take the next right."

Kaz swerved around the corner and slammed on the brakes. He jumped out of the car and brought his weapon to bear on the pursuing vehicle as it stopped. He walked slowly in its direction, both hands grasping the weapon, which was pointed at the driver.

The occupants of the vehicle remained inside. Kaz could see uncertainty on their faces. *Fantastic.* He adjusted his aim and fired two rounds, taking out the two front tires of the car. As he turned to get back into the car, he saw Aylin standing with her weapon pointed at the car, as though daring the men to get out. They apparently got the message.

As they drove away, he could see one of the men talking on the phone. He checked the mapping application on vehicle. The underground parking where their clean car waited was three blocks away. They lucked out this time.

54

The smile on Abby's face was betrayed by a look of sadness and apprehension. Janet silently wondered how a girl this age could carry so much grief on her shoulders and still remain functional. Yet she had. According to Dani, the young girl was up on time in the mornings, got dressed, and ate breakfast and arrived at school on time.

Greg and Dani sat with Janet and Abby at the small table. The smell of oregano and melted mozzarella cheese wafted through the dining room as the four of them dined on take-out pizza. Between bites, Janet asked, "How do you like your new school, Abby?" It occurred to her that she'd only seen Abby a couple of times since the school switch.

The young girl held the slice of pizza halfway between her plate and her mouth while she considered the question. Finally, she responded, "It's pretty good," and took a large bite. She put the slice back on her plate and, after chewing and swallowing, asked, "When is Grandma coming home?"

"I don't know, Abby. Do you remember how bad she felt right before she went to the hospital?"

Abby nodded without speaking.

"There's a lot of things that they need to fix. The good part, though, is that it's really good hospital and they're going to do a great job with her."

As the words came out, Janet's phone rang. She checked the display, and shivers ran up her spine. "Excuse me, please. I need to take this." She wiped her mouth, stood, and went into the living room. "Hello."

A female voice asked, "Is this Janet Polasky?"

"Yes."

The person identified themselves as a nurse at the hospital where Roberta Klein was receiving treatment. "We have you listed as the emergency contact."

"That's correct."

"She developed a respiratory infection this morning. We tried treating with IV antibiotics, but she didn't improve. We've transferred her down to Intensive Care. Her condition is currently listed as *grave*."

Janet's heart dropped. Was there no end to the grief being thrown at Abby? "What does that mean? They're treating it, right?"

"They're doing everything they can. She's on a respirator and they're continuing the IV antibiotic course. It says in her record that she's the guardian of her granddaughter. Do you happen to know what custody arrangements are in place right now?"

"Uh, yes. Abby is staying with a temporary guardian. In fact, she's here with me now."

"Could I impose on you to let her know the situation? I suspect it would be easier coming from you than from some disconnected voice over the phone."

Janet's first inclination after she ended the call was to

downplay the seriousness. Abby had had more than her share of troubles. Janet wanted to spare her any more grief. On second thought she knew it was a bad idea. The situation sounded dire. To tell Abby everything would be okay and then have it turn out badly would be a horrible betrayal.

She returned to the table and sat. Taking a deep breath, she put her hands flat on the table. "That was the hospital." She turned to face Abby. "Your grandmother got an infection in her lungs. They said that it's serious, but they're treating her."

Abby's face went flat, the emotion draining from her eyes. "Do you mean she's going to die?"

"That's not what they said." She wanted to reassure the girl, but was reluctant to build her hopes too high. "Your grandmother's getting the care she needs right now. All we can do is pray for her and be there when she comes out of it." *If she comes out of it.*

* * *

There had been little joy the rest of the evening. Most of the pizza went back into the box. Dani, Greg, and Janet had struggled to find words to keep conversations going, but with miserable results. The situation with Roberta Klein was the elephant in the room. Janet promised that she'd take Abby to the hospital to visit after school the next day. As she got ready for bed, her phone rang again. Checking the screen, her stomach turned.

The nurse said several things, but Janet heard only parts of the spiel. She was trying to organize her thoughts and come up with the words to tell Abby that her grandmother had died.

55

The first case after Val had taken over leadership nearly cost lives. If not for the quick thinking of Kaz and Aylin, all three of them might have been killed. There had to be a reckoning. This could not be the norm.

She sat with the others around the dining room table in the safe house. Kaz, Aylin, Tahira, Gwen Trent, and her father, Josh Lambert. The mood remained subdued, as though all of them knew that the colossal screw-up had to be somehow reconciled.

Val started the conversation. "I guess we start with the positive. Everyone is safe. Gwen and Josh will remain here until Aylin is ready to go."

Nods all around but no words.

"I'll go over the arrangements in place in a little while, but for now, we have to talk about the elephant in the room. I'm sorry if this comes across as overly harsh, but there's little room for error in what we do. Janet and I have both found this out the hard way."

She gestured toward Kaz and Aylin. "I'm grateful that you were able to adapt." She paused and turned her attention to Gwen. "You were told specifically not to contact your father ahead of time… for fear of exactly what happened."

Tahira spoke up, "Yes. I believe that I conveyed that accurately."

All eyes turned to Gwen. "I'm sorry about what happened, but what you asked wasn't fair. You wanted to just grab my dad with no warning. He'd have no chance to prepare and gather things he needs. On top of that, grabbing him at school… he could have fought back and made things even worse if he thought he was being kidnapped or something." Her eyes were full of defiance.

Val waved her hand gently, as though brushing aside the argument. "We can have that conversation at some point in the future. There may be things we can learn in terms of how to go about these operations. What troubles me now are not the specifics of how we went about it or even how you reacted. I will not go forward, though, if I can't trust you to follow instructions. If you don't agree with what we tell you to do, you need to make your voice heard and we can have those discussions. You cannot, though, just do whatever you want. To make this work, you and your father must be absolutely unfindable. One phone call back to a friend, colleague, or distant relative could destroy all our efforts."

Gwen sat, tense with her arms folded on her chest. The confrontational look in her eyes had not diminished. She clenched her jaw and stared at Val.

"This next month will be one of the hardest you've ever endured," Val nodded toward Gwen and her father, "for both of you. On the bright side, you've got some very dedicated people supporting you. Kaz and Aylin risked their lives to help you. We have a silent partner somewhere who has pulled out all the stops to create new identities for you. What we ask of you is to follow instructions."

Tahira spoke again. "Miz Trent, I regret if this seems excessively harsh. Miz Gomez, though, is not exaggerating the danger. I have seen this all too often, both here and in my home country. When powerful people are in pursuit, they will exploit any weakness to regain control of what they consider their personal property. Sadly, I must say, you are viewed as the personal property of the Trent family. Your husband likely does not have the wherewithal to get you back. His father, though, Randolph Trent, has more than enough power and will deploy it without hesitation. I must agree with Miz Gomez in this matter. We must be able to trust that you will follow instructions."

Josh Lambert spoke for the first time. "We get it. It was unfortunate. I don't understand, though, how they knew. It was just one phone call."

Kaz offered the explanation. "Cell phones are not that hard to intercept. They transmit their signals in the open airwaves. Unless you have an encryption app, they are there for anyone who can hone in on the frequency and has some rudimentary equipment. Since Gwen has attempted to leave before, the Trent family was on alert. Apparently, they have no intention of letting her go. It's demented but not that unusual. They simply set up cell phone surveillance of both Gwen and you. It doesn't take a lot of sophistication."

Lambert hung his head.

After a moment of silence, Val continued, "So, I need to go back to the question, Gwen. Are you willing to follow instructions?" She let the question hang.

The defiant look diminished but not gone, the woman turned her head to stare out the window. It appeared as though she were weighing her options, of which she had few.

"I guess I don't have much choice, do I?" Her words were soft but bitter.

Val shot back immediately, "Yes, you do have choices. You can go back to your husband. You can choose to go it alone. It's up to you. If you want our help and resources, though, I need that assurance from you. I almost lost two employees today."

"Okay." The word hung in the air like unfinished business.

Val started to demand a stronger affirmation. The *okay* sounded like a placating throw-away line. Considering the mood around the table, she decided to let it go. Still, she had a nagging sense that this was not a final resolution. Gwen's desire to do things her way would likely raise its head again.

56

The call came just as Janet was putting the dinner dishes away. Janet plopped into her overstuffed living room chair and connected. "Hi, Dee."

"Luellen Pickering's dead." The detective's voice sounded defeated and tired.

Somehow, the news didn't surprise Janet. Her mind briefly traveled back to when she'd met Luellen and the events of the day. From the moment that the woman had learned that her children had been murdered, it was not hard to imagine that she was living on borrowed time herself. "How?"

"Suicide. The hospital staff are all circling the wagons —not saying much. They're hiding behind patient confidentiality and the fact that there will be an investigation into the death. They aren't, as you know, able to comment on an active investigation."

Tears gathered in Janet's eyes. "I guess there are no winners here, huh?"

"Guess not." Dee's voice took on a more official tone. "We got a warrant to search her home... I mean the one she had before she jumped the rails. We were also able to search her brother's home. No gun."

"Maybe she wasn't the killer after all."

"I might have helped her, Janet, if you'd confided in me." The tone was accusatory.

Janet knew that she could easily be angry is she let herself. After all, Dee was never going to be able to help Luellen with what haunted her. Still, it hardly seemed worth the effort. She let it go. "What now?"

"It's still an active case. They'll continue to follow leads… keep digging. If the killings stop, sooner or later, they'll either close it with the assumption that Luellen was the killer, or it will become a cold case. Either way, the world moves on."

"Maybe you and I could grab a pizza and try to bury the hatchet."

Dee hesitated before responding. "Maybe. Now that Luellen is gone, is there anything else you can tell me?"

"I told you everything that she said that was relevant to the case. I can tell you that, when she came to see me, she had already had a psychotic break. You could see it in her eyes—lights on… nobody's home. She rambled about her kids, wanted to know if they were with me. It took everything I could do to get her to go to the hospital."

"What about the gun?"

The question hit Janet like a punch to the gut. "What gun? You said you didn't find one. Do you know for certain that she owned one? If she was living on the streets, as her brother suggested, she might have lost it, had it stolen, or even sold it for food money. If you're asking whether I have the gun or not, the answer is a resounding *no*. If you're asking whether I know where any such gun is, the answer again is *no*." Janet paused and softened her voice.

"Why is this so important to you? You've had these kinds of cases before. Why now?"

"I could have saved her, Janet. She didn't have to do this. If she killed those men, she could have easily gotten off on a mental illness defense."

Janet responded, "Maybe. You weren't in charge of this case, though. It could have just as easily gone in another direction. If she was the killer, do you really think that you had it in you to fight a legion of male cops who would have given anything to put her away for the rest of her life? I trust you, Dee. I know that, if it was within your power, you would have helped her. Unfortunately, you're a police officer and your allegiance is to the law. Please don't take this the wrong way, but my experience is that the law is whatever powerful and wealthy men say it is. Luellen wouldn't have stood a chance against them."

* * *

Kaz sat quietly while Janet went over what she knew about Luellen's death. "It's horrible, but I can't think of anything that we… any of us… could have done that would have changed the outcome. My sense is that her fate was sealed when she found her children murdered."

Kaz nodded. "So, it comes full circle. Her husband murdered her children. He is, in turn, killed by the police. Luellen, the last member of the family, takes her own life. I agree that, given how you came to be involved, there's likely little you could have done to change the outcome. It seems that everything turned on one simple event. Somehow, the husband managed to find out where the children were. If not for that, things would have no doubt gone much differently."

Chapter 56

Janet's curiosity got the better of her. "What did you end up doing with the gun?"

"What gun?"

57

Kaz waited with Gwen and her father at the safe house. They had decided on an early morning work-hour departure. The hope was that they would get lost in the work rush. He had no idea what was going on with the Trents—what efforts they were expending to find Gwen. The neighborhood around the safe house had been quiet. Kaz had surveilled it for several days, watching for any unusual movement. There had been nothing.

Two packed duffle bags sat in the middle of the living room floor. The two would be leaving all their other worldly possessions behind. They were indeed embarking on a new life.

"Aylin's text said that she'd be here around seven. You have a few minutes yet. Any last-minute questions for me?"

Both Gwen and her father shook their heads but remained silent. Her father averted his faze and fidgeted with his hands. Kaz wondered what might be going through their minds. The concept of completely re-inventing oneself had crossed his mind several times— what it would be like to leave his own self behind and become someone new. It was never a serious thought, though, only idle conjecture. To him, it seemed somewhat exciting. He couldn't help but believe, though, that the two of them were overcome with the fear and uncertainty.

"Aylin will decide on specific routes. That will minimize the likelihood that the Trents might try and intercept you. I don't know, myself, which way you'll be going. The only thing we know is that your final destination is Orlando. Do you have the card I gave you?"

Gwen reached into her purse and retrieved, studying it for a moment and then showing it to Kaz. "I made Dad a copy of it just in case."

Alarms went off in Kaz's head. "You didn't, by any chance, use your phone to take a photo of it and then print it, did you?"

Gwen cocked her head and narrowed her eyes as she considered the question. "Uh, no. Val took me over to an office where I made copy. Why?"

Kaz explained, "Most smart phones are set up to automatically store photos in the cloud. Although there's a great deal of security there, it's not impervious, especially if they have information about your account."

"Oh… okay. Anyway, Val gave us these new phone… *burners*, I think she called them."

Kaz stood and eased over to the window, glancing out into the half-light of the dreary winter morning. "Okay, here she is."

A minute later, Aylin opened the door. "I think we timed it just right. Traffic out there is brutal." She stood near the door for a moment before asking, "Everyone ready?"

After Gwen and her father nodded, Kaz said, "This is it, then." He turned to Aylin. "Your most important asset is anonymity. The three of you are safest when you're either invisible or forgettable. Your best strategy will be to avoid any kind of conflict, including any interaction with law enforcement."

Jason grimaced and looked away, as though something was eating at him.

Kaz asked, "Are you okay, Mister Lambert? Is something wrong?"

"Uh, no." Lambert glanced away and shook his head. "Everything's fine."

Kaz turned to Aylin. "Everything good with you?"

She seemed annoyed by the question. "Yeah, I get it. We've gone over this a hundred times. Stay out sight, no contact with anyone other than you or Val and then only on the burner. Anything else?" She seemed poised to add some snarky expletive at the end, but cut herself off.

"I guess I shouldn't need to ask, but do you have your weapon and the body armor for the three of you?"

Aylin tapped on her chest. "Got mine on. I'm ready to rumble."

Kaz rolled his eyes at the cheap cliché. "Gwen, you and your father will want to wear yours during the day. You can't predict when or where you might end up in a confrontation. The Trent family has a very long reach."

Both looked uncomfortable with the situation, but Gwen's father responded. "Got it. We understand."

"Aylin, can I speak with you for a second before you go?" Kaz gestured toward the kitchen. When he got in there, he leaned against the counter as she faced him. She had a look of boredom on her face. Her shoulders were stooped, and the corners of her mouth turned down slightly.

"What is it now?"

"You did good when we grabbed Josh. You handled yourself professionally. That's what we're counting on. If you sense trouble, your best avenue will be to get away from it. The last thing you want is to get into a gun fight. Even if you win and our clients are safe, there will be tons of questions. Any notion of a new life for them will be shattered. I need to make sure that you understand that."

She clenched her jaw and glared at him for a moment. "It's time to go."

58

The grief never seemed to end. Janet sat with Abby Miller and searched for the right words. But there were no *right words*. The young girl's mother had been murdered by her father, who had then killed himself. Now her last remaining family, her grandmother, had died. What was there to say? There were the usual platitudes that ministers pedaled—*the Lord moves in mysterious ways; God never gives us more than we can handle; We're not meant to understand everything; The Lord has a plan for all of us.*

The list goes on and on, but if they're meant to ease this kind of pain, then they must be judged as miserable failures. Janet had used all of these at one time or another when trying to comfort someone. It had never worked. At least the trite sayings hadn't. The only things that seemed effective were the love and support of family and friends and the passage of time.

Abby sat, dry-eyed and silent on Janet's sofa. The midday spring sun cut through the lace curtains to illuminate a patch of carpet in the center of the room. Janet had asked Dani to bring Abby there this morning rather than take her to school. She'd done her best to break the news to the young girl as gently but directly as she could. There was little point in beating around the bush.

"I'll fix us some lunch. Would you like soup and sandwich?" Janet didn't expect an enthusiastic answer. Still, Abby had to eat something.

"Do I have to live by myself now?" Abby's voice sounded empty and ambivalent.

Janet moved over onto the sofa and put her arms around the young girl. "No, of course you're not going to live by yourself. Right now, you're staying here with me. The people down at the Children's Services office will help us figure out what all to do." Janet decided to go out on a limb. "Would you like to live with me from now on?" She didn't know whether that was actually an option or not, since she was single.

"No." The words came out hard with a sharp edge— no hesitation.

The answer took Janet aback. "Well, okay, that's fine. I just thought that since we're already friends, it might be a good thing. If it's not what you want, though, that's perfectly fine." She held Abby tighter.

Abby responded with a softer tone. "Everyone I live with dies. I don't want you to die, too."

"Oh, Honey, death is a part of life. Everyone goes through it at some point. It's not your fault. Your grandmother was very sick. It didn't have anything to do with you."

"She was okay before my mom died. Then when I had to live with her, that's when she got sick. If I had gone somewhere else, she'd still be alive."

Janet took Abby's hands and turned the girl so that the two of them faced each other on the sofa. "I know that it seems that way, but it's not the way it works. I promise you.

Your grandmother loved you very much. She was sad that your mother died, but that wasn't your fault, and it wasn't your fault that your grandmother got sick."

Abby fell silent. The look on her face, though, told Janet that the young girl was not convinced. Her gaze wandered in a way that suggested disinterest.

"Abby, Hon, the next few days are going to be hard, but I'll be here to help you through. And Dani will be here too. We'll get through this, the three of us. We're in this together.

59

An unnatural quietness blanketed the room. Kaz had asked to meet with Janet and Val to go over a few things. With Gwen and her father on the road with Aylin, a lull had settled over the three. There was nothing to do except wait.

Kaz tapped his finger on the corner of Janet's desk as he mentally organized the discussions he needed to have. "First up—Janet. As far as we can figure out, you're still on the hit list. Things have been noticeably quiet, though, since the near-miss with Aylin. It may be the case that they've closed up operations for the time being. The other possibility is that they're trying to engage a new hitter. We can't afford to take any chances."

Janet sighed with obvious exasperation. "We've covered this ground time and again. I understand all of this. What I don't understand, though, is what you expect me to do about it. I can't quit work and go into hiding indefinitely. Do you have any new ideas at all?"

"I'm working a different angle with Detective Wharton. We're trying to identify the assassin. If we can get to him, we might be able pry out enough information to shut the entire thing down. It's going to take some time, though."

Janet shot back, "Then we're really no further along than we were before."

"I know. Is there any chance at all that I can convince you to take a short vacation... maybe a couple of weeks? That would give us little breathing room."

"What makes you think two weeks will make a difference? What if I take the time off and then come back to the same situation? Besides, I have Abby Miller staying with me now."

Kaz focused. He'd handled situations much worse than this one. Why, then, was it eating at him? Why did he feel so powerless? "That's all the more reason that we need to take additional precautions. I don't have answers for you, Janet. I do know that the only way you're going to be safe for sure is for us to shut their operation down. I'll work with Eisen to try and get a better handle on their status. In the meantime, if you could be unfindable for a while, it would make things much easier."

"I'll consider it. Give me a day to think it over. It would mean taking Abby out of school. Right now, I think the routine of classes is one of the things keeping her going."

Kaz nodded. "I understand completely. We're just going to have to figure out how to strike the right balance." He turned to Val. "Have you heard anything from Aylin?"

"Not a peep, why? Are you expecting something?"

He felt uneasy about the conversation he wanted to have. Part of the strategy of having both Janet and Val in the same room for this conversation was that it would avoid misunderstandings if they all heard the same thing at the same time. "I know that she did a nice job there at the school when we grabbed Mister Lambert, but in other interactions with her, she seems almost upset at the security precautions we've put in place. I can chalk part of it up to the fact that I'm a man. I know it's an issue for some."

Janet waded in. "No. It's not that. She was very confrontational with me as well. She's passionate about the work. I'm certain that there's nothing she wouldn't do to help a woman in trouble. You're right about her being upset with the security, though. She was quite explicit with me about it."

Kaz was about to respond when Janet's burner cell rang. She locked eyes with Kaz, who nodded.

"Hello."

Janet listened for a second, her mouth moving once or twice as though she were trying to interrupt the speaker. Finally she said, "Wait, please wait, Aylin. I've got Kaz and Val here in the office. I'm going to put you on speaker."

A look of incredulity washed over Janet's face. "What do you mean *no*? Val runs the operation and Kaz is responsible for security. They need to hear this." Without waiting for a response, Janet pressed the screen and set the phone on her desk. "Okay, Aylin, run through that again."

After a few seconds of uncomfortable silence, the voice came over the speaker. "Like I said, we've had an incident here… just outside Missoula, Montana." Aylin paused briefly before continuing.

"There was a guy who looked like he was tailing us. I tried to evade him, taking odd turns. He kept on us. Finally, I pulled into a vacant lot. He pulled in right behind me. I got out of the car and confronted him." She fell silent.

Kaz felt his face grow hotter, certain that he was flushed. He fought back the anger. He responded in a quiet, controlled voice. "Was anyone hurt?"

"No, but the police are here interviewing both of us."

Kaz clenched his jaw and closed his eyes tightly. After a moment, he asked, "Are you in a place where you can speak without anyone hearing?"

"Yeah, the cops are talking to the guy right now. They told me to stay with my car."

"Okay. What about Gwen and her father? Where are they?"

Another moment of silence. "When I got out of the car, I told them to get out the other side and go into a small bookstore across the street. So far, they aren't involved. I assume, though, that this guy who was tailing me knows they're with me."

Kaz took a deep breath. He noticed that both Val and Janet sat staring at the phone. "Good. Now, describe this confrontation."

Aylin's voice softened and slowed. "I wanted to make sure that we were all safe, so… uh… I drew my weapon and pointed it at him. I asked him why he was following me."

"Did he pull a gun?"

"No. I didn't give him a chance. He claimed he thought I was someone else—a bullshit story for sure. He was following us."

Kaz shook his head. "Do you know if he had a weapon on him?"

"He says he didn't, but I'm not sure I believe him. He just didn't have a chance to pull it."

"Did the police ask him? I mean, that would be the first thing they want to know… where the weapons are."

"They're holding onto my gun. They didn't get a gun from him, I guess."

"Okay, Aylin. Here's the best advice I can give you without being there onsite. Tell them you felt frightened. Tell them that you've been assaulted before, and you carry a weapon for self-defense. All of that it is true. Tell them you're driving cross country. Here's the important part. You're going to have to be humble. You owe the guy an apology and you apologize to the cops as well. Admit that you might have overreacted. Try to avoid any conversation that might involve Gwen and her father."

Aylin's response was filled with rage. "That's a gigantic pile of dog shit. I don't owe anybody an apology. I was defending myself."

Kaz kept his tone soft but firm. "You were not defending yourself. You created the confrontation. You drew a weapon despite the other guy not having one. Trust me, if you screw around with this, you're liable to find yourself in lockup until they sort it out. Your best bet is to play meek and mild, promising never to do it again. With any luck, they'll call *no harm, no foul*. At least you'd better hope that's what they do."

"Let me talk to Janet." The tone remained confrontational.

"I'm here, Aylin. What is it that you want from me?" Janet sat with a stony face.

"I mean talk to you in private." Aylin's voice had become meeker.

"We can talk later, once this whole thing is resolved. Until we're all clear on what's going to happen, it's better that all three of us here are part of the conversation."

After a few seconds of silence, Aylin spoke again. This time, her voice sounded devoid of any emotion at all. "I'll let you know when we're back on the road." She disconnected after this.

Kaz was the first to speak. "I don't want to pile on, here, but when she calls back, you need to confront her on why she called you and not Val or me. This isn't a turf issue. It's just that, if Val is going to be responsible for operations, she needs to be at the top of the call list."

Janet hung her head. "I think it's simply because Aylin and I go back a ways."

"Yeah, I get that, but it still doesn't justify her shutting Val out. Something else to consider is that she's still not out of the woods with this incident. With some good people skills and humility, she might be able to walk away unscathed and continue. If, on the other hand, she gets herself crosswise with the cops, it's hard to see how this turns out well."

Val asked, "Switching gears for a minute. It seems to me that the elephant in the room is that someone was tailing Aylin. How did that happen? We've had at least one security breach as well as the episode with at the school. Is it possible that they were able to ID Aylin and plant a tracking device?"

Kaz responded. "It's possible. At any rate, whatever secrecy we had is gone now. They obviously know the vehicle. She may have shaken this one guy loose, but I think it would be naïve to assume that she's in the clear. We have to assume that they know pretty much everything. I'll give this one some thought and get back to you."

After thinking about it for another few seconds, he added, "As for this particular incident, I'm going to see if Eisen can use his magic to see how the cops wrote it up."

60

With Aylin on the road escorting Gwen and her father, Val's life had slowed down. The panic that she'd felt when first taking over management of the project subsided, as she fell into a routine. She and Dee were living together again and talking marriage. The memories of her shooting haunted her nights, but even they were beginning to ease. Things weren't so bad.

"You're awfully quiet tonight. Something bothering you?" Val had noticed that Dee seemed distant since coming home from work.

"The usual stuff, I guess." Dee idly chopped vegetables that would become part of a stir fry.

Val probed, "What kind of *usual stuff*?"

"Look, I know that you can't talk about the details of your work. I understand. It's just that something happened today, and I worry it has something to do with you."

Alarmed, Val asked, "What was it?"

Dee set the knife down on the counter and turned to face Val. "Do you know a woman name Tahira Kushk?"

"Why?"

"She was murdered today. It's a Seattle case, so I don't have a lot of information. From what I could learn, though, it was execution style—a single bullet to the back of the head at close range."

Val felt her legs wobble as her knees threatened to give way. "How… I mean, what…?"

"I take it you know her."

Val nodded. "Yeah, she connected us with our current client and helped her get away. Do they have any idea how it happened?"

Dee stared for a few seconds before turning away. "Do you mean other than someone putting a gun at the base of her skull and pulling the trigger? I don't know much, Val, honestly. I've heard a couple of different rumors."

"Like what?"

"Well, the first version I heard was that she was involved in some kind of terrorist activity and her own people killed her."

Val spat out a venomous response. "That's a load of shit. She was here helping women get away from violent husbands, same as we do."

Dee continued on a though she hadn't heard. "Then someone said it was a drug deal gone bad."

Val turned without speaking, walked into the living room, and plopped down in a large chair. Tears filled her eyes. She wanted to scream at the top of her lungs. Instead, she grabbed her burner phone and called Kaz and Janet.

Going back into the kitchen, she hugged Dee. "I'm sorry. I have to go. This changes things."

Dee returned the hug briefly and then disengaged. "I don't suppose I could go along?"

Val stared at her for a moment and then responded, "Sure, why not?"

* * *

The four of them sat in the church parsonage where Janet lived. Val studied Janet as Dee related what she knew. The minister had seen so much death in the past year, and yet seemed profoundly shocked at this one. Was there something special about this woman, compared to the others or was it just that she never got used to the violence?

When the detective finished, silence washed over the room for a few minutes. Janet sat and shook her head, appearing at a loss for words.

Kaz broke the spell. "We'll each have to deal with the tragedy as we can, but we have a bigger problem. The competing cover stories about the drug deal and the terrorism are flimsy concoctions. The fact that they're circulating, though, tells me that this was not some random killing. If I had to guess, I'd say the Trent thugs caught up with her. The question that we're faced with is whether they learned anything from her. She knew most the details of Gwen and her father's new life. She didn't know their new names... none of us do. If Trent learned about their destination, though, it wouldn't take a lot of effort to find them, at least for someone with his resources."

Val asked, "Given that we don't know the answer to the question, what's our best course of action?"

Janet added, in a meek voice, "If they knew about Tahira, then we have to assume they know about the three of us as well. If they didn't get the details they wanted from her, they'll come for us."

Kaz spoke again. "That raises yet another problem. If they know about the three of us, then they likely know about Aylin as well. It's complicated because we know that Aylin was detained by the Missoula Police the other day. While they didn't arrest her, they certainly have a record of the call. That information will likely find its way into some database that, if searched properly, will give the Trent clan yet another piece of the puzzle."

Val thought about the problem for a moment. "Did you hear anything back from Eisen? You were going to ask him to find out what he could about the incident."

"I haven't heard anything yet. Let me give him a call." He punched in some numbers and waited, the phone to his ear.

"Hey, you have anything for me yet?"

Kaz listened for a moment before responding. "Okay, that's good. I may have something else for you later, but that's it for now."

After disconnecting, he set his phone aside. "He confirmed most of what we already knew. The cops were called to the scene, interviewed Aylin and the guy, and cut them both loose. There's a twist, though. Aylin's sense of the guy was probably right. His version of the story sounded suspect to me. He claimed that he thought he knew her and was just wanting to say hi. He acted like it was some kind of joke. The police warned both of them—him about those kinds of stunts and her about overreacting with a weapon."

Janet said, "I guess I don't understand. If you think that maybe the guy was following her, how did he find her? She's been gone for days. Did he follow her from Seattle or... what?"

Kaz leaned back in his chair, his hands laced behind the back of his head. "Good question. The only thing I can think of is that maybe someone planted a tracking device on her car. I did a sweep the night before she left, so unless somebody put it on that night, I'm not sure how that would have worked."

Dee spoke for the first time since recounting what she'd

heard. "It seems a stretch to me. It would take some really good luck on their part to know that Aylin was going to be doing the escort and then locating her. With any savvy at all, they'd know that her vehicle would be checked for devices, which would mean that they waited until you swept it. I'm sorry, but if I had to come up with an explanation, a leak from someone on our side would have to be part of it."

The statement landed like a bomb in the center of the room. Finally, Kaz responded. "I have to agree. I think we can safely say that no one in this room was the source of the leak, even an unintended leak." He paused and appeared to study the faces.

"That means that either Aylin, Gwen, or her father was the source. As much as I think Aylin can be a loose cannon, I don't think she's inclined to discuss something like this on the phone."

The statement was met with silence, although it felt to Val as though everyone agreed. "That means that either Gwen or her father leaked it. Is there a way to confirm it or rule it out?"

Kaz answered, "I'll have to talk to our resident tech genius." With that, he took out his phone again.

"Hey, got another for you. The burner phones that you provided for Gwen Trent and her father, is there any way you can check those accounts for activity?"

Kaz listened for a moment and then responded, "Thanks. I appreciate it." Tossing the phone onto the couch beside him, he briefed the group. "He can find out if they were used. He also has both of their original cell phone numbers and will check those accounts as well. I would be shocked if either of them were stupid enough to use those phones, but they might have used a burner."

Ten minutes later, the news came from Eisen. A fifteen-minute call had been placed from one of the burners to a local Seattle number. Kaz pushed a piece of paper with a phone number across the coffee table toward Val. "We have to assume that they know much of what we know. For starters, I think we have to assume that they managed to get a tracking device on Aylin's car. I'll get in touch with her about that, but we now have a bigger problem. Gwen may not be up to this. She could get herself, and her father killed, along with Aylin."

61

Kaz sat huddled beside Val in the small office. "If she's kept the app running in the background like she's supposed to, the connection should be more or less instantaneous."

"Let's do it, then." Val, who appeared calm and collected in spite of all that had happened, leaned back and waited.

Kaz brought up the encryption app on his own phone and punched in Aylin's number. She picked up after only two rings. "Yeah?"

Kaz sat the phone on the table to his right. "Are you someplace where you can talk, I mean, privately?"

"Gimme a sec."

The faint sound of shuffling and a door opening and closing came across. "Okay, I'm good. What's up?"

"We've got several things to discuss, but first, how are the two of them doing?"

Aylin's tone was very *matter of fact*. "Okay, I guess, all things considered."

Kaz took a deep breath. "Good. Things may get a little rough from here on out. First up, turns out you were probably right about the guy following you. Eisen hacked into the Missoula Police network and downloaded everything related to your case. The guy's explanation didn't make any sense at all, on top of the fact that he's a Washington state resident."

He could almost hear her gloating on the other end. He continued before she could respond. "We'll talk about the incident more later, but we have more pressing issues right now. If he was following you, then the only real explanation is that you've got a tracking device hidden somewhere on your vehicle. I checked the night before you left, and it was clean. That means that, if it's there, they installed it sometime later that night or early the next morning."

"How did they even know how to find me?"

Kaz forced a laugh. "It's not that hard. Your address is on your driver's license, which is public record. Very likely when we had the confrontation after we grabbed Lambert at the school, one of them probably took photos of both of us. They could have run those through facial recognition software and compared it to license photos. That's high-end stuff, but I'm betting that Trent wouldn't bat an eyelid at the expense."

"I assume that you want me to find and remove it."

He thought about for a long moment before answering. "No. We're going to try something else. There are some other complicating issues. First, things have gotten rough here. Tahira was killed—executed, I presume by some of Trent's guys."

"Fuck!"

Kaz responded, "Yeah, exactly. That information, by

the way, is for you only. We can speak with Gwen and her father later. For now, let's not drive up the anxiety any more than we have to."

He could sense mild disapproval, although she gave it no voice.

"The issue right now is that we can't know for certain whether they got any information from her or not. We have to assume, then, that they at least know your final destination. That may be why they didn't pull out all the stops to grab them the other day. It would be easier for them to plan an operation in advance for the destination."

Aylin's voice sounded defeated. "I guess that puts us back at the beginning."

"Yeah, I don't think that's gonna work. It's a lot to ask of anyone—Gwen, her father, or the people who arranged all of this. Val and I have discussed it and feel that our best bet is to make them understand... make Randolph Trent himself understand that it's not in his best interest to pursue you."

Aylin laughed. "Just how do you intend to pull that one off?"

"I'll fill you in when we meet."

"Really, you're coming here to meet us?"

Kaz responded, "We'll rendezvous. I'll send you directions in a secure text. If I'm right, they won't bother you again until they're in a position where they believe they control the situation. If things remain the way they are, they'll most likely set up in Orlando, since they know where we're headed. We have to resolve it before we get there."

"Okay, then. I'll wait for your instructions."

Kaz paused and looked at Val, who nodded. "One more thing, Aylin, and do not mention this to either of them. We're certain that either Gwen or her father used one of the burner phones to call someone, presumably an acquaintance, before they left Seattle. Watch them closely. I hate to say it, but they seem to be their own worst enemies."

62

K az picked the perfect location. He stood on a busy street in front of a large department store on the outskirts of Salina, Kansas. Aylin would turn right onto the street and drive ten yards before picking him up. She would be out of sight to anyone following her more than a few cars back for a good minute or so—long enough for him to jump into the car without being seen.

He had told her 12:15 pm—early in the lunch hour. There would be lots of people on the sidewalks and traffic in the streets. Kaz checked his watch. Five minutes to go. He scanned the sidewalks on both sides of the street. Nothing seemed out of place. There were a couple of visible video surveillance cameras, but there was no reason to believe that the Trent thugs would randomly check those.

The blue Toyota Highlander rounded the corner right on time. She eased to a rolling stop in front of him and he hopped into the backseat. Glancing up at Gwen, who sat on the other side of the car, he forced a smile. "Fancy meeting you here."

She didn't appear amused.

Aylin maneuvered through traffic, making several turns before heading up an onramp for Interstate 70 eastbound. Once on the freeway, she accelerated to speed. "Okay, would you like to tell me what's going on now?"

Kaz turned around and studied the traffic behind. He was certain that somewhere back there, a vehicle was tailing them at a respectable distance. For now, though, he wasn't able to spot it. "The situation is as described on the phone. We have to assume that they know the destination and, absent some compelling situation, won't risk action while you're in transit. We have to force their hand."

"What exactly does that mean?"

"It means that we have to present them with a situation that's too good to be true. We need for them to feel confident in engaging us. That means that we have to make clear to them that we're in one place and we're going to stick around for a day or two. It has to be a remote place that works for their purposes. We might also try to convey that we're changing destinations. We'll give them enough time to scope it out and so some rough planning but not enough time to get reinforcements in place. We want them to think that engagement here is the only viable option. My guess is that we're probably going to be dealing with anywhere from two to four people. With the element of surprise, we should be able to control the encounter."

Aylin laughed. "*Encounter.* That sounds a lot like euphemism to me. Do you mean a full-on gun fight?"

Kaz responded softly. "I hope it doesn't come to that. I would prefer to simply get the drop on them and give them a message for Trent. We want to leave no doubt in their minds that we're willing to take this fight to them if necessary. We'll have to follow it up with a rather compelling communication to Trent himself. I'll work that out with

Chapter 62

Val, though. For right now, it's up to you and me to orchestrate this."

"What if it goes sideways or if they choose to fight?"

"Then we fight. We have the element of surprise so we can position ourselves for an advantage. We'll make sure Gwen and Jason are out of the immediate area."

After a moment's silence, Aylin asked, "In the event that things go badly, that's going to leave Gwen and Jason at the mercy those guys. Any suggestions?"

Kaz glanced at Gwen across from him. Jason, in the front seat, had turned around to listen. "They have phones. If it goes badly, they can call nine-one-one and scream for help. If you have a better idea, I'm willing to listen."

Aylin's voice was soft. "Do you think we can do this without a fight?"

"Yes, I think it's possible. That's what I'm hoping for. If it turns out otherwise, though, we'll have only seconds to react. The question is, are you ready for this?"

A dry, humorless laugh escaped her. "You bet I am. Bring it on."

63

Kaz craned his neck to see out the front window across the Kansas landscape. "Take the next exit onto Route forty-three south. We'll stay on that road for about twenty miles. There are a few small hotels that suit our purpose down near Hope."

Once Aylin turned off the Interstate and was settled into the drive south, she asked, "How's this going to work?"

"It'll start out pretty routine. Drop me off about a quarter mile before the motel. I'll walk the rest of the way. You pull in, get two rooms—one for you and one for Gwen and Jason. I'll check in separately. Once things are settled, we can talk. I'm pretty sure that the spots we're looking at don't have surveillance cameras and, with their relatively small size, the parking lot would be too obvious a place for our pursuit to be parked. If things look clear, you and I can get together later this evening and lay out the plan."

* * *

Chapter 63

Kaz sat in a large corner chair with cracked leather—the room and its furniture had seen better days. The odor of stale tobacco smoke overwhelmed everything despite the sign assuring them that this was a non-smoking room. "Before we lay out the plan, there's another matter that we have to attend to." He took a folded sheet of paper from his shirt pocket. Unfolding it, he sat it on the low coffee table that the group had huddled around.

"Do either of you recognize the name and number of the paper?"

An awkward silence enveloped the room. Gwen stared at the paper for a moment and then abruptly glared at her father. "Dad?"

Jason squinted his eyes as though trying to make out the detail on the paper. He alternately opened his mouth to respond and then closed it. The confusion and fear on his face made it seem as though he wanted to vanish in that moment.

Kaz intervened. "A fifteen-minute phone call was placed to this number from one of your two cellphones before you left Seattle."

"What did you do, Dad?" Gwen seemed frantic.

Her father hung his head and muttered, "Yeah, it was me. I called her to let know we were leaving."

Kaz paused for a moment and forced his tone into a neutral, non-accusatory one. "This is important, Mister Lambert. What exactly did you tell her?"

Lambert's eyes widened. "You don't think she…?"

"No, but I'm pretty sure that your phone call was monitored."

"But I used the burner phone." He held his cellphone up.

"Doesn't matter. It's not fitted with an encryption app, so whatever went out was unsecure. If they knew where you were, they could have easily intercepted it. I think I mentioned this before. The required technology isn't that sophisticated. Now, what did you say?"

Lambert exhaled and shook his head. "I don't know… I told her we had to move, that it was an emergency. I told her… I mean, she and I were about ready to announce our engagement. I couldn't just run off and leave her hanging."

Kaz persisted. "Exactly what did you tell her?"

"I said that we were going to Orlando and that I'd send for her when thing settled down." His words trailed off at the end.

Kaz stared at him. "Surely you understand that this plan of yours is out of the question. The entire point of all this is that you disappear without a trace leaving no way for anyone to find you. Bringing someone in from you past life would destroy everything we worked for. You know that, right?"

Jason shrugged. "It doesn't matter. She's not willing to do it anyway."

"Okay. Now that we have that out there, we can deal with the rest of this. We have to assume they know where you're headed. I'm relatively certain that they're planning on moving on you there, where they can prepare and control. Here's what we're going to do. Mister Lambert, I need you to call your lady friend again. Tell her that you can't say your current location because of security stuff but tell her that you're going to be here for a few days, and you may be changing your destination. Tell her that you just wanted her to be aware. Keep the conversation short and try to give the impression that you're worried about security."

Jason shot back, "I just told you that she said *no*. Calling her again wouldn't make sense."

Kaz laughed. "Of course it would. Think about it. She said no. You're calling back telling her that you're going to a different place, hoping maybe she changed her mind. Her reaction doesn't matter. The important thing is what you say. That's what we want them to hear."

Aylin stared wide-eyed. "That's your plan? You're betting that they have that woman's phone under surveillance?"

Kaz leaned back in the chair, his hands laced behind his head. "I'd say that's a pretty safe bet."

64

Kaz knew it was a long shot. Success required that Trent's men in the area felt they had the leisure of time to scope out the place and plan but not enough time to get reinforcements flown in. Besides, as far as the men knew, it was only Aylin and her two charges.

They sat in Aylin's room. The father and daughter had remained in their own room. Kaz hoped they'd be able to make some peace. Gwen had been furious while her father maintained that he was doing his best to accommodate her. It seemed that neither had an inkling of just how dangerous this was going to be. Kaz had purposely withheld the information about Tahira's murder. They would deal with that later.

"The conditions are in our favor. The parking lot's well-plowed but was ringed with a berm nearly five feet high. That will give me decent cover."

Aylin had unloaded her weapon and taken it apart, rubbing down the individual parts with gun oil and generally remaining quiet. Finally, she spoke softly. "How's this going to work?"

Chapter 64

Kaz considered her for a moment. She didn't look quite so confrontational now. "Before we start, something you need to accept. Everything we come up with will be premised on assumptions. We'll do the best we can to consider the possibilities. First, I think it's safe to assume that they've been on the phone with their home base. Right now, they're probably making a crucial decision— move here or wait for a better opportunity. If they were monitoring the phone call, they will get the sense that the destination is changing but won't know where it is. That's incentive for them to strike here."

"Probably right." Aylin set the weapon part on the table, wiped her hands with a rag, and took a long drink from her water bottle.

"Assuming they decide to strike here, my money's on a first light rush, evening at dusk, or something in the middle of the night. I doubt they'll risk a scene here in broad daylight. Even though it's a back road there's still a fair amount of traffic. I tend rule out the middle of the night option—they'd have to break down doors, which would cause one hell of a ruckus."

Aylin nodded. "I guess that leaves either dawn or dusk."

"That's my bet. We can sweeten the deal, though. If they feel they can neutralize you without causing a scene, it makes their work so much easier."

Her next question came out bathed in dread. "Are you planning on killing them?"

"No. I'd rather not. Unfortunately, we are going to have to lure them into a confrontation. If they force my hand, I won't hesitate… and I'm counting on you not to hesitate either."

She stared at him as though trying to read his mind.

"I'm sorry, Aylin, but I don't know any other way.

They've declared war and it's clear that they don't have any problem killing. They know about you, Val, Janet, and me. We're all potential targets along with Gwen and her father. I know that I've probably said this too many times, but in a conflict like this, defense is ultimately a losing strategy. We have to go on the offensive. The problem is that it's hard to do that while, at the same time trying to avoid killing. Ultimately, it'll be up to them. If they force me, I'll take them."

She nodded, paused for a moment, and then went back to cleaning her gun.

Kaz focused back on the technical. "My guess is their going to set up surveillance. I'll try to get eyes on them. The rub is that you're going to have to draw them out. Here's what I suggest."

* * *

Two days had passed. Kaz had spotted the surveillance right away, but the two men appeared to be in no hurry. Aylin went to the main office just before sunrise to get a cup of coffee. She visited the office again after sunset on the pretext of doing some kind of business. The pursuers didn't budge.

Kaz's room was located on the far end of the motel. He'd taken care never to approach Aylin or their rooms. He went from his room into the motel registration lounge for coffee and then made his way out the back door. He climbed over the snow berm and into the thick brush of the field beside the lot. After a slow and deliberate trek through calf-deep snow, he found himself behind the surveillance vehicle. The sun would be up in another twenty minutes. Aylin would leave her room and head for the office.

It unfolded as he thought it would. She left her room and started down the walkway toward the office. Kaz saw the surveillance team car doors open—driver's and passenger's side at the same time. He took a deep breath and took out his weapon—a Glock 9 mm fitted with a noise suppressor. He'd given Aylin a silencer for her weapon as well.

Rather than starting towards Aylin, though, they stood in front of their car. Then things went sideways. A second car pulled into the lot, much closer to the father and daughter's room. Two men leapt from that car, weapons drawn, and started at a trot down the walkway after Aylin. Neither pair of men had spotted Kaz.

He climbed over the berm and eased up behind the first surveillance car. Creeping around the side, he drew down on the two. "Freeze! Don't move a fucking inch or you'll drop in your tracks."

He turned his gaze toward the motel and yelled, "Aylin, behind you!"

She whirled around, her weapon drawn. Going into a crouch she aimed but held her fire, just as he'd instructed.

Maybe this'll actually work out. He spoke to the men, who remained standing with their backs to him. "Okay. Walk slowly, ten steps and then stop. When you get there, lay your guns on the ground and kick them away. If we all just keep our cool, nobody get's hurt."

The two men remained frozen in place.

Kaz looked again at Aylin. The two men who had been approaching her had stopped about fifteen yards away and had separated, standing about ten feet apart.

He turned his attention back to his two men. "Move it. Now!"

One of them started forward, the other stepped to side.

Fuck. He's going to do it.

The man who stepped to side suddenly whirled,

dropping to a crouch. Everything went into slow motion. Kaz saw the gun coming up to bear on him. He squeezed off three quick rounds. Blood splattered as the man fell backwards, his weapon bouncing off the frozen surface of the parking lot.

The other man spun and fired. The shot went wide. Kaz crouched and fired off another three rounds. The man dropped in his tracks.

When he turned toward Aylin, he saw her lying on her back, her weapon held out in both hands. She fired continuously and both men fell.

He ran, dropping to his knees as he reached her. Blood had soaked through her jacket. He opened it up and could see two bullet wounds. One in her shoulder that looked as though it might have passed through her. The other was in her side and appeared to be nothing more than a graze. He glanced over at the two men that she'd shot. Neither was moving.

"Aylin, can you hear me?" He took a handkerchief out and stuffed it in her jacket over her shoulder wound. She wasn't bleeding extensively from her side.

She forced a laugh. "You know, I gotta stop getting shot." She passed out.

Kaz stood for a minute and surveyed the lot. No one was moving. No lights were on. The office was dark. *Now the serious shit begins.*

65

From experience, Kaz understood that things would happen fast, but care must be taken to ensure correct sequencing. There was a definite order to things. He pulled out his cellphone and dialed 9-1-1.

Emergency medical help would be on the way, but so would the police. Slipping on a pair of rubber gloves, he picked up Aylin's weapon and removed the noise suppressor. After putting his coat over the woman, he took both silencers around the back of the motel and stashed them among some snow-covered brush. Hopefully, the cops wouldn't have the need to search that area.

Next he knocked on Gwen and Jason's door. When the man answered, still his pajamas, Kaz pushed past him into the room. "Listen up. Things are going move quick. You're safe for now. Aylin's been shot and I need to get back out there to her. The cops are on their way. They'll interview you. Tell them the truth. Don't hold anything back. Don't lie to them. It's going to get messy, but we'll get through it."

They both stared as though in disbelief. Before either could say anything, Kaz turned and walked away.

* * *

Kaz observed the two detectives with no small amount of amusement. They were truly a study in caricatures. The Kansas state cops had shown up about ten minutes after Kaz had placed the call along with a few uniformed officers. The male and female both appeared to come into the investigation with what seemed an appropriate level of curiosity and objectivity. That didn't last long.

Sitting in the backseat of the cruiser with the door opened, he spoke with the detectives who stood outside. As Kaz poured out the story, the male became more hardened and confrontational while the woman seemed to soften. A writer of TV procedural cop shows couldn't have scripted it better.

"Let me see if I have this straight," the man whose badge showed the name Robert Sullivan said. "You were transporting a woman and her father... let's see... you were helping them escape a violent husband. I don't get it. Why didn't the father just drive them. Why did they need you?"

Kaz shook his head. He knew this was a pointless discussion. Detective Sullivan had already decided that somehow the dead men were the victims while Kaz and Aylin were the perps. Still, he had to play along. "The woman's husband is part of the Trent family in Washington state. They are extremely rich and powerful. They'll stop at nothing to get her back."

"Says you." The tone was dismissive.

"You might check with Seattle PD. A woman named Tahira Khushk was murdered less than a week ago. She was also helping us and was killed execution style."

Sullivan turned to the woman and nodded without speaking. Apparently she understood that she was to check it out. Turning back to Kaz, he shrugged. "I have to say that your story seems farfetched. A more likely account would be that you and your partner abducted these two for ransom. It's just as likely that the deceased were there to try and rescue them." The right corner of his mouth turned upward in what could only be described as a sneer.

It had been a long time since Kaz had ever heard a comment that rose that level of stupidity. The female cop had stepped away from the car, apparently to check out the account of Tahira's murder. Kaz carefully considered the ongoing conversation. It had clearly slipped over the edge into some alternate reality. Something deep inside told him that, at the end of the day, this cop wouldn't matter much. *Might as well humor him.* "Like I told you, we were helping them escape. If you doubt that story, you can ask them yourself. Your officers out there have them isolated from us. If we abducted them against their will, then there's no reason they wouldn't tell your people that."

"Maybe." Sullivan tapped comments into his notepad. "We'll see."

At that moment, the female detective returned. "They confirmed the murder, but they have nothing to suggest it was related to any kind of domestic violence issue."

Kaz countered, "Miz Kushk was the one who brought Miz Trent to our attention. We were working with her to get her and her father away."

The woman, who had introduced herself as Detective Paisley, continued, "They said that they were pursuing two different theories, each equally likely at the moment. One is that it was a drug deal gone bad. The other was that she was a terrorist who was executed by her own people. Like I said, nothing to suggest DV."

Kaz studied the woman for a moment. Her eyes cast downward, and she shuffled her feet. She didn't believe the

Seattle PD account. "I can't comment on what the Seattle PD knows or doesn't know. I can tell you, though, that we know Tahira because of this case. My dealings with her suggested that she was exactly who she purported to be—a woman dedicated to helping other women.

He stood and stretched, taking a few steps then turning around. "I need to check on my partner. You have my statement. You can cross check everything with Gwen Trent and her father. You have all of my contact information. I'll help you in any way that I can."

Detective Paisely put her hand on his arm. "I have a couple of questions. It won't take long."

Kaz nodded and stood waiting.

You and your partner killed four men. If they attacked you, how did you manage to get the jump on them?"

It was indeed a good question. "The women we serve are not the average domestic violence victims. These are women who genuinely fear for their lives. We've had two women killed and two of our staff have been shot helping. The men they are escaping from are vicious and our experience tells us they will stop at nothing to prevent the escape. We are prepared for the worst every single day. We wear body armor as do our clients. We are armed and won't hesitate to use deadly force."

Kaz locked gazes with her, injecting dispassionate ferocity into his tone. "This is life or death, Detective. You can interrogate us. You can suspect us. Hell, you can arrest and charge us. But we will never simply sit back and watch our clients murdered."

She nodded, her eyes signaling that she truly understood.

Detective Sullivan, on the other hand, was most definitely not in their corner. "That's a great story. The fact is, though, that you killed four men here. I'm having a hard time believing that this was not premeditated. It's almost as though you set a trap and were waiting when they stepped into it."

Kaz shot back, "Think whatever you want, Detective. We didn't ask to be attacked. My partner didn't agree to be shot. If you want to charge me, go ahead. Otherwise, I need to go check on my partner."

66

Kaz lifted the covers and considered the bandage on Aylin's shoulder. "I guess they did a passable job. Looks like you're going to survive."

Aylin's laugh seemed a genuine attempt at humor under the horrendous conditions. "What can I say? I'm just an expert at getting shot."

He slouched back in the chair beside her bed. "You're going to need to stay put for at least a few days, and take it easy after that."

She shifted in the bed. "What are the cops saying about all this?"

He smiled and shook his head. "They're not happy. My guess is that they'll be here shortly to grill you."

"Anything I should know?"

"Answer their questions truthfully." He laughed half-heartedly. "And by the way, the male cop, named Sullivan, is an asshole. He's going to bait you. Don't rise to it. Yeah, it's going to piss you off. Just let it ride. In the end, they really don't have anything they can hold against us. The other cop, the female, is okay. I think you'll find her a bit more receptive."

She closed her eyes for a moment and then nodded.

Kaz continued, "So let's go over a few things. The most important is that you didn't cause this. We deal with the issue of blame later, but for now, it has nothing to do with you. You handled yourself very professionally back there. I've seen guys die in those circumstances without ever getting off a shot. That you took both of them down and survived says a lot."

Aylin nodded, a single tear rolling down her cheek.

"Another thing that's going to rear its ugly head. You killed two guys. Yes, it was self-defense and, yes, they likely deserved it. They would have done the same to you. Nonetheless, it's going to eat at you. You took human lives. You'll have to sort that out and it'll take time."

"I'm okay." The look of uncertainty on her face conflicted with her words. "What next then?" Kaz could see that haunted look in her eyes.

Kaz considered the question, which was far more complicated than it seemed. "We have to work several avenues at once. First order of business will be to revise our strategy. Trent declared war when he killed Kushk. He came after us with the same obsession. We can't sit back and play defense. We have to take the fight to him in a way that it convinces him to leave us alone."

She chuckled. "You never told me that you're a miracle worker."

"Yeah, well, sometimes you need miracles. We can talk about it more later, but for now, we're going to have to find temporary lodging for you, Gwen, and her father. I'm probably going to have to return to Seattle to finish this up."

"I'm part of this. I'll go too."

Kaz shot back, "No. Your first obligation is their safety. Don't forget that, as of now, Trent probably realizes his efforts didn't work out and is planning something new. You're going to have to go completely dark. That means we probably have to confiscate their phones. We simply can't trust them."

She asked meekly, "When are you going to tell them about Tahira?"

"I suppose that I should tell them now. Keeping it a secret won't ease the pain. Actually, it might make it worse when they find out."

* * *

The three of them sat in silence. They had talked about Aylin's condition, their immediate plans to remain in temporary shelter, and the possibility of long-term plan changes. Kaz knew it was time to fill in the blanks.

"We saw it coming this time. Next time, we might not be so lucky." It was a throwaway line. Kaz was certain that they knew it. He moved on the topic he'd avoided.

"There's something else—something that happened back in Seattle that I haven't had a chance to talk to you about yet." He paused to let the words sink in.

Jason spoke up. "If you're referring to other phone calls we might have made, I can promise you that I didn't make any others. That was the only one." He acted as though that was something to be proud of.

"Me neither," Gwen added.

"Nothing to do with that. About a week ago, Tahira Kushk was murdered. As it turned out, her killing alerted us to the fact that something was amiss. I don't have any idea how they identified her, but I doubt it had anything to do with your phone call. Most likely, they spotted her while she was working with Gwen. We might find out more later, but I wouldn't count on it."

Gwen's eyes widened. "You think Trent could have done this?"

Kaz nodded. "I guess there's a slim possibility that it had nothing to do with you, but I find that unlikely. Besides, if we assume that it was connected, being cautious will only help us."

Gwen seemed unwilling to let it go. "Why didn't you tell us sooner?"

"Quite frankly, we had a lot on our plate trying to keep you safe. I saw no upside in telling you. Also, and I don't mean to pile on here, but you" he nodded toward Jason, "did exactly what we told you not to. Before you say anything, yes, I know we were asking a lot. Hopefully, you can understand now why it was important. The last thing I needed to be saddled with leading up to our little shootout was sorting out Tahira's death. It happened. My guess is that it will come to nothing legally... just another unsolved murder."

Gwen slouched back in her chair with her eyes closed. "Is this what we have to look forward to for the rest of our lives?"

Kaz held silent for a moment before answering softly. "We take it as it comes."

67

Kaz sat in the Kansas City airport pondering the task ahead. He had no idea how he would convince Trent to give up, which was exactly what was needed. He had the driver's licenses of the four unfortunate men who had been sent to ambush Aylin and take her charges back to Seattle. They stood as proof to Trent that his efforts had been thwarted, for all the good that would do. He sighed, leaned back in the uncomfortable chair and closed his eyes for a moment.

His cellphone interrupted his attempt at respite. The call was coming through on his encryption app, but it wasn't a number he recognized. "Yes?"

"I have something for you." The voice belong to Dylan Strauss, a mercenary with whom he'd had a rather serious conflict some months back.

"Of all the people I thought might contact me, I have to admit that you're at the bottom of the list."

Strauss didn't rise to the bait. "You've attracted a lot of attention, my friend—the wrong kind of attention."

Kaz sighed. "So, what's new?"

Chapter 67

"Somebody wants you bad. They're offering one mil."

"Anyone I know?"

Strauss' voice sounded as though he were forcing the casual tone. "No idea. I only have an account number."

"You took the contract and then called to tell me? Seems awfully gentleman-like. I didn't know you were wired that way."

The laugh came across as genuine. "Not me, my friend. I only saw the posting. I'm not interested myself." He took a breath and continued, "Another bit of interesting info—your old pal Janet Polasky is on the list as well, although she's only worth a half-mil. Two other women— Valentina Gomez and Aylin Fryberg are included at a half-mil each."

"What board did the posting show up on?" Kaz knew that different types of hit contracts appeared on different boards. The experienced assassin knew how to comb all the different posting mechanisms in search of business.

"U. S. Domestic-medium grade." The grade referred to the sensitivity of the assignment. Some required the ultimate in discretion. His contract apparently didn't rise to that level.

Kaz's mind raced. Was this the hit list that they already knew about or something new? "Do you have any idea how long the posting's been up?"

"Popped this morning."

Shit. Janet and Aylin were now officially on two lists, with presumably different funding sources. "I appreciate the info, but why tell me? The way we left things, you don't owe me."

"Consider it an investment. The day will come when I'll need the same kind of favor. I like to keep all the friends I can, at least the ones I can rely on."

"I guess in this case, then, I owe you." Kaz paused for a

moment before asking, "Any idea who might be taking the job?"

"Can't say for sure, but I saw two inquiries. I'll send you the info by encrypted text. If this blows up, though, you didn't hear it from me."

Kaz laughed. "If this blows up, I'm probably not going to be in a position to tell anybody anything."

"Forewarned is forearmed."

Kaz shook his head. "Catchy phrase. Did you just come up with that?"

"Take care, my friend."

He considered probing for likely fund sources, but he already knew where the contract likely originated. *Better to be sure.*

Kaz brought up his phone encryption app and selected a number.

"Yeah?"

"Hey Eisen, this Kaz."

"I know."

Kaz shrugged off his annoyance at the flip answer. "I need you to check something for me."

68

He expected to wait days or even a week. The call caught Kaz by surprise. "Hey, that was quick." After all, to get the confirmation on the source of the hit contract funds, the tech genius needed to hack into an account that was specifically designed by experts such as Eisen to prevent exactly that kind of intrusion.

"It wasn't that hard. So, yeah, the source of the contract funds is Randolph Trent, although it's being filtered through several shell corporations."

"Okay, then. I guess that's it. Thanks, I appreciate."

"No problem, I'm being well compensated." The ensuing laugh sounded genuine.

"Take care."

"Oh, wait. There's more. Yeah, Trent is funding the contract on you and the others. Here's the really interesting part, though. He's also the money behind the *Truth is Strength* group."

The revelation stunned Kaz. "Are you sure?" Even as he asked the questions, though, the pieces fell into place. Trent was a staunch, even hardcore right-wing guy. His public image was limited to advocacy and sound bites. Behind the scenes, though, he was working to shape the world more to his liking. DV workers being assassinated fit in. His own son was a batterer. What else was in the making?

Eisen's response confirmed the realization. "No doubt. The only part that I haven't figured out yet is how they move the funds from electronic to cash and how the cash gets distributed. From what I can tell, this organization that we're talking about isn't confined to the northwest. It's national, maybe even international. If I had to guess, I'd say that the operation involves at least one offshore bank. I'll get back to you when I have more."

Kaz brooded over his next steps. In his heart, he knew that taking the fight directly to Trent was inevitable. He couldn't simply wait for the next foray. If things remained as they were, sooner or later the bullet would hit its mark. It's the nature of defensive strategy. You have to thwart every single attempt. By contrast, the enemy has to succeed only once.

This new information changed things. This wasn't some random guy using his wealth to solve some personal problem. Trent had forged an organization that was systemically eliminating what he considered undesirable elements of society—people that helped battered women.

To eliminate the threat completely, he would need to eliminate both Trent and the organization. A thought suddenly occurred. He now had two points from which to work. He knew the source of funds. The other point was the assassin who had targeted the women. His efforts thus far had pointed to somewhere in Boise, Idaho or within easy driving distance. On top that, he felt confident that he would soon have a name and address.

Chapter 68

Kaz sat across the bistro table from Wharton, mentally composing how he'd lay this out for her. She'd left no doubt that she was unwilling to outright step over the legal line. He, on the other hand, was certain that success was only possible if they did.

"I've managed to acquire some crucial information." He paused, studying her face for reaction. Her eyes signaled interest, although she remained motionless and silent.

"I told you when we started that I'd respect your choices, whatever they were. I also understand your need to remain on your side of the legal line. Unfortunately, as sometimes happens, it may become necessary for us to part ways. I'll tell you what I can for now. If you need to disengage, I hate to see you go but wish you well."

She stared directly into his eyes. "Would you please stop talking in circles. I'm a big girl and I know how to make decisions."

"Okay, got it. So, here's what I know. The organization that we're after is funded and probably controlled by Randolph Trent." He allowed the new information to sink in.

She exhaled and shifted her stare to the drizzle outside the coffee shop. After a moment, she spoke quietly. "That certainly changes the game. I suppose it would be stupid to ask if you're certain."

Kaz didn't respond. He took a sip of coffee and placed his cup back on the table, giving her the space to speak again.

"I assume that this organization includes the assassin that's targeting women."

He nodded.

"It doesn't get us any closer to knowing who the hitter is or if he's connected to Robinson in any way."

"Yeah, that's why I figure you might be in a spot where this isn't a road you want to go down. We have a bead on the power behind it all. I can work the assassin angle, as well. Tying it back to Billy Robinson, though, doesn't tell us anything of value. I figured that since that was your interest, it's a moot point."

She ran her finger around the rim of her mug as she seemed to consider the situation. "Where do you go from here?"

Kaz leaned back in his chair and thought about it for a moment. "My answer to that depends a lot on what your intentions are. I've given you the objective information I have. That I came by it through questionable channels may or may not disturb you. Where I go next, though, may well be a bridge too far. I'm posing this to you now so that you can bail without the burden of information that might compromise you."

She laughed. "That sounds like double talk. What is it you're trying to say, Kaz?"

That was the first time that she'd called him that. He chose his words carefully. "My loyalty and obligation is to my client. I'm charged with their safety; their lives. Make no mistake. I'll do whatever I have to. You're bound by a different set of rules than I am."

"I'm interpreting that vague explanation to mean that you're going to take them down yourself rather than go to the cops."

Kaz had expected the words, but her tone was not at all accusatory. It sounded like a simple question. He bowed his head for a moment before responding. "About a week and a half ago, a woman named Tahira Kushk was murdered—shot in the back of the head execution style.

She was helping Trent's daughter-in-law escape her violent husband. That in itself is nothing unique. Men like that have used their money and power this way for centuries. The worrisome part is that the Seattle Police response thus far has been to suggest either terrorism gone awry, or a drug deal gone bad. This shit doesn't happen by accident. There's no way that Trent's not pulling the strings. The cops are going to be of no help."

Wharton nodded. "Money and power buy justice that's not available to the rest of us. We can like it or not, but that's the reality."

The words surprised Kaz. "Hmmm, not the response I expected." He paused and collected his thoughts. "Given enough time and energy, we could likely neutralize him while remaining on the right side of the law. My fear is that this strategy would produce some casualties along the way. I'm sorry, Charlotte, but I'm going to have to take care of this myself." He let it drop without further explanation.

After a moment's thought, she responded, "I'm not sure how I feel about getting into a fight with Trent directly. I'll think about it. I will, though, commit to the pursuit of the assassin. I'd like to think we can do it legally, but if not, so be it."

69

The Sniper had graduated to the big leagues. He'd made contract hits before. In fact, he so many kills under his belt he had trouble remembering them all. If you threw in all his work in Afghanistan, it was an overwhelming work history. This was different, though. It would be a first.

Randolph Palmer Trent. The man bathed in money and power. He was a charter member of the one percenter club. The Sniper's other hits were typically reported on the local evening news. Any further mention of them was usually limited to comments about how the police had no leads.

This one would be on the national news. *Hell, they'll interrupt regularly scheduled programming for this news special.* The President of the United States would go on national television during prime time to express his condolences and remind the country that they had lost a hero.

Speculation would be rampant. Was it terrorism? Were leftists rising up and turning to violence to bring about their Marxist Utopia? Was it a secret cabal of intellectuals from around the world who were terrified that Trent had grown too strong?

The Sniper relished the possibilities. All he had to do was kill the man and get away with it. *Easy enough.*

He set aside the fantasy daydreams and turned his attention to the computer screen. The high-end mapping program had cost a serious outlay of cash, but it was proving to be worth it. It ran circles around Google Earth and, because he accessed it through the dark web, there would be no way for anyone to track the inquiries back to him.

The mansion was more like a fortress than a house. It was set in a secluded area. The grounds, which covered more than ten acres, were surrounded by what appeared to be a brick wall approximately ten feet high and topped with razor wire. Security cameras adorned every corner of the house as well as key spots along the wall. There were even video cams mounted on the wall facing out. Whoever monitored these would be able to track activity outside the compound as well as inside.

Fortunately, he'd located a spot outside the compound from which he could see Trent depart and arrive each day. The Sniper was able to access a large, low-hanging limb of a monstrous oak tree from heavy brush, which obscured him. From his observation and calculations, it would be a one-hundred-yard shot. He'd never taken anyone out from that range. It would be a challenge.

Trent was driven back and forth to his offices in down-town Seattle by what appeared to be a heavily armored limo. In addition to the driver, two bodyguards accompanied the man wherever he went.

The Sniper had abandoned the idea of a hit at the offices. The underground parking was closely controlled and offered direct access to the building, which itself was a locked institution. No, the hit would of necessity either be at his home when he departed or arrived or at some other random event. Random situations could not be predicted in advance, so planning was nearly impossible. It would happen at his home.

After a week of observation, the Sniper was as ready as he was likely to be. He decided at the outset that it would be an evening hit. First thing in the morning, the body-guards would be fresh and alert. They didn't appear appreciably more relaxed in the evening, but there would, undoubtedly, be some level of fatigue. What little it might be would work in his favor.

Another factor in favor of an late afternoon hit was the fact that the sun would be behind the Sniper. It would illuminate his target while, at the same time, blinding the bodyguards.

Finally, he would have a short window, only one or two seconds, to make the hit. Trent's bodyguards were not rent-a-cops. They appeared to be battle-tested and hardened. They did an excellent job of obscuring a clear shot at the man. The only opening was typically right as Trent exited the limo. It took one to two seconds from the guards to position themselves.

It would have to do.

* * *

The Sniper dressed in fleece camo clothing that roughly approximated bare tree branches against a gray sky. The barrel of his rifle was swathed in similar fabric and fitted with a noise suppressor. He eased into position just after 1:00 p.m. and settled in. It would be at least a three and a half hour wait, during which he would need to remain relatively still. *Patience.*

Trent typically arrived home around four-thirty. Sunset on January 28 was right around five o'clock. There would be plenty of light and, given the cloudless day, the sun would be in the eyes of the bodyguards if they looked in his direction.

The Sniper was well aware that he was in the field of view of at least one camera. He counted on not being seen as he crawled into position. Once there, his camo and lack of motion should render him nearly invisible. And so he waited.

Right on time—just like clockwork. The limo pulled through the front gate at ten minutes after five, coming to stop at the front door of the mansion. As expected, the two bodyguards got out first and scanned the area.

The right side back door opened, just as always. It was at that moment that things went sideways. The man that exited the car was not Trent. The Sniper didn't recognize him, but he looked a good twenty years younger than the target.

The stranger turned around, stretching his arms as though weary from sitting. He eased away from the door and said something to one of the bodyguards.

The left side passenger door opened, and Trent got out of the car. This screwed everything up. There was no clear shot. The Sniper could see the top of his head, but nothing else. The bodyguards moved around the car to take position.

Fuck! Fuck! Fuck! The Sniper clenched his jaw, wanting to scream. All the planning and everything had gone to hell. He muttered, "Just plain fuck."

He calmed himself. A temper tantrum would solve nothing. If he missed this opportunity, he would just have to try another day. Apparently, nothing he'd done had alerted anyone. One day wouldn't make a difference.

The Sniper aimed the rifle at where he thought Trent's body should be, although it was obscured by the bodyguard. Peering through the scope, he kept the weapon trained, hoping for an opening. The four men—two bodyguards, mister unknown, and Trent—walked briskly toward the front door.

As they reached the top step, it happened. One of the bodyguards stepped aside and looked down at the bushes beside the porch. It was a fucking miracle. Something must have caught his attention, because, in that instant, Trent's body appeared in the Sniper's scope.

Smiling, the Sniper squeezed… a little more… a little more until he heard the muted pop and felt the reassuring recoil of the rifle.

Trent dropped in his tracks. A brief look revealed blood spreading from a hole in the man's upper back. The unidentified man went down on his hands and knees as though to protect Trent. The two bodyguards had their weapons in hand. They scanned in the Sniper's direction, but it was clearly to no avail. The sun in their eyes, the distance, and the Sniper's camo clothing worked in his favor.

After a moment, he eased back on the large branch of the tree and slid down the trunk into the bushes. Backing out, he disassembled his rifle as he walked and stuffed the pieces into the backpack he'd left on the ground.

After a short walk to his truck, he was away. He stopped in a secluded area a couple of miles away to stash the rifle in the hidden compartment in the back of the truck. Cop cars flew past, their lights flashing and sirens sounding. As always, the Sniper kept his composure, remained just slightly under the speed limit, and made his way into the flow of traffic. The stolen Washington plates were a nice touch.

Chapter 69

He tried to suppress his giddiness. He'd done it. He'd pulled off the hit that, if managed properly, could make him a legend. That, combined with his share of the cash haul that was stored in one of his caches back in Idaho, could set him on the path to a new life.

Allowing a genuine smile onto his face, he stopped for dinner.

70

Kaz poured heavy cream into the oatmeal, inhaling the aroma of cinnamon and apples. He tossed in a heaping spoonful of brown sugar and stirred it in. The breakfast was simply a distraction though. His mind focused on how he was going to bring Randolph Trent down.

He stared out the breakfast room window in the winter darkness. The only evidence of rain was the occasional splat on the window. It was an early morning, even for him. After a sleepless night, he'd finally quit trying at 5:00 am. Up and showered, he turned his full attention to the task before him. He'd already spoken to Val, Janet, and Greg about the contracts that were out and who was behind them. Now he had to come up with a plan.

His cellphone interrupted his thoughts. He checked the display and thought to himself, *what on earth gets you up so early, Detective Wharton?*

Kaz pressed the connect icon. "A little early, isn't it?"

Her voice sounded cold as ice. "I knew you moved

quickly, but I didn't think you'd do it without at least letting me in on it."

"Okay, I give up. What is it that I moved so quickly on?" He honestly couldn't imagine what she was talking about.

"So, you're going to tell me that you had nothing to do with it and don't know anything about it?"

Kaz exhaled and shook his head. "Again, what is the *it* that I supposedly did."

The line went silent for a moment. "I need you to be honest with me, Kaz. Did you have anything to do with Randolph Trent's death?"

The words stunned him. "Death? Are you shitting me? Trent's dead? No, absolutely… I had nothing at all to do with and, no, I don't know a goddamned thing about it."

Her tone softened. "Yeah, he was killed last night. Someone got him as he got out of the car at his mansion. It's a Seattle PD case, so I don't have a lot of details. They're keeping it close. What seems likely, at least from what I've heard, is that it was a professional hit—long range sniper. I guess I just figured it was you."

He quickly evaluated what he'd just learned. "Thanks for the compliment, but, no, it wasn't me… although, if I find out who it was, I might just send them a case of expensive scotch."

She retorted, "Maybe we should sit down and talk this through. It changes things, but we'd be stupid to think that it solves all the problems."

Kaz found himself liking this woman more and more. "Yup, you got it. Let me touch base with Val and the others this morning. How about we meet after work. I can throw together some pasta and a salad here at my place if you want to come over for dinner."

* * *

Val took the revelation in stride and remained focused on how to proceed with Aylin and her clients. Greg had wanted to celebrate until Kaz reminded him that it left a lot of questions, not the least of which how all this affected the hit list that Janet and Aylin had already been on. The real conversation, though, came with Janet.

Sitting in her office with Kaz in a chair beside her desk, she listened to his account without interrupting. When he was done, she sighed and moved a few papers around her desk, as though she was composing her answer. "There's something else going on and I'm not sure what it is. Do you remember the men from the church association, you know, the ones that we suspected were tied to the *Truth is Strength* organization?"

"Yeah, let's see, Broward and... I think... Conyers, right?"

"They're both reported as missing. That can't be a coincidence."

Kaz laughed. "That's rich. Maybe we caught a string of good luck."

Janet shook her head. "I guess... I thought that... maybe you might be somehow involved in it but just not telling us." She seemed ashamed of the accusation.

"As much as I'd like to take credit, no. I've not done anything other than gather information. The only thing I've heard is that the hit on Trent seemed like a professional job. If I had to guess, I'd say that the same assassin who was hitting the DV workers did Trent as well. For what reason, I have no idea. I don't know of anyone on our side that would do it and, if you tie the other two disappearances in, then that's how it looks."

Janet's eyes grew intense. She tapped her pen on the

desktop. "Do you think that somehow takes us off that hit list?"

Kaz considered the question for a moment. It was more complicated than it sounded. "Well, first, as bad as it sounds, you and Aylin were actually on two lists. Val was on the latest. The short answer is 'I don't know.' The contract let by Trent himself was posted to a clearing board. He would have had to deposit the funds to secure services. That means that the money is likely still there to be claimed. There's nothing to suggest that hitters who might be interested would care about Trent's death one way or the other."

"What can we do about it?"

"The most surefire way of defusing it is to provide proof of death for the three of you and collect the funds."

Janet laughed darkly. "That would seem an inconvenient approach, to say the least."

Kaz considered it in more depth. "No, actually it could work. We might need some help from Eisen, but we might be able to pull it off. Remember, the guy who actually wanted you dead is no longer around. That means that the contract broker will verify evidence and release the funds. It's nothing to them. We just have to make it easy."

71

Kaz felt it was a long shot, but they had to try. He asked Eisen, "Is there any way that we can remove our people from those two hit lists?"

Eisen scratched his chin as he mulled over the question. "I guess it depends on what you mean by *remove from the list*. In term of simply making their names disappear from the lists, it's doubtful. Even with the funding source gone, the money has already been put up. The way it normally works is that, with the way they account for the money, it's tied to data fields. If the data in the fields go away, it leaves them with money that has no anchor, so to speak. It would be a red flag."

Tapping his fingers on his knee, he narrowed his eyes. "On the other hand, your idea about claiming the money has merit. Of course, if you go that route, you'll have to go all the way and actually take the money. I can create an alias for you that will allow you to get it without anyone knowing who you are. Since the guy Trent is dead, no one's much gonna care, so long as all the accounting threads are neatly tied together."

Chapter 71

Janet and Val sat quietly listening to the discussion without comment.

Kaz asked, "Okay, let's say we go that route. How do we do it?"

"Easy. Once I create your online identity, just access the site and post your evidence."

"Which is?"

Eisen laughed. "Okay, first thing. We take photos of everyone laying out on the floor, obviously in different locations. Then we get someone to do their photo editing magic and add the blood and special effects. This could be easily detected but, since Trent is dead, there's probably no one with enough interest to do it."

He paused for a moment before continuing, "The next part is mine. I'll create bogus news stories about the killings and create links so that it looks like the stories are on reputable news outlets, such as the Seattle newspaper. Again, it could easily be debunked, but hopefully, no one will notice."

"How does the collection of the money work?"

"Easy enough. You provide an account number, routing number, etc. and, when the verification is complete, they transfer the funds. So, you're gonna have to set up the account and, as soon as the money is available, move it. I'd say move it three or four times using offshore banks. That should be enough. Again, the only people interested will be those contractors who didn't get the kill. Once you collect the funds, there's no more money to be had with the funder out of the way. Even if someone discovers the con, there's really no upside to pursuing it."

* * *

Janet was the first to react to the doctored photos. "My God! Those are gruesome." She stared at the pictures arrayed before her. She'd seen the raw ones, where they had posed lying in various positions on the floor. At the time, it had seemed a stupid joke. The edited copies were realistic enough that they made her sick.

Val said nothing, although the shock painted her face.

Kaz, on the other hand, marveled at the technological accomplishment. They even had one for Aylin, who had sent a posed photo taken by either Gwen or her father. "These look real enough. Like I said, anyone taking the time to examine them closely would see through the ruse. This should work well enough, though."

Eisen dropped four sheets of paper on the table. "These are the news stories. Kaz, I'll send you links, which you can submit."

Kaz nodded. "Okay, I have the account set up. Actually, I have five accounts, all in offshore banks. The final question, then… what do we do with the money? I wouldn't try to move it into your main project accounts. It'll stand out like a sore thumb."

Val turned and stared out the window for a moment before responding. "We could leave it in one of the offshore accounts. That way, if we need to come up with cash that we don't want traced back to the organization, we could use that."

Kaz thought about it for a moment and then shrugged. "So be it. It'll be our little slush fund."

72

Wharton looked tired. The bags under her red eyes spoke of sleepless nights and no small amount of pressure. She'd been subdued since arriving, a marked difference from her usual contentious demeanor.

"You seem quiet tonight." Kaz tossed the salad with a light helping of oil and balsamic vinegar.

"Things have gotten complicated a lot faster than I expected. With so much floating around, I'm finding it hard to know who to trust." She picked at a bread stick on her plate. The glass of Chianti in front of her remained untouched.

He set the salad tongs down and eased over into the chair across from her. "Yeah, I get it. I have to admit I've been there on more than one occasion. Sometimes things just get screwed up beyond all recognition. What I think is true turns out to be an illusion. People I trust abandon me or, even worse, turn on me."

She stared into his eyes for a moment. Her eyes signaled that she had another question or comment on the topic. Finally, though, she broke eye contact and picked up her wine.

He stood and retrieved the salad from the kitchen counter. "We'd better eat or salad's gonna wilt and the pasta will get cold." He handed her the tongs.

Kaz continued speaking as she dished salad onto her plate. "Whether you trust me or not is something you have to decide. I've never lied to you or tried to deceive you in any way. On the other hand, I do cavort with some unsavory types when it suits me."

If the comment bothered her, she didn't show it. "I guess we need to decide where to go next."

Kaz took a forkful of pasta, chewing it as he considered the proposition. "From where I sit, our goal hasn't changed. Trent's death makes it easier and, I believe, might even provide us with some avenues for investigation."

"How so?"

"Your sources suggested it looked like a professional hit —a sniper. That's exactly the kind of shooter we're looking for. The possibility that our assassin killed Trent is intriguing. It fits. The old man's got money… or rather *had money*. His reputation as an extreme conservative puts him in the same company as our bad guys. Finally, his son is a batterer."

"Okay…." She sat still, her eyes fixed on him as though she was waiting for *the rest of the story*.

"You may not have heard this other piece. There are a couple of guys from the Bellevue area that we learned were associated with the organization—Carl Broward and Millard Conyers. They're both ministers… and they've both gone missing."

"And you think it's all connected?"

Kaz scooted his chair closer to the table and set his plate aside. "It all leads back to the assassin."

Chapter 72

"What makes you say that?"

"Think about it. His last hit, well, before Trent, was botched. He shot Aylin Freyberg but didn't kill her. If I'm right, he was also the guy who waited outside when Billy Robinson came for Greg Stottman. Remember, whoever hit Robinson was a pro."

He paused and patted the tabletop gently as he spoke. "Here's how I see it… and, yes, it's just conjecture at this point. The assassin worked for *Truth is Strength*, both as a hitter and doing some other odd jobs. He screwed up the Freyberg hit—very amateurish. He ended up killing Robinson in what also turned out to be a failed hit. This guy had to be seen as a growing liability. The organization turned on him. He went after them before they could get him."

A light went on in Wharton's eyes. "The Robinson connection seems more likely now."

Kaz leaned back. "Honestly, that connection doesn't matter much anymore. We have a line on the guy. The ones who were paying him are dead. He's the only loose end. And the best part is that he's most likely flying solo."

"Assuming you're right, how do we proceed?"

"I'm going to talk to someone. These events change the landscape, and I need a better read on it."

"Who are we going to meet with?"

Kaz shook his head. "*I'm* going to meet with them."

She glared. "What about all that *trust* crap you were throwing out earlier?"

"It's not that I don't trust you. I'm just pretty sure that you wouldn't want meet with this individual."

73

The e-mail showed up in the Sniper's ISP account two days after the Trent hit. The *from* line failed to provide any identification of who sent it. The message was simple and to the point—*We need to talk. Please visit our website.*

What little he could surmise from the e-mail told him that it originated with the organization with whom he had been at war for the past few months. He half-laughed as he mumbled to himself, "I'll just bet you'd like to talk."

He closed the dark web browser and shut his computer down. He needed to focus on his immediate problem—vacating his cabin and finding a new permanent place to live. He'd been searching the web to identify a region that might best suit his needs. His current thoughts were Missouri and Arkansas. He could easily get lost in both.

The e-mail kept popping back into his mind. The old adage came to him—*keep your friends close but your enemies closer*. It might be worthwhile keeping tabs on what they were doing. Clearly, he was on their mind and there was little doubt they wanted their money back… most likely along with his head.

Still, it wouldn't hurt to at least visit the website and see what they had to say. It's not like they could kill him through the web.

The next morning, he pulled into a Burger King restaurant just inside the Boise city limits. He preferred McDonald's, but he feared that others might know of his preference and be waiting in ambush. Better to play it safe.

As he sat down with his order, he opened his notebook and signed into their free wi-fi. Taking a generous bite of the Whopper, he navigated to the website and, using the code system he'd used before, identified the photo he needed. After downloading it, he opened it up in his editing program and studied the metadata.

The coded message, like the original contact, was simple. They wanted to meet under a flag of truce and have a discussion. They were confident that a mutually agreeable resolution could be reached. The meeting would be at the same McDonald's in Spokane where he'd first met with Broward.

He mumbled to himself, "Hmm. I'll have to think about that."

He closed the file and powered down his computer. The website would have recorded his visit and the fact that he'd opened the photo. Whoever was behind this would know that he'd read the message.

He turned the problem over in his mind as he munched on the burger and fries. No doubt they would kill him without missing a beat. On the other hand, they were missing eight million dollars. They wouldn't do anything right away that might jeopardize their ability to get that back. Plus, it wasn't as though they didn't know it was him.

Popping the last fry into his mouth, he powered up the computer again. "Fuck it, why not?"

* * *

The wind coming out of the southwest was cold and raw on that early February afternoon. The Sniper pulled his coat tighter as he hurried for the nearest door. Inside, he stopped and scanned the dining area. A man in a corner booth held up his hand and motioned the Sniper over.

The Sniper scanned the room again—no apparent threats, although that meant little. It would be easy to conceal a small handgun... all that was needed to send him on his way to hell. Still, it was a little late to back out. He approached the table but didn't sit down. "I'm gonna grab a burger. Can I get you anything?" Might as well be nice about things.

The man shook his head. "I'm good."

Once seated with his order, the Sniper unwrapped the quarter pounder and stuck the straw into the lid of the soda. "Okay, you wanted to talk. Talk."

"First things first. I know who you are, although you probably aren't aware of me. My name is Nicholas Trowbridge." The man was medium build with wavy dark hair. He had a touch of gray at the temples. He was dressed in jeans, a light blue button-up shirt, and a navy-blue fleece vest. He nursed a cup of coffee in front of him.

"Okay." The Sniper took another bite of his burger and waited.

After a moment, Trowbridge said, "You have something of ours. We'd like it back."

"Hmm." The Sniper shook his head. "You could have told me that in the e-mail."

Trowbridge idly rotated the coffee cup on the table,

staring at it as though it offered some mystical wisdom. "I believe in finding solutions. Anyone, no matter how incompetent, can complain about things or find problems. The key is setting a direction that will solve those problems. To be more precise, I prefer solutions that work for everyone. I think I can offer you something that will work."

"Such as?"

"Return the money. You walk away; we each go about our own business. No harm… no foul."

The Sniper took a sip of his soda. "That doesn't sound like a very good deal to me. I lose a bunch of money but get nothing in return. And before you say that I can get assurances of my safety, I'll tell you that I'm not stupid. Once you get your hands on the money, there's nothing to prevent you coming after me."

Trowbridge held up his coffee up as if in toast to the Sniper. "You raise a couple of points, so let me address each separately. First what do you get out of this? You killed five people, including a very wealthy, influential man. You get to walk away with no consequences. I'd say that's a big win for you. You get to put this incident behind you as though it never happened."

The Sniper stifled the urge to tell the man how ignorant that sounded. Instead, he remained silent.

"As to your observation that, once you return the money, we could still pursue you. That reminds me of the old Prisoner's Dilemma exercise."

The reference was lost on the Sniper. He'd never heard of it. He arched his eyebrows in expectation.

Trowbridge continued, "Goes like this. There are two bank robbers. They are both told by a reliable source that the police are on their way to arrest them. Their source also tells them that the police have no evidence and will have to rely on a confession by one or both of them. The two robbers quickly agree that the best solution is for both of them to remain silent."

He waited, as though expecting some reaction or question from the Sniper. When none came, he went on, "Sure enough, the cops get there and take them both into custody. They separate them for interrogation. The gist of the conversation is predictable. The cops offer the same deal to both men. If one cooperates and agrees to testify against the other, that one will get off with only a six-month sentence. The other, if convicted, will likely get a twenty-year sentence. The question is, then, what will each man do?"

The Sniper shrugged. "I give up."

Trowbridge tapped his fingers on the tabletop as he spoke. "Well, we can agree that the smart move is for both men to say nothing. That way, they both go free. Remember, the cops have no evidence. People are funny, though. Rather than maximizing benefit, most will opt to minimize harm. In this case, maximizing benefit would be for them to trust each other and say nothing. If, however, they choose to minimize harm, they will fall all over themselves to be the first to cut a deal."

"Interesting story, but I'm not sure how that applies." The Sniper took another bite of his burger.

"If the two of us are minimizing potential harm, we would seek to destroy the other. You know that I have the resources to pursue you, so you might believe it in your best interest to get me first. I, of course, would feel the same. If, on the other hand, we just agree to trust each other and walk away, it saves us both a great deal of trouble and worry."

The Sniper laughed. "Therein lies the problem. We have to trust each other, although we have no reason to do such a thing."

Trowbridge stared at him for a moment before changing the subject. "You killed the wrong guy, you know."

"Do tell."

"Unless I miss my mark, you killed Trent thinking he was the money and the power behind our group. You were only partially right. He certainly was the money, but he never involved himself in the operations or even strategy. He was completely hands-off.

"Tough luck for him."

Trowbridge's eyes bore in on the Sniper's like focused laser beams. "And for you as well. You tried to take out the command and control but only succeeded in pissing people off. I am the one that you should have gone after. I call all the shots."

The Sniper forced a laugh. "Well, you have to admit that losing that funding will hurt more than a little."

Trowbridge broke into a laugh. "That's priceless, just priceless. You truly think you cut off our money." He grew serious as he leaned in closer to the table. "Mister Trent funded the organization years ago through a generous donation to a foundation—a foundation that has but a single purpose. The fact that he's gone changes nothing."

"Then you don't need my measly few dollars."

"It's the principle of the thing. You took money that didn't belong to you. If I allow that to stand, I invite every member of our organization to do the same. That's not going to happen."

The Sniper pondered the threat. "Why not consider my take as a severance package. Your man, Broward, tried to double-cross and kill me. That's gotta be worth something."

"We can talk about a severance package, after you return what you've stolen."

The Sniper stared at Trowbridge in silence for a moment. "It's a compelling argument. I'll give it some thought and get back to you." It was a throwaway line. He knew it and he could see from Trowbridge's face that the other man knew it as well.

"These things spin out of control. You have the chance here to lock in some degree of certainty and safety. The longer this goes unresolved, the more dangerous it gets."

The Sniper wadded up the napkins and stuffed them in the empty burger container. Standing, he picked up his plastic tray. "For both of us."

74

K az watched as Leah Bowman nodded discreetly to her bodyguards, who turned and left. After they were gone, he spoke. "Thanks. I appreciate you meeting with me."

The black woman, dressed in dark charcoal woolen slacks with a burgundy blazer over a cream-colored silk blouse, smiled warmly. "One hand washes the other, Mister Kazarian. What can I do for you?"

The room they sat in was small and sparsely furnished. Kaz was certain this wasn't her main office. "The last time we spoke, you mentioned an organization and we talked about a certain assassin. Information that I've come into suggests that the landscape has changed."

"Very astute." She offered no details.

"My best guess, and you might have better information than me, is that this sniper is out in the cold. Several top figures in the organization are no longer with us, courtesy of our friend, I believe. That would suggest that the overall operation of the group has been, let's say, interrupted."

She laughed. "That would be a fair statement."

"To be clear, I'm not interested in whether any other organization is stepping up to fill the void. I am, however, interested in the whereabouts and activities of the assassin."

"He doesn't work for me, if that's what you're asking. He's not been in contact with us. I can tell you that he's not capable of resuming operations within the *organization*, as you call them. As best I can figure, they are regrouping with a greater focus on social and political strategy. Frankly, I don't care as long as they leave me alone."

"Is he a part of this *regrouping*?"

Leah seemed to ponder the question for a moment. "As you yourself said, he appears to be out in the cold. If he was the hitter, then there's no way that others in the group would ever trust him. Here's something that might interest you, though. It seems as though someone, quite possibly our assassin friend, also hit a cash distribution site for the group and walked away with a tidy sum of money—high seven figures, I'm told. With that kind of liquidity, he might be hard to flush out."

Kaz exhaled. "Any ideas on the best way for me to proceed?"

"Nothing specific. You know as well as I do, though, that when people are faced with crises, they tend to seek situations and environs that are comfortable. It gives them a sense of control. If I were a betting woman," she paused and laughed, "and I am, I'd be scouring the area around where you first noticed him. I believe we were talking about southern or central Idaho."

* * *

Chapter 74

"It's pretty much what I thought." Kaz folded his hands in his lap as he sat on the couch across from Wharton. "*Truth is Strength*, as an organization, is in shambles. Most likely, our hitter is on his own, although I understand that he may have come into a rather tidy sum of money recently."

"How did you learn this?" There was a trace of uneasiness in her question.

"As I told you before, information is the common currency. I got it from someone who's in a position to know."

"And who would that be?"

Kaz eyed her for a moment. "Do you really want to know?"

"If you're in bed with the devil, yeah, I do. This kind of thing could come back and bite us in the ass."

"Well, I wouldn't say that I'm *in bed with the devil*. I ask questions. I get answers. People ask me questions. I answer when I can do so without stepping over my own moral boundaries. What I can assure you, is that I didn't engage in anything illegal."

She cocked an eyebrow and waited.

"I spoke with Leah Bowman, you know, the——"

Wharton cut him off. "Leah Bowman? I know who she is. Every cop in the Pacific Northwest knows who she is. She's your secret partner?"

"We're not partners. I think I mentioned to you that sometimes I talk to unsavory types. She's just one of them. Cops have snitches. I simply take it to a more sophisticated level. Believe me, Charlotte, I'm not her colleague or friend. She's a source of information and what I tell her doesn't involve breaking the law or even stepping across moral lines."

She glared. "Let's let it go for a while. What now?"

"We have enough information to get out into the weeds. We know generally where he lives. We have a good idea what he looks like. We know the kind of vehicle he drives and the kind of places he frequents. I think a road trip of Boise and surroundings is the next logical step."

75

Kaz and Wharton sat silently in the car with steaming cups of coffee. The small coffee hut parking lot was mostly deserted. With the car engine running and the heater cranked up, the windows remained clear and the temperature comfortable. "The residence is a long shot. We can only hope that since he took out the organization's leadership, he's not worried about them."

Wharton opened the file folder and looked at a printed image of a small cabin obviously taken from Google Earth. "Looks like a dirt road leading to the place is obscured by trees and brush, although this time of year, it won't help much."

"Assuming that he is Robinson's cousin, he didn't escape Afghanistan and reboot his life easily. It took planning, resources, and attention to detail. We're not likely to catch him unaware during the middle of the day."

Wharton shot back, "I'm not sure that evening, night, or early morning will be much better. If he's as good as you say, he's probably got surveillance cameras and alarms set up all along the dirt road. He's gonna know the minute we drive up that road."

Kaz smiled. "Then we'd better not drive up the road." He nodded toward the parking lot entrance to the south. "Let's head back to Boise, grab a couple of rooms, and get some dinner. We'll come up with a plan tonight."

* * *

Kaz put his finger on the map. "Right here. You can see there's a ravine. It drops off about a hundred and fifty feet. The cabin is here." He indicated another part of the map. "That means that we have about fifty yards behind the house before it falls away."

"Any chance we could go north, access the ravine, and follow it south to this point?" Wharton indicated a spot on the map.

"Maybe, but that would presume that we could climb up. I can't tell from this photo whether there's a viable route or not." Kaz moved his plate aside.

The small restaurant in the north Boise suburbs had few diners, although six in the evening was prime dinner hour. The smell of garlic, grilled meat, and fish wafted through the dining room.

Wharton took a sip of water. "The alternative would be to follow the ravine either from the north or south along the top edge. You can see that there are several pull-offs in each direction. The one immediately to the north looks like it extends back into the woods... maybe a park of sorts. We could leave the vehicle there."

Kaz studied the photo for a few minutes and then laughed. "What if we go to all this trouble and he isn't even there?"

"At least we'll be alive... and we'll know at least one place that he's not."

He agreed. "One other problem that we're going to have to deal with. If he has surveillance cameras on the drive in, he'd be stupid not to have a few on the side approaches as well. Too much at stake for him."

Wharton responded, "Here's a thought. This time of year, there's no foliage. Any cameras he might have should be visible. Let's start up north during daylight and work our way south. We can scan for anything as we go."

"Okay, let's say we do it that way. How do you want to handle the confrontation?"

Wharton bit on the corner of her mouth as she stared at the photo. "Easiest, safest way would be to position outside and wait for him to come out."

Kaz laughed. "It could be a long wait."

She retorted, "If we get there just after dark, we should be able to see any signs of light from inside the house. With some patience, we could make out movement by watching for shadows. If the place is dark and nothing stirs overnight, we can probably assume he's not there."

"So, your thinking is that, if he's there, he'll come out at some point over the course of a day or so."

Kaz probed, "And if he's not there, do we go in and have a look?"

"I say no."

He chuckled. "What, too big of a leap across the legal line?"

"Nothing like that. If this guy is who we think he is, he'll have the place booby-trapped. He's never going to leave it completely undefended."

Kaz considered the reasoning. "I agree."

Wharton leaned back in her chair and bit into a piece

of garlic bread. "I say we take it one step at a time. If we get there and there's no sign of him, we can regroup and come up with another plan. There's just no way to know all the contingencies right now."

After a brief pause, she continued, "We still haven't talked about what we do when we find him. If we do it by the book, we should be notifying the Idaho state cops. If we confront him ourselves, there's almost certainly going to be a shootout."

Kaz had known it would come down to this. "Yeah, that's where we are. Unless we're willing to put our cards on the table, I don't see them being anxious to jump into this. After all, neither of us have any standing over here. I'm just a contractor and you're a county cop from Washington state—well outside your jurisdiction. It would take a lot more than a subtle tip to get them onboard. Here's what I think, Charlotte. Up to this point, you haven't broken any laws or gone outside the bounds of your department policies. Walk away. Take the car, go back to Seattle, and let me deal with it."

She stared at him, mouth open and eyes wide. After a few seconds, she shook her head and looked away. "Really? That's it? We do all this work... come all this way, and when things start to get sticky, you want to ditch me?"

"That's not what I said." Kaz moved his chair in closer to the table and spoke with a soft voice. "You're a law enforcement officer. There's an implicit expectation that you will remain within legal constraints yourself. If we go in, you're already outside the boundary. If we get into a shootout, you're in deeper." He paused a moment before continuing.

"Unless I'm missing something, I won't be able to wait and see if this guy makes a move. This is likely going to be one of those situations where I end up shooting first. I can do that with the element of surprise. If, however, I hesitate and give him a chance to react, all bets are off. He's a pro. This probably won't be the first time that he's either had to react or die. You have to know that this could be construed as first degree pre-meditated murder. No self-defense or stand your ground. Unless I'm reading it wrong, you didn't sign up for this."

She quickly countered, "Even if I didn't go in with you, I'd still be an accomplice, given that I've helped you out."

"Only if I tell… and I won't."

Her face softened and her eyes moistened. "How did you not see this coming?"

"When we started out, it wasn't real. Everything was conjecture and speculation. You said it yourself. We spoke in contingencies—*what if?* Now we're into the weeds. I'm not trying to ditch you. I'm trying to do what's right by you."

She responded, "If you're not able to take him alone, do you think that will be right for me?"

He half-heartedly laughed. "At least you would have a life and a job to go back to."

"What about you?"

Kaz pondered the question for a moment and turned it back on her. "What about me? This is what I do. If there were any other way to protect Val and Janet, I'd jump on it. As long as this guy's alive and free, though, they will never be truly safe."

"You can't be sure of that. His organization—the one that was paying the tab for those hits—is in disarray. Their leadership is gone. It could well be the case that he's cutting his losses and intends to disappear again."

Kaz shook his head. "It could be the case, but the

stakes are too high for me to take the chance. This guy has killed repeatedly with cold calculation. I can't leave this to luck."

He reached across and touched her arm. "Go back to Seattle. I'll give you a call when I get back."

76

A simple plan. Kaz would make his way along the top edge of the ravine from a point two miles north of the cabin. The sky was overcast, and the temperature hovered in the mid-twenties with a slight wind out of the southeast. A major winter storm was forecast to move into the area by nightfall. He started in around noon with the idea of approaching the cabin at dusk. His white and gray camo gear would help if he moved slowly.

What seemed simple quickly became more complicated. The soft snow was nearly two feet deep making the going very slow. There were no natural game trails to be seen, so he was breaking new trail along the way. In the back of his mind, he knew he would arrive completely worn out. As he plodded along, a new plan began to take shape. He could hunker down and ride out the storm that was forecast to come through later that night. He would make his assault on the cabin at first light.

Kaz weaved through the heavy timber, trying to stick close to the trees as he went—there was less snow and the cover was better. He sipped water as he walked and stopped mid-afternoon for a snack—almonds, chocolate chips, and raisins.

He checked the GPS on his watch around 4:00 pm and figured he was about a quarter mile from the cabin. He put his binoculars to his eyes and scanned the area ahead, looking for any signs of surveillance cameras or traps of any type—nothing.

His thoughts strayed to Charlotte Wharton—mixed feelings. It would have been nice to have help, and he had complete faith in her abilities. On the other hand, the assassin he was stalking was no fool. This had a real chance of turning out badly. It was not her fight. The thought of her dying on this mission forced his stomach into somersaults. Yes, he was glad that she agreed to bail out. At least if things went south, she would be safe.

He turned his attention to finding a spot that would afford him some minimal amount of shelter from the storm which, by his reckoning, was still an hour away. He figured he'd look for a spot within sight of the cabin.

Forty-five minutes later, Kaz spotted it. In the gathering dusk, he could make out the straight vertical sides, which contrasted with the natural shapes around the area. He stood still for a moment while he surveyed the area. The low light obscured details. He could make out the sides of the cabin. There were no windows. He stared at the dark, forbidding shape.

Then something caught his eye. Just to the right, mounted on a tree limb about eight feet off the ground—a video camera. "Fuck me," he muttered under his breath. But it had been inevitable. There was no way that someone as successful as his prey would not have loads of surveillance on his primary abode. Sure as hell, this was not the only camera.

His thoughts were shattered. A force slammed his left

Chapter 76

shoulder. The attack knocked him backwards. He slumped against a tree and slid to the ground. He surveyed the area, holding his weapon held firmly in his right hand. His left arm hung limp at his side. Kaz saw nothing through the blaze of psychedelic colors that flashed in his head.

His hearing, though, was clear. When the voice came, it sent chills up his spine. "If you'll kindly drop the weapon and sit still, perhaps we can avoid any more unpleasantness."

Kaz wasn't certain, but it sounded like a chuckle followed the statement. He still could not see his assailant. Considering his options, he decided to play along… somewhat… at least for the moment. He allowed his handgun to drop to the ground beside him. "Okay…it's down."

"Nice try. How's about you push it down toward your right foot and then kick it away, you know, just to be on the safe side."

No. Not gonna happen. Kaz thoughts sped up. If this guy had wanted him dead, he would have done it with his first shot. No. He needed… or at least wanted something. He muttered with as much confidence as he could muster, "I did what you asked. It's your turn. Why don't you tell me what you want."

A laugh came out of the darkness. "I'll give you this. You got one set of balls on you. Here's what I want. I want you to kick the fucking gun away. Is that clear enough? If you can avoid the urge to play stupid games, who knows… you might live to see the sunrise."

Kaz knew better. This guy was not going to leave him alive. On the other hand, the gun beside him was doing little good, since he couldn't even see the man. He pushed the gun toward his foot, which he used to shove it about another foot away.

"Ever the optimist, huh. You think you can move it far

enough to satisfy me but not so far that you can possibly get to it. I give you credit for not giving up."

Out of the shadows, a figure moved lithely, pausing to kick the gun across the clearing. "There, that's better. Now we can talk."

Kaz watched the figure closely. From what he could see, nothing about the man looked special. He looked as though he could easily blend into a crowd and never be noticed. The thought crossed Kaz's mind that it was that very characteristic that was, in many ways, responsible for his own success over the years. He sighed and shrugged. All he could do at this point was to let it playout and hope for some opening along the way.

"Good. Now, first things first, where's the bitch?"

Kaz did his best to toss a disinterested smirk back at his assailant. "No idea what you're talking about."

"Now, you see, that's your first problem. You think I'm as stupid as the rest of the dimwits around this neck of the woods. Lose the attitude, friend. I saw the two you today when you slowed passed by the entrance to the place. Now, where is she?"

Playing for time—that's was all he could do. He turned his head toward the south as though search for something in the dark. Finally, he responded, "And why would I tell you?"

Another laugh. "Because if you don't, then you obviously have nothing I want and I have no reason to keep you around."

It was Kaz's turn to laugh. "You're going to kill me anyway."

"That's quite possible, but as I see it, your only hope, as slim as it is, is to give me what I want." The figure skirted around Kaz, peering south along the rim of the ravine. "Hmmm, coming at me from opposite directions? Seems like a dumb idea to me. Too easy to shoot each other in the low light. Still, given that you were stupid enough not to check surveillance, I guess it's not far reach."

Kaz sensed uncertainty in the man. Snow flurries began. The sniper needed to be in total control and Charlotte Wharton was the missing piece. Switching approaches, the man asked, "I guess that I could ask who sent you, but that would be kind of a useless exercise. I'm just a little surprised that Trowbridge reacted this quickly." He knelt beside Kaz and crammed the barrel of this handgun into the shoulder wound. "What's it gonna be? Where's the woman?"

Kaz forced a laugh even as his brain tried to process what he'd heard. *Trowbridge?* He'd heard the name before but couldn't recall where, not that it mattered at this point. "Ah… what's the matter—dissention in the little boys' club?"

The sniper's voice contained a tone of urgency. "You're choice, Pal. You jumped into the wrong bed."

The sniper stood and circled around and stood with his back toward the rim of the ravine. He took a quick look around. The dim illumination came from reflection off the snow. Night had arrived. The snow fell harder. "As much as I'd like to continue this conversation, I'm afraid we've both run out of time." He raised his handgun, holding it with both hands.

Kaz was on the verge of lunging for his own weapon with two shots rang out. What shocked him is that he felt nothing. Is that the way it worked when you were killed? You could hear things but not feel them? *No, it's the other way around, stupid. You never hear the shot that kills you.*

In the swirling snow, wrapped in darkness, he barely made out the figure of the sniper stumbling backwards over the rim of the ravine. *What the fuck?*

"Nice plan you had, there, Kaz." The voice sounded familiar. Wharton's face appeared before his. "Were you just going to waltz in and ask him to go peacefully with you?" She laughed grimly.

He shot back as best he could, "It seemed like a good idea at the time."

"I'm gonna go down after him and make sure."

Kaz grabbed her wrist before she could stand. "No." The word came out more harshly than he intended. He spoke softly, "No. It's nearly full-on night and the storm's here. If he's dead, you accomplish nothing. If he's not dead, he'll have the advantage of hearing you descend. Besides, you have no idea how deep that ravine his or what's at the bottom. He lives here, so he knows it."

Wharton relaxed and knelt beside him. "What then? We just let him go? If he survives, he'll probably come after us."

"First, he's not likely to survive. You hit him and presumably did some serious damage. He probably suffered more injury with the fall. On top of that, he's gonna get about a foot of snow on top of him before the night's over."

"I agree that the odds aren't on his side. Still, it's not impossible."

Kaz responded, "Second, he's not gonna come after us. This guy's a pro. There's no upside to him coming after us. If he survives, he'll spend every ounce of effort and ingenuity to get away and reinvent himself. Remember, he's already done that once. He knows how to do it and that's his best chance of survival. If anything, he'll go after Trowbridge—the guy he thinks sent us."

Wharton shook her head. "So we let him off, free as the wind? What about all the women he's killed. Don't they deserve justice?"

"I'm not saying they don't. That's a job for law enforcement. My job was to protect my employer. I believe we've done that. He's no longer a welcome soul within his organization. That means that the hit list he was working from no longer means anything to him. I'm telling you, Wharton, he doesn't live in the past. He moves forward. We can give everything we have to the Washington and Idaho cops and even the FBI. They can take it from there."

"In case you haven't noticed, I *am* law enforcement, and I'm here. This is what I do."

Kaz almost laughed but squelched it to a smile. "You are somewhat out of your jurisdiction, Detective. If you go down there and put another bullet in him, you're going to have a lot of really, really hard questions to answer."

It was her turn to laugh. "And your solution is just to pretend it never happened? You know that the minute you show up at an emergency room with that gunshot wound, they're gonna call the local police, and you're going to have a lot of explaining to do."

Kaz propped himself up on one elbow, grimacing with the pain. "Here's what we do. I have some medical resources I can call on that are discreet—no law enforcement involvement at all. If anyone questions where you've been, in the unlikely event they even missed you, just tell them that you went for a holiday weekend with your boyfriend. That'll shut 'em up."

"My boyfriend? Seriously? Do you honestly believe that anyone will buy that story—me going away for a weekend with a boyfriend that I've never mentioned before?"

"You could do worse."

She fell silent for a moment. Taking his hand in hers, she replied, "I guess you're right. I could do a lot worse."

77

The Sniper figured he had at least two or three days. His response to Trowbridge's offer—*I'll think about it*—would certainly not have been taken seriously. Despite that, he figured that it would take the man a couple of days to finalize whatever plan he was going to execute.

He spent the entire morning repositioning video cameras to cover the drive in as well as both north and south approaches to his cabin along the bluff. Whoever came for him would at least stop at the road and confirm the target. After that, they'd likely try to approach from either side along the bluff. There was no other way in.

In the afternoon, he reorganized his caches, making sure that his latest haul was secure. When he finished, there was nothing in the cabin but food, dishes, and a few items of clothing. He's parked the cash in an underground storage some fifty miles north of the cabin.

As he unenthusiastically ate a plate of beans and sausage for dinner, he took measure of the cabin. He had a few clean-up items to take care of before he left. By his estimation, he could finish the next day and leave before dusk. He could take what he needed from the caches on the way north and be in Coeur d'Alene before midnight. That was as far ahead as he could think at the moment.

The next morning brought a storm warning. Heavy snow followed by below zero temperatures would arrive by nightfall. It would make for shitty driving between the cabin and the city but there was nothing to be done. He set about the final tasks. Breaking out C-4, he began to set out explosive charges around the cabin. Connecting a 12-volt car battery, he detonation to be triggered by opening the storage chest in the main living area. Anyone coming for him and not finding him, would search the place. This would certainly light up their life.

The audible alarm sounded around mid-morning. The Sniper turned his attention to the camera feed from the front drive. A late model SUV with two people—a man and a woman—had stopped beside the dirt road leading to the cabin. They sat there for about ten minutes before driving on.

This was unexpected, but certainly not a fatal development. He had two choices. He could either bolt right then and simply avoid the conflict or set a trap and eliminate the pursuit immediately. Fortunately, he would have the element of surprise. He decided to take care of the problem before it became a critical one.

It was about an hour before sunset when he saw the movement on the north approach to the cabin along the bluff. A man crept along, stopping frequently to scope things out. *This guy's no amateur.*

The Sniper checked all the other cameras. Where was the woman? Was she coming behind him or perhaps from the south so that they could prevent his escape? He could see no signs of her on any of the video feeds.

Shit! Not ideal, but he'd have to make the best of it.

The guy's partner was nowhere to be seen. The Sniper would deal with the man first.

He strafed north a good twenty yards in from the bluff. After about fifteen minutes, he estimated that he'd moved beyond where the man was. He banked in and quietly followed the bluff back toward the cabin. He spotted the man after only a couple of minutes.

His target was still headed away from him. The Sniper took a step closer and brought his pistol to bear. He reminded himself that the man probably had body armor on. Rather than a killing shot, the Sniper took aim at the man's right shoulder and squeezed off a round.

It found its mark as the man was thrown forward against a tree trunk. He fumbled around for a minute, reaching for his weapon and then turning.

The Sniper moved in, his handgun trained on the man's head. "If you'll kindly drop the weapon and sit still, perhaps we can avoid any more unpleasantness."

The man's gun dropped to the ground. "Okay…it's down."

"Nice try. How's about you push it down toward your right foot and then kick it away, you know, just to be on the safe side."

The Sniper thought he could see the man grimace. "I did what you asked. It's your turn. Why don't you tell me what you want."

The Sniper laughed and shook his head. "I'll give you this. You got one set of balls on you. Here's what I want. I want you to kick the fucking gun away. Is that clear enough? If you can avoid the urge to play stupid games, who knows… you might live to see the sunrise."

The man pushed the gun toward his foot, which he used to shove it about another foot away.

"Ever the optimist, huh. You think you can move it far

enough to satisfy me but not so far that you can possibly get to it. I give you credit for not giving up."

The Sniper came out of the shadows, pausing to kick the gun across the clearing. "There, that's better. Now we can talk."

The man laid back against the tree trunk, watching the Sniper's every move. Everything he did screamed that he'd seen a lot of action. He was not new to this kind of thing.

"Good. Now, first things first, where's the bitch?"

"No idea what you're talking about."

"Now, you see, that's your first problem. You think I'm as stupid as the rest of the dimwits around this neck of the woods. Lose the attitude, friend. I saw the two you today when you slowed passed by the entrance to the place. Now, where is she?" The Sniper continued to scan to the north and south but saw nothing.

"And why would I tell you?"

The Sniper shrugged and waved his gun. "Because if you don't, then you obviously have nothing I want and I have no reason to keep you around."

The intruder offered a weak laugh. "You're going to kill me anyway."

"That's quite possible, but as I see it, your only hope, as slim as it is, is to give me what I want." He skirted around Kaz, continuing to scan north and south. "Hmmm, coming at me from opposite directions? Seems like a dumb idea. Too easy to shoot each other in the low light. Still, given that you were stupid enough not to check surveillance, I guess it's not far reach."

Snow flurries began. The Sniper needed to be in control and the woman was the missing piece. Switching approaches, he asked, "I guess that I could ask who sent you, but that would be kind of a useless exercise. I'm just a little surprised that Trowbridge reacted this quickly." He knelt beside Kaz and crammed the barrel of this handgun into the shoulder wound. "What's it gonna be? Where's the woman?"

Another forced laugh. "Ah... what's the matter— dissention in the little boys' club?"

The sniper gave up. "You're choice, Pal. You jumped into the wrong bed."

He stood and circled around and stood with his back toward the rim of the ravine. He took a quick look around. The dim illumination came from reflection off the snow. Night had arrived. The snow fell harder. "As much as I'd like to continue this conversation, I'm afraid we've both run out of time." He raised his handgun, holding it with both hands.

The Sniper wasn't sure about the sequence. A couple of light flashes from his right followed almost immediately by two loud cracks. Searing pain shot through his shoulder. Something slammed his chest, which was protected by body armor.

The Sniper stumbled backwards. Swirling colors cut through the darkness as the Sniper tumbled back over the bluff and into the ravine.

78

Kaz forced himself to sit up straight on the couch. His shoulder ached and he was drowsy from the pain meds. He wanted nothing more than to sleep. He'd spent the entire prior evening digesting the volumes of information that Eisen had given him on Trowbridge. The name had meant nothing to him when the assassin had said it. Now it appeared as though he was at the center of things.

Janet and Val sat in the two chairs on either side of the couch. "I could make some tea if you'd like it." Kaz's heart was not in the offer, but he tried to be a good host.

"What happened?" Val sat in the overstuffed chair, leaning forward toward Kaz.

"Long story." He didn't feel like recounting the entire thing.

"I got time." Val didn't crack a smile.

Janet seemed softer, more concerned for his injuries.

"It was the assassin, the sniper guy that was targeting the women.

Janet asked, "The same guy that tried to get Aylin and had me on the list as well?"

"The same. I cornered him over in Idaho. Unfortunately, he drew first blood."

Val queried, "And?"

Kaz sighed. "I got off a couple of rounds. It was dark but I think it got a shoulder hit. I also hit him mid-section, chest maybe, but I think he was wearing body armor." He avoided bringing Wharton's name into the discussion.

"Anyway, he fell down into a ravine. I was shot, it was night, and a major snowstorm was blowing in, so I didn't chase him down. I doubt that he survived, especially if he had to spend the night exposed."

"But you're not sure?"

Kaz thought about protesting the question but decided to let it go. "No. If he did survive, he's on the run and will probably focus more on survival than anything else."

Val continued, "Even if he's out of the picture, is it possible that the organization will just employ another killer?"

"Maybe, but they're in kind of a tough spot right now. They've lost elements of their leadership along with a key contractor, who went rogue on them. My guess is that their priority will be on cleaning up their own house right now."

Janet asked, "Anything else?"

It came back to Kaz in a flash. "Yeah, there is. Does the name Trowbridge ring a bell with either of you?"

Even before the answer came, Kaz could see the reaction in Janet's eyes.

"Yes, it does. We've crossed paths a couple of times and we're not exactly on the best of terms. Why?"

"We got some things wrong. Trent was never calling the shots. He provided money but Trowbridge was always the boss."

Chapter 78

Janet stared as in disbelief. "That's a serious allegation. Are you sure?"

Kaz nodded toward the stack of papers. "It's all there. Eisen spent the last few days dredging every source he could find."

The minister shook her head. "I guess this is going to make a splash."

Val stood. "One more thing. This series of events with the killer... are you going to turn it over to law enforcement?"

"I think not." He started to go into his reasoning and logic but decided against it. "No, not at the moment."

Janet and Val had been gone less than thirty minutes when his cellphone rang. He felt a tinge of happiness as he noted the number. "Good evening," he forced a pleasant tone.

Detective Wharton voice floated out of the speaker. "I thought I'd drop by to check on the sick, lame, and lazy. You up for visitors?"

"Are you bringing dinner?"

"Gyros okay?"

"Sounds great."

"Good. I'm the parking lot now."

As he opened the door for her, he resisted the unexpected urge to kiss her. *Where the fuck did that come from?* "Smells good. My cook took the month off."

"You should fire him."

They opted to eat sitting on the couch. Wharton seemed pre-occupied, inspecting her sandwich after each bite. For a few minutes, they ate in silence.

Finally, Kaz asked, "How did it go back at work?"

They hadn't discussed what she would be telling her bosses.

"Like you said, I took a long weekend off with my boyfriend." Her tone was matter-of-factly, although there was a slight hint of anticipation. An important point, though, was that she didn't share the information she had about the Sniper. Detective Wharton had definitely stepped over a line.

He laughed. "If it means anything, you sure know how to show your boyfriend a good time."

She smiled and took his hand in hers. After a moment, she grew more serious. "I'm thinking about giving up on law enforcement. Somehow, the ideals and principles never seem to work from a practical perspective. I might look for something in the private sector."

An idea shot through his head. "How would you feel about security work for women on the run from violent husbands?"

"If you're my boyfriend, wouldn't that be unethical?" She shot him a sly smile.

He squeezed her hand. "We're not much on nepotism rules."

79

J anet turned the corner and checked the rearview mirror again—nothing. She was certain, though, that she'd seen it earlier in the evening. A knot formed in her stomach.

Greg gazed out the passenger side window. "I could get used to this, you know, being driven around." He turned and smiled warmly at her. "Especially by you."

She nodded curtly and glanced again at the rearview mirror—again, nothing.

"You seem preoccupied. Did I say something wrong?" Greg had twisted slightly in his seat to face her.

"No, no, it's nothing, really. I just have a lot on my mind." She really wanted it to be nothing.

He considered her for a moment. "I don't want to seem argumentative, but it sure seems like something is wrong. You've been someplace else all evening. If something I've done, please tell me."

She sighed deeply. "No, Greg, it's not you. It has nothing to do with you. It's just that late this afternoon, I thought I saw… something."

"Something… what?"

"I don't know, it just looked like Rob Young's car, you know, my old board president."

Greg's voice suddenly sounded serious. "Yeah, I do remember. He's the husband of your first client, as I recall. Where did you see him?"

"First of all, I'm not absolutely certain it was him. Second, even if it was, it could well have been a coincidence. It was on the way to the restaurant. The car was behind us for a couple of blocks then turned off."

"You need to notify the police, Janet. You know how dangerous people like that can be."

Janet offered a mirthless laugh. "What exactly would I tell the police? That a silver SUV that looked like a former board president was behind me on a public street for two blocks? It doesn't mean anything."

Greg shot back, "It must mean something given your reaction. I'm serious, at least tell that detective friend of yours, Dee. Maybe she can give you some suggestions."

"I'm sorry, Greg." She conjured up her best smile. "With everything that's gone on over the past year, I'm starting to see danger everywhere. I'm sure it's nothing."

They pulled up into the parsonage driveway. "I need to grab a few things if I'm going to stay over at your place tonight." She turned off the ignition and got out. Greg walked around and took her hand as they started for the front door.

A man jumped out of the bushes. Before Janet could react, he aimed the gun at her chest.

"Time to pay your debts, Reverend Polasky."

She stepped back and tried to compose herself. "Rob, what're you doing?"

His laughter sounded more like howl. "Now what does it look like I'm doing? I'm going to extract payment for all the wonderful things you've done for me. And look what we have here. It's two for one night. I get the cunt and the money man that's fucking her. I didn't plan on this but, what the hell, I'll take the freebie." He shifted, aiming the gun alternatively at the two of them.

Before Janet could say anything, the world exploded. Greg hurled himself at Rob and the two of them tumbled onto the lawn. Janet started for the two, intent on gouging Rob's eyes or something… anything.

A shot rang out. The two stopped tumbling. Greg, who was on top, rolled off and lay still. Rob struggled getting out from beneath him.

The gun landed on the grass. Janet stared at it for a moment. Rob evidently saw it and scrambled to get it. Janet dove onto the lawn, reaching the gun an instant before he did. She twisted around, bringing the gun to bear on her attacker.

Her mind became a twisted mass of thoughts and emotions. She saw Greg lying, probably dead, on the ground. The man who had killed him was coming for her. She screamed at the top of her lungs. "Noooooooooo!"

She pulled the trigger. In that instant, she had clarity of mind. It was not a reaction. It was not a mistake. It was not the heat of the moment. She became the hunter. She fired again and again.

Rob Young stopped moving. She fired again. Dark stains spread from two places on his light shirt. She dropped the gun and fell on her knees over Greg. His shirt was soaked with blood.

She took off her jacket and put it over what appeared to be his wound and pressed. He didn't move. "Help," she screamed at the top of her lungs. "Somebody help!"

She reached into her purse for her phone and quickly dialed 9-1-1, placing the phone on the ground and yelling into while she worked on Greg. She reached up and brushed the hair from her face leaving a swath of blood across her forehead and cheek. The smell of sulfur and copper overwhelmed her.

Janet heard the first siren, followed by others. Soon she felt hands on her shoulders, gently moving her to the side.

"We got this now. Are you okay? Are you hurt?"

She stared at Greg's motionless body for a moment before rolling over. Staring at the sky, she asked God, "Why?"

80

How did she get to the hospital? Janet didn't remember driving. Maybe she rode with the ambulance. A uniformed police officer sat beside her asking questions. Janet had no idea what the man was saying. His voice droned on.

Someone else sat down on the other side of her. A moment of quiet and then another voice. More people. The world spun. The overhead lights pulsed bright and then dim. The noise of unintelligible voices ramped up.

She sat staring at her hands, covered with the Greg Stottman's blood. Her black pants and lavender blouse were both soaked with the sticky residue. It was all that was left of him.

An arm found its way around her shoulders. She felt as though she would collapse. More noise, but this time a few words came through. "They're working on him, Janet. He's in good hands."

Consciousness slipped away.

The light came first. It was more like a lightening of the darkness rather than actual light. The transition from black to gray to moving shapes. A din of noise washed over her followed by a few words that she could make out. "Dani's here."

Janet opened her eyes as she felt arms wrap around her shoulders and neck. She could hear and feel sobbing. "Dani?"

The arms tightened around her. She reached up and touched them. Words struggled to get out, but none came. None were necessary.

After what seemed an eternity, a different voice spoke to her. "It's me, Janet, Dee. Can you talk?"

Janet started to nod then shook her head. She couldn't speak.

"It's okay. Just listen. They got him stabilized. He's out of surgery and they're moving him to ICU."

Janet struggled to make sense of the words. *Stabilized? Out of surgery? ICU?* Who were they talking about?

A different voice. "It's Dani. Come on, Janet, open your eyes."

Janet blinked a couple of times and then opened them. People surrounded her—Dee, Val, Aylin, Dani, and Kaz. "What...?"

Dani took her hand. "Come on, Janet. We need to get you cleaned up." The young woman wiped the tears from her eyes. "You're creating a spectacle here in the waiting room." She tried to force a laugh that sounded phony.

It felt more like wobbling than walking as the two of the navigated toward the women's room. Janet struggled to put the pieces together. "Greg, he's...?"

Dani's voice sounded on the verge of breaking. "I don't know. They operated and now he's going to ICU. They won't tell us any more than that."

"He's not... dead?"

Dani made another vain attempt at laughter. "He's to

ornery to die. Besides, he can't just leave now that he's got this great thing going on. I've been waiting most of my life to see him married off."

"I don't understand. He was…." She remembered the blood and the still body.

"Maybe they'll tell us something when we get up to ICU."

Janet had no idea of the time. The endless parade of people came and went. Val and Dee had stayed until sometime after midnight. Greg's business partner, Melissa, had spent several hours there. Dani stayed by her side.

The sky was beginning to brighten with morning twilight when Kaz came and sat beside her. "How you doing?"

Janet looked at him, not sure what to say. She shook her head.

He smiled. "That's about right. I'll let you in on a secret. When they stay alive this long, it usually takes. He's going to be fine. Trust me."

She wrung her hands in her lap. "I don't know what happened. We were just… and then…."

"You'll get it sorted out. It takes time. It's never easy but you have lots of friends. You just need to lean on them."

Another thought stole its way into her mind. "Rob Young. What…?"

"He's dead." Kaz's voice was kind and reassuring, but the words were stark.

"I want to feel sorry about that, but I don't. I pulled the trigger, and it felt right." Tears came and blurred her vision. "God, Kaz, I don't want to feel this way. I killed him and somehow, I'm okay with it."

He took her hand. "You'll deal with it when the time is right. Now isn't that time. Only you will know when it is.

Until then, focus on yourself, Greg, and your friends. That'll get you through."

* * *

Janet went home shortly after noon. As she walked from the driveway to the porch, she avoided looking at the lawn where it had happened. Yellow crime scene tape cordoned off the small area. She went immediately inside, showered, and made some oatmeal. After a few bites, she gave up. Grabbing her purse and keys, she headed back to the hospital.

Greg's condition had been upgraded from grave to critical. Janet wondered about these terms. Did they really mean anything? She leaned heavily on what Kaz had told her that morning. He had promised that Greg would be fine.

Late that afternoon, she found her way down to the chapel. There were candles burning in the front, but the pews all sat empty. She took a seat in the front row. With her hands in her lap, she bowed her head. She remembered that she'd questioned God the night before, while lying on the grass next to Greg's bleeding body. He hadn't died, so maybe God had intervened. Why did it happen at all? Why didn't God stop these thing before they got out of hand?

No answers came. Instead, she found herself remembering the days and nights she'd spent in the hospital chapel praying in vain for Mark's recovery. Despite fervent pleas, her husband had died. Now here she was praying for someone else—someone who had touched her heart in a way that no one had since Mark. She felt a pang of guilt. It was as though she was betraying her husband, being unfaithful. Yes, she still loved Mark. She always would. And yet, she loved Greg Stottman fiercely. *Is that even possible?*

"Of course it's possible."

Janet eyes opened as she jerked her head around. Sitting next to her was an ethereal figure bathed in golden light. "Mark? How is this…?"

"You asked a question, Janet. I am here to answer it for you. Yes, you can love again. It's not betrayal. In fact, it's wonderful. I'm happy for you."

"But… are you… I mean, are you here… really?"

He smiled but didn't speak.

"Did God send you back to tell me this?"

Mark's laugh was the same as it always was when she asked a question to which the answer should be obvious. "No, of course not. You called me."

"I don't understand. Where…?"

"I'm a part of you, Janet. I always will be. Now, you should get back. I suspect that the doctor has some good news for you." With that, his image faded.

81

J anet sat stiffly in the wingback chair staring at the untouched plate of Russian tea biscuits as though they might offer up some heretofore absent meaning. She noticed that she had unconsciously placed her hands between her knees and gently rocked as she struggled for something else to say.

Maddie Kavanaugh, her long-time friend and mentor, had listened to Janet's story with sadness in her eyes and without the quick-witted humor. "You have to know, Dearie, in your heart, that you had no choice. Had you not acted, he would have killed both you and Greg."

Janet offered an unenthusiastic, "I know." Her gaze never strayed from the plate of biscuits sitting on the coffee table. She had somehow thought that the ritual of the snack cookies along with Maddie's sense of perspective, would *put things right.* Some things, though, could never be made right. Some people could never be made whole again.

After a moment of silence, Janet wandered into the deep woods that so frightened her. "I understand that,

Maddie, and I know that, if I had to do it again, I would do the same thing. As much as taking a human life weighs on me, that's not the problem."

Her friend nodded gently but remained quiet.

Janet heard the ticking of the antique clock on the mantle as its pendulum swung back and forth. Time marched on regardless of the troubles and cares of humans. She forced herself to speak. "In that moment, when I had the gun in my hand, something in me snapped. As Rob came for me, his face changed. He became Todd Miller as he killed his wife, Hanna. He was Luellen Pickering's husband as he killed their children. Then he became Thomas Corel as he battered his wife. He was every man that battered and murdered partners and children. In that moment, I was ecstatic. The fear and anger were gone. It was a sensation that was as close to pure pleasure as I can imagine. I didn't just want to shoot him. I wanted to keep shooting him. I wanted to see the life drain from his eyes. I wanted to hear screams of pain. With every pull of the trigger, I felt better."

Tears flowed from her eyes. "God, Maddie. I became a monster. I became the very thing that I fear the most."

Maddie slid down to the end of the couch and took both of Janet's hands in hers. "Finding the right words is a challenge in times like these. If I mess this up, please forgive me. First, I'm not trained therapist or psychologist so take what I say with a grain of salt. Second, you just described for me a set of very complex feelings and emotions that, by your telling, occurred during a desperate struggle to save both your life and Greg's. You say that you understand the necessity of that action, so I'm going to pass that by. We've been sitting here for a good half-hour. You've no doubt turned these issues over in your mind countless times. Keep in mind, though, that the incident that you described probably took no more than about fifteen seconds."

She smiled warmly at Janet and squeezed her hands gently. "I suspect that these emotions that you describe are ones that you've come up with since the incident in an attempt to make sense of everything that happened. I think that your mind is somehow still trying to justify the action. I'd say, during the incident, you experienced surprise, fear, anger, grief, and finally relief when it was over, It seems to me that there just wasn't enough time for anything else."

Janet looked up from the tea biscuits and struggled to see the details of Maddie's face through the blinding tears. "Whatever else I can say about what happened, the truth is that I took a human life. I'm a killer."

Maddie laughed softly as she shook her head. "Tell me, Dearie, have you ever told a lie?"

The question struck Janet as an odd one. "I guess… maybe."

"Does that make you a liar? When you were a kid, did you ever steal anything?"

Janet found herself smiling in spite of the crushing weight of her guilt. "Once or twice… maybe more."

"And does that make you a thief?" Maddie leaned back on the couch and swept the white hair from back from her temple. "What you *are* is a very complex human being. Objectively, you're a Methodist minister, and woman with a conscience and a life ahead of her. Had you not done what you did, you would be nothing more than a memory and a corpse."

Janet made a feeble attempt at humor. "No need to sugar-coat it."

Maddie sighed. "How's Greg doing?"

"He's out of the hospital but the doctor's say that he can't return to work for another few weeks. We haven't

346

really had a chance to talk about what happened in any detail."

The old woman cleared her throat and picked up a tea biscuit. She took a bite, followed by a sip of tea. Swallowing, she said, "There is something you're going to have to consider. It's possible, even likely, that he's going to feel far more guilt than you. He was shot and would have died had you not acted. He didn't protect you. I'm not trying to be the chauvinist here, but the fact that you had to kill someone to protect him will probably hit him pretty hard. Be prepared for that."

Janet hadn't even considered that angle, but it made sense. Greg had always tried to look after her.

Maddie set her teacup down and leaned forward, her eyes locked on Janet's. "I'm going to be blunt with you, Dearie, because I think you need to hear this. As tragic as all this was, you do not have the luxury of playing the victim. Not only do you have Greg to take care of, but you also have an organization that depends on your wisdom and encouragement. You have that young girl, Abby, who is going to need you. You have to be there for her, Janet. I rather suspect that you will be her lifeline."

82

J anet nestled closer to Greg, resting her head on his chest. His arms held her tightly despite his still weakened state. "Are you sure this doesn't hurt?"

He winced as he shifted in place. Even his voice sounded painful. "This is perfect." He held her even tighter and rested is chin on her head.

They sat together on his couch in the fading light of day. Shadows crossed the room but neither of them made a move to get up and turn on a light. Janet closed her eyes and felt herself melt into Greg's embrace.

After what seemed like an eternity of silence, Janet put the words together—what she needed to say. "Greg, we haven't talked about that night yet."

She started to continue but he interrupted her. "Which night? Do you mean the first night that we...." His words trailed off. She could almost hear the smile in his voice.

"The shooting." Janet remembered Maddie's words and her caution. "There's something I need to say. That night... when he came at us, if you hadn't jumped in like that, I wouldn't be alive. You got shot, almost killed, to protect me."

His voice sounded pensive, almost reluctant. "And yet, you're the one that saved both of us."

"If you mean that I'm the one that shot him, yes, I did. That's not what saved us, though. You knocked him off balance. You made it possible for me to get the gun in the first place. You gave me… gave *us* the time. I may have pulled the trigger, but by that time, it's not like I had any other choice. Please don't try to minimize what you did. Not a day goes by that I don't think about how differently it could have gone if you hadn't acted. Thank you."

There was a part of her that wanted to confess her emotional stress, but it simply wasn't the time or place. Given the tone of his response, she was certain that he was in a worse place than she was. "I want you to promise me something, Greg. Please… please don't try to work through this alone. We were both there. It happened to both of us. We need to do this together."

His response was muted and serious. "I'm sorry, Janet. This is just going to take some time. Yes, though, I won't go off on my own."

Janet thought about his answer, along with his overall demeanor for a moment. "I need to ask you something, and I need for you to be completely honest with me. No joking and no deflection, okay?"

He made a half-hearted attempt at humor. "When have you know me to deflect?"

"With the shooting and all, does this change things between us?"

His face went through several different looks. His first reaction appeared as though he .would continue with the humor. That look morphed, though, into a quieter, more thoughtful one. He took a deep breath. "Yes, absolutely."

Janet's heart fell, although she couldn't blame him. It was one thing to be in a regular relationship, but the near-death experience they had both gone through was over and above what most couples experienced. "I understand, I really do, and I appreciate your honesty."

He continued on as though he hadn't heard her. "Life is so precarious. One minute, things are great—not a care in the world. Then everything caves in. It was like that when my parents and my brother were killed." His eyes had that faraway look.

Suddenly, he squeezed her in his embrace. "I'm sorry, but it just seems to me that we can't afford to take it slow, like we talked about. We almost lost each other, just like I lost my family. We only have the present, so we have to make the most of it. I want to build a life together, Janet, and I don't want to put it off until later."

Janet nestled closer to him. That wasn't the answer she expected from him, but his sentiments reflected hers. "I know that we briefly discussed this earlier, but given the circumstances, I need to bring it up again. There is a strong likelihood that Abby Miller will end up living with me at some point. How do you feel about a ready-made family?"

He laughed, a genuine laugh that she hadn't heard from him in some time. "It's perfect. I mean, I won't have to change poopy diapers."

83

Janet sat across from Detective Dee Martin at the Crusty Loaf bistro. This was the first social interaction they'd had in the last few months. Things had been tense and Janet wasn't sure this would actually turn out any better.

On the bright side, she was hungry. The aroma of fresh baked bread filled the eatery. Silverware clinked on porcelain plates and the low din of constant conversation provided a pleasant backdrop. The wait staff scurried about serving this particularly heavy Thursday lunch crowd. Janet ordered a half turkey-avocado club sandwich with a cup of corn chowder. Dee opted for a halibut burger with a side salad. With their orders in, the two drifted into casual conversation.

Dee observed, "It's strange to see such a large crowd on a Thursday." She munched on a breadstick as she surveyed the dining area.

"I guess lunch is their main offering. The place is nearly dead in the evening." The bistro was less than a half-mile from St. Luke's and she passed by it on the way to and from work each day.

They shifted to the weather, then talked about Abby Miller for a while. Finally, Dee waded into more serious matters, although it wasn't what Janet expected. "I don't know whether Val told you or not, but we're getting married."

"Congratulations." Janet reached across the table and took both Dee's hands and squeezed. "That's wonderful. When's the wedding?"

Dee laughed. "We're going to be June brides." The sparkle in her eyes complemented her smile. "We were wondering if you would perform the ceremony for us."

"I'd be honored. Are you looking at a civil ceremony or a church affair?"

Dee chewed slowly on her breadstick for a moment. "You know, we haven't given it much thought. Neither of us is particularly religious, but I have to admit, a nice big church wedding would be cool. Does the Methodist church allow same-sex marriages?"

Janet shrugged. "The church as a whole is divided on the topic. Saint Luke's would welcome you."

After another brief lull in the conversation, Dee brought up the subject that Janet hadn't expected. "They're putting the vigilante murder case on the back burner."

Janet arched an eyebrow. "Oh? I thought that was already gone."

Dee shook her head. "There's a strong suspicion that Luellen Pickering was the killer. Since she committed suicide and didn't leave a note, there's not a lot of evidence. We never found a gun."

Janet asked, "Okay, well, then, what now?"

Chapter 83

"I don't know. I'm still trying to figure it out… how things might have gone if you'd been more open with me."

"We've already covered this ground, Dee.

Dee responded, "I know. I believe in my heart that she truly was mentally ill. Whether she was able to distinguish right from wrong, I can't say."

"Then why not let this go?"

"Like I said, it's complicated. I was certain that the detectives working the case would look at all the angles, including what she'd been through. When they got into it, though, all they wanted was to lock her up in prison for the rest of her life. She was nothing more than a murderer to them."

Janet reached across the table and held Dee's hand. "You did the best you could. What the other detectives would or wouldn't have done really doesn't matter anymore. Luellen is gone."

Dee continued as though she hadn't heard. "I was wrong about it. This has shown me that you can't trust the system to do the right thing. It will always take the path that makes the police, and the prosecutor look the best. No one is going to look out for the Luellens of the world."

84

Janet set out early that morning, before 7:00 am. She had several stops to make before her 2:00 p.m. appointment. First up, the Governor's office in Olympia. In the reception area, she managed to talk her way into an audience with the Governor's executive assistant.

"Have a seat, please. Would you like a cup of coffee or tea?" The middle-aged woman offered a warm smile, one that Janet suspected had been finely honed with years of practice.

"No, thank you. I have some other stops to make." Janet handed the woman a one-inch thick manila envelope that weighed a few pounds. "This is for the governor. It's personal." She knew, of course, that the executive assistant would surely open it first. "I wanted to give him the benefit of seeing this before anyone else does. That way, if he chooses to act, he can get out in front of the publicity. I will be providing copies of this to several media outlets."

The assistant stared at her for a moment, as though

trying to decide how to respond. Finally, she said, "Thank you. May I ask to what this is pertaining?"

Janet shrugged nonchalantly. "It's some new information that has come to light about Nicholas Trowbridge, the governor's assistant for faith-based initiatives. The governor should be aware of these issues before the journalists get hold of these documents."

The assistant fingered the sealed flap on the envelope. "I see. And what's the nature of this information?"

"The documents speak for themselves. I've included source citations, and I encourage you or the governor to verify the information."

"The governor will be in this afternoon. I'll see that he gets these." She sat the envelope on top of a stack of other documents.

Janet turned toward the door. "I need to be going. I have several other stops to make this morning." The comment was meant to underscore the fact that the contents of the envelope would be delivered to others.

The next stop was the Post Office, where she mailed three more copies of the envelope to select journalists. The postal clerk assured her that, since it was Friday morning, the envelopes would likely not be delivered until the following Tuesday. That was perfect. It would give the governor the weekend plus a couple of days to decide how to proceed with the information about Trowbridge.

Checking her watch as she left the Post Office, Janet decided that she had time for a quick coffee and scone before her next appointment.

* * *

Reba Stillings' office could be described as nothing short of spectacular. From the top floor of one of the tallest buildings in the Seattle area, it offered a stunning view of the Seattle skyline, including the Space Needle, along with a sweeping vista of the Olympic Mountain range. The furniture and appointments were on par with the view.

"Have a seat, please. Can I offer you something—coffee, tea, or perhaps something a bit more robust?" The attorney offered a practiced, pro forma smile that, to the uninitiated, might even seem sincere.

Janet sat in an overstuffed chair facing Stillings' desk. "I'm fine, thank you. I appreciate you making time to meet with me. I'll try to make this quick. As you know, my name is Reverend Janet Polasky. I'm the minister at Saint Luke's Methodist Church in Bellevue."

Stillings nodded, the smile never leaving her face.

"I felt that, after a lot of what's happened over the past year, it might be fruitful to sit down and talk with you."

The attorney toyed with the handle of the delicate China teacup as she seemed to process the information. "I'm not sure what you're talking about."

Janet had expected this. Reba Stillings was a seasoned attorney renowned for her composure under pressure. "As you well know, I've been involved in helping women get away from their violent partners. In fact, you represented some of these men."

"I provide legal representation for many people."

Janet folded her hands in her lap and returned Stillings' practiced smile. "There are no cameras or recording devices here, Miz Stillings. Naiveté doesn't suit you. If we can be honest here for a few minutes, I'll be done and get out of your hair."

Stillings nodded once.

"You represent men who batter their partners. While I find that distasteful, I suppose they are as entitled to counsel as much as anyone else. You also advocate for men's rights. I'm not certain that men, as a whole, need that kind of advocacy. Again, though, what you're doing is legal."

The attorney leaned forward, putting up her hand as though to get Janet's attention. "Let me briefly interrupt you, Reverend Polasky. I appreciate your candor, but I really don't need your approval for my business conduct."

Janet continued as though she hadn't heard. "On occasion, though, you step over a line beyond these basic business functions. For example, last year you bugged an accountant's office to learn about my activities. As a result, that placed my client in danger. I understand that you provided legal services, if not more, to Senator Thomas Corel. As a result of his activities, at least three women were killed."

Stillings' voice grew louder. "First, I don't bug offices. I'm an attorney and I do legal work."

"As I said, Miz Stillings, don't play dumb. I know exactly who bugged those offices and I know who paid them to do it."

The attorney continued, her voice raised almost to fever pitch. "As for Corel, I had absolutely nothing to do with whatever he did."

"Here's my point. Rob Young, the man you represented when those offices were bugged, is dead."

"I know. You killed him. Are you here to threaten me too?"

Janet continued unfazed, "Senator Corel died a… how should I put it… a suspicious death. Several other men have met similar fates over the past year. Things are changing, Miz Stillings. The women that we serve are no longer willing to cower in the shadows hoping for the best. We are fighting back. At a bare minimum, you may want to advise your clients that should they choose to go down the violence path, they could be in for a very unpleasant surprise."

Stillings smirked. "Vigilantism is an ugly thing."

"Domestic violence and murdering innocent and defenseless women and children is a much uglier thing."

"What is it that you want from me, Reverend Polasky? I'm quite busy and would like to bring this little party to a close."

Janet leaned forward, locking gazes with the attorney. "I don't want anything from you. I came here to convey some information, which I have done. What you do with it is up to you." She paused for a moment and then continued.

"One other thing. I understand that you have a professional relationship with a Nicholas Trowbridge."

"I am, of course, bound by client confidentiality and therefore cannot respond."

"No need to. I would just like to advise you that Mister Trowbridge is about to experience a rather dramatic change of fortune, and not for the better. Your interests might best be served if you didn't hitch your wagon to his particular star."

Stillings shuffled some papers on her desk. "I'll take all this under advisement. Now, if there's nothing else, I need to get back to work."

Janet left feeling a huge weight lifted from her shoulders. She'd made decisions and taken action. Things would play out somehow.

* * *

Reba Stillings seethed with anger as she forced herself to focus on routine tasks the remainder of the morning. As the afternoon progressed, though, she'd parsed through the messages delivered by Reverend Polasky, taken note of relevant information, and discarded the rest.

Just after 4:00 p.m., her cellphone rang. Checking the display, she allowed the call to go directly to voice mail. Ten minutes later, it rang again. Once more to voice mail. At 4:30, her office intercom beeped. "Yes?"

"Miz Stillings, I have Nicholas Trowbridge on line one for you. He says he was unable to get you on your direct cellphone line."

Stillings did a quick mental risk calculation. "Thanks. Would you tell him that I'm on my way out of town for an extended vacation. If he needs legal assistance right away, we can refer him out." *That should do it for now. I can figure out the rest later.*

85

There were so many things happening so quickly. Janet and Greg were involved the intricate dance of figuring out the relationship. Meanwhile, she was still coming to grips with his being shot and her killing Rob Young. The revelation that Nicholas Trowbridge, the man who sat at the Governor's right hand and who oversaw the state's faith-based initiatives turned out to be the very man responsible for Janet and Aylin being placed on a hit list. Life had turned completely upside down.

And then there was Abby. The Office of Children Services staff were only too happy to approve Janet as a foster parent, allowing her to take the young girl in. The issue of adoption remained on the horizon. There simply needed to be some time in which Abby could heal and find herself. This was, of course, complicated by the fact that marriage was a distinct possibility for Janet and Greg, which would impact her status. Nothing was ever easy.

"We'll hang the posters on the wall. You can keep these photos either on your chest of drawers or your night table." Janet held a small framed photo of Abby's mom as she spoke. She was a little surprised that Abby had no been interested in pop culture-themed posters, but rather soft, pastel landscapes—a style associated with much older people.

"Are you going to be my mom now?" Some of the flatness in Abby's demeanor had disappeared, but she still came across as depressed.

Janet held out the photo of Hanna Miller. "Do you see this? This is your mom. She will always be your mom. She loved you dearly and that's something you can never let slip from your life. That's why you have these photos."

Abby took the framed picture and studied it for a moment. Sitting on the bed, she moved her finger slowly over the glass, tracing the outline of her mother's face. After a few moments, she handed the frame back to Janet. Her hands began to gently rub the satin fabric of her bed comforter. "Is Dani going to live here too?"

Janet laughed. Greg's niece and Abby had become almost inseparable, especially during the brief period when Roberta Klein was hospitalized. "No, I'm afraid not. She'll go back to her apartment, but she'll be coming over every morning to pick you up for school and then bring you home.

"What about her uncle? What will he do?"

That was a question that Janet had not expected, at least not at this stage. Her relationship with Greg had not been a point of discussion with Abby. "What do you mean?"

A slight grin escaped onto Abby's face. "Dani says that he likes you, you know, as a girlfriend."

Janet felt the blush. "Well, yes, I suppose he does."

"Do you like him too?"

"He's a really nice man."

Abby became more insistent. "No, I mean, *do you like him?*"

Janet fell silent for a moment. It wasn't that she didn't know the answer. She wondered, though, how this would affect Abby. "Yes, I like him very much."

Abby looked away for a moment, as though lost in thought. As she turned back, a look of concern swept across her face. "I hope he doesn't hit you like my dad hit my mom."

Janet took Abby in her arms. "No, he's not like that. I can't explain why your father did what he did. I can tell you though, for certain, that not all men are like that. In fact, most of them are good, gentle people. You'll see."

86

The call came late on a Friday. Val sat in the office dutifully producing a to-do list for the following week. Things had settled down. They had two new prospective clients and they would need to find at least one more escort employee… maybe two. The burner phone rang. She connected and said, "Yes?"

"It's me, Aylin. We made it. We're at the condo now."

"Any hitches?"

Aylin's voice sounded remarkably calm… even pleasant. "None. Everything's just as expected. You guys have any luck on getting us off the hit list?"

Val laughed. "Yeah, we did. I'll tell you about it when you get back." She paused and continued, "How are you feeling. I really wasn't sure about you making the rest of the trip after the shooting."

It was Aylin's turn to laugh. "I've gotten to be a real pro at getting shot." Her voice turned serious. "Actually, Gwen and her father did most of the driving. I'm better now, but I have to say that things were dicey there for a day or two. Thank God for drugs."

After a moment's silence, Aylin spoke in a soft voice. "Hey look, I want you to know that I'm sorry about things, I mean, the way I acted in the beginning. No excuses or explanations, I was just wrong."

Val responded, "Thanks. It was hard on all of us, I guess. We just have to keep feeling our way along as best we can." She swiveled her chair around to look out the office window. "Take a few days to rest before you start back. Whatever you do, don't push it. Take your time and enjoy the road trip. I have one other thing to do here to put the finishing touches on Gwen's case."

* * *

Val sat on what appeared to be a prohibitively expensive leather sofa. The assistant, if that's what the young woman was, had offered a drink, which Val had declined. Edward Trent was on a phone call and would be with her when he was done.

It was apparent at first glance that Judge Trent knew exactly who Val was. "I confess I didn't expect to see you here at my home. What do you want."

Val had carefully constructed her presentation. There were certain things she needed to convey, but she knew that it would be too easy to get carried away. "I won't take much of your time, Judge Trent. We share a common interest, and I want to make sure that we're both on the same page."

His words were coated with disdain. "I have a hard time believing that you and I would ever share anything of interest."

She let the comment slide. "Your wife no longer exists. You can report her missing. You can file for divorce saying she deserted you. You can say whatever you like. The bottom line, though, is that she no longer exists. Your father expended some pretty intensive resources to locate her and bring her back. It didn't go well."

"I assure you, Miz Gomez, if you had anything to do with my father's death, we will uncover it and you'll never see the light of day again." He glared at her as he spat the words out. A sadistic grin found its way onto his face. "From what I understand, you're no stranger to prison life anyway."

She ignored the *prison life* shot and kept on script. "You have it wrong. I had nothing to do with that, nor did anyone with whom I'm involved. If you'd bothered to do any research, I think you'd discover that an assassin with which your father was formally associated did the deed. One can only turn their back on their friends so many times before one of them takes offense."

His face remained hard. "Is there anything else?"

Val put on what she felt was her best sarcastic smile. "As a matter of fact, yes, there is. Things are changing. What was once commonly accepted in the good old boys club will no longer fly. We've set up warning loops that will alert us if you attempt to find your wife. I promise you, Judge, we will not allow that to happen."

He smirked, "What's that supposed to mean?"

"Try me and find out."

87

The hymn ended with a resonant swell and the congregation fell silent. Reverend Janet Polasky rose from her seat and ascended the pulpit. Offering a warm smile to the faces in front of her, she raised her arms as though in welcome.

"Welcome to Saint Luke's on this holiest of our Christian holidays." Her eyes sought out and locked on the occupants of the second row on the right—Greg, Abby, and Dani. She was surprised to find her eyes brimming with joy. She nodded and then, as an afterthought, winked at Abby. The young girl beamed in return.

Continuing to scan the sanctuary, she found Maddie Kavanaugh, who sat up straight, her eyes fixed on Janet and an expecting look on her face. Another special smile for Maddie.

Then she saw a couple that wasn't familiar. They appeared older, perhaps in their seventies. There was something about them. As best she could tell while they were sitting, he was tall, maybe six feet and a few inches.

The woman beside him shorter by a good foot and trim. He had a full head of silver hair, perfectly coifed and wore what appeared to be an expensive, tailored charcoal suit with a subtle maroon tie. Her hair, also silver, was trimmed short. She wore a sapphire blue dress with a gray shawl draped over her shoulders. Their faces were focused and serious, although not unpleasant. Janet made a note to seek them out and welcome them after the service.

"I'm sure that you all know the Easter story—Christ was crucified and died for our sins. On the third day thereafter, he rose from the dead and ascended into Heaven to sit at the right hand of the Father. I won't be spending any more time on that today."

Janet noted the look of confusion on many of the faces in the congregation. It was customary for the Easter sermon to actually be about Easter.

"Instead, I'd would beg your indulgence to look at this holy day in a different light." She gestured with her hands toward the stained-glass windows.

"Spring is here. It's been a long, dark winter. Indeed, it's been a challenging year filled with tragedy and sorrow. Families have suffered illnesses and death. Violence has visited on more than one occasion."

Janet paused and smiled. "And yet, here we are—all together, caught up in the arrival of spring and brimming with hope. Was this God's plan?"

The let the question sit for a moment. "Honestly, I don't know. Maybe… or maybe there is no plan."

A murmur coursed through the congregation as though in disapproval. "What I want to talk about, though, is not the presence or absence of a plan, be it one from God or one that we've constructed on our own. No. What I want to talk about today are God's greatest gifts."

She let out a soft laugh. "No one that I know has the gift of prophesy. We cannot know the future. The past, as we can all attest, lives only in our memories. What we have —what is certain for us—is this moment. That is the first of God's great gifts. With it, we have a responsibility to not squander or waste the moment. I urge all of you to recognize this and be grateful. Never let a day go by that you without acknowledging this."

She turned the page of her notebook and cleared her throat. "The second of God's great gifts is this wonderful earth that we call home. We must never take it for granted. In addition, we should all strive to be good stewards of the land and seas."

She nodded, again, breaking into a knowing smile. "As much as I'd like to believe that humankind will eventually travel among the stars, our first responsibility should be to taking care of this wonderful gift of a planet that we've been given."

Janet noticed that nods of approval had replaced the looks of confusion on the faces of many in the congregation. "Finally, we have the greatest gift of all—each other. We can and should pray to God for guidance, mercy, or even salvation. Remember, though, the Lord has given us the gift of other human beings. These connections with our loved ones—friends, family, colleagues—they are what make life worth living. These people are with us through the darkest times. I can tell you from personal experience... and most of you know exactly what I'm talking about... that I simply would have dissolved into nothingness if not for the love and support I've received this past year."

Her gaze returned to Abby, Greg, and Dani. "Here before God on this holiest of days, I make a vow to always be there for you. I humbly ask that each of you, in your own heart and in your own way, make that same commitment. We, after all, God's greatest gift to each other."

She paused and lowered her head. "Let us pray."

88

The man who had been Millard Conyers sat in his
Cadillac sedan staring at the rundown church. It had
apparently not seen a congregation in decades. A portion
of the roof was collapsed, the steps leading up to the front
entrance were all be rotted away, and the paint was mostly
peeled off. Perfect!

Just about this time, a BMW sedan pulled up next to
him. A bleach-blonde woman in her late thirties got out.
She was dressed in tight-fitting slacks, a cream-colored silky
blouse, and a black blazer. She wore gobs of makeup, and
her lips were painted bright red.

He got out of his car and approached her, offering his
hand. "Good afternoon. Reverend Tommy Patterson."

The woman introduced herself and nodded toward the
dilapidated building. "Don't let the outward appearance
fool you. You're getting a great deal on this. The foundation is solid and all the original furnishings, you know, pews
and such, are all there. It's a steal." Her heavy drawl left no
doubt that she was local.

He had chosen Brookhaven, Mississippi, a small town

about fifty miles south of Jackson on Interstate 55 as his new home. Equipped with his new ID, he was ready to build a new congregation in the heart of the Bible-belt. The town was close enough to pull from the more well-to-do suburbs of Jackson as well as the rural towns in the area. A perfect location.

The previous night, he'd journeyed down to New Orleans in search of fun. As it turned out, with money, there was plenty to be had. He was close enough to go down and play from time to time and still maintain his pious appearance in this devout, picturesque community.

He smiled warmly at the woman. "This is perfect."

* * *

The man who was between identities sat in the wooden chair next to an archaic desk in a musty Seattle office. "Good to see you again, Mister Enretti"

Rico Enretti nodded and smiled. "What brings you to my humble abode?"

"The identity you got for me a while back—it worked out well, but I think it's time to move on. I need a new one —same as last time. Is the price still a hundred?"

Enretti shook his head and laughed. "Inflation bites at us all. It's one fifteen now. Same caveats. It'll get you through a traffic stop or job application, but if you get into any kind of serious shit, it won't hold up. As long as you understand that, should be no problem."

"I assume you take cash?" The man placed a cheap brown briefcase on the desk.

"Cash is king. So, tell me, is all the information the same? You still looking for Idaho documents?"

"I think not. I'm going to try Missouri."

* * *

Back on Interstate 70 headed east, the Sniper fell deep into thought. What would he do next? Regardless of what he found in Missouri, there would still be the burning need to fill his days. He'd never been one for doing nothing.

The miles rolled by. The brown grass was beginning to emerge from the snow cover as winter retreated. He tried to imagine what burning cause would draw him back into the fray. Nothing came. Instead, his mind kept returning the source of income and purpose that had never failed him—the assassin's contract boards. Here everything was as it seemed. Names popped up along with prices. It was a simple calculus—was the effort worth the money?

Then there was the thrill of the planning and the hunt, culminating with that squeeze of the trigger, followed by the reassuring recoil of his rifle. It was the life he was meant to live.

His mind wandered to nemeses he'd left behind. If the news outlets were to be believed, Nicholas Trowbridge would not soon be in a position to cause any more trouble. As for the two would-be assassins that come to his cabin, he wondered briefly whether he should tie up that loose end. In the end, though, they didn't matter. They'd not taken the opportunity to finish him when he was at the bottom of the ravine. There would be no reason they would try again later. Besides, he had a grudging respect for the two. They were in some ways kindred spirits.

The world was made up of predators and prey. *If you're not a predator, then you're prey.* As best he could tell, those two —the man and woman—were predators like him. He silently wished them good luck.

Epilogue

J anet hurried into the bistro, shaking the rain off her coat in the vestibule. With a quick look around, she spotted Greg. Making her way between tables, she approached as he stood. They kissed briefly before sitting. "I guess spring isn't quite as *here* as I had hoped." Janet took her coat off and hung it on the back of her chair.

"There's no snow to shovel, so it's all good." Greg had a way of finding the bright side of things. "I'm starved." He picked up the menu and began to scan it.

All of a sudden, two figures stood beside them at the table. It took a moment, but Janet recognized them—the couple that she'd seen at church on Easter. She'd meant to seek them out and talk to them, but they apparently left before she was able to connect.

The man spoke with what sounded like a heavy German accent. "We are sorry to disturb your lunch, but we want to say hello before we fly home." The slight smile seemed out of place on his severe face.

Janet nodded and gestured toward a couple of empty

chairs at the next table. "Uh, sure. There's plenty of room here." She moved her own chair around so that she sat adjacent to Greg.

"I recall seeing you at church on Easter. I meant to talk with you but wasn't able to make the connection." She offered her hand to the man. "I'm Janet Polasky."

"Your reputation precedes you, Reverend Polasky. It is my honor to meet you. My name is Reinhold Gustenfeld, and this is my lovely bride, Emma." He shook Janet's hand firmly but briefly, turning and offering his hand to Greg. "And you must be the esteemed Greg Stottman—co-founder of the quite successful firm Quant-Sys, benefactor of Reverend Polasky's efforts, and, of late, her intended. It is my pleasure, Mister Stottman."

Janet had a twinge of discomfort. What did the man mean when he referred to Greg as the benefactor of her efforts. Then it clicked—the accent and his familiarity with her. "Thank you, Mister Gustenfeld. Might I ask, is it you that we have to thank for our new identity solution?"

He gazed at her for a moment, his bright blue eyes intense. Finally, he shrugged. "There are many who contributed. They do, however, prefer to remain in the shadows, at least with regard to efforts such as this. I might add that you yourself were a substantial part of the solution. It was you who provided the vehicle for the young woman's new life. Me and my associates simply filled in the blanks."

Janet nodded. "I will tell you, though, that I was more than a little uncomfortable with the arrangement. After all, we essentially gave you a blank check with regard to future favors. I still wonder why you chose to help and what you expect in return."

"Why I chose to help should be obvious. You were

quite clear in your Easter sermon about our duties to help each other. You, or more appropriately, your client needed help that I happened to be in unique position to provide. It was my moral duty."

He took a sip of tea. "What do I expect in return. For that, I shall defer to my beloved Emma. He nodded in the direction of his wife.

She spoke for the first time. "I shall be direct. "In case you haven't noticed, we—Reinhold and I—are aging. We feel ourselves hurtling toward that wall that is the end of life. The train, sadly, doesn't slow down to allow us to finish all to which we aspire."

Emma placed her hands flat on the tabletop and leaned in, her face serious. "I would ask you to accept without discussion, Reverend Polasky, that we know what it is that you do. We've been aware of your efforts for some time."

Turned toward Greg. "We were quite heartened when we learned that you had agreed to finance this noble effort, Mister Stottman. It made our tasks and decisions much easier."

Emma returned her attention to Janet. "As was implied in our communication with you some time ago, you are not alone in what you are undertaking. There are hundreds of small organizations around the world that are doing the same and similar things. What binds us all together is our determination to see the end of this kind of violence."

Janet looked first and Greg and then back to Emma. "Do you help all of these other organizations with new identities for women?"

"Sometimes it is identities. Sometimes it is intervention with authorities. Sometimes is nothing more than financial support. On rare occasions, we deploy specialized contractors to solve the more serious problems. We noticed, though, that you have assembled a rather competent group of operatives."

Janet asked, "So again, my question is, what do you expect or want from us?"

Reinhold responded, "In the near term, we would have you continue what it is that you're already doing. We assume that, if we learn of someone in this area that needs your help, you would be willing to step up and assist them."

"Of course. That's what we do."

He smiled. "Of course it is." He took another sip of tea and broke a piece of bread in half, taking a small bite. "In the longer term, things are more complicated. As my wife so subtly noticed, we, the two of us, have relatively little time left in this world." He laughed. "I do not mean to imply that we are on our way out the door as we speak, but we would be foolish to behave as though we will live forever. To that end, in the longer term, our most important challenge ahead is succession planning. We have no children to whom we can pass on this cause of ours."

Silence swept over the table. Despite what Janet knew to be a constant din of conversation and silverware clicking on plates, she could hear nothing. The Gustenfelds sipped their tea and munched on sandwiches as though they had explained all they intended to.

Janet shook her head. "I'm sorry. You lost me. What does that have to do with my operation?"

Reinhold wiped his mouth with the cloth napkin. "With your operation—nothing. It is my understanding that you have passed the baton, so to speak. Your subordinate, a Miz Valentina Gomez now runs your operation. You have become more of a figurehead... and I use the term in the most positive of connotations. Our succession planning does not affect Miz Gomez nor your operation. It does, however, affect you and Mister Stottman"

Janet stared at him, unable to formulate a question.

Reinhold continued. "You watched a woman die. In the aftermath, you envisioned this organization. You overcame hurdles and moved others to action. You inspired, managed, and led the group. You assembled a crew of unlikely allies, organized them, and gave them purpose. It was at that point that you wisely ceded operational control to Miz Gomez."

Janet understood that the Gustenfelds knew about the operation, but she was stunned at the depth of their knowledge. "If you don't mind my asking, when and how did you come to learn about what I was doing?"

The silver-haired man responded, "Our knowledge of you came within hours of the death of the woman, Hanna Miller. I normally would protect the anonymity of my sources, but in this case, I think it hardly matters. We received a call from the director of an agency in the area— Sue Hartman. Sadly, I believe she met her death shortly after that, courtesy of Senator Corel."

"She worked for you?"

Reinholdt laughed. "Hardly. She was, to the best of my knowledge, employed by her agency. We were merely associates of a sort. We exchanged favors from time to time, much as we do with others around the world."

Janet delved deeper. "Speaking of Sue, I understand that she was actually killed by a mercenary of sorts, a guy name Dylan Strauss. Do you know of him?"

"Yes, we are acquainted with him. He is, in many respects, similar to your Mister Kazarian. He hires out to people with problems and money." Gustenfeld chuckled,

"Admittedly, Mister Kazarian is more discerning in the jobs that he takes on. Still, I wouldn't be too quick to condemn Strauss. To be honest, we've been in contact with him and have used him for some of our problems. We're still working on smoothing his rough edges."

Janet shook her head. "I don't know. I mean, it seems to me that he's too far over the line."

"Yes… and no. Context is everything. Mister Kazarian has, himself, pulled the trigger a number of times. Granted that he has better judgment, but in the end, what makes one killing virtuous and another evil can be quite subjective. It is an ambiguity that you will, unfortunately, have to live with."

"One other thing, if you don't mind. When we were talking to the person who contacted us about your help, he referred to the efforts around the world as a *Garden if Lilies.* Do you know how he came to this name? It seems odd, since I had a similar vision early on."

The old man smiled warmly. "Of course you did. We learned of this indirectly from you. At Miz Miller's funeral, you had lilies in your church. You spoke with several people about the symbolism. Those words eventually found their way back to us and we thought it an ideal metaphor. I hope you don't mind that we plagiarized."

Janet shook her head, marveling at how much these people knew about her. "Of course not."

"And so it is, Reverend Polasky, that you are now ready for the next chapter of this life you've chosen. Unless I miss my mark, you have found yourself in an uncomfortable relationship with your church. You have done a remarkable job with the congregation, but events in your life have forced you down a different path. We are here, Emma and I, to offer you the opportunity to do more of what your life has become about… only on a much larger, global scale."

He smiled and added, "What makes this work especially well is that Mister Stottman is no stranger to money. With control of our endeavor comes a great deal of money and power. Despite your personal fortune, you will find that you'll need to adjust to the magnitude of resources that you will inherit. I trust you will manage them well."

Greg looked bewildered. "I'm sorry. You lost me. What is it you intend to do?"

Gustenfeld's smile came across as sad. "It is, for the moment, quite simple, Mister Stottman. We are placing all of our considerable assets into a trust with you and Reverend Polasky as beneficiaries. We have, of course, added intent language. Our intent is that you be the stewards of the assets and use them to combat family violence and violence against women around the world."

Greg's bewildered look turned to disbelief. "That's what you call *simple*? It seems to me like you're asking something of us akin to negotiating world peace."

The old man laughed softly. "I do believe you have the gist of it."

The conversation ended and silence swooped in. The four of them munched on their food. To Janet, it seemed as though each of them was lost in their own thoughts. She was mildly amused that Greg had been speechless. She'd never seen him without a quick comment or answer. Here at the table though, he finally seemed to be faced with something that he'd never anticipated.

Finally, Reinhold pushed his plate back and took one last sip of tea. "I know this comes as a surprise. I assure you, this is not something you need to worry about today. Emma and I hopefully have a few years of productivity remaining. It will give me great comfort, though, if you agree to our proposition. In the meantime, we will be in touch."

Janet and Greg sat and stared. Janet, for her part, felt as though the world had turned upside down. At her very core, though, she understood that their life together would be nothing like they planned.

With that, the two of the stood. Emma bent over and kissed Janet on the cheek. "It has been lovely to meet you."